CC Gibbs was born and lives in the USA.

Breaking the Limits is the second instalment in the Reckless series which stars Rafe, a striking playboy heir with a secret, and Nicole – the beautiful and headstrong niece of CC Gibbs' infamous hero Dominic Knight from her bestselling *Knight* trilogy.

ALSO BY CC GIBBS

THE KNIGHT TRILOGY

Knight's Mistress
Knight's Game
Knight Takes Queen

THE RECKLESS SERIES

Pushing the Limits

AVAILABLE IN EBOOK

Forbidden Pleasure
Wicked Fascination
Insatiable Desire

Burning Touch
Lovers and Rivals

Promise Laid Bare
Desire Laid Bare
Temptation Laid Bare
Venus Laid Bare

Touch of Sin
At Your Mercy
At Her Command

Indecent Attraction
Surrender to You
To Please a Lady

Our Bodies Entwined

BREAKING THE LIMITS

CC Gibbs

Quercus

First published in Great Britain in 2015 by

Quercus Publishing Ltd
Carmelite House
50 Victoria Embankment
London EC4Y 0DZ

An Hachette UK company

A CIP catalogue record for this book is available
from the British Library

PB ISBN 978 178429 085 6
EBOOK ISBN 978 1 78429 059 7

10 9 8 7 6 5 4 3 2 1

Typeset by CC Book Production

Printed and bound in Great Britain by Clays Ltd, St Ives plc

BREAKING
THE
LIMITS

CHAPTER 1

August – Split, Croatia

No one said taking down Zou Yao, Director of Cyber Surveillance Unit 21986, was going to be easy. They knew it was going to be a bitch. But the latest news ripped a hole in their initial planning.

'Fuck.' Rafe Contini stared at his fixer, Carlos, standing beside him on the airport tarmac. 'When?'

'Sometime last night. The Hong Kong apartment was tossed so we're not the only ones looking for Zou's mistress and child. Small compensation for missing them, but—'

'Useful,' Rafe said softly.

'Right.' A scrap of satisfaction in Carlos' voice. 'Zou's going to be fighting on two fronts.'

Rafe Contini, billionaire CEO of Contini Pharmaceuticals, had just landed in Split and he and his party were waiting for their luggage to be transferred to a chopper

1

that would ferry them to Rafe's private island where the operation against Zou would be finalized. The two tall men standing off to one side were keeping their voices down. Rafe's girlfriend – a term everyone would have regarded with irony only days ago – was talking to her mother on the phone, nodding as she listened, responding mostly with yeses and okays, taking her Uncle Dominic's advice and being super-agreeable.

After a quick glance at Nicole to check that she was still involved in her conversation, Rafe raised a brow in query. 'Does Ganz have any idea who went after Zou's second family?' Zou's young mistress and child were critical to the success of their mission.

'Uh-uh. He says the possibilities are endless. Especially with the premier's new anti-corruption campaign that has everyone covering their asses by pointing fingers at their rivals. Even Politburo membership isn't protection against indictment, prison or worse. It's insanity over there.'

'Understatement. How about word on the street?'

'So far nothing. Leo's monitoring the chatter.'

Rafe almost smiled. 'At least we're not the only ones with an unpleasant number of enemies closing in for the kill. When Ganz destroyed the unit's cyber system, Zou's blood in the water brought out the sharks.'

'No shit. If we're lucky, one of Zou's enemies might take him out first and we can all go home.'

'Wouldn't that be sweet,' Rafe drawled. 'In the absence

of that dream being realized,' he added, a sudden coolness in his voice, 'tell Gina we're putting on a special team of analysts to help her narrow the search for Zou's mistress and child. Webster's ready, right? He's unstoppable. Zou couldn't have sent his secret family far. He didn't have time.' Rafe's face suddenly lit up as Nicole approached; long-legged, curvy, fuck-me gorgeous in a summery, sleeveless, mini-skirted dress that had him thinking about finding a quiet corner, flipping up that little purple skirt, bending her over and making them both happy. Sucking in a breath of restraint, he smiled instead. 'So is your mom all content and pacified?' As she came within reach, he wrapped his arm around her shoulder and pulled her close. 'Everything good back home?'

Looking up, she gave him a relaxed grin. 'Everything's cool. Dominic spoke to Mom so I didn't have to give many details about our holiday. She said to send pictures.'

A lift of one brow. 'Yeah?' He'd recently gotten the impression that Dominic Knight thought he wasn't exactly boyfriend material.

'Not you.' Nicole smiled at the dark-haired, wildly hand-some man looking at her, his amber gaze watchful. 'Even though you light up my world. But I know you like your privacy. I just said there's a bunch of us here. No lie, right? Anyway, my mom likes scenery. She's never been to Croatia.'

For a man who'd been in the front ranks of eligible bachelors his entire adult life, it was a novel experience to be invisible. It wasn't a problem, just a data point. He understood. 'Scenery we have,' Rafe said with a warm smile. 'Picture postcard stuff, I'm told. It looks like the chopper's almost loaded. Give me a minute to say goodbye to Milo. He's always accommodating.'

The small group looked like anyone else on holiday; the men in shorts and T-shirts, Nicole's designer dress simple enough to have come off the rack, everyone in sandals – including the pilot. It wasn't even so unusual to fly in on a private jet; the Adriatic was popular with the privileged set in August. Not everyone had a 1.2 billion-dollar helicopter at the Split airport, however, or a personal acquaintance with the young customs official who'd greeted them. But then Rafe actually liked Milo and he travelled here a lot. The buildings on his island had been more or less under constant construction for years. He was one of the major employers in the area.

Rafe explained to Milo that he had a large contingent of guests arriving; Milo smiled and agreed that a good many had already flown in. 'It's high season,' Rafe said with a little eye roll. 'Try to keep them away, right? Are you playing at the music festival next week?'

'Wouldn't miss it.'

'Good. No one handles a keyboard like you. Thursday, right? I think Simon's bought tickets for us. Thanks again for your help. It's always appreciated.' They had an arrangement: Milo never asked for passports or went through their luggage and Rafe had seen that a large gambling debt Milo had incurred with the wrong people had been paid. Leaving Milo's fingers intact.

Twenty minutes later, the helicopter banked steeply to the right and the pilot pointed as Rafe's private island rose out of the Adriatic Sea and spread slowly across the horizon – a sizeable expanse of mountainous landscape visible through the shimmering mist, a faint silhouette of a distant castle materializing out of the haze.

Nicole's brows shot up in surprise. 'A *castle*?' Leaning in close to Rafe so he could hear her over the rhythmic thump, thump, thump of the rotors, she felt a spiking shiver run up her spine. 'You didn't mention a castle.' *Castles had dungeons!* Kink and dungeons were practically a stereotype, her overactive imagination pointed out, even as a flashback of images from way too many horror films suddenly had her heart tripping. *Jesus, get a grip!* She was on holiday with the most ridiculously beautiful, shamelessly loveable man; life couldn't be better. Okay?

'It's not exactly a castle yet.' Rafe smiled. 'It's closer to a rock pile that's burning through money. I call it my hobby. My accountant calls it a nightmare.'

'Speaking of nightmares,' Nicole said, apprehension flaring again at the reference to things that go bump in the night. 'Reassure me about dungeons. Don't ask. It's stupid, I know, but . . .'

Taking note of Nicole's trepidation, Rafe chose a marginal lie rather than argue reality versus her wild imagination. 'No dungeons. Don't worry. And you'll love the room that's been restored in the tower,' he offered, avoiding further discussions of dungeons. 'You can pretend you're a twelfth-century demoiselle. I'll pretend I'm the crusader who never reached the Holy Land, built this castle instead and chose the lucrative life of a pirate.' He grinned. 'So wanna play? I'll make it worth your while.'

A small frown mirrored her lurking anxiety. 'I don't know – maybe, probably, let me think.' Rafe's unencumbered views on wealth always gave her pause to consider – how he could buy anything and anyone, for pleasure and perversion alike, no hassle, no questions. And the words pirate and play weren't particularly reassuring as they approached this remote island with its spectacular limestone cliffs, wind-swept, twisted pines and medieval ruins.

'Maybe?' A teasing query.

'Look, if you must know – and don't you dare laugh – your castle ruin is kinda creepy. It reminds me of Frankenstein monsters.'

Rafe's brows rose. 'Seriously? You believe in that shit?'

'I'm trying not to. Oh God, is that the tower?' As the distance to the island narrowed, the castle tower loomed, half derelict, dark and gloomy against the blue sky. She squinted, took a small breath, muttered, 'That's scary.'

He stared at her. 'You're kidding.'

'Okay, how about it makes me a little unsettled?'

'Good.'

His smile was so wide his goddamned dimples showed. 'Meaning?' she said, half guarded, wishing she hadn't watched so many spooky movies.

'Come on, pussycat, relax,' he said, pleasantly. 'I promise you'll have fun.'

Nicole gave him a hard, steady look. 'No offence, but I'm in the middle of fucking nowhere. I'm allowed to wuss out.'

He flicked a glance at the passengers behind them. 'You're in the middle of nowhere with beaucoup bodyguards. You're safe as hell.' A small smile. 'If that's what you want.'

'They're *your* bodyguards.' Her eyes grew wide. 'Jesus, don't look at me like that.'

His smile was pure bad-boy brilliance. 'Like what?'

'Like you're going to eat me alive.'

'As I recall, you like—'

She put her hand over his mouth then because the pilot was grinning and she wasn't anywhere near as blasé as he was.

He licked her palm, she jerked her hand back and tried to glare at him, but he was smiling at her now like she was the best thing that had ever happened to him and her frustration fell away before the flat-out beauty of his smile.

Recognizing her capitulation, he leaned in, tucked a dark curl behind her ear and kissed her cheek softly. 'Consider me your guardian angel,' he murmured and, at her sceptical look, amended it to, 'Personal guardian – how about that? And we'll have privacy once we land.' He flicked a glance toward the pilot. 'Just you and me. No one else.'

'Except for those down there.' She pointed at a small village of white-washed, blue-roofed houses spilling down the hillside from the castle gates. 'And the staff required for that.' A sprawling peach-coloured Venetian-style palazzo surrounded by gardens came into view beyond the castle walls.

Rafe touched her ear with his lips. 'Everyone will keep their distance. I've given orders. So you're free to scream as loud as you like, wherever and whenever you like.'

She turned, grinning. 'Appreciate your foresight and planning.'

'I'm here to make you happy, Tiger.' Dropping a kiss on her nose, he turned to the pilot as the landing pad came into sight. 'Take it easy, Davey. No showboating.'

The pilot gave Rafe a thumbs up. And instead of skimming the tops of the large palms bordering the pad as usual, he set the chopper down so gently it practically floated to earth.

The small party alighted into the brilliant sunshine, Rafe first so he could help Nicole down. Then Ganz, Rafe's childhood friend, Mongolian hacker extraordinaire, and current target for Shanghai's assassination squads. Carlos stepped out next, followed by Dominic and Rafe's security men – Leo and Simon respectively.

After deplaning, Simon glanced at Rafe. 'I'm assuming guests are allowed up to a point.'

'As long as she's willing to leave on short notice.' Simon had a girlfriend in Split.

'Understood. Not a problem.'

'Go for it then.' Rafe nodded at Carlos. 'We'll see you tomorrow. My phone's on.' He'd insisted on twenty-four uninterrupted hours with Nicole, or as uninterrupted as possible considering the circumstances. Rafe gave Ganz a narrowed look. 'That means you're not to bother me unless the sky's falling. Got it?'

Ganz frowned, looked at Rafe through a tumble of straight black hair. 'Am I allowed to decide when the sky's falling or am I at the mercy of my minders?' Jerking his chin up, he flipped his hair out of his eyes.

'All you have to do is limit the blow, dude,' Rafe drawled, 'and you won't have minders.'

'If only,' Ganz drawled back.

Rafe laughed. 'Gotcha. Then listen to Carlos. And if you need coddling, I believe some of the women at the spa might be willing to help you out.'

Ganz flashed a broad smile. 'You really do love me, don't you?'

'Fucking A,' Rafe murmured. 'You're the love of my life. Now play nice with the ladies and behave, okay? I know you can do it.'

Nicole was always touched by the warm, teasing affection between Rafe and his friends. It was rare and unselfconscious.

'Ration my blow, behave, don't piss off the women at the spa. Fuck, I'm gonna have to set my timer so I know there's an end to the fucking rules. Twenty-four hours, right?' Party to Rafe's conversation with Carlos, Ganz punched his timer icon a couple times and shoved his cell phone toward Rafe.

Rafe arched one brow. 'Cute. Now remember to eat something.' He took Nicole's hand. 'Come on, Tiger. We've got things to do.'

'Such as?' she murmured playfully as he drew her away from the men.

His grip tightened on her hand. 'Such as anything your little heart desires. I'm all yours.'

She glanced up. 'For twenty-four hours.' She'd noticed the grim-faced look on Carlos when Rafe had said, *We'll see you tomorrow.*

Rafe shrugged. 'It's a half-assed deal. My phone's still on.'

'You don't have to coddle *me*. I understand you're dealing with ... ' She paused, quickly discarded several comments on precarious reality. 'Lots of stuff.'

'It can wait until tomorrow.' His smile was a slow unfurling of tenderness. 'That's my gift to myself. Twenty-four hours. Fuck the world till then.'

'I shouldn't be so selfish, but thanks. Really.' Her heart beat harder and faster because she knew how little time they had. 'Thanks a lot.'

'I'm totally selfish myself but, hey, why change now,' he said with a grin. 'Ready for a climb? I'm going to take you to the best view on the island.'

CHAPTER 2

Ganz twitched his broad shoulders, gave his head a shake, then surveyed the grounds beyond the landing pad for a second as though getting his bearings. Then he turned to Carlos.'Who came in before us?' he asked, crisply and clearly.

'The tech team. Or most of them. Three security teams. A couple cleaners.'

Ganz frowned. 'Zou's mobilizing every fucking resource at his command. So tell me more are coming or I might as well shoot myself now.'

'No need for that,' Carlos said with a tic of a smile. 'A fucking army's on its way. Ours, Dominic Knight's, Gora's – his includes every thug in eastern Europe. He's called in his markers back to the Dark Ages.'

'For Rafe's mother.'

'Yeah. Word has it Gora would take on the world single-handedly for Camelia.' Carlos smiled faintly. 'And apparently has; maybe even her late husband.'

12

'Gora got tired of waiting for his happy ending?'

'*Their* happy ending the story goes. This from a man who's racked up more professional hits than he can remember,' Carlos murmured. 'Love is strange – or maybe not so strange.' A slice of laughter. 'Gina's volunteered to help; I'm guessing she's on board to help protect her favourite lover boy.'

'Then don't tell her Rafe might be considering a change in his role as stud to the world,' Ganz said with a grin. ''Cause we need Gina's mad skills. Hell, her intelligence contacts are almost as good as yours, Sanz. She found Timur when no one else could.'

'And slit his throat *after* he fucked her; talk about dying happy,' Carlos noted with a flicker of his brows. 'She might actually be half in love with Rafe, though, so keeping him alive is real personal.'

'Love?' Ganz snorted. 'It's just raw sex.'

'Au contraire,' Simon interposed, catching the last of the comments. 'Not that Rafe doesn't give her what she wants, but she's really into him. He *is* fucking loveable. I don't often say that of a guy. Never, as a matter of fact.'

Carlos grunted. 'Love, sex, kink up the ass – who cares. Right now, we need to focus to survive.'

'Then show me our tech capacity and I'll let you know if it's adequate, fixable or we're totally fucked,' Ganz said, sharp, tight, fast.

Carlos recognized the C-rush in that staccato delivery. 'Think you can make it up the hill? It's steep.'

'No problem. I'll be wired for—' Ganz glanced at his watch and grinned. 'At least three hours. Wanna race?'

'Save your fucking energy,' Carlos said, drily. 'You're gonna need it.'

By the time the men reached the castle gates, Rafe and Nicole had disappeared. The huge iron-strapped doors were open, the inner court fully restored to the last polished cobblestone. The entrance hall was equally resplendent, the high-timbered ceiling a hybrid Gothic/Saracen design so intricate it could have been patterned on a spider's web. And as for the painting alone, it had taken six Florentine workmen two years to fully redecorate the ceiling timbers. Other artisans had also been hard at work on the castle; not that the project was anywhere near finished, but portions of the castle were livable. Carlos led the men to the back of the entrance hall, then down a flight of stairs to an elevator. 'The tech equipment can withstand a nuclear attack,' he explained. 'We're five stories down in the dungeons.'

While the four men were descending underground, Rafe and Nicole were climbing a circular staircase winding up the inner walls of the tower. Despite the original design being built for defence, a railing had been installed for safety.

Rafe held Nicole's hand as he guided her up the stairs, explaining the various restoration projects in detail, his obvious reverence for the historic structure gradually eliminating the last vestiges of Nicole's paranoia. By the time they reached the small landing at the top of the stairs, she was relatively satisfied no monsters lurked and acutely aware of the tower's antiquity, the sense of history in the weathered stones so vivid she could almost visualize the previous occupants who'd travelled these stairs. 'Do you ever think of all those who've lived here before? You must,' she said, answering her own question.

'It's impossible not to.' Turning the large key in the lock, Rafe pushed open the centuries'-old, iron-studded door and waved Nicole in. 'I don't believe in ghosts, but you can feel the spirits in these old walls, in the worn stair treads, in this room that served as the last bastion against enemies.'

'Seriously?' She scanned the large, airy, elegant space. 'Here?'

'Yeah. This was the final sanctuary from attack, the top floor, the ultimate defensive position. The stairway was deliberately narrow in order to thwart invaders. And this door . . . ' He rapped his knuckles on the much-worn, four-inch-thick oak. 'Shows evidence of some hard-fought battles.' He smiled. 'No sword marks on the inside though. The castle survived intact until the palazzo was built in 1507; after that the comte's descendants allowed this to fall into decay.'

'You must have had a decorator.' Nicole surveyed the circular area, carpeted with layers of antique rugs, the walls hung with colourful tapestries, the furniture richly carved, gilded and upholstered in sumptuous Venetian velvets. 'This is posh for a medieval interior.'

'Not in this part of the world. Byzantium's trade with the East was flourishing, every luxury was available. The furniture is original, although most of the fabrics had to be replaced. Miraculously, the tapestries were transferred to the palazzo and escaped destruction. Legend has it the original French comte had an eye for beauty and extravagance.' *And lush women who he housed in this: his tower harem.* With Nicole's declared misgivings about the tower, Rafe chose not to mention that bit of history. 'Apparently, the comte's free-booting life gave him the wherewithal to live in comfort. Take a look at the view though,' he added, changing the subject. 'It's the reason I had this room finished first.'

Resting his shoulder against the door jamb, Rafe watched Nicole cross the room to the windows overlooking the sea and briefly considered locking the door, shutting out the world with all its lethal consequences and indulging his sexual appetites as the original comte had. It was only a fleeting thought; those on Ganz's trail were tenacious. They had to be. The price of failure was high.

With a soft sigh, Rafe eased the door shut, resolved to forget the precarious future for the next twenty-four hours and simply gratify their wild, mad, soul-stirring desires until the clock ran out.

Sharply aware of the limited time, Rafe followed Nicole

to the new large windows he'd had installed, wrapped his arms around her, and drew her back against his hard body. 'God, you feel good,' he whispered, tightening his grip. 'We should just stay here. Fuck everything. What'd you think?'

She turned slightly to meet his gaze and smiled. 'Count me in.'

He laughed. 'Wouldn't that be nice.' He slid his fingers through hers, smooth and easy, his voice when he spoke so soft she had to strain to hear. 'If only the world wasn't ready to wreck everything good, grind it up and throw it away. If there actually was a second first time.' *Or better yet, a way to overcome their numerical disadvantage in this war*, he thought, a muscle in his jaw twitching. 'As if, right?' He shrugged, winced; his shoulders were coiled tight. 'Screw it. Let's just play hard till we flame out and go down for the count. Whadda you say?' No beat beforehand, no advance notice, a raw-edged, flaring pressure in his voice. 'Oh shit, forget it. I shouldn't have asked.'

You shouldn't have asked like that, she wanted to say. But he was breathing fast, like he'd been running and his fingers were folding and unfolding around hers in taut restraint. 'I don't mind,' she said, feeling the urgency too, the swirling danger spinning in the air, the reeling sense of imminent loss. 'How about a small wager on who flames out first?' she added, wanting to make him smile even for an instant.

'You can't be serious.'

The smile she was looking for drifted through his words. 'So far I've been able to keep up, Contini.' Her voice was soft as silk, a hum of pleasure beneath her words, the smallest hint of backward thrust against his crotch.

Anyone less familiar with her impatience would have missed the slight movement of her ass. 'We're talkin' pro leagues, Tiger.' A playful note rang in his voice now, the sharpness and tension gone.

'Sign me up.'

His husky laugh warmed her to her toes, sent a spiralling heat racing downward, brought a flush to her cheeks.

He liked that she blushed; his barely chained testosterone liked it even more. 'No ground rules,' he said softly. 'You okay with that?'

There was an unmistakable warning in the low-pitched statement; an irresistible invitation as well. He offered rich, flamboyant pleasure with virtuoso ease, the thick, straining length of his dick against her back the ultimate temptation. 'I'll let you know if I'm not okay.'

The silence lasted three seconds too long. 'I may not listen. I'm a moody, selfish fuck. Just so you know.'

'Wow, newsflash,' she said, drily.

'Keep it up, Pussycat,' he whispered, bending to nip at her ear, 'and you'll get a newsflash right up your tight little ass.' Slipping his hands free, he swivelled her enough to get a firm grip on her bottom. Then, kissing his way up her cheek, he put his thumbs on her hips for leverage, flexed his fingers over the curves of her butt and gently squeezed; the weight of his broad palms, the faint pressure so slight she shouldn't instantly feel a rush of desire burn through her senses nor find herself suddenly breathless.

'You're always ready to rock, aren't you?' He told himself there were advantages to her slam-bang sexual response, that her past and his were irrelevant, that he should be gratified. But an inescapable outrage was never far from the surface when he thought of Nicole with other men. 'With you, it's Christmas every day.' His voice was lightly abrasive at the last, his fingers tightening cruelly on her ass.

'Hey!' She flinched, tried to jerk away. 'That hurts.'

He told himself to be reasonable and he was for two seconds more. 'But how much does it hurt – isn't that the question?' His voice was silken, his grip relentless; reasonableness had never been his strong suit. 'Sometimes you like it a little rough. Even ask for it.'

Her entire body was rigid, her breathing ragged. 'Stop it,' she hissed, trying to ignore the sensational size of his erection pressing into her stomach, the blazing desire drumming through her senses, the frantic throbbing inside her that confirmed the exasperating truth of his observation. 'I'm not asking now, okay?'

'Such a liar,' he whispered, stroking her bottom through the soft fabric of her dress, gently, back and forth, unhurried, like he knew how to do this job; it wasn't complicated. 'Tell me this sweet ass is all mine and I'll help you calm down.' A second passed, two, then one palm came down on her butt with a well-placed, expert smack that registered in every high-octane, stressed out, sexually deprived nerve in her body.

She flinched, then softly moaned as a wayward thrill spiked through her body in flame-hot waves. 'Damn you,' she whispered, her face warm with embarrassment.

He suddenly flashed a smile. 'It's okay to give in once in a while, Pussycat. When you need it, you need it. No one's keeping score.'

Now who was the liar? The too-beautiful-for-words control freak who also happened to be her favourite, blissed-out, orgasmic high, that's who. She sighed. 'You do have a stellar dick.'

The side of his mouth kicked up. 'Appreciate your interest.' Then he unleashed the full power of a truly wicked smile. 'Just a suggestion, but if you'd like to ramp up the game, we could try a little more wildness, make you even wetter and hornier.'

'You're in a mood.' She smiled back. 'So, no thanks.'

He gave her ass a sharp, open-handed slap gauged to hurt *so good*.

She yelped, the high-pitched sound melting into a breathy, fevered whimper as pleasure spread like wildfire through her senses.

Rafe's golden eyes flickered with amusement. 'I don't

know why you keep saying no. You never mean it. Most—'

'Don't you dare say "most women"!' Although her protest would have been more effective if her body hadn't been aglow, buzzing, slick with need; if her nipples weren't beaded hard.

His gaze lifted from her nipples, his smile indulgent. 'What I was about to point out,' he said, mildly, 'is that *most* of the time you come faster, harder, scream louder when I push you to the wall.'

Oh God, and no one did it better. Sure, smooth, gauging her meltdown with maddening ease, his long, slender fingers splayed across her ass, the provocative pressure just enough to send the requisite tingles to every eager, throbbing, sexed-up, fuck-me portion of her anatomy, to remind her how good it felt to be pushed to the wall by the living legend Rafe Contini. Wishing she wasn't such a pushover for him, that she had some of his nerveless discipline, she heard herself say, 'That's not always true,' when they both knew she was lying, when she'd barely had breath to finish the sentence, when the agitated rise and fall of her breasts was a patent display of primed, X-rated need.

'Whatever you say.' A pleasant vibe to his voice. 'Your call.' *But mostly mine*, he thought with customary arrogance, his gaze on her lavish, quivering tits, recalling their soft, weighty resilience with a tantalizing rush of memory.

Selfishly intent on cupping that warm, silken flesh in his palms, he moved her effortlessly, arranging her back to his front once again and reaching around her, began unbuttoning her dress.

'Wait a minute, wait, wait.' Rafe was always capable of such restraint like some abstemious monk. If this was the pro-leagues, if she wanted even a chance in hell of winning their wager, she couldn't just cave. 'Hey.' She shot him a look over her shoulder. 'You said, my call . . . what are you doing?'

He raised his dark brows fractionally. 'Getting ready to fuck you. Remember – no rules.' Capturing Nicole's hands, he circled her wrists with one hand, and started freeing buttons with his other. 'And I'm guaranteeing unlimited orgasms. What's not to like?'

'Your damned arrogance for starters.' But her nipples were drilling holes in the fine linen of her dress, her breathing unquiet, restless, her body opening the door wide for those promised orgasms.

'Fuck my arrogance.' He spoke with stunning indifference. 'As if that's gonna stop you from coming.' Freeing another button, he glanced at her stiff, peaked nipples. 'Christ, you're almost there, aren't you? All I have to do is touch these impressively sexed-up nipples and you'll go off like a rocket.'

She gritted her teeth, looked back at him through a haze of lust and shook her head.

He laughed. 'We've met before, remember? Even on a good day, you've got a short fuse when it comes to sex. Don't get me wrong, I like that, but I'm running this show. That means you're going to lose your little wager,' he said with a lazy smile. 'In just a few seconds.' Slipping free the last of the row of pearl buttons, he eased open the dress top. 'Jesus, Tiger,' he whispered, a small heat in his voice. 'You have the *nicest* tits – best in the world, no shit.' He slid his fingers down her warm cleavage, under the ripe abundance of her breasts, lifted slightly, his fingertips sinking into the yielding softness, his erection surging in stark appreciation.

'Fuck – just the feel of these cushy boobs makes me so hard it hurts.' His voice was tightly leashed, a hushed expectancy in his words. 'Change of plans. You're gonna have to jack me with your tits first.'

He heard her muffled sob, bent forward, saw that her eyes were glittering with wetness. 'Christ, don't cry. We'll talk about it, okay?'

She sniffled, drew in a deep breath, embarrassed and angry with herself for dissolving into tears with a man like Rafe who was the poster boy for casual sex. 'I don't feel like talking,' she said, biting her bottom lip to stifle her tears. 'I'm fine.'

She looked so lost and confused, making her happy was a no-brainer. 'Look, that was a dickhead thing to say.' Her eyes were still shiny with tears, her little hiccupy sniffs witness to his dickheadness. 'From now on, if I'm doing something you don't like, just let me know. We good?'

His offer to accept input during sex didn't go unnoticed by his psyche – the word pussy-whipped came to mind, startling in its novelty. But when Nicole blinked away her tears, then nodded and smiled, he suddenly felt as though he'd been given a prize. 'That's my girl,' he whispered. 'Yeah?'

'You betcha.'

Her smile this time was warm and heady and he had to tell his dick to cool it a little longer. Too many years of women giving him what he wanted had made him callous. Insensitive. He almost smiled. Fuck, new world order. Behave.

Sliding his fingertips over the soft fullness of her breasts to her nipples, he caressed the sensitive crests with feather-light delicacy, up and down, around and around, tugging a little, squeezing gently, taking his time until her breathing turned into erratic little pants. Then, capturing the ostentatious, jewel-hard tips in his fingers, he slowly compressed the tender flesh.

She shuddered, the exquisite pressure streaking downward, coiling hot and achy between her legs and, with a frantic little groan, she pushed back against his engorged dick. 'Rafe, please, I'm dying.'

'Just a second,' he whispered. Moving his hands down her stomach, beneath her short skirt, he slid his fingers under the edge of her panties, twisted his wrist, pushed two fingers into her slippery sex to her G-spot, placed his thumb on her clit, said, 'Take a breath' and exerted an irresistibly subtle pressure.

She moaned, a fevered, hysterical sound.

Liquid desire instantly drenched his fingers. 'More?' It was a promise of pleasure he took pains to deliver, stroking her sleek, pulsing tissue with tenderness and skill, with targeted ingenuity, with just the right degree of pressure and depth. Until she was squirming hard against his hand and so close to climax, her whimpers were rising into audible demands. 'Done waiting?' A gentle question not likely to be answered when she was trembling, her eyes shut tight. With a hand on her shoulder, he turned her back facing him, his fingers still buried in her sweet, throbbing sex rotating sleekly. Dragging his fingertips over the tender nub of her G-spot, he waited a pulse beat while she shuddered, then slid his other hand under one soft, plump breast and, lifting it high, bent to lick her nipple. Lightly at first, a few nibbles, a little sucking, a drift of up and down strokes with the flat of his tongue, estimating her readiness, her soft moans, choppy breaths – waiting.

Until she suddenly arched her back against the sharp, raw feeling, grabbed huge handfuls of his hair, hauled him close and pleaded, 'Now, now, now!'

Showtime.

Spreading his fingers wider, he tightened his grip on

her tit, sank the fingers of his other hand deep into her hot, slick pussy and, holding her securely, drew her taut, peaked nipple into his mouth and sucked the life out of it.

Nicole groaned as lust punched downward with lightning speed, turned into hot, blazing rapture, and exploded a pulse beat later into the opening throes of an orgasm so stunning, she gasped. The soft, smothered sound swiftly escalated into a more familiar overwrought cry that rose in volume until it reached the adrenalin-powered scream of full-out, orgasmic ecstasy that always made Rafe smile. She had no restraint, her emotions raw: hot/cold; sweet/sulky; plenty of stubborn, but easy too. She laid it all out there. White lightning. Take it or leave it.

Taking it made his world perfect, made his heart rate tick up, made him feel lucky as hell.

She was still trembling when he carefully eased his fingers free, drew her into the warmth of his body. Running his hands up and down her back as she slowly calmed, he felt a pure, unspoiled content he only felt with her. Picture postcard nice. Good enough to pin up and remember with wonder when the world blew up to shit.

By slow degrees, Nicole's senses returned to planet earth and, with a blissful sigh, she stretched up and kissed his throat. 'You're so good to me, I think I'm in love. No, I definitely am. Really truly.'

Her teasing tone effectively silenced any alarm bells apropos the word love and, dipping his head, he kissed her lightly. 'Does that mean I get a turn?' Because playing at love and roseate postcard scenarios were going to be winding down real fucking soon. 'If you're still going another few rounds though,' he added, politely, forcibly suppressing stark reality. 'Not a problem.' But he was sliding her dress off her shoulders and down her arms as he spoke, baring her breasts a moment later, his dick fixed on getting into the game regardless of her answer or his offered politesse.

A small flicker of coolness drifted over her heated skin as the dress dropped to her waist, a wild, spiking pleasure coursing through her, his touch instantly igniting her cravings as if she'd not just climaxed moments ago. 'You inside me ASAP. My turn, your turn, we both get turns,' she said in a heated rush, her need for Rafe unquenched, insatiable. Terrifying. 'I feel as though I should apologize for my breathless frenzy, explain – if I could. Fuck it. I can't. I'm hopelessly addicted, not that you haven't heard that a thousand times, but—'

'I haven't,' he interrupted, not about to get into a discussion of the women in his past. 'Where? Here, the bed or—'

'Right here, right now. Right the fuck *now*!' Nicole was fevered, impatient, beginning to tremble. Just like all the other women who lusted after Rafe Contini's celebrated dick, she thought, reaching for the zipper on his shorts. 'I don't suppose you ever fall apart, crazed with lust?'

She was staring at him with a fretful, narrowed gaze and his dick was rock hard, so he chose a tactful middle ground answer. 'Not often, no.'

'You mean not *ever*,' she said, tight-lipped, struggling with the zipper caught in the chino cloth.

Okaaay. Try again. 'Look, Pussycat, don't take it personally, but coming from my family I learned early on to keep my shit together. Falling apart was never an option.'

She was sprung so tight, she was practically twitching; he, on the other hand, was un-fucking-believably composed. 'I never fell apart before. That's all I'm saying. What the hell are you smiling for?'

'It pleases me, that's why.'

'It unnerves the hell out of me,' she grumbled, jerking on the zipper. 'And just so you know, I resent your permanently aroused dick, I resent my inability to resist it, I despise all the women in your past . . . for no good reason, okay – I get it, the past's the past.' She raised her chin contentiously. 'But you know, sometimes I forget that. What I really hate though, is feeling this irrational lust whenever I'm within fifty feet of you and if you don't help me with this zipper right this fucking second,' she snapped, her voice cracking at the end, 'I'm going to *scream*! I want you inside me. Now!'

If he was in the habit of expressing his feelings, he could have said they were both in the same schizoid boat – simultaneously sexed up and resentful. He also could have said that he wasn't accustomed to women screaming at

28

him. He should tell her to go fuck herself. He should tell her he knew a couple of therapists. He should refuse her undiluted command. 'How far inside?' he said instead, his voice dangerously soft.

'Zipper,' she said with a little bite.

'No problem,' he said, calm as hell, brushing her hands aside. His shorts were off a second later and, kicking them away, he spun Nicole around so her back was to him. 'Hands on the window sill.' Shoving her skirt up over her wiggling, squirming ass, he suddenly went motionless – irrationally offended by her goddamn eagerness. All his festering jealousies instantly reignited at the thought of other men who'd seen her like this.

He dragged in a breath. *Let it go.* This was about play, nothing serious; the clock was ticking for Christ's sake. This wasn't the time to overthink; this was about hot sex, and getting off until his dick gave out. *As if.* Rational thought hadn't had a fucking chance since he'd first set eyes on Nicole. 'I have a few questions,' he muttered, jerking her upright and spinning her around.

She blinked. 'You're kidding!' But his expression was so grim she quickly adjusted her response to something more likely to keep her on her impassioned path to nirvana. 'Look, if you want me to apologize, consider it done, okay? Whatever I said, I take it back.'

'I'm not looking for an apology.' His expression was unreadable. 'I need to ask you something.'

'Could we do this later—' She drew in a steadying breath. 'When I'm not so stressed out – lust wise?'

A flash of impatience. 'No.'

'I'd like to be agreeable, but—' She smiled, fluttered her hands in voiceless apology, then slid them between her legs. 'This really isn't a good time.'

He jerked her hands up so fast her jaw dropped. Holding her hands in a deceptively loose grip, he smiled tightly. 'It's a good time for me.' He spoke softly, without inflection. 'And if you ever want to come again, you might want to answer my questions.'

Her eyes instantly narrowed into slits. 'What's your problem?'

'I don't have a problem. You have a problem. Me. So . . .' His nostrils flared. 'First, don't fucking scream at me. Second, consider learning a little sexual restraint.' His gaze passed over her briefly, without expression. 'Third, I want to know how many men have . . .' He sucked in a breath, suddenly questioning his sanity. His world was about to come crashing down around him for Christ's sake and he was looking for some ridiculous head count. *What the fuck?* Dropping her hands, he exhaled loudly, quickly raked his fingers through his hair, then gave her a curt nod. 'Look, screw it. Just don't scream at me, okay, and we'll get along.'

'Does getting along mean I can have sex with you?' Feeling as though the storm had passed, and she'd survived, her sexed-up psyche was wilfully back on target. Her eyes locked in on his blatant erection lifting the fabric of his boxers. 'Are you going to take it out or should I?'

She sure as hell had balls. But he was still smarting from almost losing it over some totally unacceptable jealousy. 'It depends.'

She smiled. 'Come on, can we cut the drama?'

He shrugged. 'You tell me. You're the screaming drama queen.'

She squared her shoulders, inhaled, offered him a tentative smile. 'Okay, here goes, I'm going to lay it all out – every confused, conflicted emotion. And even though you've heard it from me before, remember, women like to talk things to death. I've always preferred things simple, no strings, no craziness. And until I met you, the pattern never changed. So I dislike, loathe, maybe even hate feeling this out-of-control about a man – you in particular. I don't, as a rule, think about men and all I *do* is think about you, want you, need you . . . in me, over me, around me . . . every goddamn minute.'

'Sex, you mean.' A noticeable growl vibrated through the words, his recent reflections on being reasonable about head counts going up in smoke.

She grimaced. 'I don't know, maybe, could be. But you of all people can't take issue with that.'

'I find I do with you. It annoys me. Not often.' He smiled his first warm smile since she'd screamed at him, thinking that was about as close to contrite as his little hot-headed girl could manage. 'Look ... you've brought me a kind of happiness I didn't know existed. But dealing with this – sex ... relationship – whatever it is between us, processing all the strange, new feelings; good and bad, the wanting ... ' A quick, boyish smile. 'Which is fanatical, by the way, is messing with my head too.'

'Also, you don't like women who talk back. I worry about that.'

He laughed so long, she was scowling up a storm by the time he wiped his hand over his face and composed himself. 'Sorry, but that was so fucking deluded.' He chuckled, caught himself. 'Sorry, really.'

'And you're always completely transparent, I suppose,' she said with a little flash of annoyance.

No way he was going there, his entire life shrouded in layers of reticence. 'With you, I'll try, okay? Ask me something. I'll answer if I can.'

'But not why we're here.'

'It's too dangerous for you to know. That's why your uncle was freaking. Ask me something easier.'

'Do you believe in love?'

He cleared his throat. 'That's a pretty loaded word.'

'Doesn't have to be.'

She waited, a smile lifting her perfect mouth. Understanding this was in the way of a test, he was careful with his answer. 'Before you, I would have said, emphatically, no. Now? I'm thinking, maybe.'

She laughed. 'Men. So predictable. Scared as shit about love.'

'Predictable this, Pussycat,' he said, reaching out for her, putting an end to a conversation that couldn't possibly end well. Grabbing her skirt, he jerked it up, ripped off her lace panties with a snap of his wrist, dropped them, shoved his boxers down, then spun her around. 'Hands on the sill, Tiger. You wouldn't want to fall.' His voice was soft, the finger he slid up her slick pussy practised, professional, smoothly efficient in its results.

With a quivering sigh, she leaned over and set her hands on the sill.

'Good girl.' But even as he slid the swollen head of his dick into her sleek, pulsing sex, he experienced a sharp, bitter taste in his mouth at the feel of her ever-ready, slick pussy. A second later, he reminded himself that he'd always considered wantonness an asset in a women; get over it. So he did in his habitual fashion – deny the problem – fuck instead. Splaying his fingers around her slim hips, he secured his grip, and without preliminaries, drove in hilt deep, ignoring her startled cry, begrudging her low moan of pleasure that followed, not sure any of this was even close to habitual.

Nicole had never been a casual lay.

More like an obsession.

And in his current reproachful frame of mind, undeterred by reason or logic, he blamed the beautiful, captivating, unpredictable woman for making unclear what had always been clear in his life, for trashing his long-held custom of sex as entertainment, for the bloody unwelcome cluster-fuck in his brain. Rankled and sullen, wanting her to somehow pay for his obsession, he gave her ass a slap. 'Show me what you've got, babe. Give me a good ride and I might let you come first.'

His fuck-all tone was so outrageous, her pulse was suddenly loud in her ears for reasons other than her feverish arousal. 'You're confusing me with all the women who put up with your bullshit,' Nicole snapped. Pushing hard on the window sill, she tried to rise, ignoring her wildly aroused libido that was screaming, *No, no, no! Don't do this to me!* Shutting down the hysterical voice in her head, she flung herself back against the immovable force holding her down. 'Get the fuck off me!'

Motionless, tense, his dick buried deep inside her, he didn't move, with the exception of tightening his grip on her hips, his fingers leaving marks on her skin. Assailed with an overwhelming need to finish what he started, her hot, pulsing pussy wetter than hell, there was no doubt in his mind she wanted to come as much as he did. Rocked with indecision, thoroughly selfish, sexual denial previously unknown, he quickly debated his options. With anyone else, debate would have been a non-starter. Also, if he wasn't so fucking ready to explode, if his fucked-up life didn't make true enlightenment impossible, he might have seen the humour in the situation.

Really, what woman says 'stop' when she's impaled on your dick and panting? The Princess of the Universe, of course. Who the fuck else?

Dragging in a steadying breath, he took a moment to deal with his rancor, quickly calculated a sexual cost/benefit analysis and decided Nicole couldn't go long without an orgasm. So what the hell – he could afford to be polite a few minutes more.

But he was still damn near explosive, his dick in particular, and it required another moment or two to drain the snarl from his voice. 'Sorry, my fault,' he said, tightly. Shutting his eyes briefly, he summoned every shred of willpower he possessed, then withdrew from the sweetest, hottest piece of ass this side of paradise. His libido was still raging, his erection hard enough to cut steel. Life sucked.

'Oh, hell, I'm sorry too.' Standing up and turning to face him, Nicole offered a small deprecating smile. 'I get pissed when you play God.' She twitched her nose. 'Jeez, sorry again – really – that would have been super good too. Damn.' She smiled. 'I apologize for my freaking temper.'

'Not a problem. I deserved it,' he said, not defensive, patient, being an adult now that his pulse rate was diminishing. 'I shouldn't have said what I did.'

'Look, it's supposed to be just a game.' Nicole sighed. 'I overreacted.'

He shrugged. 'We both did. For what it's worth, I don't mind your temper. It's different.'

A playful twinkle warmed her eyes. 'Different from all your compliant lays?'

'Something like that.' Although she was so much more, different in countless ways – all good, shiny bright and dazzling.

'You've had it easy too long.' She held up her hands to stop his protest. 'Not that I don't understand. Smart, handsome billionaire with a legendary dick. Hell, *I'm* willing to be agreeable for access to your inked magnificence.'

He chuckled. 'You agreeable? Hey, joke, relax. You're perfect.' Pulling her close, he slid his hands down her back, rested them at the base of her spine, smiled his most winning smile. 'However.' A lift of his brows. 'At the risk of returning to the war zone, I don't much feel like conversation. I'm barely keeping my shit together you noticed, yeah? Anyway, under stress, my normal go-to setting is to smash something or else fuck till I drop. Old habits, sorry. If I'm scaring the shit out of you, you're off the hook. I can do myself.'

'I don't scare. Also, in case you haven't noticed, I'm horny too. Capisce?'

Having noticed her horniness wasn't the issue so much as his curious disapproval of it. But apparently she was willing to overlook his behaviour for her own selfish reasons. He understood; selfishness his mantra too. 'Our bet still on, then?' he asked with a truly lovely smile.

'Fuck, yeah.' Damned if he couldn't be sweet. And, honestly, he had major reasons for his bad-ass mood. 'I'll even raise you one. Me at your complete disposal. That should give me extra points on the scoreboard.'

He sucked in a breath. 'You sure you know what you're doing?'

'I thought you were the one who did,' she purred.

He was beginning to have a real good feeling about the next twenty-four hours. 'Seeing how you're magnanimously offering me my drug of choice, you have to tell me what I can buy you in return – name it . . . anything in the world. Don't even think about frowning because you deserve a ton of gifts. You make everything better in my fucked-up world.'

'I don't need presents.' She grinned. 'But there are some things I want.'

He looked at her from under his dark lashes. 'I can afford the fucking gifts, okay? So decide. That's an order.' He dipped his head and gave her back a lazy grin that was pure, undiluted sex. 'The other things you want are free.'

She shrugged. 'Okay then, if you insist, I'll decide on a gift *after* the wedding.'

His eyes went from stunned shock to anger in an instant. 'Very fucking amusing,' he growled.

Her little giggle was one of triumph. 'You said *anything.*'

'Very well,' he said with a small despairing sigh. 'If that's what you want – no point in waiting. We might as well call your mother and father and give them the good news.'

Nicole immediately went ashen and Rafe grinned, made a little check mark in the air and whispered, 'Gotcha.'

'You're so on my shit list,' she grumbled. 'You almost gave me a heart attack.'

'I can give you something else you'll like better,' he murmured, flexing his hips so she felt the rigid length of his dick against her stomach.

Still sulky, she tried to swat his hands away; he pulled her back, his palms hard on her ass. 'I'm done fucking around, Tiger. No more talking, no more arguing, no more playing around. If you're not interested in fucking, I'm going solo.' Motionless, he waited, not interested in trying to read her mind, needing a clear-cut answer. Because a blinding neon sign was lighting up his brain, blinking – TWENTY-FOUR HOURS – and he was real fucking close to scaring the shit out of her.

She recognized the line in the sand, the grim set of his mouth, the taut muscles of his throat visible above his T-shirt. 'Definitely interested,' she murmured. 'Now pay attention.' Rising on tiptoe, she slid her hands up his black T-shirt with the logo of some band she'd never heard of, slipped her arms around his neck, locked her fingers under the dark silken curls laying at his nape and stretched to kiss his chin.

Every cell in his body was paying attention, fresh blood

rushing to his dick at dizzying speed. Dipping his head, he touched her lips, whispered, 'Ummm . . . nice – sexy.' The kiss quickly deepened, his dick started doing the happy dance, Nicole began to pant and, under normal circumstances, he would have had them on the bullet train to orgasm. But the deliberative part of his brain wouldn't shut down. It kept reverting to the imminent dangers facing them, reminding him that the clock was ticking down, his world was shrinking by the minute, destruction was fast approaching and regardless his feelings and wishes, including the fierce delirium of flame hot sex – nothing mattered if they lost this war.

'Hey.' Nicole leaned back enough to give him a perplexed look.

'Sorry.' Dragging himself back from the brink of the abyss, he smiled. 'I apologize for zoning out, but there's a ton of shit going down right now. You have my permission to smack me back to reality when I drift off.'

'Oh God, I'm so selfish. Would you rather be with your friends? I'd understand completely.'

'Hell, no. I just want to be with you, and forget everything except the good stuff.' He was back in reality, the hard pull of disaster fading, the complications facing him boiling down, running out of steam, cooling. He had a day, a wisp and flicker of innocence still left him and a woman he really liked and wanted; he'd never wanted anyone more.

'Okay then, here's what we're going to do,' Nicole said, firmly, unwrapping her arms from his neck, easing down from her tiptoes and stepping away.

He frowned, his voice sharpened. 'Get back here.'

She stared at him.

Recognizing that stubborn tilt to her chin, he ducked his head, watched her from under his eyelids. 'Please?'

Her smile slowly appeared. 'You have manners after all.'

In the interest of détente, he bit back his remark about not needing manners when you had billions. 'I'm sorry if I offended you. Now come back and kiss me.'

'I was thinking, since you're obviously tense – with reason,' she noted, as if he hadn't spoken, 'why don't I see if your dick would like some kisses. You know, help you relax.'

Everything except his dick instantly relaxed. 'Thank you,' he said, politely, as if his turn in croquet had just come up. 'I'd like that.'

'Let me take this dress off so it doesn't get—'

'Messy?' He grinned. 'Or are you going to swallow?'

She grinned back. 'It depends how polite you are.'

'Give me a hint. What do you want? Please and thank you? Actually, that would work, wouldn't it? I'll say please now and thank you later.'

'I'm trying to do you a favour and I get sarcasm?'

He looked amused. 'You don't have to do me any favours. Just come a little closer and I'll do us both some favours. Repetitive favours – you know, the kind you like best.'

CHAPTER 3

'Finish undressing for me – slowly. Calm my nerves.' He pointed. 'You there. Me here.' He turned and walked to a chair, pulling off his T-shirt as he went. Dropping the shirt on the floor, he sat, looked up and lifted his brows. 'What?'

'I don't know if you've noticed, but you give orders. A lot.'

He smiled. 'Sorry. Remind me when I revert to asshole mode. I can adapt.'

'For me.'

'Yeah. Just for you.' He paused, debating how to politely decline her offer of oral. Practically every woman he met offered to go down on him. It was common as shit in his world – the modern equivalent of hello. 'Look.' He ran his hands over his hair, took a breath. 'I appreciate you trying to be nice to me. But I've had less practice, so let *me* work on being nice.' His smile was a thing of beauty, visual poetry come to life. 'So come here.' He patted his thigh. 'I just want to feel you – everywhere. You can be my security blanket.'

'Did you have one?' she asked, moving toward him.

He shook his head. No point in mentioning the nannies his father had hired who'd made his young life so miserable that his mother finally had stood up to Maso and insisted on taking care of Rafe herself. At the age of four he'd first come to know the meaning of salvation.

'I had a blankey,' Nicole said, unbuttoning the last few buttons on the dress. 'Mine was white with bunnies on it, silky and worn down to a scrap before I gave it up. I couldn't go to sleep without it.'

He smiled. 'That's probably why my life went off the rails. You'll have to tell me what it was like to have a security blanket.'

'I'd be happy to show you.' She slowly slid her dress down her hips, let it slither to the floor, stepped over the puddle of purple linen and grinned. 'Consider me here for your edification.'

He laughed and held out his arms.

She'd never been drawn to men by their looks alone. It was too often a façade for banality. Yet it was impossible to ignore the physical munificence that was Rafe Contini. His dark hair fell in disarray over his shoulders, framed the high cheekbones of his handsome face, the beauty of his golden wolf eyes, the hard line of his jaw. He was sprawled in the carved and gilded chair, big, tall, nude – enough energy running through his sleek muscles to power the world, his colourful, inked dick arched high, tapping his stomach. His smile clean as the sun.

Nicole caught a huge breath.

He offered her a slow, lazy grin. 'Everything good?'

A tiny smile tugged at the corners of her mouth. 'Oh yeah.'

He crooked his finger, his smile swelled. 'Come. Talk to me.'

She closed the distance to the chair in a slow catwalk.

'Fancy that.' His eyes sparkled. 'A little sex-bomb tease.'

'Didn't know I was a sex bomb.'

'You're every man's fantasy, Pussycat.' Huge blue eyes, rosy skin, soft mouth, dark curls all raggedy and messy from the wind, a body that could stop traffic; the kind of lovely that would last for ever. He raised one finger from the chair arm where his hand rested. 'Were. Past tense.'

Her grin had a glint. 'We putting up fences?'

'I am.'

'We'll have to see how that goes.' Coming to a stop, she took his outstretched hands, put one knee on the turquoise velvet of the chair cushion, then the other, straddled his thighs, leaned forward, kissed him, then sat back with a smile. 'What do you want to talk about?'

'About how many times you want to come.' Sliding a hand under her bottom, he lifted her slightly, guided the head of his dick into place and, leaning back, held her gaze as she slowly sank down his rock-hard erection. 'I'm real sorry I missed out on security blankets.' His voice was a low rasp, his hands closing over her hips. 'If they make you feel this bloody fine.' A small hooded smile as she came to rest on his thighs, shut her eyes and softly sighed. 'Don't move.'

She couldn't if she wanted to, his steely grip nailing her in place, an incredible pleasure whooshing through her like a strong, hot rush of E. Uttering a small, dreamy sound, she slowly opened her eyes. 'More.'

He grunted. 'Greedy.'

'Always.' She wrapped her arms around his neck. 'Or should I do myself?'

'You'll like this better.' Holding her immobile, he flexed his quads and gluts, thrust his huge dick upward hard and zeroed in on all her sweet spots with perfect understanding and absolute precision – offering her the first generous hint of promised favours.

Her head tipped back, pleasure sharp enough to make her gasp.

Her pussy convulsed around his dick with sheer perfection.

And a breath-held moment passed in an electric, fast-beating silence.

Then, well-trained and accomplished, Rafe raised her slowly up his dick and started over again.

He watched her from under his lashes, monitoring the nuances of her arousal, the little panting groans, the flush on her cheeks, the way she sank her nails into his shoulders when he was forcing his dick all the way up into her tight little pussy.

There. Like that.

Now wait for her gasp, her greedy swivelling grind, her lush moan. He smiled. There was something about that soft, breathy sound that made him feel invincible.

With every lustful cell in her body offering infinite devotion to her sexual benefactor, Nicole recognized that if there was a contest for the best dick in the world and how to use it, Rafe would win it hands down. Not that she was a major authority but, at the moment, she was as close to an earthly paradise as any opium-crazed poet could imagine. She was drowning in happiness, bliss was exploding in her brain and her body was quivering on the brink of another spectacular, mind-blowing orgasm. Oh. My. God. How does he know that when he touches her right *there*, her entire nervous system melts into a puddle of love.

'You like that?' A deep, low whisper. 'Try it again?'

If she could override the fevered pleasure scorching her brain, the synapses powering her speech functions would be screaming, *Yes, yes, yes!* But coherent thought had short circuited, carnal desperation held sway, ravenous lust was flooding her body and the best she could manage was a hot little pant.

Good enough. He hadn't really expected an answer anyway. He pushed deeper, dragged his dick slowly over the soft cushiony nerves of her G-spot, up and down, one, twice, three times, super gently. Gave her clit a tender massage with his thumb for good measure. He was just about to begin an encore riff when she arched her back, uttered a low, strung-out moan and started to climax.

He'd never before contemplated the word *finally*, when it came to Nicole's pedal-to-the-metal orgasms but, tense as hell, wired to the max with lethal threats coming from every direction, he'd been waiting his turn. So the second she sucked in that little breath in prelude to her scream, he did a quick mental check that all her erogenous pussy zones were feeling the pressure of his big, stiff cock and raced to catch up. As she began shuddering against his body, he blanked out everything but immediate sensation, jumped on the orgasmic rocket and climaxed in a powerful surge, flooding her pussy with wave after wave of white-hot come.

Before he'd even stopped breathing hard, a jarring memory prompt replayed Nicole's strangely subdued orgasm; no wild cry, only a few stifled whimpers. Jesus, had he hurt her? An instant spike of worry shot through him. Bending his head, he took her face in his hands and quickly scanned her features, as if evidence of her affliction might be visible. 'Something's wrong.'

'Not true.' Her eyes were shut.

Brushing away a tear escaping from under her lashes, he said, 'You expect me to believe that when you're crying? If I hurt you, I'm sorry. Just tell me what I did and I won't do it again. If it's something else, I'll fix it, buy it or make it go away.'

She slowly opened her eyes. 'You can't do any of that.'

'Try me,' he said, gently.

Struggling not to burst into tears and scare him off by saying something stupidly romantic about how perfect he was to her, she forced a smile. 'It's nothing – nerves, hormones, fatigue, the alignment of the planets – fuck, I don't know. Don't worry about it.' Rafe had too much on his plate right now, scary shit that had Dominic sending Leo along to guard her. This wasn't the time for her to get all needy and emotional. Although with Rafe there probably was never a good time for that.

'Sleep if you want.' She didn't want to talk – fine, although with her, he would have listened. 'I'll just hold you.'

She squirmed a tiny bit. 'What about him?' His dick was still hard inside her or hard again or if the last few days were any indication, perpetually hard.

'Ignore him.' Reaching down over the chair arm, he picked up his T-shirt, mopped up some of the come seeping onto his thighs, then dropped the T-shirt on the carpet.

She smiled. 'How exactly should I ignore him – like, realistically?'

47

'He likes you. I'm sorry. He's sorry. Don't worry, we'll behave.'

'Or we could think about a slow, lazy, sleepy fuck. When was the last time you slept?'

He shrugged. 'No time for that.'

'You'll collapse.'

He laughed. 'Sweet child.'

'And you're the big bad wolf?'

'More or less, last time I checked. You know, Tiger,' he said, softly, brushing a fingertip across her mouth, 'I wasn't completely joking about the security blanket. You remind me there's a normal world out there. More peaceful. Relaxed. Even when you're being a drama queen, it's real, not some fake act of cunning. You're my comfort and joy, my very own security blanket. Seriously.' He dragged in a breath, dropped his hand. 'Jesus, stupid. Forget it.'

'Uh-uh. That was nice of you to say. All of it, especially about me reminding you of something peaceful.' Her eyes twinkled and she spoke in a teasing tone to mitigate his obvious discomfort. 'Could I get that in writing for my family?'

He laughed, grateful for her rescue from a potentially awkward conversation. 'As if my opinions matter. Your Uncle Dominic's counting the days until you escape my clutches.'

'He should talk. We both know a little about his wildness.'

One of them considerably more than the other. 'Any requests?' he asked, interested in changing the subject. 'Want something to eat, want to sleep, a drink, we could go for a swim. Or,' he said, charmed by her flirty grin, 'we could *try* a sleepy fuck.'

Her grin widened. 'So accommodating.'

'Just trying to keep up with your shocking interest in sex.'

'I've never underestimated your ability to keep up. Rumour precedes you, you know. You have records. I don't.'

'Let's keep it that way.'

'Sure,' she said, smart enough not to push back when he was looking at her in that unsettling way. 'You're the boss.'

For a second, no blink, just taking her in. Then he smiled. 'You've got a deal.'

He slid his hands under her bottom, large, wide, long-fingered hands, remarkably gentle. With a smooth ripple of honed muscle, he lifted her just a little, the smallest adjustment of male and female parts, a yin/yang subtlety of great richness.

She felt the warm glow, a shimmer of heat slipped into every secret corner of her brain and body, the starry-eyed feeling of bliss so real she couldn't help but smile. 'It's always good with you. Layers of sweet hotness.' She sighed. 'Swear to God.'

The pale curve of her cheek was suddenly limned by sunshine and a feeling he didn't recognize caught him off guard. He blinked away the odd sensation, cupped her ass and smiled back. 'Same here. Sweet through and through.' And holding her lightly in his hands, he flexed his hips upward an almost invisible distance, she melted around him and for a stark, fleeting moment, they stopped breathing.

He managed to get himself together first, but then self-control had been critical to his survival. 'Hey, you okay?' he asked, quietly, watching her with laser vision after her recent tears. 'More, less, call it a day?'

'More.' Eyes at half mast, shuttered.

Her voice was eerily docile for the Princess of the Universe and he cautioned himself not to fuck this up. *Seriously, don't get this wrong.*

He moved her first in an effortless, gentle rise and fall lift and descent, her weight incidental to the strong flex and flow of his muscled arms. The feel of her warm, silken skin, the sweet scent of her, her soft curves no one else should see brought out his predatory instincts, made him swell harder and bigger. His sensations were both raw-edged and tender; this brief, golden time the best of all possible worlds.

Nicole eyes finally opened, the electric-blue gleam like a drug to his senses.

'I won't break,' she said with a smile.

'Good to know.' His voice was gentle. 'Just didn't want to take any chances. Make you cry again.'

Reaching up, she slipped his dark hair behind his ears, eased upward a little and brushed his lips with a kiss. 'No worries, okay?'

He took her hands, placed them on his shoulders, smiled. 'I'll worry if I want. And since this is a sleepy fuck, you're allowed to doze off any time.'

She gave him a sexy wink. 'You aren't.'

'Not a chance.' His fingers trailed down her back in a warm flow, settled low over the curve of her ass, held her like she belonged there, like maybe she actually belonged right the fuck there for a very long time.

His hands were warm, strong, *relentless* – not in a negative way; there was just a certainty and courage in him, Nicole reflected. Trouble waiting for him and he was going to face it, head on. Without her, unfortunately. Dominic had made that clear in his usual roundabout way; Rafe didn't want to talk about it. An irrevocable life waited for him somewhere else. She shivered at the thought of losing him, even though she knew it was childish to wish for the moon.

'You're cold.'

She shook her head. 'Kiss me,' she said with a straight-out blaze of longing, her voice sharp and clear. 'Kiss me like you mean it.'

It was like a punch in the jaw, it hit him so hard.

Although the fact that he couldn't fool himself about what she meant to him didn't mean he could change the trajectory of his life. And his tone was halfway to earnest before he caught himself, eased off and smiled. 'If I kiss you that way, Pussycat, I'll scare the hell out of you. How about a no-bruises kiss?'

'Sure. Why not?' Nothing in her voice to catch anyone off guard. Score one for salvaging a dicey situation. If she burst into tears, he'd leave her, she told herself; it was the only thing that kept her from spinning out of control.

They kissed in a slow unfurling of tenderness, in a cascade of breath-held rapture, faces tilting together, mouths open, eyes closed at times, witness to something special, both taking chances because they couldn't help themselves. Even though they both understood that life was too frail and brittle now, too loaded with might-have-beens. With danger and uncertainty.

But burning hot with something truly amazing too, something beautiful.

And at the end, when kisses weren't enough, when their hearts were pumping, when Nicole was whimpering and Rafe was gently moving inside her, when the sheer joy they were feeling lit them from within—

A ring tone shattered their paradise.

Rafe recognized the ring tone, ignored it, didn't miss a beat. Nicole was seconds away from climax so he was seconds away from climax.

The phone rang again.

Nicole shivered, flinched, glanced up at him.

'It's nothing, shut your eyes, feel me? There?'

On the fifth ring though, Nicole murmured, 'Should you—'

'No. Am I deep enough here – or *here*?'

She gasped, then moaned.

'Take just a little more?' he whispered, working to keep them both in the moment despite the distracting ringing. Then her sleek pussy begin to ripple up his cock in the initial stage of orgasm and, solidly committed to bringing this off to their mutual benefit, he angled his head down, drew a sweet, stiff nipple into his mouth and sucked so hard her little whimpers reached fever pitch in seconds flat.

She came with a muted cry.

He was right behind her, his mind inconveniently counting fourteen rings at that point. But a climax was a climax, thank you very much. And he poured into his all-time favourite pussy with a smart-ass smile on his face.

Moments later, Nicole lay limply in his arms, her cheek resting on his chest.

His smile faded like snow in the desert. Christ, maybe something *was* wrong. Maybe two non-screaming orgasms in a row meant something. 'Hey, talk to me. You okay?'

'Tired.'

'You wanna sleep?'

'Maybe.' Her voice was muffled against his skin. 'Answer your phone.'

He hesitated. Gina was calling.

She felt him tense. 'I'm wallowing in feel-good endorphins,' she said, lifting her head enough to give him a smile. 'So if some woman's calling you, I don't care.'

He blew out a quick breath, brushed her nose with a kiss. 'Thanks.' He knew better than to start explaining Gina. Holding Nicole close, he smoothly rose from the chair, set her back down gently, braced his hands on the chair arms, and leaning forward, held her gaze. 'It's business in case you were wondering.'

Her smile was soft and girly; it made him wish he'd known her at sixteen.

'It's okay. Really.'

'This won't take long.' He walked over to the window where he'd left his shorts and pulled the ringing cell phone from a pocket.

CHAPTER 4

Hitting the answer icon, Rafe put the phone to his ear. 'Sorry, I was busy.'

'I know what you were busy doing. I already talked to Carlos.'

'Then you should have left a message. I would have called you back.'

'Maybe I'm just a bitch.'

'I wouldn't disagree right now,' he said, rubbing his forehead with two fingers. 'What's up?'

'We changed the flight plan, mid flight. Webster's a goddamn star. I'm halfway across India, on the way to Brisbane.'

'No shit. Fill me in.' He held up five fingers to Nicole, then turned and, listening, walked across the room to the windows. He nodded a few times at Gina's recital, braced one hand on the window jamb, leaned forward and stared at the sparkling blue sea as she ran through the search methodology. 'Your contact in Manila gave up the first information, right? He's paid, I assume.'

'Enough so he's still covering the streets for more info. We're not the only ones after Zou's mistress and child. But once my man in Manila connected the dots, Webster found two likely names on a passenger manifest – false, of course – but a video feed showed them boarding a Macau–Brisbane flight. Your tech wizard accomplished this feat in under five minutes. If he's as hot in bed, I need to fuck him.'

'He's married. Happily, I might add.'

'You never know.'

'True. But he's been vetted down to the beer he drinks. No side action. Sorry.'

'Damn. You sure know how to ruin a good mood. You know how I love expertise.'

'It's a big world out there,' Rafe said. 'I'm sure you'll find someone to get you back in a good mood.'

'I gather you're not available at the moment.'

'No.'

The simplicity of his answer was more startling than the actual answer. But Gina had known Rafe for a long time. Leopard's spots and all that shit. He'd be back on the market soon. 'Well, since Carlos is paying top euros, even if you're currently unavailable, I'll keep working the case.'

No way he was going to discuss anything personal with Gina. 'We both appreciate your help – you know that. Ask

Carlos for whatever you need once you get to Brisbane. What's your gut feeling on whether the woman and child stay there or move on?'

'It's a strange place to go unless you have good reason. The usual escapees end up in Dubai, Cyprus, South America, some island nation with no extradition treaties. So I'll give it at least fifty-fifty Zou has a hideaway there in some better-than-average suburban neighbourhood. With his money stashed somewhere else.'

'Money he's not going to live to enjoy.'

'You and I know that, but he's hopeful. All the crooks are bloody optimists, well protected or both. Otherwise they wouldn't keep sending money out of whatever country they're plundering.'

'Seems that way. Now, don't take any risks. Seriously, Gina, no heroics, okay? We'll close this deal without you putting your life on the line.'

'Easier said than done. You know what you're up against.'

'Fuck, yeah. But my order still stands. Be careful. All you have to do is find the woman and child, then back off. We'll do the rest. I have no intention of losing this one.'

'That's what Carlos tells me.'

'Believe it. I'll be back on line tomorrow.'

'If only you could dismiss me so easily,' she said, a smile in her voice.

'Piss me off, I might not answer your calls.'

'Ooooh, threats. I love it. Are you going to whip me?'

'Jesus, shut the fuck up. I'm ending this conversation.' But he didn't move from the window for a few moments after the call, his mind racing, contemplating all the actors in play, their motives, constraints, tactics, how many others were on their way to Brisbane, possibly there already. He was fully aware that he should be discussing this with Carlos and Ganz instead of indulging his passions. The consequences of losing an entire day were substantial with Zou and his killers breathing down their necks. He was walking a fucking tightrope here. One foot wrong and it was over.

Nicole hadn't heard the conversation, only the resonance and cadence of Rafe's deep voice. But he hadn't moved since ending the call, his large frame silhouetted against the brilliant sun, his tension palpable even from across the room. His underlying musculature was taut beneath his graceful stance – from his lightly braced arm to his broad shoulders, down his strong back, over his fine ass and long, powerful legs, to his feet planted firmly on the carpet.

No matter the dizzy white light pouring in the windows, the full-on view was so explicitly defensive, so cold and distant that a sudden sharp panic gripped her senses. She could already feel him drifting away, a shadow of loss strong enough to take her breath away.

As if responding to her unease, Rafe turned, smiled. 'It's always something, right?'

'You've got a lot going on.' She gave herself kudos for keeping her voice steady.

His eyes were cool and unblinking for a moment as though her simple statement required more than a cursory response. Then a little furrow formed between his eyes, followed by a tiny pause where Nicole felt as though time stopped. 'I thought I could do this,' Rafe said. 'Take off a little time. But I can't turn it off.' His brows flicked upward. 'Sorry.'

For the first time, the phrase 'your heart drops' hit home. But Nicole managed to keep the crushing sadness at bay and offered him what she hoped was a sympathetic smile. 'Hey, I'm a big girl. You're dealing with high stakes. Go do what you have to do.'

'I'll think about it.' His look had softened now, his voice too, all the emotional cross-currents deliberately subdued. 'Or I'll think about it later,' he said, a warmth in his sudden smile, telling himself this was a self-indulgence he could afford. 'Carlos can handle things a little longer. If he can't, he'll let me know,' he added, walking toward her with an easy stride.

Her heart moved back where it belonged, her shoulders imperceptibly relaxed. 'I know you're trying to strike a balance between your responsibilities and me. So I can be mature and unselfish. Stay out of your way.'

'I hope that doesn't mean you're cutting me off.' His voice was calm, but a predatory spark lit his eyes.

'As if I could.'

'That's my girl.' A big grin broke across his face. 'Dutiful and compliant.'

'You're such an asshole. No offence.'

'None taken.' He came to a stop in front of the chair. 'Now.' He glanced at a large standing clock that had been telling time since Copernicus. 'Should we try out the bed?'

'Right after you apologize.'

A short stare. 'Always prickly as fuck, aren't you?' A flash of a smile. 'I love our chemistry. I apologize. We okay?'

Huge-eyed, she took a long, shaky breath, told herself not to be reckless. But she said it anyway. 'We're always okay. Always.'

Curiously, he experienced no alarm seeing the wistfulness in her eyes, felt no need for a customary smooth withdrawal. In fact, he considered asking her again so he could hear her say it again, so his world could rock just a little again. *Always.* Such a grand word. Impossible though. Now more than ever.

But not right this second. He held out his hand. 'Come. I need to feel you.'

She should have qualified her response, made sure he knew she wasn't looking for anything permanent. That she understood *always* wasn't an approved word. But when she wove her fingers through his and he pulled her to her feet, she found she couldn't pretend. It was a character flaw Dominic had always contended with himself, a master of omission. 'I have no clue how to deal with this any more,' she said with a ghost of a smile.

'Us, you mean.' There was a small catch in his voice.

She nodded.

His grip tightened on her hand. 'All I know is it feels right. I have no idea why. I don't give a shit why.' This might be his one and only shot. He was going to take it. 'The rest of the world can stay on fucking hold for a while.'

He towered above her, his strong hand holding hers, a ready-for-anything sexy man. A beautiful, capable man who'd stopped her meltdown with a few simple words. Her smile was a flash of sweetness. 'We're running out of road, so make me a miracle.'

He laughed. 'You got it. A well-fucked, epic miracle, Pussycat. Guaranteed.'

A moment later, he was lifting her up on the high gilded bed when his cell rang. Recognizing the ring tone, he quickly lowered Nicole onto the crocus-yellow damask coverlet, then straightened, and gave her a nod. 'Family. I have to take this.'

Picking up the phone from the nightstand, he asked, 'Where are you?' He then winced in response to the answer given, began pacing and, for the next few minutes, circled the room like a caged animal, alternately listening and speaking, his voice cold and flat. 'Okay, okay; Yes, I said I would; No I won't forget; Of course, no problem; No comment, no comment, *no* comment, keep asking me that you'll get the same fucking answer.' His frown was in place throughout the conversation and after a last, terse 'No problem', he came to a stop and slam-dunked his phone on the bed so hard it bounced.

'Sounds like a problem. Sorry!' Nicole giggled. 'I couldn't resist.'

'Not now, okay?' he said in a don't-fuck-with-me tone.

'That bad, hey? Is there anything I can do to help?'

'I'm sure there will be later,' he said with just the smallest inkling of a smile. 'But right now, we're screwed.' A note of resignation in his voice echoed his one shoulder shrug. 'We have to get dressed. My mum, step-dad and little brother just anchored in the harbour and we're invited aboard for drinks and dinner. My step-dad was being a major prick. He doesn't want my mother to worry. It's my fault she's worried, blah, blah, blah. So I have to fix the problem, which means lying to her non-stop. Anton knows that but doesn't care. All he cares about is protecting my mother. Not that I'd consider involving my mum in any of this mess but, still, it's gonna be a long evening.' He dragged in a breath. 'And I have to talk to Carlos first.'

'How much time do we have?'

'None. Bath or shower?'

'Shower.' She surveyed the circular space. 'Downstairs?'

He lifted his chin. 'On the other side of that bookcase.'

'Such an interesting life you lead,' she said with a little laugh. 'Secret doors in castle towers. Am I in a movie?'

He gave her a look from under his lashes. 'Only if it's my private film. I don't believe in sharing.' A novel concept specific to the lady in his bed, but one he no longer viewed as incredulous. Scooping her up off the bed, he moved toward the bookcase on the far wall. 'We gotta make this fast. Anton's got my mum freaking.'

CHAPTER 5

Sliding the bookcase aside on well-oiled hinges, Rafe set Nicole down in what was essentially a glass structure cantilevered out over the original garderobe. The area was considerably larger than most medieval toilets but then the comte had been a man given to luxury. With the exception of the original mosaic floor, however, the space now resembled a glass eyrie, albeit a bulletproof one, with one-way glass available at the flick of a switch.

'Wow! What a glorious sight!' Nicole stared, transfixed, as the entire island and miles of azure sea lay spread out beneath her.

'It's relaxing, isn't it?'

Her gaze swung to Rafe. 'Not exactly the word I'd use unless you consider the view from the Eiffel Tower relaxing. This is stunning!'

Since he actually did think the view from the Eiffel Tower was relaxing, a reply would entail more discussion than they had time for. 'Glad you like it,' he said, politely. 'But . . .' He tapped the sports watch on his wrist, then motioned to the shower. 'We're on a tight schedule.'

'So no playing in the shower?' One brow arched in playful query. 'Is that what you're saying?'

He laughed. 'You're gonna kill me.'

'Oh.' A tiny start. 'Sorry. It's just that you make me feel so . . . ' Her voice trailed off, her cheeks flushing pink.

'Hey, I was joking.' He leaned in close. 'Same here, twenty-four/seven. But you want this now, we're gonna have to set records.'

Her smile was so alight with pleasure he decided never to make stupid jokes when she needed him. Nice thought. Being needed by Nicole.

She winked. 'Think you can keep up?'

'Why don't I try,' he drawled, a man with a sexual skill-set honed to perfection by considerable schooling and even more practice.

It wasn't a fair contest; it never would be.

Turning on the shower, he had her inside and up against the glass wall a few seconds later, her legs wrapped around his waist a second after that and in one smooth move his dick filled her completely. The view over her shoulder included the harbour and Anton's yacht – at least until the shower steamed up. Not that he needed added incentive. His selfish interlude wasn't going to last much longer.

Too many people needed his attention.

Including Nicole who was part confident, part defence-less, pure magic and *his*. Trapping her between his hard body and the wall, he drove into her slick pussy over and over, plunging deep, then deeper still, his fingers sinking into her ass, holding her in place so he could zero in on all her special party zones. So he could make her pant faster and louder, so she got hotter and wetter, so his dick slid in and out smooth as silk.

'Oh God, oh God, oh God.' Breathy, gasping, shuddering from the rush of pleasure lighting up her nerve endings, she tightened her arms around his neck, stretched up to kiss him, impatient to feel him everywhere, trembling, heady with need, wanting to eat him alive.

At first he smiled against her wild, frantic kisses, then growled when she nipped his lip. 'Careful,' he warned.

She nodded, then shook her head. 'Can't.' And bit him again.

He went motionless for a stark moment. 'You need some training.' His voice was taut with restraint.

'No.'

He gazed at her, exhaled a long, slow breath. 'Just fuck-ing behave, okay?'

'Yes, yes,' she whispered, breathless. 'You're the boss.'

The subliminal outrage in her voice warred with her incandescent gaze; he should have let it go. If he didn't have tooth marks on his lip, he might have. Or if his default setting wasn't seriously autocratic. 'Tell me you mean it,' he muttered, absolutism in every syllable.

She looked startled at first, then her gaze sharpened and if she'd had breath to speak she would have told him to fuck off.

He exhaled hard, told himself to relax, told himself not to even think about going Neanderthal; seriously, there was no excuse for that kind of asshole behaviour. Other than *his wanting to own her, he supposed*. He lasted maybe five seconds more before he thought, *fuck it all to hell*, and bracing his feet, flexed his powerful legs, and rammed his dick up her slick, pulsing heat with the entire force of his lower body. At the stunning impact, their breathing faltered, every libidinous nerve was hammered with raw, riveting sensation and the game suddenly ticked up a notch.

Her heart racing, the hot, feverish centre of her body gorged and vibrating, overwhelmed and frantic, Nicole sucked in a breath, then bit Rafe's lip so hard that if it had been anyone else, he would have dropped her on the floor.

She wasn't anyone else though. She was his compulsion, deeply fucked up as that was with his world going to hell. She was in his heart and bones, his smart-ass, no bullshit, stubborn princess who made life worth living. He suddenly smiled – recognizing the blinding joy in what had always been a cliché.

But she was whimpering – a sound of impatient need

– so he dismissed joyful epiphanies, licked the blood off his lip and hurried the fuck up. Adjusting his dick to exert more pressure on her swollen clit and G-spot, he slid into her honeyed warmth and pressed upward gently, indulgently, deeply until she was shivering, panting, barely holding on. 'Good to go?' A rhetorical question; he was already shifting her hips to refine the sensory impact of his dick on her throbbing tissue, forcing her thighs wider, waiting patiently for her pliant flesh to slowly stretch and take him all. *Oh fuck.*

She gasped, lavishly filled with cock, sensory overload hitting her square-on and fast. Burying her face in Rafe's shoulder, she held on tightly as the next rush of blazing-hot rapture spiralled through her sex, curled her toes, made her body hum and spark.

'Close? Look at me.'

She was slick, panting, rocking gently with the pressure building inside her; it took enormous effort to look up.

'You my girl?' A bare, simple question, the undercurrent of earnestness no more than a brief wing-beat of sound.

Teetering on the edge, too overwrought to speak, she gave him a shaky nod.

'Good,' he whispered, his golden gaze transfixed for a moment. Then he winked. 'Show me how much.' Flexing his fingers, he broadened his grip on her ass, withdrew slightly, then leaned forward, forced her legs even wider, and with a soft, barbaric growl, drove in hard and fast, burying himself balls deep.

She quietly shuddered, feeling as though she might detonate any second with her body stretched taut, with an unbearable, exhilarating desire drumming through her senses.

Dragging in a rough breath, he pushed in a carefully calculated distance more, measuring her ardour, his audacity and the outer limits of sensation. 'Feel that?' he asked, husky and low. 'Right. Fucking. Here?' It wasn't really a question; the answer clear. She was trembling helplessly, her body slippery wet, hot enough to fuel the universe, beautiful enough to have him thinking of for ever. Or more realistically, beautiful enough to keep his dick epically inspired. So breathe in, breathe out, make his little princess happy and get the hell out on Anton's yacht. Here goes: he eased in just a little deeper, barely moving.

She let out a tiny shriek.

He stopped. 'Too much?'

She shook her head, the stabbing pleasure whirling raw-edged and shimmering through her senses.

He hesitated; she was incredibly tight.

She whispered, feverishly, 'Don't you dare stop!'

One of them had to be sensible; there was no question who. So despite her frantic protests, he withdrew slightly, 'Hey, hey, look I'm back', made sure to keep a tight leash on his libido and took her over the finish line with a cautious, limited penetration and a well-behaved dick that was super-attentive to Nicole's quivering, insanely hot and distractingly tight pussy.

When she climaxed, her scream was muffled by the gush of the shower.

He was only seconds behind her, although, after that carefully executed, do-no-harm, play-nice finish to their fuck, he came with such savage intensity he forgot to breathe.

Caught up in a fierce, heart-pounding orgasm, Nicole clung to Rafe against the fury of her climax tearing through her at lightning speed, rolling over her with a violence that left her dizzy. 'No more,' she whispered, weakly, as her body suddenly went slack.

'Good idea,' Rafe muttered, gasping for air.

'Need . . . rest,' Nicole murmured, the words half lost in his shoulder.

She was a burn-to-rubble spendthrift with her passions, wild and greedy. No messing around; expecting him to keep up. He smiled. No problem.

Still breathing hard, he shifted her into his arms with a casual strength, carried her over to one of the filigreed marble benches, set her on his lap, held her close, and wondered how he'd ever thought he could keep her at a safe distance. Hell, he was going to have a hard on and a smile on his face until the day he flew out of here.

She was a surprise.

He'd misjudged.

Nicole slowly lifted her head.

'Welcome back, Pussycat.' He looked at her with an unconcealed assessment. 'You okay?'

Sliding her arms around his neck, she gazed up at him and smiled sweetly. 'I'm crazy for you. Otherwise I'm okay. You're perfect, you know.' She gave him a wry, sideways look. 'Seriously, break-the-mould perfect.'

He grinned. 'Am I'm hearing the endorphins talking?'

'Maybe, but it's me being sincere too.' Her blue gaze slowly swept his face. 'Even if sincerity is against the rules.'

'We don't have any rules. It's just us,' he said, softly. 'And you're pretty damn perfect yourself.'

She took a deep breath. 'I like that it's just us.'

'We're in our own little bubble, Tiger.'

'Where the world can't touch us.'

'Yup.' He drew in a slow breath.

'Don't say it.' Her eyes were wide with appeal. 'Please. Not yet.' She tried to keep her lip from quivering. 'I know, we had to leave five minutes ago.'

'We'll come back.' His voice was ultra-soft.

She knew what he meant; she even understood why he'd spoken so quietly. 'We mustn't make too much noise or we might break the spell.'

'Something like that.' He smiled faintly. 'So much for sanity.'

'Much overrated,' she whispered. 'Since I met you.'

He sighed. 'I know.' But mystical feeling aside, he was a logical man and they were expected on Anton's yacht. 'One kiss, then we do have to go.' He dipped his head. 'I'll meet you halfway.'

She stretched upward and their lips met in a kiss so replete with meaning it should have been wreathed in sonnets and troubadour songs. But a moment later, he raised his head, swung her up into his arms, came to his feet and stood motionless within the cocoon of steamed glass. 'Our timing could have been better,' he said, quietly.

Nicole trailed a finger down his strong neck. 'I'll take what I can get.'

'You have it all, Pussycat. Everything I've got.'

Until I don't. But she smiled. 'Good. You can't back out.'

'Never. My word on it.'

They were both playing the game, unwilling to shatter the dream until cold reality intruded. Their dinner tonight perhaps prelude to the widening complexities.

'We're going to be late. So,' he said with another sigh, setting her on her feet. 'How fast can you shower?'

Nicole grinned. 'Watch and learn, dude.'

A few minutes later, Rafe opened the shower door, waved her through, found them towels, then showed Nicole into his dressing room next door. 'Clothes over there.' He indicated a long span of teak cabinets on the tower wall, his voice one of simple clarification. 'His and hers.'

Her eyes flared wide. 'My clothes are here?' Had her screams been heard?

He was beginning to recognize her unease with servants. 'Relax. Our luggage was carried up while we were still at the landing pad talking to Ganz and Carlos.'

'Whew.'

He smiled. 'You'll get used to having staff.'

'No I won't.'

'They're always around, Pussycat. You have a problem with anyone, let me know. I'll fire them,' he added, playfully. After all, it wasn't as though she was poverty-stricken herself. Despite his warning, Carlos had done a minimum vetting of Nicole.

'I hope you're not patronising me.'

'I wouldn't dare.' He looked amused. 'But we're late, so let's leave this discussion until some other time. Would you like help dressing?'

She laughed. 'You never like to argue.'

'Waste of time.'

'I like speaking my mind.'

A lift of his brows. 'I've noticed.' He held out his hands. 'Help or not?'

She knew when to quit. 'I don't need help. I'm a speed dresser.'

Not that he didn't know that by now, but if there *had*

been time to argue, he would have had her explain exactly what she meant by speed dresser – a concept he was overly familiar with. Instead, he controlled his temper, gave her a bland smile and moved toward his closets. Anton had been snappish when he normally wasn't. No point in aggravating him; his mother wouldn't approve.

Rafe dressed more quickly than Nicole, but then he'd set records exiting beds, bedrooms, and sundry fucking venues. He knew the drill.

Running a brush through his wet hair, he tied it back with a short black cord, then slipped on a custom-made white shirt from Borelli in Naples, no tie, boxers, threw on a navy linen bespoke suit, and carried a pair of black sandals with him as he left the dressing room. 'I need a drink,' he said over his shoulder. 'Take your time.'

A casual courtesy, a selfish impulse as well. He needed alcohol before facing the inquisition.

Nicole found her clothes; along with those Rafe had given her, they were hanging in the closets designated as hers, or folded away in drawers. Debating her choices, she decided on one of the two dresses she'd brought with her and stepped into the bareback navy silk Céline dress. Pulling it up over her hips, she zipped it to the waist at the back, slid her arms into the long sleeves, slipped the dress over her shoulders and buttoned the two buttons at her nape. Since time was limited, she twisted her damp hair into a loose, fishtail braid, chose pearls for her ears and stepped into her silver heels. She took one last look in the wall of mirrored doors before she walked through the bookcase door Rafe had left open.

He was halfway through his second stiff whiskey. 'We're colour coordinated.' He raised his glass in Nicole's direction. 'Is that one of Alessandra's dresses?'

'No, it's mine.'

His gaze narrowed slightly. 'They're all yours.'

A small silence.

'Tell me you understand,' he said a moment later.

'I like this dress. It's comfortable.'

'That's not what I meant.'

'Don't be difficult.' The glint in her eyes matched his.

'I don't buy women presents as a rule. When I do, I sure as hell don't want them refused.'

'I didn't say I refused them.'

Rafe raised one eyebrow and tilted his head. 'So I can buy you some more?'

She gave him a dirty look. 'Do we have time for this? I thought you were in a hurry.'

'They can fucking wait all night,' he growled. 'Answer me. Is it a problem if I buy you more clothes.'

'You didn't actually buy them,' she said, levelly.

'Then I'll go shopping myself next time. We'll fly to Split tomorrow. That okay with you?'

'Why are you doing this?'

'Why are you?' he demanded, staring at her.

'Because I'm getting the impression this is about power, not gifts.'

'It isn't.' He drained his drink, grabbed a bottle and splashed another few inches into the glass. 'So what kind of gifts do you like?'

'Jesus Christ,' she muttered. 'Look, I love what you gave me. Can we stop now?'

His nostrils flared and he set down his untouched drink. 'I've never, ever, *ever* bought a gift for a woman before,' he said, very softly. 'So we can parse the meaning of buy, but that doesn't nullify my impulse. I want to give you things. You make me happy. If that's a major problem for you, too fucking bad.'

She smiled at his artlessness, but was warmed by his sincerity. 'No, it's all good.'

'Okay, then, we'll go shopping tomorrow.'

'Fine.'

He rubbed one hand up the side of his jaw, stared at her. 'In the morning. First thing.'

'Whatever you say.'

He laughed. 'Jesus, Tiger, now I'm worried. You okay?'

CHAPTER 6

'Come here,' Rafe said, holding out his hand and smiling. 'You're the only sweetness and joy in my life. Everything else is senseless tribal shit, including dinner tonight.' Folding Nicole's hand in his as she reached him, he leaned down and kissed her cheek. 'Thanks for coming along.'

'I'd miss you otherwise.'

His heart did a little stammer. She'd said it so simply. That he liked what she said was less simple. 'Good. Beautiful.' His voice was easy, contained – a natural defence after twenty-six years of locking away his feelings. 'First, though, I need a few minutes with Carlos. Get my stories straight for Anton.' Pulling his cell from his jacket pocket, he punched in a number with his thumb, waited for the answer, then said, 'We're coming down. We'll meet you in the hall.'

'You're not involving her, are you?' There was an edge to Carlos' voice.

'No.' Rafe slid his phone back in his pocket, then gently squeezed Nicole's hand. 'Ignore Anton if he's a prick. He has no say in my personal life. Be nice to my mother, although she's easy to like. Try to listen politely to Titus' non-stop chatter. He's six. What can I say? That's about it.'

'So is this a for real . . . ' She held up her hand with the ring Rafe had given her and grinned. 'Like . . . meeting the parents?'

'Oh shit,' he said, remembering.

'Hey, just teasing. Really.' She lifted her chin a tiny fraction, looked at him calmly. 'Want me to take it off? You can have it back.'

'I know.' Mentally checking off several true but unfixable answers, he chose a middle ground reply. 'I just don't want a lot of questions right now.' He paused, struck by the sheer number of lies he was obliged to deliver tonight; about corruption, criminal activity, assassination squads – the reasons he was on the island. That he was quietly happy even in the midst of such ugliness made him change his mind. 'Look, leave the ring on. Tell them whatever you want. We're engaged, if you like.'

In a normal life she would have answered differently. She would have had a clear idea of what she wanted, whether she loved Rafe or, if she was honest with herself, how much she loved him. Whether he was capable of loving anyone. 'If your parents ask, I'll just say it was a gift and leave it at that.'

He should have been more pleased that she was being sensible. He was disappointed instead – or irritated; he didn't know which. 'It's probably for the best.' He smiled. 'Saves trouble.' Rafe looked at the door, then back to Nicole. 'Ready?'

Rafe led the way down the narrow stairs, holding Nicole's hand in case she stumbled on the worn stone in her strappy heels. When they reached the entrance hall, he waved at Carlos who was striding toward them. 'Sit for a minute.' Rafe drew Nicole to a chair near the courtyard door. 'I won't be long.'

Rafe walked away with a long, easy, balanced lope like a rider or surfer, Nicole thought; she'd have to ask him if he owned horses. He was clearly comfortable in his own skin, tall and rangy, sleek with muscle, his navy linen suit cut to perfection by the best Italian or Savile Row tailor. He was beautiful from any angle, bone deep and indelible. She felt like some groupie lusting after some sports star or rocker. She couldn't help it; he was that splendid. And, of course, the sex was so extraordinary she knew she'd never even come close to finding a replacement. Priceless, once-in-a-lifetime memories. And, with Rafe's security ramping up big time, as temporary as snowflakes in summer

Nicole grimaced. How many times in the past had she been the one walking away? Being polite, smiling, offering the usual excuse: *It's not you, it's me.* Never finding *the one*, never having that *OhmyGod* moment about some guy that

79

all her friends had. Not really believing her mom when she'd say, *Don't worry, you'll find him someday*. Now that it looked as though that someday might have arrived, it had come with a firm expiration date. Although she'd known from the beginning that Rafe wasn't a hearts and flowers kind of guy, still . . . it just went to show you . . . life could be a bitch.

She had to give Fiona, her BFF, a call to whine about the vast injustices of the world and the sad reality of 'too little, too late'. Fiona was always non-judgmental, a good listener and, right now, she needed an objective sounding board for all her new, strange, happy, sad, baffling, convoluted feelings about Rafe. If there had been time, she would have called Fiona now – as in instant phone therapy. Tomorrow, right after Rafe returned to his crisis-management agenda, she'd call her.

In the meantime, Nicole surveyed the grandeur of the large hall, taking in the colourful ceiling, the high stone walls and clerestory windows, the fireplace big enough to roast an ox, the forty-foot table holding centre stage, the huge carpet woven to fit the shape of the room.

When Rafe had said, *burning through money*, he wasn't kidding.

With their dinner engagement pressing, Rafe was issuing instructions to Carlos in a brisk staccato. 'Text me when Gina gets to Brisbane. Same with Zou's Swiss bank accounts and wire transfers when they're found. The names of the bank directors. Zou's location, should we get that lucky. And if Dominic Knight contacts Leo, I want to know.'

'So far, progress but nothing definitive on all of the above. You'll be down in the morning, right? Don't look at me like that.' Carlos stared right back. 'This is the craziest thing you've ever done and I've seen a helluva a lot of your crazy. Fuck her *after* this is over. If you still want to. If *she* still wants to.'

'If *she* wants to?' Rafe scowled. 'What the hell does that mean?'

'Gora sent over his vetting report on Miss Parrish. Unlike mine, his goes way back. Let's just say, she's had an impressive number of boyfriends.'

'Jesus, are you the purity patrol?'

'Hardly.'

'Then shut the fuck up.'

'We're working round the clock,' Carlos said, ignoring Rafe's scowl. 'So whenever you come down in the morning, we'll be there.'

'Am I supposed to feel guilty?'

'Goddamn right.'

Rafe shut his eyes, exhaled, then slowly opened his eyes. 'I might be down later tonight.' He nodded, his voice dropped in volume. 'And thank you.'

Carlos sighed. 'Look, I know this isn't necessarily your fight, but you made it your fight. So—'

'Let's win it.'

'Yeah. And Gora's mad as hell. Old battles, I think, with him, but prepare yourself for a fun evening.'

Rafe nodded. 'I already got that message when he called. All he did was bitch about Nicole. As if I give a shit about his history with Dominic Knight. But apparently my mother is worried. I have no idea why, unless he was stupid enough to bring her into the loop.'

'I doubt it.'

'Me too. He protects her from a bad weather report, for Christ's sake. I'm glad he cares that much, but I don't need his bullshit right now. I've got enough going on.'

'Stop fucking your brains out, you'll have more time.'

Rafe laughed. 'Remind me to give you the same advice when you're hot for some woman.'

'Not gonna happen.'

'That's what I thought,' Rafe said with a grin. 'Just sayin'.'

Carlos watched while Rafe moved across the large room, stopped before Nicole, put his hands out, pulled her to her feet, and bent to give her a kiss. Carlos felt his stomach tighten the same way it would if he received an email in his private, anonymous, encrypted email account from someone he didn't know.

Fuck – as if they didn't have enough trouble already.

CHAPTER 7

A launch was waiting for them quayside. Gora's yacht was anchored a half mile out in the bay, long and sleek, low to the water. Built for speed.

As they approached the *Flora*, they could see Gora, Camelia and Titus waiting for them on the deck off the main salon. Titus was standing on the first rung of the railing, waving and shouting Rafe's name.

'Now, be polite to the girl,' Camelia quietly warned Gora as they briefly lost sight of their guests when the launch docked at the stern. 'Rafail has never brought anyone on holiday with him. I mean, any particular young woman.' Camelia wasn't naïve about her son's notoriety. Not with the tabloids' thirst for scandal.

'This one's like her uncle,' Gora said, gruffly. 'Selfish.'

'You don't know that. And surely,' Camelia added with a lift of her brow. 'You owe a debt of gratitude to Dominic Knight.'

'It was business,' Gora said, briefly.

'It was a problem of your own making.'

He looked at her sideways, their backstory hanging in the air between them. 'One I wouldn't have had,' he said, very quietly, 'if you'd told me I had a son.'

'I wanted to, a thousand times or more.' Camelia sighed. 'I just couldn't see a way out. You know that.'

They'd discussed and debated the subject countless times: Maso's tyranny and instability; the constant danger to Rafe; Gora's wretched marriage; the fact that his daughters likely weren't his. Gora's failure, one day in Venice, to refuse the invitation when Bianca had *accidentally* stumbled into his arms at the Hotel Cipriani. He'd recognized the fraud from the first, but his dream for happiness had died years ago, and he'd begun wishing for a son like some knight errant seeking the Holy Grail. A crucial factor in his decision. Not an excuse but a reason.

Gora touched Camelia's hand, twined his fingers through hers. 'It's over now,' he said, very softly. 'We have two sons and I love you more than life itself. I always have. I will until the end of my days.' His smile warmed his eyes and, for a moment, lightened the burden of his years. 'And I'll be polite to Rafail's friend. I promise.'

Barefoot, Titus was racing toward the lower deck staircase, and the moment Rafe crested the rise, the youngster took a flying leap at his brother. With impeccable reflexes, Rafe caught his little brother mid-vault, shifted him to one arm, and turned back to Nicole as Titus immediately launched into a description of his new video game in French. Grabbing Nicole's hand, Rafe drew her up the last few steps. 'Titus, say hello to Nicole – in English,' he instructed. 'Nicole, my brother. And my parents,' he added, with a nod to his mother and step-father. 'Nicole, Anton and Camelia. Nicole's on holiday with me,' he added, holding his step-father's gaze for a moment. 'I couldn't be happier.' A blunt warning, no matter the mildness of his tone.

With a smile for her son, Rafe's mother stepped forward. 'How lovely to meet you,' she said, taking Nicole's hand.

Gora dipped his head in a small courtly gesture. 'Our pleasure,' he said, his smile well mannered. 'Welcome aboard.'

'Rafe has to see my new game right now, now, now!' Titus shouted, pounding Rafe's shoulder with his fist, patience non-existent at his age. 'I can beat you for sure this time!'

Rafe grinned. 'What do you mean, this time? You beat me every time. But we're going to have a drink first.' Rafe winked at his young step-brother. 'You can show me how the game works while we visit.' Carrying Titus, drawing Nicole along with his other hand, he moved toward the main salon as he spoke, interested in speeding the evening along. This was an obligatory visit and he didn't intend to stay any longer than necessary. Especially since he was planning on joining Carlos and Ganz in the war room once Nicole fell asleep.

Rafe placed Titus on his feet in front of the large flat screen. 'Set up the game, then explain the rules to me.' Leading Nicole to a small salmon-coloured sofa, he took a seat beside her. 'A quick game and a drink. You okay with that?'

His parents exchanged a glance at Rafe's behavior. He wasn't solicitous by nature, or at least not *that* solicitous, particularly to women. 'You know what Rafail wants, Andrei,' Camelia said to the short, elderly man wearing a white shirt with short sleeves and grey slacks. 'What would you like to drink, Nicole?' Moving a few steps, she joined her husband on another sofa, one of several in the large salon.

'Whatever Rafe is having is fine,' Nicole said, smiling at Rafe's mother across the coffee table separating the matching sofas.

The retainer dipped his head in Nicole's direction and spoke in heavily accented English. 'Macallan 32, no ice?'

'Ice for me, please. Just a little.'

'Yes, miss. The usual?' he enquired with a meticulous bow for his employers.

Rafe snorted. 'Jesus, Andrei, cut out the servile crap. Nicole doesn't care if you have manners, do you, Tiger?'

Nicole shook her head and smiled at the stout man with a fuzz of white hair around his bald head like a monk's tonsure, pink cheeks, a ready smile and a weight-lifter's body despite his age.

'Andrei is my mum's cousin three or four times removed, and he's been telling us what to do as long as I can remember. Are we having steak for dinner?'

'Of course, it's your favourite. Strawberry trifle too. Cook insisted.'

Rafe grinned. 'Your wife, you mean.' He turned to Nicole. 'Elena's in charge of the kitchen. No one dares get in her way. Not that I'm complaining when she cooks what I like.'

'Mrs B. runs my mom's house. I know all about doing what you're told, believe me.'

Rafe went very still for a moment, opened his mouth, then closed it.

'Good idea,' Nicole whispered.

He winked at her. 'Private joke,' he said blandly to his parents. 'Nicole has a real sense of humour.'

Gora's mouth set in a grim line at the small intimacy. Camelia noticed too, smiled at her son's unusual show of affection; the young lady had made an impression on him. She'd have to find out Nicole's secret beyond her obvious beauty. 'How nice,' she said. 'Did you hear that, Anton?' She patted her husband's hand. 'You must smile more.'

'Yes, dear.' His mouth relaxed and he captured her hand in his. 'Your mother is trying to teach an old dog new tricks,' he said, amusement in his voice.

She glanced up at him, fondness in her gaze. 'I'm making progress.'

Gora rested against the sofa back, his tall, thin frame unique in its easy power, battle-hardened. His mouth twitched into a small smile. 'I'm enjoying the schooling.'

Camelia laughed. 'Enough silliness. Now tell Rafail and Nicole about your new sailboat. I've lost Anton to the boatyard,' she added, lightly. 'He's there more than he's home.'

Rafe knew better. Gora was rarely far from his mother's side, having embraced the maxim *making up for lost time* with a zealot's fervour. Taking his and Nicole's drink from Andrei with a nod of thanks, Rafe turned back, handed Nicole her drink, then asked, 'Who's building your boat? Luca?'

Gora nodded, accepted a shot glass from Andrei. The ten-year-old pearlescent-yellow plum liquor from Romania, Tuica Batrana, was his drink of choice. 'Forty-eight metre, all aluminum, single mast.'

'With a library for Mum?'

Gora smiled. 'It was the first thing I specified.'

'With big windows for me too,' Camelia added, taking a glass of champagne from Andrei. 'We'll have room for eight guests, so you and Nicole should join us when the ship is finished.'

'Good idea,' Rafe said smoothly. 'When?'

'Next spring.' Gora's smile wasn't really a smile. 'If

your schedule allows, of course.' He lifted his shot glass in salute. 'To family.' After waiting for everyone to raise their glass, he tossed back the plum liquor, balanced the shot glass in his palm for a moment, then added, 'We sail April 1st.'

'Why don't I pencil it in?' Rafe turned to Nicole. 'Think you can get away, Tiger?'

Rafe was playing his step-father for whatever reason or, more likely, appeasing his mother. 'I probably could,' Nicole said, going along with it, her voice pleasant. 'My school schedule is flexible.'

'There, that's settled, then. Hand me one of those controllers, Titus.' Rafe deliberately changed the subject to something more innocuous. 'Let's see if I can beat you. Give me a quick run-down first.' Draining his drink in one swallow, he set down the glass.

Titus's explanation turned out to be a six-year-old's rambling, uninterrupted exercise of detail over substance. Another only child like Rafe, Nicole decided – with two doting parents this time, not just one. A little prince. He was still in his swimming trunks, his only concession to company a cartoon T-shirt. So not entirely sure whether Titus dictated the game players as well, Nicole gently elbowed Rafe and lifted her brows.

He smiled. 'You want to play too?'

'If Titus doesn't mind.'

'Sure, I have plenty of controllers. Lemme find another

one,' Titus replied, rummaging through a shelf of electronic gadgets and tangled wires.

'I have a sister who's just a few years older than you,' Nicole said. 'She lives for video games. This is a war game, right?'

'Course.' Titus's voice came from inside the shelf, the carpet littered with discarded game pieces. 'Here's a good one,' he said, turning with a controller in his hand, picking up another one from the floor. 'Which one you want?'

Rafe pointed at a third controller. 'That one for Nicole.'

When the boy hesitated, Rafe said, 'Be nice. Give her your good one.'

'Really, any of them is fine.' Nicole had had considerable experience with young children's reluctant generosity. 'It doesn't matter.'

'Come on,' Rafe insisted, staring at his little brother. 'Nicole's company.'

Titus ran his fingers over the controller as if it were a favourite pet then, with a sigh, looked up from under his dark, floppy hair, leaned forward and dropped it into Rafe's outstretched palm. 'Your good deed might be worth a prize,' Rafe said with a grin. 'On that website you showed me.'

Titus's gaze snapped up and his eyes widened. 'You mean the robot?'

'Yup. I'll order it when I get back on the island.'

'Tonight?'

'Absolutely.'

'What do you say to your brother, Titus?' Camelia prompted.

'Wow! Thanks, Rafe. Thanks a million!'

'You got it. Now, let's see if Nicole's any good at gaming. Girls never are,' Rafe said with a playful wink at Nicole.

'Not true, dude.' She winked back. 'You're gonna get smoked.'

Rafe leaned in, kissed her cheek and murmured, 'As long as Titus wins.'

She arched one brow. 'I told you I have five brothers and sisters, didn't I? And I'm the oldest?'

'Ah, yes. My mistake.' Then his voice dropped low. 'So you're going to let me win?'

'Hey, Titus,' Nicole said, with a flashing smile. 'How long do you think it'll take us to beat your brother?'

Rafe was laughing as he dropped down onto the floor. 'You're on, Tiger.' He patted a spot beside him and grinned. 'Let's find out who's good and who's better.'

It was a thing of beauty to see – Rafe and Nicole's fine-tuned expertise, their competitive drive, their sharp, skilful moves and deft, flying thumbs that continually allowed Titus just the slightest advantage. It wasn't obvious they were letting him win, so the young boy experienced a genuine thrill of accomplishment.

The older adults watched with interest as Rafe engaged with Nicole for second place behind Titus's winning score.

It was strictly a numbers game; the player who annihilated the most opponents won, the next highest score came in second, then third to the one with the least number of hits. The fact that both Rafe and Nicole could respond to Titus's moves and to each other simultaneously was an astonishing display of fast-twitch muscles. As adoring parents to a video gaming child, Camelia and Gora understood the level of skill necessary for such a feat.

Titus was good.

Rafe was a prodigy.

Nicole kept pace with ease.

'Is she winning or is Rafail letting her win?' Camelia whispered.

Gora leaned in close. 'Hard to tell. She's good.'

'Rafail's enjoying the competition.' Camelia looked up when Gora didn't answer. 'What?'

'You might be right,' Gora said, feeling a jolt of unease, wondering whether to interfere. He had old-fashioned ideas about women; he'd also had a lifetime of imposing his will on others.

When the game ended a few minutes later, Titus was squealing in triumph.

Nicole handed her controller to Rafe. 'You let us both win,' she murmured. 'My troops were dead meat and you didn't attack. You punted.'

His smile was choir boy innocent, his voice low like hers. 'I disagree.'

'Nevertheless, you'll receive a reward for your compassion.' She winked. 'Later.'

He laughed softly. 'I was hoping you'd say that.'

'Ewww ... are you gonna kiss her?' Titus said with childish disgust.

'Not in a gazillion years,' Rafe said with a grin. 'Kissing is gross and, even if it wasn't, I don't have time. I'm hungry.' He glanced at his mother. 'Will Elena take offence if we sit down now?'

'Sweetheart, as far as Elena's concerned, you can do no wrong.' She came to her feet. 'Andrei, will you tell Elena we're ready?'

As they reached the table, Titus insisted on sitting beside Rafe. 'Sure. We'll just move a few plates,' Rafe said.

Nicole surveyed the place settings, two side by side, one across the table, one at either end. 'Don't bother. I can sit anywhere.'

'As long as it's beside me,' Rafe said, calmly, beginning to make room for another plate on one side of the table.

A few minutes later, with the staff helping, the table was reset and Rafe was sitting between Titus and Nicole. 'Perfect.' Smiling at his brother, he reached for Nicole's hand. 'Now, when does your school start again?' Titus began answering in French, Rafe reminded him to speak English, then listened patiently to a protracted, at times fretful, discourse about all the fun Titus would have if he could go away to school like his friends, but Papa wouldn't allow it.

'Your father's right,' Rafe interposed, gently. 'If you wait a few years, you'll have even more fun. Believe me, I know.' Titus was too fragile at six, perhaps too indulged as well; he had to be tougher and stronger to stand up to the bullies. 'If you get bored at home, come visit me for a change.'

'Can I, can I really? Wow, really, for real?' Bursting with excitement, the young boy's gaze whipped back and forth between Rafe and his father.

'Of course you can,' Rafe replied without waiting for Gora's answer. 'Anytime.' He glanced at Gora. 'I'll hire tutors. He won't miss anything. Titus should be a little bigger before he goes away to school. Just a suggestion, of course,' he added, softly. 'Andrei, would you mind?' Turning, he held up his empty glass as a flood of cruel memories from his schooldays hit a raw nerve. 'Make it a double.' His expression didn't change, nor the softness of his tone, the raging cluster-fuck in his brain hidden behind a bland mask.

Andrei delivered Rafe's drink and as he drained it quickly, Andrei signalled for the servers to begin the meal. Andrei had helped raise Rafe. He'd seen enough bruises and scars from the contact sport of survival when Rafe had come home from boarding school on vacation. He recognized that shuttered look.

Seafood antipasto was served first, along with a sparkling Franciacorta Brut Bellavista, followed by a simple linguine parmesan and a wine from the family vineyard on the Croatian coast. With Titus at the table, conversation wasn't an issue. Familiar with being the centre of attention, he chattered on while the adults responded as needed and quietly carried on their own conversation. Rafe asked about the state of the local vineyard the family owned, Anton's new sailboat was discussed in some detail, Andrei's son, who was in medical school in Paris, was the topic of conversation for a time, Andrei beaming as he detailed his son's successes.

No one asked Nicole any personal questions; she wondered if Rafe had warned them off or they simply knew better than to enquire into their son's friendships. Although, after her whiskey, and wine with each course, she was more than content to just listen. The family dynamic was warm and cordial, Titus a continual buzz of childhood exuberance.

Rafe's mother preferred quail for her entrée. Everyone else enjoyed Elena's version of steak Florentine, with a Conterno Barolo Riserva of incredible beauty and several vegetable side dishes, including pommes frites; another of Rafe's favourites, apparently. The strawberry trifle, beautifully displayed in small glass tumblers, was served with coffee and grappa.

As they were finishing dessert, Rafe leaned over to speak to Nicole.

'If you have a moment, Rafe,' Gora said, anticipating his guests' early departure. 'I'd like to see you in my study.'

Rafe's first impulse was to answer no. 'Of course,' he said instead and gave Nicole a nod. 'I won't be long.'

'Nicole and I will have our coffee and grappa in the salon while we wait,' Camelia said, coming to her feet. 'Bring your trifle if you like, Titus. Ah, thank you Andrei, the carpet was saved. Come, Nicole, you must tell me how you met Rafe. It's obvious you've charmed him completely.'

Following Gora, Rafe was nearly to the hallway when his mother spoke. He spun around. 'Don't grill her, Mother.'

Nicole gave her head a little shake. 'I'm fine, Rafe.'

'We're just going to chat.' Camelia waved him off.

A muscle twitched in his jaw. 'I'll be back in a few minutes,' he said, his voice measured.

His mother smiled. 'Oh dear, that sounds like a warning.'

'It is. Don't embarrass me.'

'I didn't think that was possible,' Gora said under his breath, waiting in the doorway for Rafe.

'Then we're both surprised,' Rafe said, equally softly, turning to Gora. 'I didn't think you'd be sailing down here.'

'That's what we have to discuss.'

Rafe grimaced. 'As long as it doesn't take long. Mother's making me nervous.'

'She's never had a female friend of yours to chat with before.' Gora moved down the hall. 'Considering your friendships,' he said over his shoulder, 'it's probably for the best.'

'I don't think we want to start comparing morals.'

'Certainly not. I am, however,' Gora said, opening the door to his study, 'concerned with the imminent dangers you face. Come in, sit down. I'll make this brief.' Gora walked behind his desk, dropped into a green leather chair and unbuttoned his taupe linen sports jacket. 'A man I hired found those bank account numbers you need.'

'Christ, that's great. Thank you.' Rafe moved to a modern sculpted chair, all Ergo curves in brilliant orange leather, and sat. 'Anyone I know?'

'Probably not. A Russian. He's worth his weight in gold. Literally. That's his price. Here.' Gora slid a computer printout across the desk.

'Fucking A.' Rafe scanned a list of roughly thirty numbered accounts.

'As you see, they aren't all Swiss.'

'I see that. Jesus, Zou must have been looting his department funds long before Ganz took his share. That's one helluva lot of money.'

Gora ran his hands through his cropped salt and pepper hair in a quick, restless gesture, then dropped his arms on his desk and leaned forward. 'The urgent question is: should I send my men to talk to the bankers? Or do you have the proper operatives? Those accounts have to be shut down quickly.'

'I have some men who can deal with the bankers but, fuck, thirty or more accounts. And they have to be dealt with simultaneously or someone will spook and call in the authorities.'

'Exactly.' Gora's grey gaze was cool. 'What do you need from me?'

Aware of Gora's Balkan mafia background, Rafe wasn't sure of the fit. 'No offence, but a certain subtlety is required. The men have to be able to get in the door, and into those offices.'

Gora smiled. 'I might have a bit more experience than you. Tell me who you need and I'll find them. I know when to be subtle and when not to be. This isn't a gentlemen's game – if it ever was. Zou has his back to the wall. That makes him unpredictable, and, God willing, careless.'

'We should be so lucky. Look, find me half the agents to deal with the bankers. I'll get the rest. Have your people here sometime tomorrow, if possible. It's not complicated threatening men who have a lot to lose,' he murmured, studying the list as he spoke. 'They're not going to risk their lives for Zou. Fuck, I know who runs Nederman & Ney. I'll speak to Balthus. He can block that account. Now, a question for you. When you said Mother was worried. What does she know?'

Gora sat back and flicked his fingers. 'None of this. She heard me talking to Dominic Knight late one night. I'd raised my voice and she woke up when she heard your name. I told her it was just this little affaire of yours that's problematic for Nicole's uncle. But any issue, no matter how small, if you're involved, she worries.' His brows lifted. 'Although I'm getting the impression this is more than a small issue.'

'No comment,' Rafe said, flatly. 'I'm not discussing Nicole.'

'Fair enough. Although, you should find someone more—'

'Don't say it. You have no right.'

The subject of his rights was forbidden, although it hurt to hear his son reject him. But Camelia had to be protected, Rafe's inheritance protected, the company protected. He accepted the responsibility, along with the pain. 'Very well,' Gora replied, mildly. 'Now, if you have any specifics regarding the quality of the operatives you need to deal with the bankers, let me know.'

'Anyone who looks capable of handling a hundred million or more for their client. Not that the bankers haven't seen all kinds come in, but I don't want them to give our people a second look. No visual red flags.'

'I'll start recruiting tonight. And indulge your mother when it comes to her acquaintance with Nicole. She's pleased you brought her to dinner. Your mother blames herself for your – how shall I put it – callous indifference to women. She's afraid all the difficulties you've endured have inoculated you against love.' He shrugged. 'Women are more romantic, and she doesn't know the full extent of Maso's depravities. You, unfortunately, saw them at close range. He should have died years ago. I'm sorry he didn't.'

'You, me and a lot of other people. Look,' Rafe said, softly, 'we might not always agree, but I want you to know how much I appreciate your love for Mother. She deserves it. You deserve it. The world can be seriously fucked up at times.' He sighed. 'Now particularly.' Rafe came to his feet. 'I'll talk to Carlos and Ganz after Nicole goes to sleep. I don't want her anywhere near this dangerous shit.'

'Agreed. Will she be here long? I'm only asking in terms of risk to her. I'm taking your mother back to Trieste tomorrow.'

Rafe blew out a breath. 'I shouldn't have even brought her. That said, I'll send her home when I have to. The timing's moot.'

'She's very lovely,' Gora said, softly, rising from his chair. 'I understand your dilemma. Now then,' Gora said with a faint smile, 'let's see if your mother has discovered all your and Nicole's secrets.'

Rafe groaned.

Gora laughed. 'I don't think you have to worry. Miss Parrish looks as though she can take care of herself. You almost lost to her in that video game.'

'Yeah.' Rafe smiled. 'Nicole's good at a whole lot of things.'

'How fortunate for you,' Gora said, gently.

CHAPTER 8

Titus was offered his choice of movies by Andrei and settled in front of the TV with his trifle while Camelia and Nicole decided to enjoy the evening air on the deck outside. Andrei served the ladies coffee and grappas at a small table under an awning, then returned to the salon to be within calling distance.

'Since I have orders not to grill you ... ' Camelia said with a smile, pulling out a chair from the table. 'Allow me to at least tell you how pleased I am that you came to dinner.' She looked up as she sat. 'Rafe's happy. I expect it's because of you.'

'I'm not sure, but thank you.' Sitting opposite Camelia, Nicole reached for her grappa. 'He has your eyes.' *And stunning looks*, she thought, taking a sip of her grappa instead of mentioning what might have been construed as unctuous flattery. Camelia was tall, dark-haired, flawlessly beautiful and elegantly dressed in a simple sleeveless, full-skirted chartreuse silk and scarlet poppy print dress. Her skin, a sun-kissed golden hue, was a lighter version of her son's darker complexion but, in all else, the resemblance was strong.

'I confess, it pleases me that we have features in common.' Camelia smiled. 'A mother's vanity. By the way, I recognize your dress. Céline designs are lovely.'

'And comfortable. I don't like to fuss with clothes.'

'Rafe spends a good deal of time in shorts and sandals.' A little curl of a grin. 'The young generation. Even in business, a suit and tie is no longer obligatory.'

'Rafe wore a suit for you tonight, then?'

Camelia nodded. 'He's a sweet boy.'

A phrase only a mother would use for Rafe Contini, better known for his audacity and vices. But Nicole had to admit, he could be endearing. More than that, loveable; a major problem considering the transient nature of their stay.

'Titus is sweet as well,' Nicole remarked, making a smooth U-turn from her train wreck speculation. 'I have three brothers, all in high school now, but I remember them young and bubbly like Titus.'

'You're the only girl?'

Nicole shook her head. 'I have two sisters. My mom came from a small family, so she wanted a big family. My dad wanted whatever my mom wanted. They get along. And Dad has eight brothers and sisters so it wasn't a stretch.' Nicole grinned. 'Holidays are a zoo. Everyone gets together. The din is unreal.'

'I can imagine.' Camelia suspected Nicole's openness appealed to Rafe; a change from her son's usual female companions who were accommodating for a variety of reasons; marriage to a billionaire preeminent. 'It sounds like fun though. When Rafe was young, it was generally just the two of us. Maso was away from home a good deal. Then Rafe went away to school . . . ' She exhaled softly. 'And he grew up overnight.'

'When was that?' Rafe and his friends' references to boarding school had been shocking to someone educated in neighbourhood schools.

'He was nine. Maso wanted to send him away at eight, but . . . Her voice died away for a moment. Drawing in a breath, she said very softly, 'I convinced him to wait another year.'

Wow, thrown out into the world at nine. 'Rafe seems to have managed well,' Nicole said, keeping her voice neutral with effort.

Camelia sighed. 'I'm afraid it's all past mending now. But Rafail made some dear friends in those difficult years. The boys are very close. For that I'm grateful.'

'I met Henny, Basil and Ganz in Monte Carlo. They have their own special bond, joking and teasing, yet intensely private beneath all the banter. My best friend from primary school and I have that kind of friendship. And in a large family like mine, if you want someone to talk to, whine to, need a shoulder to cry on, take your pick.'

Camilla smiled faintly. 'How nice to have a supportive family. I hope you appreciate it.'

'Most of the time.' Nicole grinned. 'We fight too, but no one holds a grudge. Mom won't allow it; her mother was or is really difficult. Long story. Our housekeeper, Mrs B., is even more adamant about forgiveness; what goes around, comes around is her favourite saying. And she has the chops to enforce her philosophy.'

A small, considering look. 'Chops?'

'Authority. She orders everyone around. Even my Uncle Dominic doesn't argue with Mrs B. and he likes to think he's the ruler of the world.'

'Some men do, I've found,' Camelia said.

No way was she was replying to that soft, underlying fury in Rafe's mother's voice. 'I figure it's a testosterone thing.' Nicole smiled. 'I try to ignore it.'

'Ignore what?'

Nicole turned at the sound of Rafe's voice.

'That second dessert. Or I try at least.'

Rafe grinned. 'No you don't.'

'I said try, okay? You wanna argue?' she purred.

His smile was dazzling. 'Not on your life.' He held out his hand. 'Come on, Tiger, we're leaving.'

A moment later, Rafe leaned down, gave his mother a kiss goodbye, thanked her for dinner, tossed a glance back to Gora standing in the doorway of the salon and waved. Drawing Nicole to the stairway, he descended so swiftly that Nicole stumbled. Sweeping her up in his arms, he leaped down the last two steps without missing a beat. 'How about I'm always here to catch you, Pussycat?' he said with a grin. 'You okay with that?' He lifted a brow when she didn't answer quickly enough. 'Only one answer allowed.'

'Yes, yes, yes.' The word, for ever, had been hovering restively on the tip of her tongue and required a moment to restrain.

'Perfect. Good girl.' And he carried her – a full on grin on his face – to the waiting launch.

Camelia and Gora stood at the rail, hand in hand, waiting for the launch to get underway.

'What do you think?' Gora murmured in their native language.

Camelia didn't have to ask what Gora meant. 'She's caught him. Or Rafe's caught her. I can't tell.'

'I'm not sure it's permanent.'

'I noticed. They're both being extremely careful. Why?' She looked up. 'I expect you know.'

'I don't.' Gora's answer wasn't entirely false. The present danger impacted on their relationship, but if there were other reasons, he wasn't privy to them. 'Rafe never shares his feelings. Apparently, Nicole didn't either.'

'They have that in common,' Camelia said with a shake of her head.

Gora laughed. 'I wonder how they converse.'

'I don't,' Camelia said, bluntly. 'But he likes her. That's plain. So regardless of your reservations, I insist you like her too.'

'Of course, dear. Whatever you say.'

'I mean it, Anton.' She held his gaze. 'Don't give me platitudes. Rafe deserves happiness. You understand?'

'I do,' Gora said very softly. Camelia as mother lioness reminded him of all the times he'd been unable to protect them. 'If Rafe is serious about Miss Parrish, I wish them happiness.'

'We had to wait so long. I want a better life for him.' Tears suddenly filled her eyes.

'Hush, sweetheart,' he whispered, taking her in his arms. 'Don't worry. I'll see that Rafe's happy.'

But first, he had to see that his son survived, he thought, watching the launch speeding toward shore.

CHAPTER 9

Nicole woke at the sound of the door closing. She wasn't surprised. Rafe had been especially tender and attentive making love, wanting to please and satisfy her. But he'd been tense in small ways: his teasing more subdued; his smiles fewer; the occasional tic over his cheekbone a tell. She should have just said, 'Go. I don't mind.' From now on, she would.

Reaching out, she ran her fingers over the sheet where Rafe had lain, but his warmth was gone and a small shiver of grief slid up her spine. She'd always known he'd leave someday; she'd thought she could deal with it rationally. Hadn't she always in the past?

But, from the first, Rafe had been a contradiction, a singular fingerprint on her psyche; deep, strong, capable of leaving emotional debris in his wake. And she'd struggled to stay whole. Unreasonably at times. With bonehead stupidity at other times. Stubbornly. But her freedom and independence had been at risk.

And now without him for the first time, she suddenly felt lost and alone; her equilibrium gone.

It was terrifying.

She'd never felt alone. In fact, she'd often searched for a moment of quiet in a household as busy as hers, in a family as large as hers. It had never occurred to her, not for a second, that this could happen.

Her confidence was shaken.

Rolling out of bed, she grabbed her phone and quickly walked away from the bed where Rafe so recently had given her untold delight. Crossing the large room, she curled up on one of the sofas, pulled a white angora throw over her legs and dialled Fiona. If ever she needed a voice of reason, a fixed point in a shifting, tilting world, it was now.

'Jesus,' Nicole muttered when Fiona answered, the music in the background deafening. 'Can you hear me?' she shouted.

'Wait, wait, I see your ID, give me a minute.'

If Fiona was wasted, her call would be useless. She needed Fiona semi-coherent. She needed someone to steer her clear of this disbelieving moment and world-class mess.

'There,' Fiona said. 'Now I can hear you. I'm in the bathroom.'

'Whose bathroom?'

'One of your billionaire boyfriend's bathrooms in Ibiza. Jack has some friends over. What's up?'

'Are you sober?'

'Gimme a break. It's midnight. Hey, hey, relax,' Fiona added, hearing the sudden, stark silence and Nicole's fast breathing. 'I'm clear-headed. I stopped imbibing various things a while ago when some bitch started climbing all over Jack. I figured I'd better take it easy. You know what my temper's like when I'm loaded. But Jack was sweet, shoved the skank off him so everything's good. Paradise is still golden here. How's it going wherever you are?'

'I'm somewhere in Croatia and I think I'm in love.'

'Jesus! Let me sit down. Okay, run that by me again. I may have been hallucinating.'

'Don't give me shit. I'm officially in shock. You have to talk me down.'

'Hell, that's easy. First, Rafe Contini wouldn't know what love was if it showed up at his door wearing gold sequins, a pink feather boa and a neon sign flashing the word, LOVE. He'd figure it was someone from a costume party who'd lost their way. Second, even if he recognized the word, love, the naked babes draped all over him would divert his attention in a New York second. And third, baby girl, have you lost your motherfucking mind. His name is Rafe Contini and he screws every woman in sight just as hard as he works at being CEO. Have I made my point?'

'I wish.'

'Then you need a brain transplant.'

'I know.'

'Oh God, don't cry. I can't help you from this far away. Come on, please?'

'I'm not crying . . . or maybe just a little – it's so stupid . . . I'll stop, gimme a second. There.' A few more quick breaths, a couple of sniffles. 'Jesus, emotional involvement really sucks. But I'll survive. I know the trope. No one dies of love. Scars all over, but life goes on, right? How's it going with Jack?'

'Look, my therapy sign's still on the door. Spill your guts. I'll listen all night if it helps. By the way, where is the billionaire? Oh, shit, is he gone, gone? Is that what this is about?'

'No – or he's gone temporarily. He's downstairs. But he's been unimaginably sweet and gentle, so damned perfect that it takes your breath away. Makes you realize how fragile happiness is.' She couldn't speak of the dangers Rafe was facing. But the level of activity on the island frightened her. 'I'm trying really hard not to fall any deeper in love. I'm mentally rehearsing every cliché about broken hearts and unrequited love to remind me not to be a complete fool.'

'Good for you, because Rafe's probably the same sweet, gentle, perfect guy with every woman he knows. Practice makes perfect. Just sayin'.'

'You think I haven't told 1 myself that? But Rafe says it's different for him too. Like slammed-by-a-freight-train different.'

'Come on,' Fiona said, softly. 'What do you expect him to say? He's good at this, okay? He knows all the moves, all the words, what works and doesn't work. He's a pro.'

'Is Jack like that?'

'He's awesome, but I'm keeping my feet on the ground. You better do the same. This is a summer break. We go home when it's over. Don't forget the plan.'

'Yeah, yeah.' Nicole drew in a deep breath, slowly exhaled. 'Thanks for the reminder. Summer break, me still not registered for fall semester, shit to be done. Okay, I'm back on track. Feet on the ground, braced against the gale-force winds. Got it.'

'Rafe won't give a shit if you're crying over him, that's all I'm saying. And there isn't a bookie who'd bet against him taking off sooner or later, 'cause that's what he does. He doesn't do permanent. So stiff upper lip, babe. Don't forget who you're dealing with. The billionaire with the legendary dick. He's not like the boys you've left behind.'

'Yeah,' Nicole said. 'Boys. Bless my naïve little heart, that's the irrevocable difference. Look, thanks for listening. I'm under control, in full self-preservation mode. Have you heard anything from back home? I talked to my mom earlier today.'

'My mom's having a meltdown over my little sister. Wrong boyfriend, I guess.' Fiona laughed. 'You'd know about that.'

'Oh, Rafe's not wrong. He's right in a thousand beautiful, dissolute ways,' Nicole murmured. 'That's the problem.'

'My advice. Take pictures. For your scrapbook.'

'Fuck you.' But they were finished.

'Not when I have Jack. Maybe later you and I could get together and check out the L-world,' she teased. 'Hey, Jack's knocking on the door. Ciao, baby girl. Keep on keeping on. It's the only way. Oh, by the way, if Sarah calls, don't feel you have to answer. I slipped up and told her you were with Rafe.'

Whether serendipity or just bad luck, Nicole had no more than ended Fiona's call when her phone rang and Sarah's name came up on her display. She hesitated for a fraction of a second, not sure she wanted to talk. On the other hand, she didn't have to say anything about anything if she didn't want.

Hitting the Answer button, she quickly counted backward to San Francisco time – three in the afternoon – picked up and jerked the phone away from her ear for a second. Ear-splitting music was blaring in the background. 'Where are you?' Nicole asked, loud enough to be heard over the din. 'Party or bar?'

'Party on the beach,' her friend Sarah shouted. 'The surf is prime. Just a sec. I'm gonna walk away . . . ' Her voice settled into the normal range. 'From the speakers. Fiona just called me to gloat. Is she really partying in Ibiza with some prince?'

'I think so.' Sarah was a Twitter slut, so the less said, the better. 'I haven't talked to Fiona lately,' she lied.

'Because you're too busy fucking Rafe Contini, I hear. I am sooo jealous. Seriously, I hate you right now.'

'We're just on holiday for a few days. It's no big deal.' Nicole's feelings for Rafe weren't for public consumption, particularly with the gossip queen of the world.

'Gimme a break. Everything about Rafe Contini's a big deal. He's the freaking God of Hotness. Remember when we saw him at that conference? We wanted to rip off his clothes with our teeth.'

'I don't remember.'

'Fuck if you don't. You and I both wet our panties just looking at him. So tell me every down and dirty detail of what it's like to fuck the god.'

'Look, I'll be home in a few days. I'll tell you then. I'm not alone,' Nicole said, although she was.

'Oh God, is he there? Naked? I think my heart might stop. Can I listen to him breathing at least or—'

'Jeez, relax, Sarah. Rafe's in a meeting. Hey, someone just knocked on my door,' she said, so not in the mood for this. 'I gotta go.'

Tossing her phone aside, Nicole softly exhaled. Of course she remembered the first time she'd seen Rafe.

It was at a medical conference in San Francisco. The auditorium at Stanford was packed. While the seminar topic of Targeted Chemotherapy was of interest, Nicole suspected many of the attendees found the speaker even more interesting; the gender ratio definitely skewed female. A kind of breath-held expectation was humming in the air. And it wasn't just because a free wine bar had been set up in the lobby before this last seminar of the day.

A tall, willowy blonde doctor from the Department of Medicine introduced Rafe; at the time he was head of R&D for Contini Pharmaceuticals. The doctor first expressed her admiration for Contini Pharma's innovative Research and Development division, then went on to describe her admiration for the speaker in more personal terms than appropriate for the venue. Halfway through her fawning testimonial to Rafe's impressive educational and professional credentials, he came to his feet and politely interrupted her lengthy presentation of his boy genius college degrees with a light remark about having missed his childhood. Then he deliberately moved to the podium so she had to step aside and take her seat.

For a moment he stood calmly at the podium: straight and tall, his flint-grey bespoke suit beautifully tailored to fit his lean, hard body, his long, dark, glossy hair gleaming under the spotlight, his handsome face all bones and sharp contours, his golden eyes hooded like a hawk's.

Whether he was accustomed to the rapt attention or simply waiting for the buzz to die down, it was another few moments before he smiled and said, 'Let me show you what we've been working on for the last few years.'

His presentation was erudite and definitive, first offering an overview of Contini Pharma's current research on targeted chemotherapy, then describing their newly developed drugs, moving on to detail their next-generation research that was heavily focused on immunotherapy and bioelectronics. He spoke without notes, operated the digital and visual displays himself, explained all the various graphs and charts down to their minutiae and, once he finished, opened the floor to questions.

Nothing ruffled him, no question was too difficult, the few dissenting queries – never absent from any conference seminar – were politely refuted or corrected with substantive, corroborating data.

He was a brilliant, charming technocrat.

And when he said, 'Thank you very much for your time,' he received a standing ovation.

Never underestimate the X-rated, rock-star factor no matter how stuffy the occasion, Nicole thought at the time, whistling her appreciation while Sarah beamed and clapped and elbowed her in the ribs.

Afterward, Nicole along with the other Chem students waited while their professor brought Mr Contini over for a previously arranged meeting. The blonde doctor was clinging to his arm, but Rafe casually ignored her adulation and smiled in acknowledgment as a brief round of introductions was made. Then he offered a few remarks about the relevance of a Chemistry degree to his business, answered a blunt question about Contini Pharma's hiring practices from one of the male students, then handed several of his business cards to the professor. 'I personally answer that number, so if anyone's looking for work, give me a call.' He smiled warmly. 'We like to hire alums. How many of you are seniors?'

Before anyone could answer, his adoring companion reached up, pulled his head down and whispered something in his ear.

He stiffened slightly, removed her hand, then straightened and brushed his hair back with his palm. 'If you'll excuse us,' he said, without expression. 'Dr Andrews reminded me of another engagement.'

But Nicole was standing at the edge of the group so she heard him say under his breath as he and the doctor walked past, 'For God's sake, Amy, couldn't you have waited another few minutes?' Although whatever the doctor said in reply made him laugh.

An awkward silence fell in the aftermath of the couple's abrupt exit.

Professor Norton cleared his throat. 'Now, who wants one of Mr Contini's business cards? He's willing to take a personal call. That's rare.'

'I wonder if you have to be female to get an interview?' one of the men said, drily.

'For once I might have the advantage then,' a smart-ass woman noted.

'Too bad he's rich,' Sarah had whispered to Nicole. 'I'd pay him to fuck me.'

'Maybe we could bribe one of the hotel staff to let us into his room,' Nicole had whispered back. 'He might like a foursome. We could just ignore the good doctor. She doesn't look very wild if you ask me.'

'You wouldn't!' Sarah's eyes flared wide.

'I would. Or I might for him,' Nicole said with a little shrug. 'He's hot.'

But then someone brought up a party just down the street and Sarah dragged Nicole there because she had been lusting after one of the guys in their Chem group. But soon, bored out of her mind, Nicole had actually Googled a couple of five-star hotels nearby, impersonated Rafe Contini's assistant, talked her way past the operators and found him registered at the Ritz Carlton. Whether she would have acted on the information remained a mystery because Kaz Holmes suddenly appeared at her side, gave her a wise-ass grin and said, 'Awesome eye candy as usual, Nic. I'm glad Rowdy talked me coming to this party. What say we open a bag of Doritos together?'

Instantly distracted by Kaz's super-fine weed, her plans changed.

But fate had intervened in Monte Carlo and here she was, half in love, more probably, if she chose to admit it, with a man who may or may not recognize the emotion. Or if he did, deal with it . . . God knows how.

The shadowed silence in the tower room suddenly took on a presence, or maybe it was the silver streaks of moonlight shimmering in the darkened room. Nicole gave herself a quick shake, told herself ghosts didn't exist, flicked on the lamp behind her, did some yoga breathing to calm down, lost count as usual.

But regardless of what Fiona had said, she felt as though Rafe was taking the same emotional risks; that they both had doubts, plenty of them. She also understood that it was a merciless world for Rafe right now. That every second they had together was precious.

Although, she couldn't argue with Fiona's long-term assessment. This shining moment wouldn't last. It was absolutely essential she keep that in mind. Stay calm, relax, enjoy what she had. And right now, see if there was a remote somewhere 'cause no way was she going to be able to sleep after that come-to-Jesus conversation with Fiona. Ah – a remote next to the lamp. She looked around. No visible TV. So.

Flicking on the remote, she smiled as a TV rose up from the foot of the bed. Now to find a programme in English. Unlike Rafe, who spoke God knows how many languages, she was a seriously derelict linguist. A few necessary phrases in French and Spanish, that was it.

As she walked toward the bed, she warned herself to maintain a cool, calm and collected mask for the remaining days of her holiday. Avoid disintegrating into a tearful mess. Abstain from drama, temper tantrums, hysterics.

In other words, be a mature, considerate adult until Rafe left her.

Such starry-eyed optimism.

It must be love.

CHAPTER 10

It was nearly midnight when Rafe entered the underground rooms. Despite the hour, a number of people were busy monitoring scores of computer screens, as well as live feeds from contacts around the world. Others were hunched over keyboards, accessing data on the movements of Zou and his cohorts. Or in the case of Zou, non-movements. He hadn't left his suite in the Shanghai office tower in two days.

Prior to his sudden departure from Unit 21986, Ganz had set up cameras in the suite's ceiling moulding, the devices essentially invisible, the equipment undetectable with any current scrubbing techniques. Unaware of the surveillance, Zou felt secure in his suite or he would have bolted by now. He must be waiting for something or someone. He slept in his small bedroom, ate from stockpiled food to avoid poisoning. His only communications were via an encrypted cell phone that Ganz had been trying to break into for the past four hours.

Rafe came to a stop before the monitors scanning the office suite. Zou was at his desk writing in a notebook. 'Doesn't trust his computer,' Rafe murmured. 'Can we see what he's writing?'

'Only a word here and there,' a technician muttered. 'He's shielding the notebook with his body.'

'He's had too many offices wired,' Rafe said.

'That'd be my guess. Trust no one.'

'A survivor like him. That message is etched on his liver.'

'Not just his,' Carlos said, coming up behind Rafe.

Rafe turned. 'No shit. I learned that at a young age. So what's going on? Fill me in.'

Carlos gave Rafe a quick glance from head to toe, finger-combed hair, wide smile, unbuttoned blue shirt, shorts, bare feet. 'Looks like you've been well fucked. She sleeping now?'

Rafe smiled at Carlos' snarky comment. 'She is. Is that okay with you?'

'It would be okay with me if she was sleeping in her uncle's apartment in Monte Carlo or Paris or back home in San Francisco. Then we'd have your undivided attention.'

Rafe grinned. 'Now if only I gave a shit what you wanted. And I multi-task well, so shut the fuck up.'

'You mean more than one woman at a time? I've seen you doing that kind of multi-tasking.'

'With all due respect, Carlos, I'm gonna do what I'm gonna do, so could we cut the crap?'

'Sometimes I wish you were twelve again,' Carlos grumbled.

'I was trouble then too if you recall, so tell me what's going on. What I can do to help. Can we jack Zou out of his office and get his head in the crosshairs?'

'Maybe,' Carlos said. 'I'll show you.' Turning, he moved toward a doorway across the room.

Ducking his head for a few moments, Rafe followed Carlos into what must have been a prison cell centuries ago. A single desk with a computer and six monitors above it was being manned by a technician. The remaining space held a narrow bed with a sleeping man, a short counter, small refrigerator, sink, two-burner stove and a microwave. A door led to a compact bathroom.

Carlos waved at the monitors. 'Look familiar? The exterior of the Shanghai office tower from every angle.'

'Snipers,' Rafe said, softly.

'Yeah. Even if Zou comes out from the underground garage in his armoured car, we have a shot. Armour-piercing rounds, one of the best men in the world behind that scope; a man with a grudge. Zou disappeared his brother. No trace, not a clue, the body was never found.'

'Our sniper's there for the duration then,' Rafe said quietly, understanding the nature of vengeance.

'Until hell freezes over if that's what it takes.'

'If we find Zou's second family,' Rafe said, studying the

monitor showing the garage entrance, 'he'll be coming out whether he wants to or not.'

'Unless one of Zou's enemies can muster enough support and a large enough force to go in and get him.'

'Wouldn't that be fucking great. We'd just have to send flowers.' Rafe moved closer to the desk and lowered his voice so the sleeping man didn't wake. 'Appreciate your help, Zander. How're Klara and Bo?'

'Enjoying summer at our cottage.'

'Maybe we can get you back to Stockholm soon.'

Zander glanced up and smiled. 'That's what I told Klara when I left.'

'Then we'd better make sure we don't piss her off.'

The young IT man's smile widened. 'That was the message she gave me to give you.'

Rafe laughed. He'd attended Klara and Zander's wedding two years ago. They'd married hurriedly a few days after they'd found out they were going to be parents. Klara was a programmer in Rafe's Geneva office; Zander was Rafe's personal computer hot-shot when Ganz wasn't around. The couple had met at Contini Pharma's annual Christmas party and immediately hit it off. As in, five minutes after they were introduced they were undressed and on the couch in Zander's office.

'Does it look like business as usual at the facility?' Rafe asked. 'Or is there increased activity, more people coming and going, larger contingents of military? Is Zou's siege mentality altering the schedule?' The building had been under surveillance since Ganz had decamped; the daily routine graphed down to the food delivery men and the occasional masseuse.

'Definitely more activity. Carlos has the new lists of GSD, MUCD and SIGINT staff entering and exiting. Times, dates, names. Frequency of individual activities.'

'Can we distinguish between enemies and comrades?'

'Sometimes, not always. The alliances are fluid.'

'How fluid?'

Zander looked up briefly from his monitor. 'That's the million-euro question.'

'With Zou holed up, I'm assuming no one's gained entrance to his suite.'

'Right.'

Rafe glanced at Carlos, then back to Zander. 'We have to be looking at a rapidly shrinking time frame. He can't stay in isolation long.'

Carlos nodded. 'One would assume Zou's superiors would eventually intervene.'

'Unless he keeps files on them that bite. The fact that he's being left alone even this long makes me think he has major leverage. He has enough money abroad to buy off a helluva lot of people.'

'Or he has critical data on who's lying to whom, plots and counterplots, that's keeping his enemies at bay,' Zander added.

'We'll find out when Gina tracks down his woman,' Carlos murmured.

'Maybe sooner, right?' Rafe patted Zander's shoulder. 'Thanks. I'll check in later.'

As the door closed behind them and Rafe and Carlos entered the larger operational centre, Rafe glanced at Carlos. 'The bank accounts next. You have a desk somewhere?'

Carlos pointed.

'You saw Gora's list?' Rafe had had it delivered by one of Gora's crew. 'Sweet, right?' Rafe smiled and nodded to those who looked up as they passed, gave a couple of finger gun salutes to high-fives sent his way.

'It was fucking beautiful. The man has contacts.'

'Agreed. Gora's going to find men to handle half the bankers. That leaves fifteen for us. Or fourteen. I'll talk to Balthus myself. I know how to deal with him. Did you know he's fucking his sister-in-law?'

'The young one?' Carlos pulled over a chair for Rafe.

Rafe smiled and sat. 'Of course the young one. Hugo's a fucking creep. But she's his wife's step-sister. Same father, polo player, no money. It's Hugo's wife who has the money.'

Carlos chuckled. 'He should be easy to roll.'

'No shit. You'd think he'd know better than to do his little sister-in-law when he has a jealous wife. By the way, he was one of the crew who was harassing Basil at that hell-hole school in Lucerne.'

'I thought you and Henny took care of that.'

'As much as we could. Basil had been there for almost a year before we showed up.' He lifted one brow. 'Fucked-up childhoods, I know. So I figure a little more payback for Basil, we get what *we* need, and Hugo can keep fucking his sister-in-law any way he wants if he can still get it up after I scare the shit out of him.'

'So you two have a little history.'

'Just a little.' Rafe grinned. 'I'm looking forward to our discussion.'

'In person?'

'Course. Have to.' Rafe grimaced. 'Fly out this morning. About a two-hour flight. Talk to him. Be back by one.'

'And your little sweetheart?'

'She comes with. Don't give me that look. What do I have left? A week? Probably less.'

'She might rather stay here. That's a quick turnaround.'

'I'll ask her.'

'No you won't, but she still might say no.'

Rafe smiled. 'You can't afford that bet. Now, let's set up a plan for the other fourteen accounts. They have to be shut down quickly.'

CHAPTER 11

Gina slipped her key card into the lock of her hotel suite in Brisbane, opened the door slowly, scanned the luxurious entrance hall, stepped inside and shut the door softly.

'I'm in here,' a man's voice called out. 'You can holster your Beretta. I'm Webster.'

Maybe he was and maybe he wasn't. She didn't answer, nor did she holster her handgun. She slid off her shoes, moved down the hall noiselessly on bare feet, visualized her target's location from the sound of his voice, and considered her options should this be a trap. She was on the top floor for a reason. She was in the premier suite for a reason. Private elevator, private floor, security. Anyone who got in had to work at it.

She stopped just short of the end of the hall, blinked against the early morning light pouring in the floor-to-ceiling windows, took a breath, dropped into a crouch, spun around the corner and targeted the man sitting in a chair across the large room, his hands up in the air, a smile on his face.

'Fucker!' Gina exploded, easing up out of her crouch, her handgun still trained on the space between the man's eyes. 'How did you get in?'

'There was a nice young lady at the reception desk,' Webster said, his smile tipping the corners of his eyes upward just a little. 'I told her I was your brother, I'd gotten in from Hong Kong ahead of you and you were expecting me to have champagne chilling for you when you arrived.' He lifted his chin in the direction of an ice bucket with champagne on a nearby table. 'I told her you drink any time of day. It's kinda sad but I take care of you.'

She frowned. 'The receptionist bought your stupid story? No questions?'

He nodded. 'Gullible does not begin to describe Miss Kelly's lack of judgment. We should move out quickly. May I put my hands down?'

'We?' She flicked up the barrel of her Beretta as he began lowering his hands and he stopped. 'Show me some ID. One hand, slowly.'

He laughed. 'You spies. Trust issues.'

She took her time; let him wait. 'Tell me my original destination.'

'Cold,' he said, clamping back a smile. 'Original destination, Hong Kong. Your flight diverted over India. I was already at the airport in Hong Kong when I talked to you. Do I pass the test or are you gonna pull out my fingernails?'

'A comedian,' she said, nothing in her voice, her expression blank. 'You didn't think to tell me you were coming here?' He'd reeled off his explanation like he might have rehearsed it.

He thought about saying, *We're both on the same side.* But he understood her suspicions so he answered, simply. 'I wasn't sure. I was on hold with a contact in Shanghai when I spoke to you and later, I still didn't know if I'd land here or somewhere else. Bao Yu *is* here by the way. Face-recognition software picked her up at the mall of all places. So I landed.' He slowly withdrew his wallet from his inside jacket pocket, tossed it on the floor at Gina's feet and raised his hand again.

Stooping to pick up the wallet without taking her eyes off him, Gina flipped it open, scanned the ID, then him, then the photo again, slid out the card with her thumb, rubbed it. It felt real. Slid it back in. 'So the little twit at reception really let you sweet-talk her.'

The start of a grin. 'I can be charming.'

A flash of amusement in her eyes, gone in a blink. 'And you look like a rugby player.' A big handsome man, well-dressed, expensive sport coat, expensive jeans, lean, muscled, brown hair cut short military-style; she'd have to ask. He knew his way around the world of covert operations.

'That's because I was a rugby player.'

'Which team?'

'Melbourne at the last. Go Rebels.'

'I thought you were UK.'

'My wife. She likes Kent.'

'Christ, so I might have been whacked by some Aussie rugby player who knows how to chat up the ladies into giving him their panties.'

'Just a key card. I'm happily married.'

'Yeah, I heard. Rafe warned me off.'

Webster's brows rose faintly. 'You into strangers?'

'Don't tell me a rugby player doesn't know about strange stuff.'

'I've sworn off.' He grinned. 'True love. It's not just a myth.'

'My loss. But you were such an incredible computer whiz, it turned me on. I love clever men. Relax, Rafe was pretty clear. You're off limits.'

'I can take care of myself. But Rafe as duenna – definitely novel. I'm getting up now. Don't shoot. We have to leave. Zou's hit squads wouldn't even have to break a sweat to get past Miss Kelly and associates. I know a better place to wait for Bao Yu to surface again. You know she's an artist, right? I thought we could scope out some galleries later. Not that I'm expecting her to just land in our net, but she was at the fucking *mall*. Seriously.'

'Do I get a say in this plan of yours?'

'You're the lady with the gun. Talk all you want. But the longer we stay here, the closer Zou's hitmen are getting. They're in town. Zou's babe needs protection from people like us.'

'And from Zou's enemies.'

'Them most of all. So?'

'I don't like men telling me what to do.'

'I heard different.'

'During business hours, then, okay? Are we done with the gossip?'

'You handed me that line. I couldn't resist. Won't happen again.' He mimed locking his lips. 'Now, could we get the fuck out of here? I have a life back home, a good one. Dying in Brisbane isn't on my agenda.'

Gina lowered her weapon, shoved it back in her shoulder holster, turned and, buttoning up her jacket, walked away.

Webster caught up with her in a few long strides. 'Where's your luggage?'

'In a storage locker. Yours?'

'At the house.' At her raised brows, he added, 'If you fire up a computer in a hotel you might as well send out a message to the world. Even with encryption, your location's likely to be compromised. I don't take chances, even miniscule ones.'

'I'll go first,' Gina said, slipping her shoes back on. 'We don't want to be seen together on the camera feed.'

'I'll take the stairs. What? Miss Kelly liked me. I have the code. There's a coffee shop two blocks down on the right. Take a cab there. I'll be at a table in the back room.'

She gave him a sharp glance. 'How long have you been here?'

'Couple hours this time. I did some grad work at UQ.' He grinned. 'Two years that time.'

'You're just full of surprises.'

'I'm gonna find Zou's babe. That'll be my big surprise. The rest is up to you.'

CHAPTER 12

Rafe came back to the tower room at dawn, found Nicole asleep, the TV on and, leaning over, woke her with a kiss.

Her eyes fluttered open. 'You can't leave me again,' she said, her voice soft with sleep.

'I won't.'

A tiny smile. 'Liar.'

'Not about everything.' He kissed her again. 'Not about you and me,' he murmured, his mouth lifting from hers. A lingering sigh at the toxic state of his world, then he straightened. 'Feel like a short trip?'

'Sure.'

'Thanks.'

His soft reply was straight from the heart and, regardless of what Fiona thought, Nicole heard the feeling layered in his voice, the quiet sincerity. 'Where? When? Does it matter what I wear?'

'Geneva. Now. Wear whatever. We'll be back this afternoon. And thanks, I really mean it.' His breath caught, lifted his chest slightly and a beat passed before he said softly, 'You're the only thing good in my life. I swear to God, everything else is fucked.'

Too late, too late, everything's too late, the litany ran through her mind like the voice of doom. 'I have faith in you, in your crew, your friends. Whatever you're dealing with, you'll crush it, okay? Just give me five minutes,' she said, tossing the covers aside, not giving him time to contradict or negate her fanciful dream, not wanting to hear the truth. 'I'll be back.'

The wistfulness in her voice hurt. 'You got that right, Tiger. Crush 'em for sure.' He couldn't bring himself to shape a new lie. 'I'll wait for you by the door. If I lie down, I'll fall asleep.'

But when she came out of the dressing room, he was sprawled in a chair, sleeping. He looked exhausted, his eyes shadowed with fatigue, his breathing light, his chest rising and falling faintly under his partially buttoned shirt. She'd just decided ten minutes more of sleep couldn't possibly matter when there was a brisk knock on the door. Then a shout. 'Davey's waiting!'

Rafe came awake with a start, quickly scanned the room, mornings after in strange rooms habitual. *Ah, home.* 'I'll be right down,' he called out, gave his head a shake, then heaved himself out of the chair. He smiled at Nicole like this was just a normal day. 'You look great.' He flicked a finger at her yellow summer dress and sandals. 'My Little Miss Sunshine.' He held out his hand. 'Ready?'

'As ever.'

'That's my girl.' He winked. 'Decisive, no quibbling.'

'When it comes to you, I know what I want. No reason to quibble. And you should sleep on the plane,' Nicole added as they moved toward the door. If he could pretend this was just another day, she could too.

'I will. I have a meeting with an asshole, so—'

'You'd better be alert.'

'It's not complicated but, yeah, a little sleep won't hurt. We'll stop at the house first. I have to look presentable – he's a banker. If you don't mind waiting in the car while I talk to the prick, we'll head to the airport right after, then fly back here.'

'Wow, the jet-set life.'

He stopped, his hand on the door latch. 'Would you rather not go?'

'Hey, you're not getting rid of me so don't even try.'

He laughed. 'Jesus, Tiger, seriously where have you been all my life?'

'Waiting for you to show up on Tinder. But you never did so I had to come looking for you.'

'My goddamn lucky day.' His nostrils flared as he breathed in hard, their future grim at best.

'*Our* lucky day.' Nicole squeezed his hand. 'Your pilot's waiting.' Denial was not just a river in Egypt.

He smiled, avoidance of reality high on his list too. 'Yeah, we better go.'

But even before Rafe's jet had cleared the runway in Split, he was half asleep on the bed in his cabin. 'Sorry, poor company,' he murmured, his eyelids heavy, as Nicole sat beside him. He patted her hand. 'The steward will take your order for breakfast. I'll eat later.'

'Me too, but thanks. Go to sleep.' She kissed him lightly on the cheek.

'Mmmm, nice,' he whispered, smiling faintly. 'Wake me up if you need me.'

His voice was clear and cool. He meant it. His kindness warmed her heart. She remembered him rising out of sleep one morning, stunned for a second, then seeing her, smiling and saying, 'Whadda you need, Pussycat?' But no way would she even think about waking him now. It had been days since he'd slept through the night.

Leaning back against the headboard, Nicole watched him like a mother hen would her last surviving chick. Feeling threatened and fearful, the unfamiliar emotions ripping through the gloss of what had always been a perfect life. But she was half a world away from her comfortable existence; she could hear the clock ticking down in her head, the days being checked off the calendar, the thundering apocalypse coming closer by the minute.

About to set her world ablaze.

She'd found love in the worst of times. With a man who

might consider love the last thing he wanted. When there wasn't a chance in hell that anything was going to work out. When she was not totally okay with that.

She almost touched him a hundred times, his lean, muscled strength and power, his breathtaking beauty a lavish, demanding lure to tactile contact. But each time she jerked her hand back, knowing how much he needed rest.

In his usual shorts and shirt, he was sprawled on his back, his arms over his head, his feet hanging over the foot of the bed. She would have liked to move him up so he'd be more comfortable, although she would have needed help for that; he was a foot taller and at least a hundred pounds heavier. God, she loved his big, beautiful body. She would have liked to lie on top of him and feel his hard muscled warmth. She would have liked even more to wake up with him every morning and see his smile.

But the possibility of limitless morning smiles was slim to nil. And for someone who'd been denied very little in her life, the sense of impotence was stark. She had no recourse, no alternative, no road untravelled she could take to alter the future. No power or control over events. She only had now and a few days more. She blinked back the tears that threatened to spill over. As if Rafe needed more problems to deal with. As if her crying would change a thing.

It wouldn't, it couldn't, and she refused to add to his

burdens. This would be her *carpe diem* holiday. No hoping or wishing, no useless speculation beyond that simple fact. She smiled. She might take Fiona's snarky advice and snap some pictures.

Should she ask or do it on the sly?

Both as it turned out.

She'd decided to take a few pictures as the plane began its descent into Geneva. It might be her last chance. Click, click, click, whoops – she was suddenly looking at a wide-eyed image of Rafe through her cell phone camera lens.

He rubbed his eyes, blinked, said huskily, 'What are you doing?'

'Taking some pictures.' It was too late to lie. 'Do you mind?'

'For yourself?' He was camera-shy after years of being tabloid fodder.

'Just me.' She smiled, knew what he was asking. 'I don't need the money.'

'Okay, then, me too.' He held out his hand. 'I'll send them to my phone.'

They were both storing memories against a bleak, uncertain future.

CHAPTER 13

Forty minutes later, Rafe's car was idling outside the private bank, Nederman & Ney. The neo-baroque building had no sign on the door or plaque on the wall to indicate it was home to a two-hundred-year-old banking firm. Their clients preferred anonymity; the business partners did as well. Founded shortly after the Napoleonic Wars when war profiteering had left a great number of men with fortunes to hide, Nederman & Ney had continued doing business with despots and criminals of every persuasion through several subsequent wars, world crises and hostile financial environments. Even today with stricter governmental pressures aimed at transparency, the bank continued their cloistered style of business.

'This shouldn't take long – ten, fifteen minutes.' Rafe leaned over, kissed Nicole's cheek and smiled. 'Gonna miss me?'

'Every second.' She ran her hand down the hand-stitched lapel of his bespoke, café au lait-coloured suit, smoothed the knot in his moss-green tie, glanced up and grinned. 'You look like a genuine billionaire today in your power suit, with your hair slicked back, wearing a fancy watch,' she added, tapping the platinum World Time Patek Philippe on his strong wrist. 'Go slay the dragon.'

Rafe brought her hand up to his lips, kissed her knuckles. 'He's only a rat. Piece of cake.' Dropping her hand, he reached for the door handle. 'If you get bored, Simon can give you a city tour. I'll call when I come back down.'

'I'm good. I'll check my messages, listen to some music.' She pulled her phone from her pocket. 'I'm currently infatuated with Alabama Shakes, so take your time.'

Rafe swung out of the car, leaned back in. 'Want me to bring the band to the island?'

How sweet was that? Nicole smiled. 'Maybe when your life slows down.'

'You got a deal.' Blowing her a kiss, he shut the door, loped across the small stretch of pavement, nodded to the door man who held open the door, then spoke to a smiling, well-dressed young woman at the desk in the lobby. Someone had made an appointment for him with Mr Balthus at eleven, he explained in French, the predominant language in Geneva.

Taking the manned elevator up two floors, Rafe walked into Balthus's anteroom more or less on time, smiled at another glossy, well-dressed receptionist, said, 'Hugo's expecting me. Rafe Contini.'

'Just a minute, Mr Contini. I'll let Mr Balthus know you're here.'

The beautiful blonde was model perfect, although in this business, she had to have academic credentials too. But knowing Hugo, she served more than one purpose. Not that he was particularly virtuous, but then he wasn't married for a reason.

She looked up from the intercom. 'Would you like coffee, espresso, tea, Mr Contini?'

'No thank you.' Another smile, a glance at his watch to let her know he didn't want to wait.

She hesitated.

Knowing Hugo, he was going to be kept waiting out of sheer boorishness. 'Why don't I just go in,' he said, moving toward the inner door.

Startled, she jumped to her feet, and lifted her hand as though to deter him.

'Hugo and I are old friends,' Rafe murmured, walking past her. 'He won't mind. Will you, Hugo,' he said a second later, shutting the door behind him, and smiling at the man who'd jumped to his feet and was scowling at him. 'I'm afraid I frightened your receptionist. I don't like to wait.' Giving credence to his statement, he strode directly toward the desk. 'How's everything going? I haven't seen you since the polo tournament in Deauville. Wife and children fine? You all looked cheerful that day.' Rafe waved his hand toward the framed family photos on a shelf behind the desk. 'By the way, how old are your daughters?'

The banker's gaze narrowed. 'Why the hell would you care?'

'Relax, I'm just making conversation.'

'Since you own your own bank, I doubt it. Why are you here?' Balthus didn't even attempt to hide the irritation in his voice.

Rafe came to a stop. 'Christ, not even an offer of a drink, or a chair? What kind of business do you run?'

'A very profitable one,' the banker snapped.

Unmoved by Hugo's insolence, Rafe stepped between the desk and one of the Empire chairs meant for clients, sat, leaned back and pointed. 'Sit,' he said as he pulled his phone from his jacket pocket, hit an icon, returned his phone to his pocket, looked up and smiled. 'You'll be more comfortable.'

'I'm comfortable standing,' Balthus said, indignation tightening his mouth.

Hugo was dressed in a banker's unimpeachable uniform: a double-breasted navy pinstripe suit, blue shirt with a Winchester collar, red executive tie. A big man, he'd been proud of his size at Lucerne, his bullying not confined exclusively to Basil. He stood sharply upright now, like an evangelist about to denounce sinners. Under the circumstances, Rafe found the mental image ironic.

'Suit yourself.' Rafe jabbed a finger toward a faint buzzing sound. 'You might want to look at your phone. I just sent you some photos.' Rafe saw Hugo's gaze flicker as his private phone, known only to family, vibrated in his pocket.

'And if I don't care to look?' he said, still blustering.

'Then I'll send the photos to your wife.'

Hugo's mouth twisted in a sneer. 'Blackmail?'

'Such a dirty word,' Rafe murmured. 'I like to think of it as a mutually satisfying business arrangement. Take a look. The photos might not be a problem. You know your marital situation better than I. Maybe your wife doesn't care if you're fucking her little sister. At least Monique's eighteen. It was her birthday the first time, wasn't it? Your wife was skiing at Gstaad. I like the birthday cake picture. I'd never seen that side of you, Hugo. Such a thoughtful brother-in-law.'

Rafe watched Balthus as he spoke, saw the man's face turn an unhealthy shade of pale as he flicked through the photos. Saw him sit down hard, his desk chair creaking under the sudden weight. Saw the sweat break out on his forehead.

Rafe stopped talking and looked around the room as he waited for Hugo to understand how complicated his life had become.

It was an impressive office; heavy walnut panelling, deeply carved mouldings, coffered ceiling, discreet gilding – nothing too ostentatious for this type of bank. The plush carpet was subdued in colour, the furniture genuine Empire, the upholstery subtle shades of green and umber. The framed paintings on the walls were landscapes by minor masters, as if the firm's founders were afraid their clients might be tempted to poach works of greater value.

Good God, was that a whimper?

Rafe's gaze returned to the man behind the desk. 'If you've seen enough,' he said, mildly, 'I'd like to talk business.' Nicole was waiting, Carlos was waiting, his jet was waiting. Hugo was just one small part of a much larger game.

Balthus's jaw had gone slack. He visibly pulled himself together, set down his phone and looked up. 'What do you want?' he croaked.

'I need one of your accounts shut down.' Rafe held up a finger as Hugo began to protest. 'You can keep the money. I don't want it. I just need the account holder blocked from accessing the funds. He probably won't live long, so look on the bright side. You do me a favour and your management fee on that transaction is going to be a hundred per cent.'

'I'm not sure I can do that.' The banker's voice was uneasy, his eyes full of fear. 'We have procedures that—'

'I'm sure there's an override for your more confidential transactions,' Rafe interposed quietly. 'It's your wife's family's bank after all, you're one of the directors. But your decision, of course.' Rafe sat up, leaned forward slightly.

'I'd be more than happy to send those hardcore photos to your wife. I've never liked you. If she leaves you penniless, more power to her. And consider,' he added softly, 'if that happens, little Monique will find someone richer to fuck her up the ass. Your dick isn't worth a middle-class life.' He flashed a smile. 'Just a guess from those pictures.'

'I could notify the authorities.' But even Hugo's voice indicated the lie.

'Feel free – if you want the authorities looking into your secret banking. The account I want shut down is completely illegal, the money stolen from a government without scruples, one that might decide to get it back. Think about it. Torture is a nasty business. You wouldn't last five minutes.'

'Torture?' Hugo's voice cracked.

'Count on it. I'll personally send them a note.'

'You've always been a son-of-a-bitch,' Balthus hissed, pure hatred in his eyes.

Rafe stared back. 'Takes one to know one.' Then he tapped his watch. 'I'm in a hurry. So either do it or I'm leaving. I don't have time to fuck around.'

Silence.

Rafe got to his feet. Stood for a second, then turned and walked away. He was reaching for the door latch when he finally heard what he'd always known he would.

'Wait.'

He opened the door instead because Hugo Balthus was

and always had been one of the biggest assholes in the world.

'Wait, wait!' Panic in the banker's voice. 'Don't go!'

Rafe counted slowly to ten; for Basil, he thought. Then he closed the door and turned. 'You want something?' His voice was chill.

'I'll do it. I'll do it. Jesus, come back. Fuck . . . just give me a second.'

'I don't have a second. Turn on your computer.' Rafe moved back to the desk, took out a small notecard from his coat pocket and slid it across the polished desktop. 'That's the account number.'

Hugo ran his palm over his sweaty forehead, then back over his smooth blond hair he kept longer than most bankers would out of vanity. 'Jesus, if someone notices?'

'Tell them your wife owns the fucking bank. It's a real chunk of change, Hugo. Grow a pair. Call it your retirement fund. Your wife might catch you fucking her sister someday. You haven't been very careful. Just a word to the wise. Tone it down at home, okay? You're really taking a chance whipping that little girl in your own bed.'

'How the hell did you get *those* photos?' The banker's voice was uneven, shaky.

'None of your business. What do you need – a password, finger scan, retina scan? Just do it. Right the fuck now,' Rafe growled. 'Or I'll see that you're screwed for life.'

Rafe stood behind Balthus as he logged on to his terminal, used a retina scanner to open the system, then keyed in the account number and locked it down. The no-access code was a discreet line of four numbers and two letters that Rafe had Hugo explain twice so he understood that they were specific to that account. 'A Russian found this account,' Rafe warned before he left. 'If you didn't shut it down, he'll find that out too. You wouldn't want that to happen. Clear?'

Hugo looked at him with murder in his eyes. But he answered, 'Yes.'

Rafe walked out without another word, nodded at the receptionist as he passed, took the stairs rather than the elevator. He needed a few minutes to get over the fierce rage that always overcame him when dealing with vicious, venal people like Hugo. The man was devoid of humanity or shame for that matter. His heart pounding, Rafe suddenly felt nauseous as the uncompromising violence of that year in Lucerne broke into his thoughts with total clarity. He stopped, steadied himself with a hand against the marble wall, took a deep breath and felt a powerful urge to go back upstairs and beat the living shit out of Hugo.

He could.

Zou's account was closed now.

It wouldn't matter.

He quickly calculated personal vengeance against his responsibilities, and stifled his headstrong impulse. The stupidity Hugo was engaged in with his sister-in-law would bite him in the ass soon enough anyway. Let Hugo's wife be his proxy for revenge.

Rafe was pulling off his tie with one hand, unbuttoning the top button on his shirt with the other as he strode toward his waiting car. And the moment he slid into the back seat, he pulled Nicole into his arms and softly exhaled. 'Thank God you're normal,' he whispered into her hair. Then he dragged in a breath, looked up, said to Simon, 'The airport,' and lifted her on his lap. 'Now give me a rundown of a normal day in your normal life in your normal world back home in San Francisco. Any day. Start with breakfast.'

'Bad meeting?'

'I wanted to kill the guy.'

'In that case, let me tell you about a day at the beach. And you tell me that you'll come surfing with me someday. And we'll both pretend life is grand.'

He laughed. 'You first. Hey, hey, I'm coming, I promise. I like to surf.'

'Okay, then. Where I live, the best surfing's at Half Moon Bay,' she began.

He didn't actually listen other than to the soft, melodic rhythm of her words. He just held her close, inhaled the scent of her shampoo, cologne, maybe just her natural sweetness and tried to forget he even knew people like Hugo and Zou. Only when his pulse finally stopped racing, did he realize she'd stopping talking. 'Sorry,' he murmured. 'Sorry, still coming down.' Sliding his tie around the back of her neck, he wrapped the green silk around his fist and tugged her closer in an effortless act of ownership. 'You mine?' An initial gentleness underlay his query, but before she could answer, he said brusquely, 'You're mine, Pussycat. End of story.' His fist involuntarily tightened, drawing her closer, his expression grave, intent, a narrowed slant to his eyes.

'I wouldn't have said no,' she whispered, wanting to erase the frown lines from his forehead.

He tried to smile. 'Couldn't take a chance.' Sliding a finger under her chin, he lifted her face, bent to kiss her, then just short of her lips slipped into his default setting – the one that made the world go still for a moment and let you forget. 'Feel like a nap on the flight back?'

'A nap?'

He felt her smile, felt an overwhelming relief that she was still part of his world for a few more days. 'Maybe a little personal massage thrown in,' he said, his voice lighter now, the bad shit beginning to switch off. 'Whatever you like.' He gave her lip a little nip. 'Or better yet, whatever I like . . .'

CHAPTER 14

They didn't go back to the castle tower on their return to the island, but took up residence in the palazzo.

Henny and Basil were expected soon, Carlos said. And Webster wanted Rafe to call him. 'Good news, I think,' Carlos added, standing in the doorway leading out to the terrace.

'We could use some,' Rafe said. 'If you could shift some of the operations into the east wing while we're here, it would be more convenient. I'll come over with Henny and Basil after they arrive. And let's all do dinner tonight. Just give me a head count of those coming in time for Teresa to put a menu together. I'm going to give Nicole a quick tour of the house, then I'll call Webster.'

'Hugo?' Carlos asked, cryptically.

'It went well.'

Carlos noticed Nicole's sharp glance at Rafe and wondered how much he'd told her. But he just said, 'Good. Glad that's done. I'll see you in a few hours.'

Rafe took Nicole on a brief walkthrough of the two-storey palazzo. 'So you can find me if you wake up and I'm not around,' he said. 'Our schedule is getting busy.'

Getting busy? But she only smiled and said, 'Thanks. I'll try not to bother you.'

'That would be a problem.' A slow smile curved his lips. 'Since I'm shacked up with you for a reason.'

There was a warmth in his eyes that wasn't teasing alone, that made her heart do a little butterfly flutter. 'Okay then, I'll bother the hell out of you.'

'There you go, gettin' with the programme.' He gave a slow nod, the teasing gone from his gaze, a moody seriousness in his canted brows. Then he seemed to catch himself and a quick grin flashed across his face. 'So we good now? Find me whenever you want?'

'Yup.' Only one answer was allowed; she knew that. But seriously, love sucked. If Rafe wasn't in the midst of some major battle, skirmish, whatever it was, she would have ignored all the complications of his playboy life and told him how she felt. *I love you. I've never loved anyone before. Now what are you going to do about it?* Instead, she zipped her lip and followed him with a modicum of awe through his island home.

The airy, sumptuous palazzo was a variation on a Palladian design with two large wings, a central rotunda and several large reception rooms on the main floor. The first floor east wing contained a dozen rooms, while

Rafe's suite in the west wing consisted of a palatial salon, modest-sized sitting room, two large bedrooms, a study, office, two small bathrooms and one in malachite sumptuous enough for Cleopatra.

'I am, as always,' she said, smiling at him as the tour came to an end in his light-filled sitting room, 'impressed with your princely lifestyle.'

He shrugged. 'I just like the island. The rest came with it.'

'I'll warn you now – if you come surfing, don't expect any palaces.'

'*When* I come surfing, Pussycat, I won't be looking for anything but you in a nice big bed.'

'I'll see what I can do.' But she felt a moment of giddiness that he'd said *when* so emphatically.

'You don't have to do anything but give me your address. I'll take care of all the rest.' He grinned. 'I might even find a palace with a big bed for you.'

'Now for a moment of sanity in this dream scenario,' she said with a little twitch of her nose. 'You might have to meet my parents. My dad, especially, has a thing about über-rich people.'

'Does that include your uncle?'

She did a little sideways waggle of her hand. 'He likes Dominic, but he likes him more cause my mom adores her baby brother.'

'Why don't I pick you up in a Prius? Jeans, T-shirt, something off the rack.'

'There you go.' She grinned. 'Rich *and* smart.'

His cell phone rang, saving him from a conversation that would only prove more difficult if it continued. Because he didn't know what tomorrow would bring, let alone a future that included surfing with Nicole. Pulling out his phone from his shorts pocket, he glanced at the display and grimaced. 'Sorry, business. Okay if I leave you on your own for an hour or so?'

Nicole nodded. 'Course.' She winked. 'I acquiesce to you in all things.'

He did a soft growl deep in his throat. 'Fucking tempting.' Then he sucked in a breath and walked away.

'Getting close?' he said into the phone, his voice all business as he made for the main staircase.

'At the landing pad,' Basil answered. 'I brought one of my cousins to help out. And Henny's already complaining that Teresa won't take orders from him. You can referee *that* fight.'

'Happy to. I'll be right down.'

Punching in Webster's number, he went down the wide marble staircase in running leaps and was crossing the entrance hall when Webster answered. 'Hey,' Rafe said. 'Carlos said you called.'

'Yeah. Bao Yu's here. With the child.'

'Great. And?' Rafe shoved the door open.

'We have to find her. She showed up on face-recognition

software at the mall. The city has twenty thousand surveillance cameras in public spaces. Makes my job easier.'

'She's not hiding?' Turning left, Rafe moved down the shaded loggia.

'Doesn't look like it.'

'That's strange, right?'

'Unexpected certainly. Either she's naïve to the point of stupidity or she wants to be found. I've seen some of her artwork. I wouldn't bet on stupid.'

'She has to know Zou's enemies are dangerous,' Rafe pointed out. 'Not us particularly, but she doesn't know that.'

'Gina and I'll figure it out. We have to find her first. I'm going over CCTV surveillance feeds now in all the most likely areas; the mall, of course, downtown, especially in the gallery sector. Gina and I are checking out the galleries tomorrow. There's a possibility Bao Yu's here because she's familiar with the city's art scene, not because Zou sent her. Gina just crashed but I'll be up all night in case you have any questions.'

'Not a question, but a heads-up,' Rafe noted, walking out of the shade into the sunny garden. 'Gina can be outspoken.'

'I know. Everything's fine though. She's good at what she does – the kind of partner who won't get me killed.'

'Just don't cross her. Seriously.' Gina had killed her former partner/lover when he'd tried to set her up to take a fall for him. A shot in the head at close range.

'I heard. Not a problem. We already decided this was strictly business.'

Rafe laughed, waved at his guests waiting on the palm-lined landing pad at the border of the garden. 'So she checked you out even after I'd warned her off?'

'I'm guessing that's her style.'

'True. Look, tell Gina thanks from me. And thank *you* for finding Bao Yu again. Keep me posted on your progress. The sooner we get to Zou's mistress, the sooner we can put this problem of ours to rest.'

'Got it. Once I know something, I'll be in touch.'

When Rafe reached the landing pad, Davey was already lifting off to ferry another group of men from Split to the island. Gora was sending reinforcements, more of Dominic and Max's security men were waiting for Davey at the Split airport. Carlos' colleagues from around the world had been arriving for the past few days.

Basil introduced his cousin Sasha; their mothers were sisters, he explained. Rafe knew Basil spent summer holidays at his mother's dacha near St Petersburg so he'd heard of the myriad cousins. 'Sasha's offered to help,' Basil said. 'He has a doctorate in IT from the Gorkovskij Institute. He's does tech searches without a warrant.'

'Perfect. Appreciate you coming,' Rafe said, shaking Sasha's hand. If he wasn't from such a wealthy, well-connected family, in that line of work, the man might have ended up with a body covered in prison tats. Big and solid, Sasha was muscled to the max, his blond hair cut so short his skull gleamed, his face hard-featured and austere. The two cousins couldn't have been more disparate in appearance. Basil favoured his father's tall, lean frame and aristocratic profile.

'Just so you know, Rafie, baby,' Henny drawled, punching Rafe's arm, his smile the familiar one he had after a shitload of Jägermeister. 'Mireille says if I'm killed she's coming after you.'

'Yeah, well, tell her she can take it up with Zou, 'cause if you're gone, I'll be gone.'

Henny groaned theatrically. 'Damn, then my father's estate goes to my younger brother and he has no fucking brains. He takes after father's second wife.' The old Prussian Junker estates were inherited by the eldest son, and even while titles of nobility no longer existed as legal entities in Germany, they were still inherited and carried. As in, Heinrich Graf von und zu Steindorff-Lehn. Henny was a count.

'Speaking of dying,' Basil interposed, 'Claudine and I are talking again, so I'd prefer surviving this shit storm. Let's think positive. Fill us in on what's going on now, next and whatever the hell explodes after that.'

'Come to the house. I'll bring you up to speed.'

Wanting to keep his distance from Nicole in the west wing, Rafe showed the men into what had been the steward's office. He ordered drinks, and once they were delivered, shut the double doors, walked over to his friends who were seated at a table near the windows and dropped into a chair. 'Here's what we know.' He explained Zou's seclusion, Gina's diverted flight to Brisbane, Bao Yu's sighting, the surveillance and snipers in Shanghai. He mentioned the various men who'd arrived on the island, those in current deployments or waiting to be assigned, the numbers contributing to the island security. He described the plans for targeting Zou, the teams on surveillance of Zou's wife and children, his sister, and an elderly mentor who'd retired near Shanghai.

'We've cut off most of Zou's funds,' Rafe pointed out. 'Gora found us Zou's secret bank accounts. Gora's shutting down some, we're taking care of others, and thanks to your photos, Basil, Balthus proved amenable.'

'Hugo amenable? Do tell,' Henny drawled. 'Hugo with his nuts in a vice.' He kissed his fingertips. 'Don't leave out a single heart-warming detail.'

Rafe smiled. 'I definitely wrecked his smug little world. At first though, he was all righteous outrage and bluster, but once he saw the photos, panic and fear hit him like a ton of bricks and he caved.' Rafe raised an eyebrow in Basil's direction. 'How long have you been sitting on those pictures?'

'A few months. I didn't take them. They arrived anonymously. Hugo has more enemies than just us. With my current film project on bullying well known in the small, incestuous world of documentary film, I was the logical recipient for someone bent on revenge. Who knew the prick was a bully even in the bedroom.'

'Score, score *and* score!' Henny crowed. 'Did he cry? Tell me he cried.'

'He probably would have, but I was in a hurry. I couldn't wait. Although, I'm guessing Hugo's performance is gonna be compromised if he tries fucking his little piece his usual way again. He'll be wondering who's watching.' Rafe glanced at Basil.

Basil shrugged. 'Don't look at me. I haven't a clue who set up the cameras. Could be staff he'd pissed off.'

'Just out of curiosity,' Rafe said. 'Would you have used Hugo's pictures?'

'Of course. With some identities obscured.'

'His?'

Basil shrugged again. 'Maybe. I doubt he'd sue. I'm glad they were useful to you.'

'Useful, oh yeah. Balthus turned white, sweat broke out on his forehead, he fucking whimpered. It was beautiful.'

'And they say justice is blind,' Henny murmured, raising his glass of Jägermeister.

'Not with photos that damning.' Rafe lifted his whiskey drink to his circle of friends. 'Now, some justice for Ganz's father and we can all go home and tend our gardens.'

A sudden silence fell. Each man understood the extent of the dangers they faced.

'We've done it before – survived,' Henny said, his voice quiet now. 'We'll do it again.'

Rafe half smiled. 'We're older and smarter.'

'And fucking bigger,' Basil said with a grin, his tall, lean form whip-cord tough.

'And well armed,' Basil's cousin Sasha said, his voice velvet soft.

CHAPTER 15

Feeling the need to touch base with the real world, and mildly bored as well, Nicole called Fiona.

'Still in love?' Fiona answered in a bantering tone. 'Or have you come to your senses?'

Nicole sighed. 'I'm still confused, if that's what you're asking. Who knew love was such a mind fuck – intense, wonderful, tearful. You get the picture. Add to the mix the fact that I'm beginning to feel like a kept woman. I'm in a grand palace on a private island, lying on a huge bed just waiting around while Rafe works and works and works some more. He says feel free to come and find him whenever I want, but I'm not sure he means it. So I just lie here and wait.'

'Lie there in luxury. Don't forget that.'

'Like you could forget in a place this size. He lives like Dominic – although even more extravagantly 'cause back home, Dominic and Kate live like anyone else on our street – no servants, just Patty. Rafe's lifestyle, in contrast, is completely jet set. We just returned from Geneva. Flew there this morning for a ten-minute meeting he'd scheduled, then back here two hours later. He has planes, pilots, drivers and staff everywhere; Dominic does too, but everything's more low key since he married Kate.'

'Yeah, I've seen their house in Cliffside. It's nice, but definitely not palatial.'

'That would be Rafe's Monte Carlo or Geneva house – palatial to the max. We stopped at the one in Geneva today so he could change into a suit to go see some banker. A truly majestic butler like you'd see in the movies greeted him as if he were royalty. Christ, going back to school would be like stepping off some magic cloud into the everyday, nitty-gritty world of take-out and studying all night.'

'Hey, don't break my bubble yet, okay? We still have a few more weeks of vacation. And speaking of magic clouds,' Fiona said, a smile in her voice, 'Jack's taking me to Paris.'

'Great. You're having fun. I'm glad.'

'It's super really. Not a complaint in the world. But then I'm not deep in love like you with all the will-he-or-won't-he angst that's messing with your head.'

Jarred by Fiona's deep-in-love comment or maybe just more doleful and moody in her solitude, Nicole had a sudden, unsettling thought. 'Oh, fuck, now I'm wondering how many other women have waited for Rafe on this bed?'

'You don't really want me to answer that, do you?'

Nicole sighed. 'No.' Another deeper sigh. 'I'm taking this way too seriously, aren't I?'

'Considering the man and his reputation ...' Fiona's voice trailed off. 'Hey, what does Isabelle say about your love problems? She's always more sensible than you and me.'

'I can't get hold of her. She's at one of those meditation retreats where no one talks, there's no phones, nothing. She and my mother are into yoga and shit like that, so I have to figure this out without my usual voice of reason.' There was a brief moment of silence, then Nicole spoke in a voice that one would use to convince yourself of something unpleasant. 'It's been a while since I was a four-teen-year-old teeny-bopper swooning over an untouchable celebrity. I'm a relatively intelligent, well-grounded adult now. So fuck it, I might as well be sensible and register while I'm lying around twiddling my thumbs. It's too late to get any good classes, but ask me if I care.'

'If you're talking Chem, you haven't cared for a while.' Fiona smoothly picked up on the sudden change of topic, thinking *finally* – the Nicole she knew and loved was back.

'Shit. I suppose it's too late to change my major.'

'Just a fucking little bit. Look, register, make your parents happy, you can still work for Yash on the side.'

Nicole groaned. 'I don't think happiness research is going to cut it for me right now.'

'Jesus, babe, is it really true. Love hurts?'

'Like a son-of-a-bitch.' Nicole blew out a breath. 'Hey, don't be stupid like me. Go have fun. I'm just in a blue funk. I'll get over it. I always do.'

Fiona hesitated, not sure how to respond; she'd never seen Nicole in a funk, blue or otherwise. And she was sure as hell waffling. 'If Rafe doesn't come back for a while, call me again. You can whine and I'll listen. You've done it often enough for me.'

'Sure, okay.' Another sigh. 'Maybe I'll just sleep for a while, then register.'

Holy shit. Didn't sleeping during the day equal depression? Was this like intervention time? 'You sure you're okay?' Although Fiona didn't know what she'd do if Nicole said, no, because Jack had just come into the bedroom, glanced at her unpacked suitcase on the bed and was giving her a what-the-fuck-have-you-been-doing look.

'Yeah, yeah, I'm good.' Nicole exhaled. 'I think it's just that I'm not used to being alone. Like ever. I'm fine, really.'

'Okay, I'll call you when I get to Paris,' Fiona promised. 'Bye.' Dropping her phone on the bed, she felt like the world's worst friend.

'The plane's waiting.' Since Fiona was frowning, Jack's voice was super-polite. 'We can buy you what you need in Paris if you don't feel like packing.'

'Nicole's in love,' Fiona said, more tersely than she intended.

Jack took a small breath. 'Sorry about that.'

'That's it. Sorry?' A hard flash in her eyes.

'I wish I could help you out,' he said, kindly. 'But it happens all the time. Women like Rafe.'

'Like or love?'

She was sitting up straight now, staring at him. 'Both,' Jack said, figuring there was no point in lying about Rafe's lifestyle. It wasn't a mystery. 'Actually, Rafe inspires all kinds of feelings – love, lust, like and everything in between. Since he doesn't give out his email or phone number, he keeps the postal service in business. He gets love notes, invitations to intimate dinners, invites to less-exclusive orgies, or pick-your-pleasure opportunities of every kind. You name it, he's offered it. Rafe's good with women.'

'Like a lion tamer or horse whisperer.' Each word was softly astringent.

Jack put up his hands. 'Don't get pissed at me. I have no control over his life. No one does. No one ever has. His father tried his damnedest and failed. Rafe's a law unto himself. That's it. That's the way it's always been. If it helps, Nicole has touched him more than any other woman – ever. He's altered his life for her, made adjustments those of us who know him well wouldn't have thought possible; he's shown real affection. I'm not saying it's permanent or even significant. I'm just saying it hasn't happened before.'

'Nicole's really unhappy.'

Jack raked his fingers through his sun-streaked hair, dropped his hands. 'I don't know what to say. What do you want me to say?'

'Nothing.' Fiona took a deep breath. 'Don't worry about it. I'm just feeling sorry for her.'

'Rafe's made some major changes for Nicole. That's a simple fact.' Jack shifted restlessly; defending his cousin's sense of commitment was dangerous.

'Thanks for the explanation. Whatever I think really doesn't matter anyway.' With a nod, she rolled off the bed. 'I can pack in five minutes.' She smiled. 'You wearing that?' He had on shorts, no shirt, his feet were bare.

'I'll put on a shirt. It's just us on the plane – and a steward or two. Wear whatever you like.' He grinned. 'Or nothing at all.'

'I'll need a few more drinks before I consider public nudity, although cultural mores are definitely more casual down here.' Nude beaches were common on the island.

'It's summer.' Jack smiled. 'What can I say. La dolce vita.'

CHAPTER 16

Nicole actually registered for fall semester and striking the last key to exit the programme, felt a surge of unfettered freedom. It felt good; not depending on someone else to make you happy, to give your life meaning, to bring you pleasure.

Or kinda good.

She wasn't naïve about her happiness fading fast once Rafe disappeared from her life. But she'd taken that obligatory first step and enrolled in graduate school; classes started next month and, regardless of how events transpired on the island, her life was on track. The fact that Rafe's attention span when it came to women was reputedly non-existent, the additional fact that waves of security men arriving daily spoke of coming perils had been powerful impetus.

Not to mention Fiona's blunt advice. Bask in *carpe diem* bliss while you can, but plan for tomorrow. Because Rafe Contini didn't do permanent.

Fiona may have worried about Nicole sleeping in the daytime, but Rafe just smiled when he walked into his bedroom and found her fast asleep at five o'clock. He'd been keeping Nicole awake at night too much – or she him. His smile widened. She was a greedy, impetuous little puss and his . . . the possessive pronoun no longer coming with a warning but flavoured with happiness.

His smile vanished the instant he saw her fall schedule on the bedside table. His lips clamped together in a grim line. Bloody hell. He shouldn't have been surprised, he reminded himself; it wasn't unexpected. Still, Nicole was a miracle he didn't feel like giving up just yet. If he hadn't been dealing with Ganz's war, he might have asked her to stay. *Might* the great unknown. Along with so much of what he felt with Nicole, his emotions were unfamiliar, mystifying. And whether the brilliant, high-coloured sensations were lust or something more permanent was uncertain.

What was certain, however, was the heated resentment he felt seeing Nicole's fall schedule finalized. Fuck, fuck, fuck. *Oh Christ, had he spoken aloud?* He was staring into Nicole's heavy-lidded gaze.

'Hey. You're back.'

Her voice was soft with sleep, her cheeks flushed, the blue of her eyes touched with such tenderness, he felt a flash of pure joy light up his brain. 'Sorry I woke you,' he murmured. 'Go back to sleep.'

She pushed up on her elbows, shot him a warm, crinkly smile. 'Not when you're here.'

'Then tell me something.' A sharp glance as he picked up the registration sheet and gave it a flick. 'You leaving me?'

'No, not for a while. But I had to register before it was too late.'

'You could go to the University of Geneva.' His gaze was quietly intense. 'I'm on the board. I could get you in any time.' She didn't answer for so long, he tossed the schedule on the nightstand. 'Never mind,' he said, gruffly.

Sitting up, she brushed her hair out of her eyes and smoothed her Wonder Woman T-shirt over her hips because there was a slow burn in Rafe's eyes and covering her nakedness seemed like a good idea. 'Look, in a perfect world I'd like to go to school in Geneva. It would be grand. But I'm guessing it's not a perfect world for you right now.' She moved over to make room for him and patted the bed. 'Come closer. Tell me if I'm wrong.'

'Don't be reasonable,' he grumbled, sitting beside her and pulling her into his arms. 'I prefer illusion.' Resting his chin on her head, he sighed. 'When does school start?'

'First week in September.'

Rafe did a quick count of the days, measured them against all the moving parts in the dangerous game he was playing and allowed himself a sliver of hope. If Webster came through quickly in Brisbane, if Zou could be coaxed

168

out of his hermitage to go join his mistress, if the snipers performed – a lot of ifs, but a good outcome wasn't impossible. 'Don't be surprised if I show up in New York to walk you to class.'

She flung her arms around his neck. 'Really?' She looked up at him, her eyes alight with hope. 'You mean it? Like actually?'

'Maybe,' he said, quietly. 'If I can fucking make things happen.'

She stretched up and kissed his chin. 'Thanks for even trying.' Easing back down, she drew in a small breath, opened her mouth, shut it again, then put her finger over his lips and said, 'Just listen. Don't say anything until I'm done.'

He felt his heart rate spike; those were not words a man cared to hear.

As if she knew, she moved her hand to his heart, looked up and grinned. 'Relax. You're not required to do anything. Consider this a monologue, okay?'

None of her comments were likely to relax him. They sounded like a preface to a conversation that *did* require him to do something. But he politely nodded, smiled and eased back only slightly.

She noticed though, figured now or never, don't wuss out. 'Okay, I just want to say this isn't your problem, it's mine. Oh, hell,' she added and her cheeks turned cherry red. 'Give me a second.'

He almost said, *Am I going to need an attorney?* But figured time enough once she was finished talking.

Then she straightened, took a deep breath, looked him squarely in the eye, and spoke in a rush of words. 'I'm pretty sure I love you. No, I'm sure, I'm really sure. Jesus, don't panic,' she added, uncertain whether it was shock, impatience or he was just shutting down behind that golden stare. 'You don't have to do anything. I already told you that. I just wanted you to know. That's it.' Her smile was easy now, as though she was feeling a whoosh of relief after laying all her cards on the table. 'You're surprised. I understand.'

You wouldn't understand in a fucking million years, he thought. But she was starting to say something again so he chose a polite silence in lieu of risking a response.

'I've never said I love you to anyone before, well – except to family and that's not the same. I never even knew what my girlfriends were talking about when they'd go on and on about how great love was, how amazing and fantastic, how kick-ass wonderful. How loving someone made them all trembly and weak in the knees, and . . . ' She stopped, held his amber gaze. 'Maybe you should say something so I know you're still alive.'

He drew in a small breath, gazed at her, watchful, flipping a coin; should he feel threatened or appreciative? 'How did you know?'

She wrinkled her nose. 'Just did.'

'Explain,' he said, still mostly unsettled, maybe wary too. The life he lived, the women he knew; he had reason.

'Why?'

'Because I'm trying to figure out a few things too.'

She grinned. 'Things?'

'Feelings.' His mouth twitched. 'I don't do feelings.'

'You do with me,' she said with cheerful certainty.

His eyes narrowed a little. 'I don't know. I'm not as sure as you. Spell it out for me. Give me a beginner course in love. I'll see if anything rings a bell.'

Her eyebrows lifted. 'Hey, it's not a contest. I just know I'm in love. You don't have to be, that's okay. There's no way I want you to love me because you have to.'

He smiled. 'I don't do *have to* either.'

She smiled back because he was enjoying himself now. 'Fuck you.'

He laughed. 'That I do.'

She glanced at the clock.

'There's time,' he said, smoothly, on solid ground when it came to fucking. 'As for the other stuff—'A quick breath through his nose, an infinitesimal flinch. 'I'm pretty much on board along with you.'

She grinned. 'Really – on board?'

A real flinch this time, visible from space. 'You know what I mean.'

'I don't think I do.' But her heart was beginning to rev up.

'Oh fuck. You want me to say it?'

'Not if you're gonna start bleeding from your eyes or something.'

A nanosecond later, she was lying beneath him with her Wonder Woman shirt pushed up, her legs spread, his large body resting lightly between her thighs, his dark hair brushing her cheeks, his smile very, very close. 'For what it's worth, I love you.'

'Drop the preface.' Her smile touched his lips. 'That would be super.'

He lifted his head a little, blew out a breath. 'You want everything.'

Wide blue eyes, her gaze intense, watching him. 'I do.'

Silence. Then a straightforward look. 'Okay,' he said, nodding, as though making it certifiable. 'I love you.' There was probably a whole lot more he had to figure out, but if he said too much he might fuck things up. 'Remember that happy virus line from Hafiz?' he said though, because it was buzzing in his head. 'That's me.'

Her smile was a woman-in-love smile. 'I remember. But why do you?'

'Bought a copy for myself. Now kiss me.'

'That's it? We're done with the poetry?'

'Don't push your luck, Tiger. This is a big deal for me. You want poetry, I'll think about it later. Right now— 'He glanced downward, then up. 'You can probably tell I have other things on my mind.'

'Okay.'

His brows shot up at her ready compliance. 'Okay then,' he said real quickly because he wasn't stupid. Although his voice held a rare tenderness when he said, 'No more one-day-at-a time, yeah?'

'Nope. I found you and I'm keeping you. I want to be part of your life and you part of mine. I want the Hallmark Card stuff, the passion, you holding me close twenty-four/seven, the getting up in the morning.' She stopped because his smile had dimmed slightly and she knew she was here with him because of enormous effort on his part. 'I'm talking too much.'

'No,' he said, wishing it were all possible. 'I'm listening.'

'My friend, Sarah, called while you were gone and she reminded me of where we'd first met, that's all. So I'm feeling sentimental.'

'I wish I'd remembered meeting you that time. I'm sorry. My focus was in all the wrong places then. But we've been given a second chance and if there's some grand schemer somewhere pulling the strings, I'm grateful. Although I'm not so sure anyone's minding the store with the world blowing up all to shit.'

His gaze had gone shuttered like it did when the troubles he was dealing with surfaced. She understood and her voice turned playful. 'You're being real polite.' She glanced down like he had, then up, his arousal hard and explicit against her stomach. 'Do you need an invitation?'

A second later, his hips were resting against her thighs, his erection was buried deep inside her and his mouth was warm on hers. 'Better?' he whispered.

A blissful, melting sigh.

Shifting his weight from one forearm to the other, he lifted her hands to his shoulders, said very softly, 'Hold on,' and pushed deeper.

They both caught their breaths.

Then he withdrew marginally, slowly, with a smooth upward drag over her G-spot, and she gasped, trembled, clamped her hands over his stellar butt and hauled him back. 'Freight train,' she said, low and hushed.

'Sure? Last chance.' She wasn't the only one in a covetous mood.

Eyes shut, breathless, she nodded.

Maybe it was love that made it better, or that their caring for each other was out in the open, but sex and sensation seemed to blend into one brilliant, tempestuous, dream-come-true cosmic bliss.

And Rafe answered her need, giving her what she wanted, a wild frenzy of orgasms, one after another, his penetration deep, his withdrawal swift, his hands spread wide over her ass to hold her hard against his next plunging downstroke.

Soon, their bodies were slick with sweat, their hearts pounding, both panting and impatient as they raced full speed ahead to another fast and furious orgasm.

There, there . . . there.

Fuuuck! she screamed and he exploded so effing hard the world abruptly went quiet, like the silence in the eye of a tornado. Then his heart started beating again, he sucked air into his lungs, dropped his head, covered her mouth with his and tasted her sweet, breathless wonder.

'You okay?' he whispered, lifting his head. 'You're on fire.'

'Obsessed,' she panted, her eyes slits.

'Take a little break?'

Her eyes shut for a second, then her gaze swivelled up. 'If you want.'

She didn't mean if you want. He smiled. 'I might cut you off after a while if you start shaking.'

'I might not shake.'

A grin creased his bronzed cheek. 'Someday I'll teach you how to wait.' He laughed at her pretty pout. 'But not today, okay?'

'Thank you,' she said softly. 'I happen to be in love, you know.'

'I think it's contagious,' he murmured, echoing Hafiz's words. 'And fucking arousing,' he added with a smile, smoothly rolling over on his back and taking her with him, steadying her briefly when she sat up, still gorged with his cock. He ran his fingertip over her clit that was jammed against his dick and his voice dropped to a whisper. 'Your pussy is so fucking tight.' He flexed his thighs, forced himself deeper, watched her eyes go shut. 'Last word,' he said, splaying his fingers over her hips, curling them, securing his grip. 'You want me to stop, tell me. You hear?'

He waited or thought he waited.

She nodded or thought she nodded.

They were a matched pair that afternoon – in hot-blooded passion, in wildness and breathtaking need, both caught up in a mindless flood of ravenous desire, selfish and unguarded, their endorphins spinning out of control.

They were stoked.

Happy.

Filled with unimaginable joy.

Rafe didn't think once about the deep-shit trouble coming his way.

Nicole forgot about the small army forming on the island.

They were ungrounded, deep in love, distant from reality.

For however brief a time.

CHAPTER 17

Dinner in the dining room of the palazzo was a raucous affair; everyone knew everyone. Henny in his larger-than-life fashion orchestrated the arrival of the many courses, he and Teresa having come to a workable détente thanks to Rafe's intervention. The young male staff, as casually dressed as the dinner guests in shorts and T-shirts, carried in large trays of seafood of every description, roast lamb with herbs, kebabs, polenta, pasta with white truffles, paprika-stuffed peppers, grilled summer vegetables and flatbreads, a variety of local cheeses, a dozen different desserts including baklava, strudel, caramel flan, with the pièce de résistance a huge platter of snenokle; meringues in custard cream, the Croatian version of floating islands. Magnums of champagne from the Contini family vineyards near Reims along with regional coastal wines accompanied the food, the informality of the servers reminding Nicole of their meal in the kitchen at Monte Carlo.

Although the spacious, vaulted room was far from informal, the classic Palladian design executed in muted shades of marble, the various pastel hues employed to subtly distinguish pillar from pilaster from cornice or floor. Even the ceiling mural was tempered in contrast to the usual semi-erotic mythological scenes favoured by the nobility – the overhead scene portraying fully clothed Athenian maidens moving in a measured procession toward a temple.

The single nod to tempestuous nature was the long wall of glass doors that were open to the night air and the sound of waves crashing against the rocky shore.

Rafe sat at the head of the large, candlelit table, comfortable in his role as host. He was equally at ease with Nicole on his lap, although she'd initially resisted such a public display. 'Hush,' he'd whispered at her quiet protest. 'Or I might embarrass you.'

'More than you already are?'

'Would you like to find out?' he'd murmured, one eyebrow raised.

She'd decided not to push her luck and, in return, had received a smile of such effortless beauty she'd concluded that there were times when losing wasn't really losing.

No one had noticed their brief existential tussle, the buzz of conversation and laughter flowing around them undiminished. With a brushing kiss and a whispered, 'Love you, Tiger,' Rafe turned to answer a question from Teresa who'd come up beside him.

Her heart went into overdrive when it shouldn't, when he might have meant the words in the most casual way. But she couldn't deny how she felt; all warm and glowy. Caught up in the magic.

Rafe dealt with Teresa's question, hitched Nicole closer, whispered, 'Glad you're my girl. You want anything, just ask.' Then he turned his attention to his dinner guests. He was friendly and amicable, conversing easily in any number of languages, directing the servers with a discreet nod or glance if something needed doing, making sure everyone was enjoying themselves. He was particularly friendly to Nicole, kissing her repeatedly, speaking to her softly, feeding her titbits from his plate like a cosseted pet, making her blush from time to time when he whispered in her ear.

She'd given up trying to restrain him. *As if, anyway*, she thought with a smile and opened her mouth for another forkful of sweet, flaky baklava.

'Like that, Pussycat?' His voice was softly cajoling, his eyebrows pulled together slightly.

Her mouth full, she nodded.

His face cleared, as if he were responsible for her nutritional content. 'There's my girl.' Bending his head, he licked a trickle of syrup from her bottom lip and whispered, 'I'll take care of you. Okay?'

Rich with the sweet warmth of him, fighting back tears, she nodded again.

'Hey, hey . . . none of that,' he whispered as she blinked like crazy. 'We got each other.' Dropping the fork, he bent his head, caught the single tear sliding down her cheek with the tip of his tongue, then raised his head and smiled. 'You and me, Tiger. Life's good. Now, gimme a smile.'

Rafe's friends were fascinated by his behaviour. Rafe was only vaguely attentive to a woman unless he was actually fucking her. Not tonight. He was affectionate, gentle; his attention fully engaged. All they could figure was that he was operating on the principle: *live life to the fullest before you die*. A classic impulse prior to battle.

Simon leaned toward Carlos and lifted his chin in Rafe's direction. 'Christ, how bad is it? Should I say goodbye to my mum?'

'Too soon to tell,' Carlos said. 'Zou's holed up, not moving. As for him—' Carlos gave an eye roll toward Rafe. 'He's just randy as hell.'

'No shit. I hope he doesn't spread her out on the table and go for it.'

Carlos shrugged. 'Wouldn't be the first time. If you're worried about Angelina, you can always hustle her out before the view gets too explicit.'

'I might. She teaches music to little kids, for Christ's sake. If Rafe gets out of hand—' Simon jerked his thumb toward the terrace doors. 'We're outta here.'

Both men were speaking in undertones while Simon's girlfriend was talking to the dinner guest on her right.

'You can't begrudge him his happiness,' Carlos murmured. 'I use the word advisedly. He may not know what the fuck that is, but he's enjoying himself.'

Simon glanced at Rafe, then chuckled. 'Ya think?'

The men had no more than finished their conversation when Rafe picked up a spoon and tapped his crystal goblet until silence finally settled over the table. 'I have an announcement.' He smiled at Nicole. 'We have an announcement. What?'

She was shaking her head vehemently.

Holding up a finger to his guests, he turned to Nicole and dipped his head until their eyes were level. 'It's not a damned secret. Come on, I've never been in love before.'

'Don't – please, you're drunk. You'll be sorry you said it tomorrow.'

'I don't get drunk. I'm feeling good, that's all – about us.' He patted her cheek, kissed her lightly. 'Relax. It's all good, Pussycat. They're friends. They'll be happy for us.' Lifting his head, he turned back to his guests with a grin. 'Nicole worries. Nothing to worry about, I told her.' He paused for a second, took in the breath-held silence and his grin widened. 'Apparently, I don't make announcements very often.'

'Try never, dude!' Henny bellowed.

Rafe laughed. 'In that case, I should have ordered up a fanfare of trumpets for this rare occasion. Since I didn't, I'll just lay it out nice and clear. We're in love,' he said, proudly. 'It's an amazing feeling. Right, Tiger?' Turning to a red-faced Nicole, he gave her a warm grin.

For a stunned moment, the room was still as a tomb.

Then Henny yelled, 'Way to go, Contini!'

And cheers erupted.

Nicole's blush deepened although her eyes were glowing. Rafe was cool and under control as usual, but he was holding her close as though guarding his happiness.

Then his jaw clamped shut; he saw the man running in from the loggia.

And just like that, his happiness vanished.

A moment later, the man spoke quietly near Rafe's ear, the news so shitty, it qualified for worst-case scenario in any terms, tactical or strategic. After asking two hushed questions, each answered with a no, Rafe spoke loud enough to be heard. 'Thanks, Jorge. We'll be down in a few minutes.'

His arms tightened around Nicole for a fraction of a second, then he whispered, 'Gotta go. I might be late tonight.' Looking up, he scanned the table. 'Trouble in paradise, guys. See you all in the operations room in five.'

He escorted Nicole as far as the main staircase. 'I apologize for the interruption,' he said with a faint grimace. 'Shit happens.'

'I understand. I'll see you when I see you,' she answered, smoothly. Fake as fuck. 'Good luck.'

'Yeah,' he grunted, leaned down, kissed her once, hard, then straightened and walked away.

A few minutes later, the dinner guests, minus Nicole and Simon's girlfriend, were assembled before a bank of monitors with the images frozen on the screens.

Rafe nodded at Zander. 'Start from the beginning.'

'Zou's sister and another woman entered the building early morning their time. About two hours ago. They were wearing the traditional trouser suits. Not unusual. Here.' Zander pointed and clicked to restart the action. 'The driver is waiting outside the main entrance, the car's running.' He fast forwarded the sequence until the two women re-emerged from the building. He stopped the camera again.

'Two observations in hindsight. The electricity went off for ten seconds. Entire building. A brief outage, everyone figured just a glitch. But it wasn't. The cameras were dark for a few seconds. And – two.' He aimed a laser pointer at one of the women's shoes, returned to the original shot and indicated the shoes again. 'Notice. Same colour, same style, bigger size. We missed that too.'

'Anyone would,' Rafe said. 'The presentation is meticulous. The make-up and costume are professional. Pure theatre. Where did we lose him?'

Another man answered. His team had had Zou's sister under surveillance for weeks; they'd tailed her from the Cyber Intelligence Unit. 'Although we didn't know it at the time, it was Zou with his sister. They were driven into the private underground garage at her high-rise. We'd had key cards made, but it has several levels and before we entered we lost her phone signal. Zou must have dumped his cell at his office. We never did pick that up.'

'No surprise. He had to have had this plan in place – fuck – probably for years. Politics is a dangerous business there. He had every angle covered. Not your fault, Andy. Now, Jorge said four cars came out of the parking ramp minutes after Zou entered, right?'

'Yeah. Identical. Even the plates. We had enough manpower for three of them, but not the fourth. My guess is that they were all decoys anyway. At least the three we stopped were. The drivers were useless. Hired for the day. Nada.'

Rafe exhaled softly. 'Any ideas on Zou's destination? Other than Brisbane?'

'When our crews backtracked, they interviewed a doorman in a high-rise down the block who saw a helicopter take off from the roof of his building ten, fifteen minutes after we lost Zou. There had to have been some underground tunnels he accessed 'cause Zou never exited the building. We had eyes on every exit. We're in the process of pulling building blueprints now. Not that it matters at this point, but—' Andy grimaced. 'Sorry about that.'

'If the tunnels were private, they might not appear on the prints. I'm guessing they won't. We'll just move on. Are we monitoring radar? Flight plans?'

'We're on it,' Carlos said.

Rafe surveyed the assembled group. 'Check in with your contacts. Explain what happened. What we're looking for. Zou couldn't have gotten very far yet. A helicopter's too slow for any long-range flight and I expect he's getting out of the country. So scour the docks, see if a private yacht sailed recently; he wouldn't attempt the major airports – although maybe the small ones should be considered. It's not out of the question to drive to any of the South East Asian countries. That means the search area is going to continue to expand. Meanwhile, we haven't a clue what Zou's using for a disguise or passport.' Rafe smiled tightly. 'That's it. Thanks, everyone. I'm going to call Webster and give him the bad news.'

Walking with Carlos to his desk, Rafe pointed at a leather club chair. 'Do you mind? I'm beginning to fade.'

'Be my guest. You haven't slept much.'

'No one has. Have you heard from Webster lately? He was going to check out some galleries with Gina.'

Carlos shook his head, sat at his desk and leaned back in his chair. 'Come to think of it, Lola received a text. Something about buying a painting.'

Neither man mentioned the fuck-up. Regret was useless; both had learned that the hard way.

'What time is it in Brisbane?' Rafe glanced at his watch. 'Webster should be up.' He punched in a number on his cell and didn't have long to wait. 'Sounds like you're out on the street.' Rafe's eyebrows went up. 'Nice of you to fetch and carry. Anyway, I'm calling with shit news. Zou's broken out. Anything useful there?'

'Maybe. Our gallery search turned up a small show of Bao Yu's paintings. She's using a different name but I recognized her work from the photos in her dossier. We bought a painting and she's going to redo a small section to match my office colours.'

'Your office colours?'

'Yeah, I have an office building I'm redecorating, which makes me a potential big spender. The gallery owner was impressed. He convinced Bao Yu to compromise her principles and do a little touch-up on the painting for me. Sounds like she's been showing in his gallery for about six months. Also, sounds like she needs the money.'

Rafe whistled softly. 'You don't say.'

'I do. Now to find out why. Gina and I – we're married by the way – chatted up the gallery owner while he was running one of your no-name company credit cards and getting excited about selling more paintings. Apparently Bao Yu came to Brisbane this time with her daughter and her boyfriend. Yeah, you heard that right. That's what the guy said.'

'So she might not be waiting for Zou.'

'Might not.'

'Does Zou know that? Do his enemies?'

'Good questions. We might have some answers soon. By the way, Gina's a brilliant actress. I wouldn't have gotten the information without her. Gina showed the gallery owner photos of our daughter, told him how much we missed her. Little Selena's at boarding school, by the way. My mother insists and it breaks Gina's heart. She gave a desolate little sigh and said that Bao Yu was really fortunate to have her daughter with her.'

Rafe snorted. 'Gina and children? There's a picture.'

'Don't tell the gallery owner. The man's eyes teared up.'

'Fuck me. Perfect. Where are you meeting Bao Yu?'

'At the gallery.'

'If she comes with her daughter, mission accomplished,' Rafe murmured.

'If she doesn't, or if her boyfriend's along, we'll have to follow them home.'

'Any thoughts on whether Zou arrives in Brisbane?'

'Too soon to tell,' Webster replied. 'The surprise boyfriend changes the dynamic.'

'Along with the possibility that Bao Yu needs money.'

'Zou could be heading somewhere else,' Webster noted.

'And it's a big fucking world,' Rafe grumbled.

'His money's disappearing, I hear. That should help.'

'Maybe. There's still the black banking sites. If he doesn't show up in Brisbane, I'm already thinking Dubai.'

'I have personal contacts there. If you need names, let me know,' Webster offered.

'Thanks. I'll run it by Carlos, maybe Gora too. His Russian might be able to fill us in on the banking rules in those countries that don't have any. You and Gina working together okay?'

'Are you asking me something?' Webster's voice was softly sardonic.

'Just trying to be polite. Forget it.'

'I already have. I should have some news for you later today.'

CHAPTER 18

Shortly after Rafe finished his call to Webster, a helicopter landed in a field two hundred sixty kilometres south-west of Shanghai. Two top-end, off-road Range Rovers were waiting; four men in one, three in the other, the SUV's rear compartments loaded with backpacking gear.

Stepping down from the chopper, Zou ducked his head and sprinted to the lead car. The helicopter was already airborne when Zou climbed into the front passenger seat and, minutes later, the Range Rovers were speeding down a four-lane highway in a south/south-west direction.

If all went according to plan, Zou would reach Bangkok in forty-five hours. Perhaps sooner if he flew out of Luang Prabang, the old colonial capital in northern Thailand. It would depend on the security at the airport, although it should be lax. The UNESCO world site was known for its natural beauties; the travellers who converged on the airport were armed with cameras not weapons.

Zou was on his new encrypted cell phone in a matter of minutes, his voice crisp and sharp as he spoke. He was pissed for a number of reasons aside from the current conversation furrowing his brow. A number of his bank accounts had been closed, Bao Yu wasn't answering her phone and Colonel Chen, a rival since his youth, had just been patched through by his adjunct and was now informing him that his leave had been cancelled.

'You don't know what you're talking about,' Zou snapped. He couldn't say Chen was a liar although he was.

'General Hu cancelled all leave.'

'Fuck you!' Zou exploded. 'Who the hell do you think you're talking to? If General Hu cancelled all leave, my adjunct would have informed me. Now leave me the fuck alone. I'll be back in ten days.' And he cut off his caller mid-word. 'Keep to the speed limits,' he ordered the driver. 'We don't want to draw any attention.'

The driver nodded, not talking his eyes off the road.

The all-terrain vehicles had been chosen in case they had to leave the main highways and travel rough. Zou had also taken the precaution of having a logo of a fictitious backpacking company painted on the car doors to facilitate border crossings. If they drove the entire 1,795 kilometres to Bangkok, they'd cross into Laos first, then Thailand. Eight men on a trekking holiday would be relatively innocuous. Particularly in northern Laos and

Thailand where backpackers from around the world came to holiday.

'I'm going to sleep now, Jin. Don't wake me,' Zou said.

The driver shot him a look.

'If you can't handle it, wake me,' Zou added, smiling faintly, sliding his seat back down, stretching out his legs and hiking-booted feet.

'I thought you wanted this trip to stay under the radar.'

'I do. So don't kill anyone while I'm sleeping,' Zou said, drolly. Then he shut his eyes and, within seconds, fell into a restful sleep for the first time in days.

The men in his party had been hand-picked, personally recruited years ago and were consummate professionals. Particularly his young driver whom he'd saved from a precarious life on the streets when Jin was just a boy. They all could operate with minimum orders and, most important in the fluid world of political cunning, their loyalty was beyond reproach. None had family; a necessary component to the specific activities assigned them. And, not to be discounted, Zou paid them extremely well.

Soon after Zou fell asleep, Gina and Webster entered the art gallery in Brisbane. Since they were ostensibly on holiday, they were dressed casually but expensively in slacks and jackets, Gina's large red purse slung over her shoulder: Hermès.

'We're a little early.' Webster took off his sunglasses,

sliding them into his jacket pocket and smiled at the gallery owner, a thin, youngish man in a fashionable skin-tight suit with short pant legs that displayed his colourful socks. 'But my wife is hoping to see the artist's young daughter, so she's a little anxious.' He turned his smile on Gina. 'Aren't you, darling.'

'Don't tease me.' Gina pouted prettily. 'I miss our little Selena. Seeing another young girl would be lovely, that's all.'

'Would you like me to call and see if Bao Yu is bringing her daughter?' The gallery owner was interested in pleasing the couple who might purchase several more works for their office building.

'No, no, don't bother her,' Gina murmured. 'But if I might have a cup of coffee while we wait, that would be super.'

Gina spoke with a posh, upper-class British accent that Webster found admirable for a woman raised in France. The distinctive, soft diffidence, the partially swallowed words; it was perfection. He nodded as the owner glanced at him. 'Thank you, coffee for me too. Come, dear.' He took Gina's hand. 'You were admiring that Hong Kong harbour painting the other day. Let's have another look at it while we wait.' And he drew her away toward a large work on display across the room.

'This is too easy.' Gina spoke in her normal voice as they walked away. 'I'm getting jumpy.'

Webster grimaced. 'Makes you wonder all right. Locked and loaded, babe?'

'You better believe it.' She sucked in a breath. 'Think the lady's gonna show?'

'The gallery owner's hoping like hell she does. Me too. Easy or not, I'd like to get this done.' He flicked his finger at the masterful harbour view as they approached it. 'By the way, if you want any of these paintings, I'm sure Rafe wouldn't mind.' Webster knew the two were friends.

She tipped her head, left and right, squinted at the realistic depiction. 'I might. Bao Yu's damned good. This is magnificent.'

'I like the mountain landscape.' He pointed to his right.

'Get it for your wife.'

'I'm not sure she'd like it.'

Gina glanced at Webster from under her lashes. Was that tell-tale puzzlement in his tone or nothing more than a bland statement. If he wasn't so good-looking, she wouldn't have given it a second thought. Nor should she now; he'd said he was happily married. 'If you don't want it, I might buy them both. Not with Rafe's money, my own. I get paid well.'

'We all do in this line of work.'

Maybe he wasn't just a computer genius after all. 'Hacking, you mean.' For some undefinable reason she wanted clarification.

'Yes, that,' he said.

She'd been reading nuance too long. Visual, verbal, physical tells kept her alive. And for a fleeting moment she felt like shaking the truth out of him. Not likely with his size, but there was something nakedly false in his simple reply. She wondered if Rafe would tell her if she asked.

An hour later, Bao Yu hadn't yet arrived. The gallery owner had tried calling the number she'd left many times without success. Gina and Webster had exchanged cryptic glances over several cups of coffee, conversed in a desultory fashion with the increasingly agitated gallery owner and were silently calculating their next move when the front door opened.

The eyes of all three waiting people turned to the entrance.

Bao Yu, her daughter in tow, dashed through the doorway, apologizing breathlessly in English touched with a faint Aussie twang. 'Our rental car ... broke down and for ... some reason,' she panted, moving swiftly toward the trio who'd all come to their feet, 'my mobile phone ... didn't have a signal.' Stopping a few feet from them, she drew in a breath, glanced down at her daughter who was hiding behind her skirts, gave the little girl's head a pat and looked up again. 'I'm so sorry. Thank you for waiting.'

'Not a problem. We've been enjoying your other paintings on display.' Webster's voice was well mannered, his smile polite. Although he was just beginning to question her lack of painting supplies when her yet-to-be-confirmed boyfriend strode in carrying a large wooden box.

'My husband had to pay the taxi,' Bao Yu explained, smiling fondly at the handsome young man who had more than a hint of Manchurian size in his large frame. 'He's going to watch our daughter while I work on your painting.'

'How nice,' Gina said, glancing up at Webster, the words *my husband*, *our daughter* ringing in her ears. 'Isn't that nice, darling. I'll get a chance to enjoy the company of a little girl again. Our daughter's in boarding school,' she explained.

'Speaking of our daughter,' Webster interjected, 'I promised Mother I'd get back to her with our plans for Selena's birthday and I forgot. If you'll excuse me for a minute.' He pulled his cell phone from his pocket. 'I'll be right back. You know what colour I need to match my office wall, darling. Help Bao Yu get started.'

Webster was standing outside the door a moment later, his phone to his ear, waiting for Rafe to pick up.

'Did she show or didn't she?' Rafe asked.

'She did. With a man she called her husband and *their* child.'

'Is the man for real or from central casting?'

'Good question. He could be one of Zou's bodyguards but, if he is, he must be loveable. She looks at him all starry-eyed.'

'You're kidding. Love?'

'I'd bet the bank on it. And he's a big dude, so a public snatch and run is definitely out. We'll follow them home.'

'Can you and Gina handle it or would you like help? The pilots are standing by. Or we can contract some local help.'

'Please, no strangers. We're fine. Gina's worth at least a couple of guys.'

'And you've been known to take on more than your share. I still owe you for those Triad dudes who jumped us that night in Macau. But be sensible. If you need help, ask. This is about winning, not hero-shit.'

Webster laughed. 'I gave up heroing the first time I came to a gunfight without a gun. Don't worry, I'm a pragmatic guy. Bao Yu weighs maybe ninety pounds, the little girl doesn't signify as a problem. It's just the dude who's the unknown. But Gina and I know what we're doing. We might have to wait until dark though, depending on conditions.'

'A few hours one way or another doesn't matter. You found them. That's all that counts. The plane's waiting on the tarmac whenever you're ready. And thanks. Taking Bao Yu off the board will be useful, although whether it affects Zou's plans is debatable now.'

'No shit. I'm getting a strange vibe. I can't imagine Zou allowing this.'

'Let's hope the mistress is just smarter than we think.'

'Rather than this is a wild goose chase.'

'Relax. It's too early to angst. Worst case, we at least

check off a name. A few less players on the field. That's a plus, any way you look at it.'

'True. Hear anything from Zou?'

'Radio silence. But he'll show up sooner or later. Call me when you know something. Zander is waving at me. Gotta go.'

Zander was beaming when Rafe walked into his small cell. 'It must be good,' Rafe said.

'Couldn't be better. We're hacking the highway speed cameras in all directions out of Shanghai and what do you think we saw?'

Rafe laughed. 'I'm gonna fucking kiss you.'

Zander held up his hand and grinned. 'Back off, dude. You're not my type.' He waved toward the wall of monitor screens. 'Come look though. It's a beautiful sight. Considering the odds.' At Rafe's sharp glance, Zander added, 'Speed cameras aren't plentiful in China.'

There it was. Clear as day. Two Range Rovers coming up out of a ditch onto the highway at the same time as a helicopter lifted into the air from the open field behind them.

'Jesus, tell me this isn't staged,' Rafe murmured, leaning in to scrutinize the markings on the vehicle doors.

'Nope, it's real as fuck. We checked the licence numbers on the chopper, talked to the people at the high-rise helipad downtown. Same. We might be able to zero in through the car windows with a little more work. Could take a while though.'

'Do it, just to be sure.' Rafe straightened. 'They're heading south?'

'South/south-west. Bangkok, I'm guessing.'

'Once they cross the Chinese border, let me know. I want to make sure we're there to greet Zou properly. How much time would we have once they enter Laos?'

'A day, maybe more if he stops,' Zander answered.

'He could take a flight out of Jing Hong or Luang Prabang. That would cut down our time.'

'Both are chancy. Especially Jing Hong. Zou has enemies up the whazoo.'

'Agreed. Then they might take to the back roads if they're worried about pursuit. Are we good there?'

'Yup. We're tracking on satellite now that we found him,' Zander noted. 'He's not going anywhere we can't follow.' Rafe had a partnership share in two satellites; one of many profitable business ventures in his portfolio.

'Anyone who's going to Bangkok or parts East with us better make any calls they have to make. I'll talk to Carlos, see what contacts we have on the ground in that part of the world and check in with Dao. She has informers everywhere. It's great news though.' Rafe gave Zander a thumbs up. 'Made my fucking day. Zou's back in our crosshairs.'

Carlos was on his phone when Rafe walked over. Taking a seat, he waited while Carlos finished arranging for two of his Basque friends to come in from the war zone in Libya. 'You look happy,' Carlos said, ending the call.

'Zander found Zou. He's on an expressway driving south.'

'Fucking A,' Carlos breathed. 'That was fast.'

'You'll have to go look later. Andy was right; he flew out on a chopper. We have to plan for a flight to Bangkok, Zou's most likely destination. Fingers crossed . . .' A quick gesture. ''Cause if it's Bangkok we'll have it made. Crowded as hell, lots of dark corners, bent law enforcement, a river for easy disposal. Fuck, it almost makes you believe in a god.'

'With the reach of his enemies, his bolt-holes are limited. And keep in mind, he could be gathering his troops there.'

Rafe shrugged. 'I still like the advantageous terrain. We've got him on satellite, so we can fine-tune our plans if and when he approaches the city. Another thing, someone has to look into Dubai banking. It's an extra-legal maze, I know, but Zou's gonna need money.'

'Will do. What the status on the girl and baby?'

'And her *boyfriend*. Yeah, how about that?'

Carlos blew out a breath. 'You think you're beyond surprise and—'

'Out of the blue,' Rafe said with a smile.

A nod, then a raised eyebrow. 'Complications?'

'Minor, Webster tells me. He and Gina are going to wait until dark, then visit them at their house.' Rafe slid down on his spine and studied his bare feet for a moment before he looked up. 'I tell myself that a lot of people have been working hard to succeed at this mission, so the fact that everything's falling into place shouldn't make the hairs rise on the back of my neck. But—'

'Zou's no dummy.'

'Yeah, times infinity.' Rafe slid upright. 'That means we have to scrutinize everything six different ways. No one takes chances. Especially Ganz. He wants the kill shot. So if and when we get to Bangkok, he has to be on a leash.'

'She's gotta go home now.'

Rafe gave him a flinty-eyed look.

'*Nicole* has to go home now,' Carlos corrected, his tone more polite.

'Thank you.' Rafe exhaled softly. 'And yes, I know.'

'Want me to set it up?'

Rafe shook his head. 'Let me talk to her first.' Then he smiled faintly. 'Just in case Zou decides to stop for a couple of days on his way south.'

Carlos scowled. 'You're going right up to the wire, aren't you?'

Rafe came to his feet and grinned. 'Let's just say I'm gonna try like hell.'

'Goddamn, some things never change,' Carlos muttered.

'Don't worry, when all systems are go I'll be right beside you.' Rafe's grin flashed. 'Keeping up with you ain't a problem.'

'Get the fuck out of here. You got that much energy, you might as well put it to better use.'

'That's what I was thinking. Get some sleep while Zou's on the road. It's gonna be a while.' Rafe patted his shorts pocket. 'My phone's on. I'm waiting for Webster's call.'

CHAPTER 19

Gina and Webster's plan to wait until dark to abduct Bao Yu and her child had to be adjusted on the fly, because after the repainting was finished, the small family had no more than driven away in a taxi than a grey panel van pulled out into traffic behind them.

'Another interested party,' Gina murmured as she and Webster walked to their rental.

'Worse. A don't-give-a-shit high-profile party.' Webster lengthened his stride. 'Need your door opened?'

'Not since my finishing school days,' she drawled.

He shot her a grin and sprinted for the car.

A few seconds later, Webster hit the ignition, murmured, 'Hang on,' stomped on the gas and punched his way into traffic. The driver in the car he missed by a hair's-breadth leant on his horn. Webster tossed him the finger, accelerated around three vehicles despite the narrow street and oncoming traffic, slowed only marginally before shooting

202

through a red light, then speeded up again. 'Bingo,' he said a moment later catching sight of their target two blocks ahead. Decelerating, he wove through traffic more slowly now until only three cars separated them from the van. 'Would you rather drive next time?' he asked, giving Gina a sideways glance. He'd seen her push an imaginary brake a few times.

She shook her head. 'Reflex, that's all.'

'You like to be in control?'

An undercurrent of more than simple query resonated in his voice. Or maybe it was just her libido's wishful thinking. But whether she was reading his remark correctly or not was irrelevant. Her dark gaze was cool, her voice cooler when she said, 'Yes, I do.' Looking away, she pulled her Beretta from her purse and slipped the handgun into her shoulder holster.

Webster almost smiled. She was shutting him down. He'd have to be more careful; try not to tease. Got it. 'I saw two men in the van,' he said, his tone strictly business. 'Same for you?'

'Yeah. Unless there's more in the back.' Lifting four more clips from her purse, she slipped two in each jacket pocket, shot him a glance and murmured, 'Life's a mystery.'

He shrugged. 'More of a mystery in some occupations than others.'

An eyebrow tilt. 'You're not just a hacker, are you? Don't answer if you'd rather not.'

'I've never worked with a woman before,' he said.

There was her answer. 'Why are you still in the game when you have a wife and child? You don't have to answer that either.'

He exhaled softly, debated whether he wanted this conversation or not.

'Sorry, I shouldn't have asked.'

'Actually,' he finally said, 'I'm doing this as a favour to Rafe. Sorta,' he added, still equivocating on how much to disclose; this entire profession worked on a need to know basis.

His reluctance was so pronounced, she held up her hand. 'None of my business, really.'

He gave her a tight smile. 'Make up your mind.'

'As long as you don't fuck up this operation, I'm good. The rest doesn't matter.'

He scowled. 'You can be real irritating.'

'That's because I asked you some personal questions and men don't like personal questions. Or maybe just the men I know.'

'You don't know me.'

'Keep being a prick and I won't want to know you.'

Her little sniff at the end was such a girly chick sniff, it seriously screwed with her lethal killer persona. He grinned. 'Jesus, did I just meet you in a bar and you turned me down?'

'Goddamn right,' she muttered.

'So you're not gonna give me a tumble?'

'Fuck no.' *Wait, wait, what?*

He gave her a killer smile that could have melted metal. 'Okay, here's my life story, babe. 'Cause if we're gonna stay alive, I don't want you pissed at me.'

She sucked up her sudden stab of horniness, told herself he was right and she was wrong and said, 'I'm not pissed.' At his lifted brow, she added with a smile, 'Any more.'

'Good.' Another of those heart-melting smiles. 'Here's what I got. The guys are all my friends. I met Ganz first, online, in a dark market chat room. Years ago. We were kids. So I'm doing this as a favour.' He shot her a look. 'I'm guessing you're doing Rafe a favour too.'

'Me and a lot of other people. He's a good guy; a loner like so many of us; no strong family ties, no place to really call home, a few demons in his past. But willing to go to the mat for you if you ask. And look, I apologize for being curt. I'm just trying to keep my hands off you. Not your fault in any way,' she added with a nod.

He smiled. 'No problem. I shouldn't tease you either. But you make it tempting; you're not all hard-ass shooter with a reputation for—'

She shot him a squinty-eyed look.

'Relax. I meant a reputation in this business of ours.' He grinned. 'You're a legend, babe. With a star dossier.'

'Why haven't I heard of you?'

'Because I like it that way.'

'You're not really Aussie, are you?'

'Let's just say I lived in Australia longer than I lived any-where else. My father was career Marine Corps. We lived everywhere on the globe. I was born in San Diego, but that was about it for roots. Undergrad years at Berkeley; finished my degree in three to get the hell out. Then grad-uate school and a couple years teaching at UQ. After that, rugby. Always hacking jobs on the side. That's about it.'

'And the covert shit?'

'Pretty much all along. With my family background, weapons were a way of life. Combine that with let's say, the fringe world of hacking, and you meet all kinds of people who need things done.'

'Any limits on what you do?'

'Lots. I just do white hat. You sleep better at night. Although sometimes it's hard to know who the good guys are, right?'

'You asking me?'

'No, just stating a fact. You better than most can testify to double-dealing and betrayal. By the way, I'm completely trustworthy. We're in this together.'

There was something deeply honourable in the way he spoke. A benevolence rarely seen in her occupation. She almost choked up. Not good. At all. 'Thanks,' she said, knowing better than to elaborate with the lump in her throat.

He smiled. 'Don't mention it.' He lifted his chin at the thinning traffic ahead, politely changed the subject. 'I think I know where they're headed.' Lifting a finger off the steering wheel, he pointed. 'Nice neighbourhood not too far from here.'

There was something in his voice. She looked at him. 'How nice?'

'Billionaire nice. Big houses, walled properties, gated. It's gotta be Zou's place. Unless her boyfriend's rich.'

'I doubt it. Although he's sure as hell bigger than Zou and whole lot prettier.' Comfortably back to business again, she smiled. 'A plus for her, I'd guess.'

He was tempted to say, *you like 'em big?* but knew better than to flirt now that they'd cleared the air. 'She's into him, that's a fact,' he said instead. 'Can't tell if it's reciprocated. The guy was careful. Not with the kid though, in fact—'

'Oh my fucking ass,' Gina interrupted. 'Look, look – where they're turning in. It's an humungous castle.'

'Set well back from the road, long open driveway so you can see trouble approaching and pull up the drawbridge. But first—' Webster jabbed his finger at the van as it drove past the property. 'We follow the tail and make them go away.'

'We're so far out there's no other traffic. We don't have to worry about witnesses.' Manicured estates lined the road, the architectural variety testament to the owners' whimsies, some mansions hidden behind high walls, others, like the castle, on show.

'Now to see what they're gonna do. I'm still surprised they showed their faces in broad daylight.'

'Overconfident.'

'I'm hoping stupid.' He smiled. 'They haven't been here before. Look, they're slowing down, looking for some-where to turn around. If it's okay with you, I'm all for simplicity. Provided they're not hiding a crew in back, a couple of shots and it's over.'

Gina pulled out a second handgun from her purse. A Glock 19. 'Just in case the numbers change,' she said, checking the load with a one-handed slide. 'For starters though, which one do you want? Driver or passenger?' Glancing behind them, she slid her Beretta from her shoulder holster.

'Driver.' Webster scanned the road ahead, glanced in the rear-view mirror, then reached down and pulled a custom assault rifle from under his seat.

Gina's eyes widened. 'When the hell did you put that there?'

'You were in the shower.'

'It's a beauty,' she said in breathy awe.

Webster smiled. 'A friend of mine makes these.'

'You'll have to introduce me to your friend. I could use one of those. It's purse size.'

'Will do. Heads up, babe. They're coming back.' Slipping

off the safety on the rifle, Webster hit the switch to open the car windows, slowed his speed, gripped the steering wheel with his knees and said, quietly, 'On three.'

They both surveyed their surroundings one last time – a quick, automatic glance – and, assured of their isolation, unlatched their doors and focused on their targets. Webster waited until the oncoming car was forty feet away, then gently squeezed the brakes to slow the car, but not in an obvious way. Neither spoke; this was a business they knew.

'One,' Webster said, as the van neared. 'Two.' Thirty feet. He brought the car to a stop, shifted into park. Twenty feet. 'Three.'

Kicking open the car doors, they jumped out, sighted in with a cool second's worth of professionalism and, firing full automatic, pissed bullets into the van.

Blood and brain matter sprayed the shattered windshield in a pink mist before the glass disappeared completely. Webster raked the ragged opening twice more, emptying his mag in a stream of lead, then snapped, 'Get in.'

The van was still slowly rolling forward.

As they slid back into the car, Webster slammed it into drive, jerked the wheel and steered into the path of the van, hoping like hell nothing major would be damaged. Calling a tow truck wasn't an option. The hit was only a jolt, not a crash. He let out a breath.

Gina had reloaded their weapons. Stepping out of the

car a moment later, guns drawn, they moved toward the silent van in a low, defensive posture. As they approached, Webster straightened and gave Gina a grin. 'Really, babe, right between the eyes? Showing off?' One side of the passenger's head was raw meat from Webster's rifle burst, but the entry point between his eyes was clearly visible.

'Play it safe. That's my motto. Speaking of safe,' she said, 'we have to stash this van.'

'I know a place. I'll drive the van, you follow.' Gina was already walking back to their rental when Webster opened the driver's door. Pulling latex gloves and a packet of baby wipes from his jacket pocket like someone who'd done this before, he set the wipes on the floor, slipped the gloves on and heaved the driver's bloody body over the seat. After quickly wiping off the steering wheel and seat, he tossed gloves and wipes in back, took off his jacket, folded it, slid the side panel door open and hung his jacket from a metal bracket. Then he shut the door, stepped up into the driver's seat and calmly turned the van around.

Ten minutes later, they watched the van with two dead bodies slide down the bank of the Brisbane River and slowly sink. 'We can't wait till nightfall to take Bao Yu,' Webster said. 'When these two don't return, the B team might show up.'

'Or considering Zou's enemies list, teams plural. Let's go in the castle from the back. I take one side, you the other. I'm good with door locks.'

'I was thinking we'd just drive up to the front door and knock. They know us as buyers. Come on,' Webster said to her dubious look, 'I've got a good feeling about this.'

'I don't believe in good feelings when I'm working. My mantra's logic and weapons.'

'Trust me,' Webster said with a smile. 'We bought four of Bao's paintings. They love us.'

'Trust me? You're fucking kidding.'

'Okay, then, put on Kevlar. It's in the car.'

'If I could cover my whole body, maybe.'

'Forget it. I'll just go in. You can wait somewhere.' He grinned. 'Safe.'

'As if I'm going to risk my life 'cause you're jerking my chain.'

'Sorry. I'll be serious. You don't have to do this. I mean it. But consider all the ways Bao's so-called husband was protective of her and the girl. He didn't explicitly show his feelings, but he cared for them both with a gentleness you don't normally see in a bodyguard who's just doing his job.'

'Hmmpf,' she muttered, biting her bottom lip.

'You know I'm right. And I'm not saying it because I'm some macho prick who has to be right. If you don't want to do this though, I'll drop you off at one of the coffee shops down the road and you can wait for me.'

She didn't speak again on the way to the car nor as they drove back the way they'd come. But as they neared Zou's castle, she turned and said, 'Okay, but I'm putting on a vest.'

Bringing the car to a stop at the side of the road, he reached in back and pulled out the smaller of the two Kevlar vests from the seat.

'You should too,' she said, taking off her jacket.

He shook his head. 'Told you I had this feeling.' But he pulled his handgun from his shoulder holster, checked it was loaded, slid it back.

She lifted an eyebrow in his direction.

He smiled. 'Good feelings aside, a loaded weapon is reassuring.'

A few minutes later, Webster drove slowly up the long drive so they didn't surprise anyone and came to a stop at the front door. Gina's heart was hammering in her chest; full frontal wasn't her style. 'You know they're watching us.'

'Then smile, babe. Look friendly.'

She blew out a breath. 'This is the stupidest thing I've ever done. And don't you dare say *trust me* again or I might shoot *you*.'

He held up his hands. 'Relax, this is a done deal.' Then, without waiting for an answer, he dropped his hands, opened his car door and stepped out onto the raked gravel drive. Whether she followed him or not, he was knocking on the door. He didn't get these feelings often – try never. He was going for it.

By the time he reached the door and rapped the lion

head knocker on its brass plate, Gina was at his side. He turned and smiled. 'Hiya.'

She grimaced. 'So I like crazy people.'

He was chuckling when the door opened.

'We've been waiting for you,' the bodyguard said in a perfect English he'd not used before. 'Please come in.'

Webster took note of the man's linguistic versatility but, intent on his mission, smiled anyway. 'Don't tell me we look that benign?'

'In contrast to the others?' The man's brows lifted. 'Yes.' He shut the door.

'We don't have much time,' Webster said, a new briskness to his voice. 'As soon as you're ready, we should leave. You saw the van following you.'

The man nodded. 'Bao Yu and our child are in the safe room upstairs. We were hoping to leave this evening. I've wired the house with explosives, primarily at the entrances. I was on watch till then.'

'Do you have to pack?'

'No.'

'Then we'll wait while you fetch your wife and child from the safe room,' Webster said, politely. 'We can talk on the plane.' Time enough then to discover the truth about any marital status.

While they waited in the entrance hall, Webster texted Rafe. *Found your birthday present. Wait till we get there for the party. Call you soon.*

A few minutes later, Bao Yu and her daughter were escorted out to the car by three highly trained professionals, weapons drawn.

Seated in the back with her daughter on her lap, her hand in her husband's, Bao exhaled softly as they drove away from the house. 'Thank you so much. We weren't sure you'd come for us.' She glanced up at her husband and smiled. 'Li was more confident.'

'I'm able to monitor a portion of Zou's communication,' said Li. 'Enough to know of his campaign against Ganz. So we offered to leave Hong Kong for reasons of our own and Zou agreed for his.'

'Do you know what his reasons are for letting you leave?' Webster asked, looking up and down the road before pulling out of the driveway.

'One of them is what brought you and the others to Brisbane.' Li indicated his wife and child with a nod. 'Zou's adding extra work for his enemies. Whether Bao Yu's just a decoy or not is uncertain. Zou's dealing with a tangled web of political opponents. What do you want, precious?' He leaned in to hear the little girl's whisper. 'Look, I have your kitty in my pocket.' He handed the little girl a small silky toy, then looked up. 'Could we discuss this later?'

'No problem,' Gina said, half turned in her seat, her gaze on the cell phone the man was taking out of his pocket. 'Do you mind?' She held out her hand.

'Don't touch the Blue Sky app. Not yet.'

'If I do?'

'We're not far enough away.' He raised his brows. 'Flying debris.'

'Ah.' She handed the phone back. 'I expect you'd like the honour.'

'Yes, thank you.'

'That your specialty?' Webster asked.

'No, just part of my current job. I was an English teacher a very long time ago.'

'You don't fucking say,' Webster murmured. 'Small world. I taught Chinese at UQ.' He shot a glance out the back window. 'We're far enough away now. No point in missing out on the fireworks.'

Before he finished speaking, a huge ball of fire rose in a massive cloud from what had once been Zou's castle, the sound of the powerful blast arriving a second later. When a detonation is faster than the speed of sound, heavy explosives are involved.

Webster shot a grin over his shoulder. 'That took a while to set up. I hope Zou was insured.'

'He won't live to collect,' Li said.

'That's what we're hoping.'

CHAPTER 20

Rafe was just getting out of the shower when his phone pinged and Webster's message came through. Relief washed over him. A major hurdle overcome. Whether Bao Yu was important to Zou or not, she was at the very least a distraction better to have out of the way. He replied to Webster: *Looking forward to the party.* Then he sent Carlos a text with the news, towelled off and walked to bed with a smile on his face.

'You smell good,' Nicole murmured sleepily as he slipped under the covers and pulled her into his arms.

'Shampoo. You smell like the woman I love,' he whispered, dipping his head and kissing her cheek. 'Ummm . . . candy sweet, a hint of roses. I could find you blindfolded in the dark.'

Twisting in his arms, she climbed up on his big body and kissed him; wet, passionate kisses, little biting kisses, frantic, hot kisses. 'If you're too tired,' she breathed, nipping at his smile, 'I'll be good.'

He loved her wildness, her helpless need. 'I'm not tired and I'm not looking for good.' He slid his hands down her spine, cupped her ass in his large hands. 'So what can we do for you?'

'I'm just so happy,' she said, a tiny hiccup in her voice. He was always willing to accommodate her, no matter his weariness. 'And you should sleep. Really, give me a kiss and I'm content.'

He laughed, then his smile turned intimate and his voice was that of a man in love. 'I'm here to make you happy, Pussycat. I'm guessing I can do a little better than a kiss.'

Her smile was dazzling. 'You're so good to me.'

'It gives me pleasure,' he said, this man who'd faced the world largely alone since childhood. 'You're a part of me now, Pussycat.' He ran his palms down her back, gently cupped her bottom, thought for a brief moment about how his love for her tempered his life, his immediate future. Perhaps added to his risk when his focus should be single-minded on survival.

But he shook away all the uncertainties and lifted his head to kiss the woman who gave him such pleasure. Who could make him forget his unprosperous odds, the entire world when he held her in his arms.

*

Toward morning, Rafe's phone pinged. Reading the text, he carefully slid from the bed in order not to wake Nicole, walked into his dressing room, shut the door and called Carlos. 'Did you sleep?'

'Unlike you, I did,' Carlos said, a smile in his voice.

'If you have a problem with me fucking, I'll find you a therapist.'

'Find me a good-looking one and I'll think about it. Good news though. Bao Yu et al. are airborne. Webster just called. But I have even better news for your shiny new love life. Zou stopped two hours ago.'

'That *is* good news. Any idea why?'

'He entered a compound crawling with men although, from the signs of activity, I'd guess they're not ready yet to take the offensive. If I had to bet, I'd say Zou's there for a few days at least.'

Rafe laughed. 'Jesus, is it my birthday?'

'It is for a minimum of two to three days anyway. Then, if Bangkok's their mobilization zone, that's another day or two's drive. Additionally, they'll have to space out their arrivals to mask their numbers.'

'If we have eyes on them, though, what about Zou's enemies? Those upper ranks have to have access to satellites. That's gonna widen the battlefield.'

'Or give us a miracle. Someone might take him out before he reaches Bangkok.'

'Wouldn't that be sweet. In the meantime, keep me up to date.'

'You still have to ration your playtime. We need you too.'

'I'll be down at night for sure, more often if possible. Thanks, Carlos.'

'You got it. Have some fun today. We're all taking a breather.'

It turned out to be more than a day. Zou didn't leave the compound, although the level of activity monitored by the satellite was intense. Trucks coming and going, men arriving, it was clear that he was preparing for a sizable campaign.

Zou hadn't tried to contact Bao Yu. A blessing for her, a mystery to those on the island. Both she and Li, who had turned out to genuinely be her husband, had been debriefed when they arrived. The little girl was theirs. Perhaps Zou had discovered the subterfuge; perhaps he'd known it all along. Although others hadn't or her apartment wouldn't have been trashed; nor would a hit team have been sent to Brisbane.

All Bao Yu and Li had been able to verify was that their flight to Brisbane had been arranged by Zou, and he'd offered them the use of his home there. The reasons were still obscure. Sun Li had helped compile a list of Zou's enemies, along with their capabilities. And he'd offered to accompany them to Bangkok. Ganz wasn't the only one with a vendetta against Zou.

The small family was staying in an apartment in the palazzo distant from the day-to-day activities. Rafe didn't want Nicole to see them and ask questions he couldn't answer.

Zou was continually under surveillance by satellite and on the ground. Arrangements for flights to Bangkok were in train. Everyone on the island was only waiting for Zou to move.

Until then, everything was on hold.

CHAPTER 21

After a late morning swim and a luncheon al fresco, poolside, Nicole and Rafe lay side by side on a sun-faded chaise, the too-tender-to-touch happiness they were feeling underscored by small stirrings of melancholy. After eight days in their own special paradise, they both knew time was running out.

The shadow of fear sent a shiver down Nicole's spine.

Rafe felt it, looked down. 'You okay?'

No. She hated feeling this way: restless, stifled, powerless against the future. Not knowing what was real and what was skidding mist. But the blue of her eyes suddenly flashed spotlight bright as she turned her face up to his. 'Tell me we can stay here forever.' A familiar echo of defiance rang in her voice. 'Just you and me. Say it.' A ferocious stare. 'Officially.'

He heard the small twitch of fear beneath the hard ding of her words, knew what she was asking and he cared enough to lie through his teeth. 'Why do you think I brought you to my hidden lair, Tiger? So you can't get away.' Lightly tracing the delicate arch of her brow, he wondered if he'd ever be this happy again. 'Just you and me, for ever.' His smile was a blaze of beauty. 'That's the plan.'

It was too late for anything but lies.

There was no forever.

The statute of limitations had run out.

Even knowing their world was being shaken to the core, a rush of gladness shone in Nicole's eyes. 'That works for me.'

Rafe's face closed over for a moment, before he smiled. 'We're a good pair, Pussycat. Right from the beginning. A triumph of serendipity over reason.'

'And me not taking no for an answer without a hissy fit,' she said, all playful sass, sure again.

'Yeah, that too.' A wolfish glint darkened his amber eyes; he wasn't so sure he would have let her walk away. He suddenly stifled a yawn. 'Sorry.' His voice was thick with fatigue.

'Poor baby,' Nicole murmured. 'You're not getting much sleep.' Rafe was often gone when she woke in the middle of the night, his schedule brutal. 'Don't feel you have to entertain me. Go take a nap.'

He rolled his eyes. 'Thanks, Mum. We're just dealing with the fallout from the Geneva attack. Nothing to worry about. I'll sleep when it's over.'

'You're bringing in an awful lot of men.' Security was

visibly ramping up; Leo had taken to frowning more or less full time and while she understood she was being protected from the war plans, something beyond ordinary defence was in the works.

Rafe smiled. 'Okay, it's major fallout. But we weathered their twelfth attack, so I've been to this dance before. It's pretty routine. More wine?'

'Sure. A little.' She gave herself points for responding like a mature adult. Rafe didn't wish to discuss the subject. She understood. 'Lunch was fabulous as usual.' She waved at the debris of luncheon on a nearby table.

'Henny's behaving himself and Teresa's a gem. I'm lucky to have her,' Rafe replied blandly, levering upward in a supple flex of abs to reach for a bottle of local rosé.

Nicole picked up her wine glass from a small mosaic table beside the chaise, then quickly set it down as tears suddenly welled in her eyes and all her stiff-upper-lip intentions melted away. 'Oh hell,' she whispered, incapable of Rafe's cool control with farewell and loss twisting her gut. 'How much longer before—'

Putting down the wine bottle, Rafe swung back, put his finger over her mouth. 'Come on,' he said softly. 'Don't rain on my parade. I like feeling happy.'

Sucking in a deep breath, then another, she finally managed to conjure up a wobbly smile. 'Gotcha.'

'There you go.' He gave her a sweetly wicked wink. 'Compliance. That's what I like.'

Cautioning herself not to ask for more than Rafe could give when he was only looking for a degree of normalcy in the eye of the coming storm, she grabbed handfuls of his sleek black hair and pulled him close. 'Then you better make it worth my while, Contini. Got it?'

'So you give the orders now?' A slow, lazy smile, an eyebrow lift.

'Was I somehow not clear?' she purred.

His grin was bad boy perfect. 'Just checkin'.' Although he'd been on his best behaviour the last few days, wanting to offer Nicole unalloyed pleasure, wanting what they had to matter somehow, wanting it to be better and brighter and sharper so even when the lights went out and the signals were lost, the memories would still be vivid. He had two, maybe three, days of sweet, urgent happiness left. 'Okay, now don't give me any shit, but my orders first. Shut your eyes.'

Her gaze narrowed. 'Seriously?'

'Seriously the orders or seriously shutting your eyes?' Not that it mattered; he knew how to make her obey.

'What if I say both?'

He smiled. 'It'll just delay your orgasm.'

'Hmmm.'

He knew that sound and look. 'Ready to move on? If so, I apologize for the cliché, but it's something I want to do.'

'Do what?' she asked warily.

'I said clichéd, Pussycat, not depraved. Trust me.' He waited calmly.

She finally shut one eye.

He flashed her a wide grin. 'You have trust issues, Tiger?'

'Maybe.'

'Do what you're told,' he drawled. 'You get the prize.'

'I'd better,' she said in her bossy little bitch voice that always made him smile.

He leaned forward a little, gave her a small, intimate smile. 'Have I ever let you down?'

A second later, her eyes closed and he gave himself a moment to relish the lush image of her lying on his chaise, eyes shut, her skin warm and golden, her opulent form on almost full display in a tiny red polka-dot bikini, her beauty so precious she took your breath away.

And she was his, at least for now.

Sitting up, he stretched out his arm and plucked a plump red cherry from the bowl on the table. Turning back, holding the cherry between his thumb and index finger, he said, quietly, 'Open your mouth. Uh-uh, you can't look yet. Trust, okay?' He waited until her eyelids drifted downward again, then waited a fraction of a second more – committing to memory the sweetly erotic picture of her waiting open-mouthed and expectant – before he lowered his hand.

The instant the cherry touched her tongue, her eyes flew open and her giggle warmed his heart. 'See, perfectly innocuous,' he said with a lopsided grin. 'Am I a good boy or what? Now bite.'

'You're a romantic, too,' she teased, giving him a poke in the ribs. 'How hard should I bite?'

He laughed. 'Goddamn sex fiend. No wonder we get along.'

'Did you ever doubt it?'

'Jesus, and I thought you liked me because I made you laugh and we both enjoyed walks on the beach.'

'Fuck you.'

'All in due time. You gonna eat this cherry or what? Or would you like it somewhere else?'

She grinned. 'Same old pervert.' But she pulled the cherry off the stem and began to chew.

'Yeah, well, men are fucking predictable,' he said, holding out his palm for the pit. 'Feel like another one in a different place?'

She took in his playful leer. 'So I have choices?' she said with a tantalizing glint in the blue of her eyes.

He chuckled. 'You always have choices, Tiger. The menu's large and my dick and I are always on board for whatever you want.'

'The tower room.'

He laughed. 'Walls twelve-feet thick – your kind of perfect. No one can hear you scream.'

She grinned. 'Do I detect a note of censure?'

'Hell, no. Your enthusiasm is music to my ears.' He held out his hand. 'Want me to carry you? Don't answer. I'm carrying you.' His need for her burned hotter with each passing moment, the thought that he might never hold her again so sharp it hurt.

Nicole pressed her hand to her chest as though he'd spoken aloud, as though his thoughts had scalded her skin, as though telepathy were real and not just coincidence. 'I don't want to leave,' she blurted out, her eyes huge, pleading. 'Tell me I don't have to. Oh God, I'm sorry – I shouldn't have said that. No I'm not!' Her voice pitched high, she stared at him with heated challenge in her eyes. 'I'm not one bit sorry! And I'm *not* going!'

He couldn't think of anything on earth he'd rather hear, nor anything more impossible. 'Hey, hey, it's okay,' he whispered. Leaning in, he slid a finger under her chin, dipped his head and kissed her gently. 'You don't have to leave,' he lied. 'No way.'

He felt her smile on his lips, heard her soft 'Thanks', and easing back, met her warm, sun-lit gaze.

'Fairy tales really can come true, right?'

'I'll make sure they do.' *Three days, tops*, he thought, giving her a reassuring smile because she was watching. Although there was a chance he might win this crapshoot. 'Since you walked into my life, I've become a believer in miracles. So why not a few more.' His smile was heartbreakingly beautiful this time. 'Are we all good now?'

Swallowing her tears, she nodded.

He kissed her cheek. 'That's my girl. Now, let's check out the view from the tower room. We'll slam the door on the world, you give orders this time and I'll take them,' he said, sexy and low as he started to lift her up. 'And we'll—'

He recognized the ring tone.

'Give me a second.' Slipping his arms free, he swung his legs over the side of the chaise, sat up and grabbed his cell phone from the table. With Nicole in earshot, he answered cautiously. 'Yes?'

'I'm in Split,' Dominic said crisply. 'I've come for Nicole. It has nothing to do with you. Nicole's sister was in a bad car accident. She survived, others didn't, but they don't know whether she'll live. I need you to alert your men that my chopper's coming in. Fifteen minutes.'

'I'll take care of it,' Rafe said.

'Is Nicole's phone on? I'll call her next.'

'Yes.'

'Help her out.'

'Of course.'

A second after Rafe ended his call, Nicole's cell rang. Even before she answered it, she knew something was wrong because Rafe picked up her iPhone from the table and, without looking at the caller ID, handed it to her.

After she put the phone to her ear, she didn't move, didn't say a word. Just listened. With a final nod, as though in answer to something, she handed her phone back to Rafe.

'She'll be ready,' Rafe said.

'Did she hear me?' Dominic asked.

'I don't know.' Nicole was staring into space, barely breathing, her hands palm up in her lap as if dropped there and forgotten. 'Gotta go.' Tossing the phone on the table, Rafe picked up Nicole, carefully placed her on his lap and wrapped his arms around her gently. Even in the sun, she was cool to the touch, utterly still, in shock. He'd just decided to call one of his doctors when Nicole looked up, her gaze unfocused. 'I sent Isabelle a message.' Her voice melted away in a whisper. 'She heard me. She's going to be fine.'

'I'm glad,' Rafe said, softly, pulling her closer, pressing his cheek against hers as if he could give her his warmth. 'If she answered you, that means she's getting better. You know what though? We should go inside.' *He'd have Alexei look at her, see if she needed medication.* 'There's not much time.'

Her eyes widened and she looked at him, actually saw him. 'Why isn't there time?'

'Your uncle's coming in from Split. He's going to land in a few minutes. Didn't he tell you that?'

A tiny catch of her breath. 'Did he? I don't remember.'

Rafe spoke in an even, hushed tone, not sure of her reaction. 'I'm guessing he did. So you have to get ready. What do you need?'

Nicole's eyes flicked up. 'You.'

He put his palm to her face, bent low and brushed her lips with a kiss. 'You have me, Pussycat. Always.' He let out a long breath, his thumb moved just a little on her cheek. 'I meant, do you need anything packed?'

She shook her head.

He glanced at her tiny polka-dot bikini, looked up, hoping some of the staff were around so he could send them to fetch her clothes, remembered they had orders *not* to be around and softly swore.

'What's wrong?'

'Nothing. We should probably get out of the sun so you don't burn.'

'Weren't we going to the tower room?'

He was seriously out of his depth. 'Give me a second to make a phone call.' He needed a professional opinion; he'd have Alexei come out to the pool.

'Dominic just called.'

He turned his head, his phone in his hand. 'You remember that, yeah?'

'Of course, why wouldn't I?' Her voice shifted up a gear, her brows arched. 'He said Isabelle was in a bad car accident. He's coming to get me. But I told you, she'll be fine. I said, that right?'

'Yeah, absolutely.' He set his phone back on the table. 'I'm glad she's going to be okay. Good news.' His baby was in shock, still loopy, but half there now; better than not there at all. He'd take it. 'You know, you should get some clothes on before your uncle gets here. Or I could have someone pack a few things for you.'

'Don't bother. I'll be back soon. Isabelle is strong.'

He wasn't about to bring up the Geneva attack, the ostensible reason his life was hectic of late, nor that he might not be on the island much longer. 'We'll get a jacket at least,' he said, giving her a little smile. 'How about I take you into the house and we'll see if there's anything else you need.' Coming to his feet with Nicole in his arms, he started walking toward the palazzo.

Nicole caught hold of Rafe's arm, stared up at him. 'You're not trying to get rid of me, are you?'

'God, no!' His expression of surprise quickly turned to affection. 'Hey, no way.'

She lifted her left hand. 'You sure? You want your ring back?'

'Jesus, Tiger, I couldn't be more sure.' He stepped off the pool terrace onto the garden path. 'We're engaged. You better not be changing your mind.'

Her smile was unimaginably fragile. 'I won't. Just checking on you.'

'There's nothing to check. You're my girl. Now, tomorrow, next week, next month to infinity, okay?' Without missing a stride, he dipped his head, gave the bridge of her nose a brushing kiss. 'Know what? Why don't you and Isabelle talk about our wedding while you're home? That'll give you something to do while she's recuperating.' This wasn't the time to deal with the harsh facts of life and the uncertain future. Nicole was just returning from some frightening place; she needed a distraction. 'Whatever kind of wedding you want is fine with me.'

'I want a small wedding,' Nicole said. 'Nothing fancy.'

'Great.' He shot her a grin. 'Just you and me.'

She smiled. 'Good try. But I have friends, you have friends, there's family. And Isabelle has always talked about a wedding on horseback or scuba diving off the Great Barrier Reef, or a hot air balloon wedding in Napa. She's into theatre.'

Rafe laughed. 'Whatever. Just tell me when to be there.' There was something to be said for pure fantasy. It beat reality with Nicole's sister on life support, him facing a war zone, and the possibility they might never see each other again all too fucking true.

Feeling a swift, painful pang of despair, he came to a sudden stop in the middle of the sun-filled, fragrant garden. Shifting Nicole higher in his arms, he fixed his hooded gaze on her from very close range and said, softly, 'Have I told you lately how much I love you?'

Her arms tightened around his neck, the blaze in his amber eyes spreading a life-giving warmth through her senses, his body solid and strong against her. 'Yes, but tell me again.' *Tell me that we have all the time in the world.*

'I love you Nicole Parrish. Fiercely, unconditionally.' A smile rippled across his face. 'Obsessively.'

She smiled a tiny smile. 'Crazy in love; that's always been us. I love you, Rafe Contini, bone deep, heart full and madly.' She swallowed hard. 'I'm not going to cry. You're going to come and get me soon or I'll come back here. There's nothing to cry about.'

'Not a thing. I'll be in San Francisco before you know it.' Rafe's eyes closed for a second, a flicker of tension caught the tip of his smile, but his voice was smooth when he said, 'A few more days of this mess I'm dealing with and I'll come for you. I might be out of phone range for a couple days, but I'll call as soon as I can.'

'Promise?'

The soft plea in her voice broke his heart. 'Promise. Same page now?'

'Yup.' She swallowed hard, blinked harder. Then, in her fearless way, she said, 'Come back or I'll come looking for *you*.'

He smiled, knew she was going to be okay. 'Don't worry, I'll be back. You're unforgettable, Pussycat.' Familiar with masking his feelings and moving on through a world of soul-destroying trouble, he started walking again. 'Make sure to say hi to Isabelle from me. Tell her I'm looking forward to meeting her. And don't give me any shit,' he added now that Nicole seemed rational again, 'but we're getting you some clothes. No one looks at you half naked like this but me.'

A smile flickered at the corner of her mouth. 'Wow. Is that an order?'

'Goddamn right it's an order.'

'Okay, then.' Her smile was sweet as hell. 'And Isabelle really is going to be fine. I'm not delusional. We talk to each other ESP-wise, always have, ever since we were kids. So relax.'

He didn't argue about having been worried. He just said, 'If you say so, I believe you. I'm glad you're okay. You would have freaked out your uncle.'

She smiled. 'I doubt it. Dominic's hard to freak out. But he might have blamed you. No way I want that.'

Since the sea breeze could be cool, Nicole dressed in jeans and sweater. Rafe just pulled on shorts and a T-shirt. They were waiting on the verge of the landing pad a few minutes later, her hand in Rafe's, her backpack slung over his shoulder. Dominic's chopper was just setting down.

Rafe had asked whether she wanted to take any of the clothes he'd bought her, but she'd said, 'The clothes will be here when I come back.'

Knowing better than to insist, he replied as calmly, 'I won't move a thing.'

Then she'd tucked her hand in his and looked up, clear-eyed and unflinching. 'Whatever's going on, be careful, okay?'

'I will,' he'd said.

They both should have been on the stage.

Leo and Dominic exchanged a few words after Dominic stepped off the ramp, then Leo moved aside, Dominic smiled at Nicole and walked toward her. He was thirty-seven now, tall, tanned, handsome, but still a surfer at heart, wearing blue and white chequered Vans, cargo shorts and a T-shirt from a surfing competition in Bali. 'Sorry I'm not here with better news,' he said, wrapping Nicole in a hug. 'I see you're ready. Good.' He put out his hand to Rafe. 'Appreciate your help.'

'Rafe thinks I'm nuts,' Nicole announced, 'but I'll tell you anyway. I did that ESP thing Isabelle and I have been streaming since we were like four and six and she answered. Everything's gonna be okay. But she needs me, she said, so I'm all set to go.'

'Hey, ESP, whatever it takes. I'm with you.' But Dominic was surprised at Nicole's bland assurance that Isabelle would recover. His reports had been less sanguine and he'd given Nicole a relatively accurate assessment of her sister's condition. He wasn't about to argue though, pleased that Nicole was dealing with the tragedy in whatever fashion. Not that he wasn't above hoping that ESP was the newest medical marvel.

'More good news too,' Nicole said, grinning. 'Ta da!' She held out her hand to her uncle. 'I'm engaged.' She shot a smile at Rafe. '*We're* engaged.'

'Very nice,' Dominic said, smooth and polished. 'I like your ring. Congratulations.' He glanced at Rafe, raised an eyebrow. 'You're going to surprise a lot of people.'

'Somehow that's not a concern of mine,' Rafe said drily.

He gave Nicole a one-armed hug. 'We're happy, that's all the matters.'

'Of course. I, for one, recommend marriage.' *His current one, precisely.* 'All my best to you both.'

But Dominic watched the young couple as they quietly said their goodbyes, a faint worry line on his brow. He'd been married the first time when he was about Rafe's age. For all the wrong reasons. For no reason. And he wondered if Rafe understood what he was doing. Nicole seemed so sure. Maybe women had a better grasp of their emotions, were less puzzled by all the intangibles. Or maybe his own experience was irrelevant. Apples and oranges; no two people were the same, et cetera, et cetera. Yet still – he felt a ripple of unease. Contini had been burning through women for a helluva long time.

Henny, Basil and Ganz suddenly arrived to see Nicole off and Dominic took the opportunity to draw Rafe aside. 'This engagement? Are you serious?' He spoke in an undertone, a faint prickle in his voice. 'I'm concerned for my sister, Nicole's mother, as well as Nicole. I wouldn't want either of them upset over some rash impulse of yours.'

Rafe dialled down his flash of anger. 'I told you how I felt in Paris. It hasn't changed. I'm sorry if that's a problem for you,' he said with a touch of irony when both of them knew he wasn't sorry. 'I'll come for Nicole as soon as this operation's over.'

'Leo tells me Zou's massing a lot of troops.' Dominic's expression was absolutely neutral, giving nothing away.

'Zou needs them. His enemies list is long. But Leo can go back anytime. We're in good shape.' Rafe could do emotionally uninvolved too; a life's worth of training made it easy.

'Leo was thinking about staying. If you're serious about marrying Nicole,' Dominic said, his voice just a little bit sharp, 'it's even more important that you come out of this alive.'

'I'm not one of your employees so watch your tone,' Rafe said, a hard glint in his hooded gaze. 'But for Nicole's sake – so she doesn't have to deal with your hassle – I'll say it. There's no if. I'm serious. We're getting married. And no offence, but I don't need your help with Zou.'

'Take it anyway.' Dominic finally smiled. 'Consider it an engagement gift. We both want Nicole happy. That means you showing up in San Francisco with all your limbs more or less intact.'

There was a small, taut silence.

'Look,' Dominic said into the silence. 'We got off on the wrong foot. I made a mistake. We both want what's best for Nicole.' A casual reassurance; a cryptic warning. 'We can agree on that.'

But, deep down, he was saying something else.

Rafe left a long pause before he spoke. 'I don't want to keep going over the same ground, or get bogged down in some pointless testosterone competition. I can be a prick, you can be a prick, we both have a talent for it. But here's the situation. I'm not you,' he said, flatly. 'Just because we met where we met, did what we did, doesn't mean we're the same. Clear?'

Rafe's steely resolve was different from his at that age, Dominic reflected. Not raw and wild, not even annoyed, just firm; but the message was clear. *Back off.* Dominic sighed. Max's dossier had indicated that Contini's character had been honed in a crucible of deviant circumstance and isolation. So maybe he knew how to keep his shit together even if he was young. 'Fair enough,' Dominic said, mildly. 'I'll wind down my over-protective uncle vibe.' He lifted his chin, offered a conciliatory smile. 'The problem's Nicole. You know what she's like. If you don't let me help, I won't hear the end of it. She doesn't give up.' He shrugged. 'That's both good and bad, but you know what I mean. So how about you let me lend a hand?'

Rafe exhaled softly, then dipped his head. 'Okay. But I warn you, I'm not a cheap date. We're facing one holy mess and the word winning, isn't really applicable.'

'I'm well aware,' Dominic said. Even if they were successful, it would come at a cost.

Rafe shot a quick glance toward the group around Nicole, then spoke even more quietly. 'When you called, you asked me to help Nicole. Now I'm asking you to do the same for me. I told Nicole I might be incommunicado for a few days. It could be longer. Once we leave the island, everything's in flux; there may not be time to make personal calls. I don't want her alarmed.'

Dominic nodded. 'I'll see that she doesn't panic. Once we get to San Francisco, she'll be busy with family. Everyone's camped out at the hospital with Isabelle. But if and when it's possible, call Nicole so she doesn't worry. Leo will keep me in the loop, but that's not news I can share with her.'

'How serious *are* Isabelle's injuries?' Rafe asked. 'Nicole seems to be in denial.'

'They're serious. Isabelle was thrown from the car. Her head injuries are severe. She's in an induced coma.'

'Jesus.' Rafe blew out a breath. 'Look, I have access to every kind of facility and specialist in the world, so if I can help . . .'

'She's at Stanford's Level One Trauma Center. The care's excellent.'

'Still, if you need any particular specialist, tell Leo and I'll get back to you. Oops, we're done. Here comes Nicole.'

Dominic grinned. 'Did you ever think you'd worry what a woman thought?'

'No more than you,' Rafe said, softly.

'We're both lucky men.' Dominic put out his hand. 'Stay well.'

Rafe's grip was strong and firm. 'I plan on it.'

CHAPTER 22

After Nicole left, Dominic made a quick detour to his bedroom, sat down at a small table used for a desk, opened the single drawer and pulled out a sheet of monogramed paper and an envelope. He wrote a few lines quickly, signed it, *All my love, Rafe*, folded the note, shoved it into the envelope and wrote *Nicole* on the outside. Getting to his feet, he walked into his dressing room, pushed aside his shirts in the wardrobe and opened a small wall safe. Taking a single key from several on a key-ring, he slipped it into the envelope, licked the seal and pressed the envelope shut with a swipe of his fingers.

Returning to the desk, he put the small envelope inside a larger one, scrawled his bank manager's name on the sturdy manila stock, added a short note with the necessary instructions and dropped the packet into the desk drawer. When he left for Bangkok, he'd have someone deliver the package to Geneva. Then he rose and with a last glance around the room, turned and walked out.

He was in the operations room five minutes later. After receiving updates from Zander and Carlos, he joined Webster and Gina, who had Zou's wife under surveillance on another set of monitors. She'd recently met with Colonel Chen, Webster offered, flicking over to another screen with an interior shot of a living room.

'No big surprise, I suppose,' Rafe said, dropping into a chair with a view of the screen. 'Not exactly a love match considering Zou's roving eye.'

'His wife was well connected when they married,' Gina noted, looking up from her keyboard, then leaning back in her chair. 'Zou wasn't. Old story. He moves on when he hits the big time.'

Rafe raised his lashes infinitesimally. 'Surely not a woman scorned.'

'No,' Webster replied. 'Not even close. She's looking for a pay-off. Zou thinks she's old school; submissive, long-suffering. He calls her with instructions for their daughter, household, everything. She never argues, but she's taking care of business, no doubt.'

'When's the pay-off?' Rafe sat up a little straighter.

'Tomorrow. She gives up Zou's new phone number, his fourth since he left Shanghai. She was a tough negotiator; wanted the money wired out. Their son is at Oxford so at least he might get the funds. She and the daughter . . . ' Webster shrugged. 'Who knows? I have a tap on her phone and a mike on the house. Chen's security thinks they've taken them out.' Webster grinned. 'But I'm too fucking good.'

Rafe smiled. 'No argument there. So as of tomorrow we have ears on Zou, not just eyes?'

'You got it.'

'Then we should move out. Are either of you coming to Bangkok? No pressure. You've both done your jobs.'

'I'm in,' Gina said. 'I don't have anything else going on right now.'

'I'll think about it,' Webster said.

'Davey's lining up transport.' Rafe heaved himself to his feet. 'I'll go see how he's doing. Thanks as usual.' He shut his eyes for a second. 'Fuck I'm tired.'

'Grab a nap,' Webster said, pointing at a sofa in the corner. No one mentioned Nicole, the reason for his lack of sleep, or the reason she left. Everyone was focused on the task at hand.

'Maybe later.' Rafe lifted his hand marginally in a wave, then walked from the room.

Davey filled him in on the aircraft waiting at Split, as well as their flight plans currently on hold. Afterward, Rafe joined Carlos, who was with the technicians monitoring the island security cameras.

'Anders thought he saw something a couple minutes ago, but it disappeared. Over there.' Carlos pointed. 'North of Dock Four. Now nothing.'

Rafe sat down beside Carlos, slowly scanned the twenty screens. It was nearly five, the shadows lengthening even with the late sunsets in August, the miles of shoreline empty of activity, the waves breaking on shore in a mesmerizing rhythm. The quiet hum of activity in the room was as tranquilizing as the waves. With Nicole gone, Rafe settled into a comfortable chair in front of the wall of monitors, answered questions when needed, ate when someone brought him a sandwich and dozed off from time to time. He'd been short of sleep for days.

Several hours later, Rafe caught a glimpse of movement in the far corner of the top-right screen and briefly wondered if he'd been dreaming. A light sleeper since childhood, thanks to his father's drunken visits in the middle of the night, he was instantly alert, his gaze intent on the suspicious area. *Fuck!* 'Top-right screen,' he snapped. 'Two o'clock. Coming ashore.' He was on his feet before he'd finished speaking and running for the door. Grabbing an assault rifle from a wall rack, he blew out of the operations room, took the stairs three at a time, and was racing down the hill a few seconds later, a dozen armed men in his wake.

By the time they reached the small cove, two security patrols were pulling a deflated rubber raft on shore, along with three dead men.

'Once the team was burned, they let loose. We returned

fire. One was still alive but he put a round in his head before we could get to him,' one of the security men explained. 'So no go on interrogation, but—' He held up a small rubber-sheathed electronic device.' 'Score. They were tracking something onshore.'

'A solo assault?' Rafe glanced at Carlos, who was talking into an earpiece. Carlos shook his head, held up two fingers and, a moment later, said, 'Two more rafts, assault teams all dead. Three men by choice. Wait, one still alive.'

'Keep him alive,' Rafe said, crisply. 'Not that it matters. We know what they want. But no point doing cold-blooded until we have to.'

Carlos gave orders to whomever was relaying the information to him.

'Now let's see where the transmitter was planted.' Rafe nodded to the man holding the device. 'Lead the way.'

It turned out the signal came from the diamond studs in Bao Yu's daughter's ears. A clear explanation of why Zou had allowed the mother, father and child to leave Shanghai. 'He was using them for bait to target his enemies,' Rafe said, once everyone had returned to the operations room.

'And he didn't care who went after them,' Carlos said. 'One of his rivals or us. They were useful, then expendable. Bao Yu and Li understood that so they showed themselves and hoped Ganz et al. got there first.'

'Zou was using them to buy time too,' Rafe muttered.

'But the bastard has to leave his compound eventually. Double the patrols on the island tonight. Everyone else get a good night's sleep. We leave for Bangkok in the morning.'

There was no dissent. The men recruited preferred action to waiting.

The next morning, while two aircraft took off from the airport in Split, Nicole was at her sister's bedside, talking softly, telling Isabelle about Rafe, about their wedding, about all they'd do together once she was well again.

With the induced coma, Isabelle was heavily sedated, a breathing machine taking over her lung function, her body being chilled with cooling blankets, all in an effort to reduce the swelling in her brain and mitigate cerebral damage. Under the care of a trauma team of specialists; ER doctor, neurosurgeon, orthopedic surgeon, plastic surgeon, Isabelle was being closely monitored. She had a sensor in her brain to measure cerebral pressure, a heart/pulse monitor, a special bed that altered air pressure to reduce blood clotting. After forty-eight hours, her sedation would be reduced, her vitals scrutinized and, if her body functions performed well, the sedation dose would be reduced. If, however, her response was inadequate and the swelling persisted, an operation would be necessary and a portion of her skull would be removed to relieve the pressure on her brain.

The whole family was at the hospital, taking turns sitting at Isabelle's bedside, but once Nicole arrived, Isabelle responded best to her sister's voice; she'd moved a finger an infinitesimal distance when Nicole first spoke. And her lashes fluttered once when Nicole recited a favourite poem of theirs from childhood in a gibberish intelligible only to them. Like so many children, Isabelle and Nicole had developed their own language.

Patty, the housekeeper, was taking care of Rosie and James, so Dominic and Kate could keep vigil with the family at the hospital. Dominic had food brought in from Lucia, but under orders from Kate, he curbed his take-charge instinct. 'It's not your place to give orders,' she'd reminded him. 'The doctors are excellent. Melanie needs your support, that's all. Don't make a scene.'

By the second day, Dominic was wound up tight; diffidence was never his strong suit. So when he wasn't holding Melanie's hand, he paced. 'Not here,' Kate had whispered, jumping up and leading him out into the hall the first time he'd made a restless circuit of the waiting room. 'You're going to freak out Melanie. I'll come get you if something happens.' So he wore a path out in the hall.

But when the doctors announced that an operation wasn't going to be necessary, everyone breathed a sigh of relief. The swelling had gone down, they were told, Isabelle's lungs were beginning to function again. She might even be taken off the breathing machine tomorrow if her progress continued.

Kate delivered the good news to Dominic. Soon after, knowing Dominic and his nieces and nephews had been playing chess for years, she called home and had Dominic's favourite chess set delivered to the hospital.

Shortly after starting the first game, Dominic had leaned over and given Kate a kiss. 'You know how to calm the wild beast,' he'd whispered.

She'd smiled. 'I know everything about you. Including your competitive spirit. So make sure you lose.'

He'd laughed softly. 'Are you my conscience?'

'You betcha I am.'

CHAPTER 23

As requested, Dao waited for Rafe at her office in Bangkok. With almost as many contacts as Carlos, she knew why; monkish now that he was engaged, Rafe wanted their meeting to be strictly business. His new abstinence surprised her, although perhaps it shouldn't have. Rafe had been doing exactly as he pleased for years, long before his father died.

The fact that she happened to own the hotel where Maso had died indulging his auto-erotic tastes was unfortunate, not intentional. He'd merely reserved the penthouse in the most exclusive luxury hotel in Bangkok. Whether he'd been alone in the penthouse at the time of his death was a question the police had chosen not to ask; it saved hours of manpower and paperwork. The Royal Thai Police preferred the less time-consuming 'accidental death by asphyxiation' as the cause of death. Gora had come for the body.

Dao's thoughts were interrupted by a knock on her

248

office door and, looking up, she smiled as her houseboy announced Rafe. He'd come alone. She hadn't been sure with all the plans in train.

'You're looking beautiful, as ever, Dao,' Rafe said, striding into the large room overlooking her garden.

She gave him a quick assessing glance as he approached her desk. 'You're one of the few men who do justice to the word as well, darling.' Even casually dressed in jeans and a grey T-shirt, his long, dark hair tumbled on his shoulders, he was breathtaking. She waved him to a chair. 'Would you like tea, a drink, some food?'

'No thanks. I had something on the plane.' He sat opposite her, waited for her to send the houseboy away and for the door to close. Then he leaned forward slightly, his eyes alight. 'Zou's actually on the road. Am I lucky or what?'

She laughed and sat back in her desk chair. 'You've always been lucky.'

'With a little help from you, on occasion, don't forget.'

'How could I? You gave me the seed money for all this and more.' She swept her arm in a slow circuit that took in the splendid room and estate outside the window.

'You helped me, I helped you.' Rafe leaned back. 'We both managed to survive.'

Forced against his will to take part in his first orgy at fifteen, Rafe had been stubbornly resisting and so furious with rage at his father's goading that Dao had worried about possible carnage on her white carpets or, worse, a dead body. She'd just opened the posh 'massage' parlor, and was mortgaged to the hilt to the kind of men who expected their payments on time. Also, the bribes she was paying the police were already too high. She couldn't afford a murder investigation.

So she'd taken Maso aside, convinced him to let her school his boy privately, promised him videos in the morning. Then she and Rafe had spent the night together, talking – her early life as unhappy as his. By morning, Maso was so wasted by drugs, he couldn't remember where he was, let alone a bargain he'd made with Dao. She and Rafe had been friends ever since, occasional business partners and, even more infrequently, lovers.

Dao smiled. 'We're both long past mere survival, aren't we? You look happy. Considering the circumstances, I assume it's because of your fiancée. Tell me about her. I'm curious. Do you mind?'

'No. She's wonderful.' Rafe gave her a wry smile. 'I have no idea why. She just is. I didn't want to let her go so I'm keeping her.'

A delicate lift of her brows. 'Love?'

'Oh yeah.' He did a little flicker of his brows. 'That too. I have no idea where that came from either. Although thousands of poets have written about love in a thousand different ways, so I'm guessing that's what hit me.' He smiled again. 'It's mind-boggling – in a very good way,' he added softly.

'I can tell. Congratulations.'

He gave her a glance from under his lashes. 'Have you ever been blown away by love or shouldn't I ask? It's just such a great feeling,' he said with a deprecating little shrug. 'Brilliant, urgent.' He grinned. 'Never enough.'

'A true convert.'

'Fuck yeah. So? You? Am I overstepping?' Dao had a son at boarding school in Hong Kong. Had the father been someone she cared for?

'No, darling, you're not overstepping. You've just never thought to ask. But then you've never been in love before. You've met my son, Charlie. His father lives in London. He loves me as much as he can in his position and I love him more.'

'A wife then, I'm assuming.'

She nodded. 'And three other children, almost grown now.'

'A possible divorce later?'

She shook her head. 'He's in government.'

'Now I feel bad. I shouldn't have asked. Forgive me.' He suddenly sat up straighter. 'Want me to find you someone loveable? I'm sure I could.' Dao was stunningly beautiful, at most thirty-five, wealthy, educated now that she'd made her fortune. He grimaced. 'Oh hell, you'll have to wait until I'm finished with Zou.'

'I'm content. If and when I'm interested in a permanent substitute for Charlie's father, I'll let you know.'

'No you won't.'

She laughed. 'No I won't. Now, for the business at hand, let me bring you up to date on Zou. I received a report earlier today from the men I have inside the compound. One's a mechanic, the other serves Zou and his closest advisors their meals, the third is selling them small arms. Their information is quite good.'

Rafe listened, asked questions about Zou's journey south to Bangkok. Dao brought out a map and traced the possible routes. All three of her spies were travelling with Zou's troops and would relay additional information as they could.

'Does anyone know whether he's taking a stand here or simply using Bangkok for a staging area? Ganz is tapping his phone as we speak so we should have ears on him soon. Zou has to know by now that he lost three assault teams on my island along with his signal. The cunt was using Bao Yu's little girl's earrings he'd given her as transmitters; he figured no one would toss diamonds that large.'

'He was right. Zou's sharp and, in case you forgot, surrounded by personal bodyguards. You have your work cut out for you.'

'Ganz emptied Zou's department account and blasted his operation to dust. I'm hoping Zou has other soft spots too. In the meantime, give me those reports and we'll keep adjusting our plans as needed.'

'You're at your place?'

'Yup, in fact I'm walking back.' Rafe had a small house in the expensive, leafy area of Embassy Row. A walled estate like most of the residences there.

'Do you think that's wise?'

'Carlos complained too. I'll be fine. I'm going the back way.'

'You're crazy.'

He grinned. 'Yeah, crazy in love.' Coming to his feet, he swept up the pile of reports, folded them and shoved them in his back pocket. 'I have no intention of dying today or anytime in the next fifty years. You'll have to come to the wedding.'

'Send me an invitation.' His fiancée might have other ideas.

'You got it.' He blew her a kiss and walked out.

Dao picked up her desk phone the second Rafe left, talked to her security director and ordered him to see that Rafe arrived home alive.

Rafe had just reached Dao's garden gate when he turned back, smiled at the six men standing ten yards behind him and spoke to them in the Bangkok dialect standard for the country. 'I suppose you'd better come or she'll dock your pay, right?'

'Or worse,' the leader said with a grin.

Rafe waited for them to catch up. 'You've been with Dao a long time.' He recognized the man from Dao's original massage parlor.

'We're both from the same hill tribe. We grew up together.'

'All of you?' Rafe indicated the rest of his crew as they approached.

The man nodded. 'Dao's the village patroness. Built a new school last year, a hospital the year before, set up two businesses in the village so people have jobs.'

'Dao helped me out years ago too. She has a big heart.'

'She lives up to her name. Now, are you going to let me look out the gate first in case there's trouble waiting for you?'

Rafe laughed. 'Do I have a choice?'

'She's watching so, if you don't mind, I'd better do the looking.'

'Jesus.' Rafe turned, grinned at Dao in the second floor window, gave her the finger. She gave it right back. 'What the hell,' Rafe said with a chuckle. 'Be my guest or she'll come down and smack us around.' Dao had been a dominatrix in her early career.

'No doubt. Stand back.'

As Rafe expected, his five-minute walk home was uneventful. Zou had a lot more on his plate than keeping tabs on all of Rafe's homes. After thanking his escort, Rafe entered his property through *his* garden gate and smiled at the two guards pointing assault rifles at him. 'Just me. Christ, I can hear Henny banging pots from here. Did he mention what was on the menu?'

'Something with chillis. Along with fish. We're in Bangkok, he said.'

'Sounds good. Zou's on his way south. He shouldn't be here for another day or so, but in case he has scouts out, heads up, okay?'

A huge smile from the larger of the two men. 'Finally some action.'

'Anyone who uses a little kid for bait,' the other man said, 'deserves what he gets.'

'True enough. Carlos in?'

'Upstairs. Staying out of Henny's way. I'm locking this gate now that you're in. We're doing two-hour rotations so everyone stays alert.'

'Sounds like a plan. Zou's bringing down a fucking armada. We'll just have to see how motivated his troops are.'

A few minutes later, Rafe walked into his study on the second floor where Carlos, Simon and Leo were going over maps while Webster and Sasha were setting up more monitors for their security system. Gina and Basil were seated on the floor playing chess. 'You heard. Zou's on his way. A day or two before he gets into town. Here are Dao's reports.' Rafe handed them to Carlos. 'She has three men inside. How's Ganz doing with the phone tap?'

'Almost there, he said not too long ago,' Carlos replied. 'He's next door in your bedroom. He likes to be alone when he works, he says. What he really means is he can do lines without anyone giving him a hard time. But he's starting to get tremors. It's been too long this time.'

'Yeah, Zou's been pushing hard for awhile.' Rafe sighed. 'We better check on Ganz if it gets too quiet in there. And make sure he eats something when Henny brings us food. But till then, listen up everyone. I thought it might be simpler if we could bring Zou to us rather than we go after him. If the logistics can be managed, I'd like him to get an invitation to an exclusive party when he arrives in the city. Something so bloody tempting he can't refuse; celebrities, intimate venue, lots of women, gambling.' Dropping into a chair, Rafe stretched out his legs. 'What do you think? We could use one of Dao's boutique hotels. Or if that's too close a connection, we could rent one of the smaller embassies for the night. There's probably a couple that wouldn't turn down a few mil for a social event.'

Webster turned, a terminal cable in his hand. 'I suggest a party host from Dubai, preferably a banker. There's time to fly someone in. My friend in Dubai has lists on top of lists of money-laundering financiers available for a price. And since we haven't been able to crack Zou's accounts in Dubai, he'd be more inclined to trust an invitation from an Emirate banker.'

'Call your friend,' Rafe said. 'Tell him we'll charter a plane. But whomever he commissions has to have serious credentials; a major bank, major position, right client list, smooth and glib would be helpful. The banker can name his price. Your friend can name his price. We'll have an intimate little party; good music, flashy women, roulette and a super-clean hit with only a few people involved. Fucking nirvana.'

'If Zou takes the bait,' Carlos murmured.

'We could add some celebrity pussy to our guest list. A singer, film star, fucking tennis or golf star. There must be someone who gives Zou a hard on. Find out and book them for the party.'

'Let me check with a contact in Macau,' Leo said. 'Every major celebrity plays there. Someone might remember whether Zou has lusted after any particular lady.'

'Whomever we book only has to sing or look pretty, smile, whatever. We just need her as enticement. She might have to send a couple extra smiles Zou's way once he gets there, but that's it. She'd have protection, handlers, bodyguards. Jesus fucking Christ,' Rafe said, sitting upright in his chair. 'I'm getting super-hyped. We might be able to do this with a minimum of bloodshed.'

'And you'd get to fly to San Francisco sooner rather than later,' Simon said.

Rafe smiled. 'Yeah, wouldn't that be grand?'

Henny's heavy tread could be heard coming down the hall and, a moment later, he threw open the door and bellowed, 'First course! Ganz, get your ass in here!' He waved in four young men, three carrying trays of food, one balancing a large ice bucket of bottled beer on his head.

Everyone sat on the floor and helped themselves to stir-fried chicken with cardamom, tiny krill simmered with coconut and crabmeat and a jungle curry with peppercorns. All the dishes were dominated by a fierce, perfumed, heart-thumping chilli heat that left them sweating and swigging beer to soak up some of the visceral fire.

In the aftermath, while their tongues stopped throbbing and the sweat dried on their faces, they finalized the details for Zou's party: the venue, caterers, illegal casino operator, music.

Stretched out on the floor, Henny flexed his fingers above his head and squinted at his friends. 'Remember the time we were jumped on that moonless night in St Moritz,' he murmured. 'We were what – fourteen, fifteen? I'm in the same kind of mood. I feel like strangling someone.'

'You're lucky we dragged you off before the guy croaked,' Basil said. 'And we were fourteen. That was the winter my mother forgot Christmas.'

Henny snorted. 'Did she ever remember? Mine didn't.'

'Hey, kids, we had our own Christmases after that so chill,' Rafe said with a grin. 'And, Henny, sweetheart,' he added, softly, 'I hate to shut down all your fun, but the point of this party is for all of us to go home. So no one's gonna get close enough to strangle anyone.'

Henny gave him a wicked smile. 'Maybe you can't stop me.'

'I know who can,' Rafe drawled. 'One phone call to Mireille and you're on the next flight home.'

'Low fucking blow,' Henny grumbled.

'Yeah, well, I like your food. So stay alive.' Rafe shot a glance at Webster who was blowing him an air kiss, his phone to his ear. 'Looks like we have clearance from our man in Dubai,' he murmured, turning his gaze on his lounging friends. 'Now, who wants to recruit and vet the women we need to make this party a success?'

'Wasn't that always your job?' Ganz said from somewhere in outer space, his eyes slits behind a curtain of black hair.

'Not any more,' Henny jibed, slamming Rafe for his comment about Mireille. 'He's pussy-whipped now.'

'And damned happy to be pussy-whipped,' Rafe said, cheerful as hell. 'So who's going to line up the women?' His eyes widened briefly at the hand that was suddenly raised. 'Since when?'

Gina grinned. 'Maybe I'm a switch hitter.'

'All due respect,' Rafe said softly. 'You're not.'

'What makes you think you know everything about me?'

'Sorry, my mistake.' Although he knew pretty much everything there was to know about Gina after all their no-holds-barred fucking. 'I'll get a list of agencies from Dao,' he said. 'Any preferences on nationality?'

CHAPTER 24

An hour later, Ganz had tapped Zou's new phone and between the satellite surveillance and cell monitoring, Zou was being tracked to a high-tech inch. Alexei and his colleague, Dr Oren, arrived soon after, having come in on a transport plane with a fully equipped operating room and medical staff. Dao had arranged for the medical staff to stay at one of her apartments near the small museum that would serve as their party venue.

The museum had the virtue of being semi-isolated within the urban jungle of Bangkok. Also, everyone had agreed that an embassy might give rise in Zou to memories of untrustworthy political alliances. With bribery a cardinal rule of business in Bangkok, he'd know that his whereabouts would fetch a good price from his enemies.

Two days later, as Zou's journey came to an end at a warehouse near the Noi Canal, the party plans were complete, the banker from Dubai had been given his need-to-know instructions, and Dao's spies had reported back. Zou's troops were bivouaced at the warehouse; Zou had taken up residence in a luxury apartment owned by a wealthy Chinese casino owner. The man was not only a relative, but Zou was one of his investors. And regardless that casinos were illegal in Thailand, the pay-to-play policy of the police department allowed hundreds of gambling establishments in Bangkok alone to thrive.

Shortly after he'd settled in, Zou took the elevator downstairs to a private casino, code for: only those who could afford it were admitted. Before long, he was joined at the roulette table by a banker from Dubai who started having a run of good luck. They exchanged pleasantries between spins of the wheel: weather, horse racing, the banker's heavy schedule of client meetings, the number of beautiful women accompanying him tonight – mentioned with a wink and a smile.

A brief twenty minutes later, the banker finished his drink. 'Won enough for tonight,' he said, handing his glass off without looking. 'Now for some fun.' Getting to his feet, he took a business card from his jacket pocket, handed it to Zou, told him if he was ever interested in banking in Dubai to give him a call. Waving over the five women who'd accompanied him to the club, he'd turned back to Zou and said, almost as an afterthought, 'Care to have dinner with us?' One thing led to another, he reported to Carlos the next morning; everyone had a good time. Zou had set up an account at his bank in Dubai and it was a go on Zou's party invitation.

The following evening, dressed in jeans, T-shirts, Kevlar vests, wearing boots for running and armed, Rafe stood beside Gina, looking through a two-way mirror that had – for a substantial sum – been installed in the foyer of the museum that afternoon. The elaborate gilded frame sparkled under the chandelier lights, the mirror shimmered in the lucent glow while the two people behind the glass watched a parade of beautifully dressed and coiffed women walking in through the open entrance doors.

'Kudos, babe,' Rafe said, smiling. 'You did good. Every single lady is dazzling.'

'And classy,' Gina noted. 'That's where a woman's eye comes in. Men always zero in on big boobs.'

Rafe shot a sideways glance downward at her Kevlar-covered breasts. 'Like yours.'

'I rest my case,' she said, drily.

He grinned. 'Men are such animals.'

She gave him a disgruntled look. 'Are we done with this?'

'Yes, ma'am,' Rafe said, still grinning. 'You were saying.'

'I was *saying* I wanted the whole package. Stylish, not just a sex bomb.'

'You nailed it then – *very* nice packages.'

But his voice was casual, Gina noted. He could have been

talking about a suit or a car. This wasn't the Rafe who'd always looked at a woman with fucking on his mind.

'Once Zou arrives,' Rafe said, interrupting her musing, 'Saxe will escort him into the roulette room. Shouldn't be a problem. Money before pleasure for Zou. Then the ladies will be moved to the atrium so they're out of the firing line – although ostensibly they'll be escorted there to enjoy the music until Zou's finished gambling. Zou sits down at the roulette table, is offered a drink, we wait while it's made and once he has the glass in his hand, it's game on. Did I leave anything out?'

She gave him a sideways glance. 'You left out the part about him coming in here with an armed escort.'

He flipped her a look. 'I told you our sniper from Shanghai showed up this afternoon, right?'

'Yeah, a man with a mission. Now we have two loose cannons. Ganz and whatshisname.'

'Xu Wei. And I don't blame either one of them. A family that matters – it's no small thing,' he said, his voice going soft for a second. Then he gave a little snort, letting it go and grinned. 'So – two loose cannons. You and I have our work cut out for us.'

'Webster's on it too. Ganz's escalating drug use is making him nervous. And he's known Ganz longer than any of us.'

'His father's assassination coked him out even more. Once Zou's gone, we'll get him into rehab. He's fucking brilliant and a good friend so we gotta see that he stays alive,' Rafe said, matter of factly.

She looked up, smiled faintly. 'You're always steady as a rock.'

He laughed. 'Hell, no. Hangin' on by my fingernails, babe.'

'Liar.'

His smile faded. 'You learn to close it down, that's all. Or never even open it up. Shut all the doors. Lock 'em up tight. That's been my life.'

She touched his arm lightly. 'Past tense. You hear that?'

It took him a moment to understand and another moment to tamp down the panic. 'Problem is that it makes you vulnerable.' He drew in a quick breath. 'Makes you want to live, not take chances, think too much when you shouldn't. When you should be operating on instinct alone.'

She couldn't argue. He was right. 'Our plan is good,' she said instead. 'We stick to it, everyone comes out alive.'

If only it had turned out that way.

First, Zou walked in with a woman on his arm. Not just any woman. The runner up to Miss Thailand, the daughter of the police commissioner, an Oxford-trained barrister and well known in all capacities. She couldn't be shunted off to the atrium like the ladies for rent.

Second, Xu Wei, who was out in the garden up in a tree, his back against the trunk, adjusted Zou's head in his scope crosshairs, got the bead and started squeezing the trigger before Zou even stepped through the doorway into the gaming room. If Zou hadn't suddenly bent his head to listen to something his female companion was saying, the 180 grain, full-metal jacket, 45 round would have painted the floor with his blood and brains.

Spinning around, Zou ran, dragging his terror-stricken companion with him.

The Dubai banker hit the floor and joined Dao's croupier under the roulette table. Xu Wei took out two of Zou's bodyguards, then dropped to the ground and sprinted for the front of the building.

Surrounded by a moving phalanx of bodyguards, Zou raced for the entrance and his waiting car, hauling the screaming woman along with a steely grip on her arm.

Ganz suddenly came out of the shadowed night like some apparition, took up a rigid firing position at the top of the entrance stairs, his weapon aimed straight through the open doors at Zou's sprinting figure.

'Bloody hell,' Rafe muttered and bolted from the room behind the two-way mirror, Gina on his heels, both firing at Zou and his bodyguards as they ran toward Ganz.

Ganz was standing still as a statue in the doorway, bathed in light from the chandeliers, framed by the pitch-blackness of night. The perfect target.

In two seconds Rafe had almost reached him when Zou put a gun to the lady's head and shouted in English, then in Mandarin, 'Move out of the way or she dies.'

Everything came to a stop as if someone had hit pause on a remote.

'Cool it,' Rafe hissed, hoping like hell Ganz could still hear. Gina eased back slightly and stumbled against Webster who'd come out of nowhere. Pulling her close, he murmured, 'Don't do anything stupid. Let him go.'

But as Zou walked past a growing group of silent, hindered adversaries, he glared at Ganz. 'Take him,' he ordered one of his bodyguards. 'He's mine.'

Rafe stepped forward. 'Take me instead. He's so strung out, he's already dying.' *He didn't say Ganz won't even know you're killing him, but that's what he meant.* Ganz's pupils were completely dilated, tremors racked his body, sweat poured down his face. If he didn't get help soon, paralysis would set in and he'd stop breathing. But there was still time. 'I'm worth a hefty ransom,' Rafe said. 'Ganz isn't worth a centime. And I hear you've been losing money in Switzerland and off shore,' Rafe drawled. 'I can make up that deficit.'

'Smart-ass pretty boy, aren't you?'

'Think of it as a business deal.' Rafe took another step forward as though the decision had already been made. Knowing it had. Money was always Zou's bottom line.

'Fine.' Zou nodded, but he didn't move the gun barrel from the lady's head. 'Drop your weapon. Get in the car.' He turned and spoke to one of his bodyguards.

'Call Gora,' Rafe murmured, handing his Glock 19 to

266

Webster. 'Tell him not to fuck around. I have a wedding to go to.'

But a few moments later, just as Rafe stepped into the car, he heard a gunshot, then Ganz's scream. *Two-faced motherfucker.* He hoped Alexei was close by.

Alexei was, standing beside Xu Wei, holding his rifle arm down until the cars drove away. Then he raced up the stairs to where Ganz lay, scanned him for a head shot and relaxed marginally; the entry wound was in his chest. Dropping to his knees, he ripped away Ganz's shirt. The vest had slowed the bullet, but the fifty-calibre round had gone through twenty-seven layers of Kevlar and, partially deformed, was lodged low in his right side. He was bleeding fast.

As Alexei gave orders for Ganz to be carried next door, the others on the stairs watched the two cars disappear and waited for instructions.

'That sniper has to be sent home before he fucks up something else,' Gina said under her breath.

'It was too personal for him,' Webster murmured. 'It's not for us.'

Her head whipped around. 'It is now.'

'Gotcha.' He lifted his chin. 'Carlos is on it. He'll tell us what he needs.'

CHAPTER 25

When Carlos called, Gora and Camelia were at their villa in Trieste having a drink before dinner at a table poolside. Titus was swimming.

After listening for a few seconds, Gora said, 'Wait', gave Camelia a rueful smile and get to his feet. 'Sorry, darling, business. It won't take long.'

He inhaled a few deep breaths as he strode across the terrace to the villa, trying to calm the pounding of his heart. He hadn't felt such cold-blooded terror since his first hit as an eighteen year old. Shoving open the terrace door, he stepped inside the cool quiet of his study, shut the door and prayed for the first time in his life. Then he shook off his moment of doubt and said, brusquely, 'Okay, I'm alone now. Tell me everything you know about this motherfucking prick who took my son.'

After his call with Carlos was over, Gora phoned some men he'd known since his youth, made arrangements with them to fly to Bangkok, gave orders to have a bag packed, then glanced at the clock and hesitated. He knew Dominic was in San Francisco with his extended family. Did he want a call at five in the morning? Or, more to the point, was Rafe's fiancée significant enough to be given notice of the disastrous events? He sighed. Real engagement or not, Rafe cared about her. Picking up his phone, Gora punched a number.

'It's early,' he said in Italian, their common language years ago in Rome. 'I apologize.'

'It's fine,' Dominic replied in fluent Italian. 'No one's sleeping much. Let me go out in the hall.'

Gora waited while Dominic spoke quietly to someone.

'We're all still at the hospital, although things are much better,' Dominic said, walking out into the hall. 'What's going on?' He knew Gora wasn't calling to chat.

'A serious fuck-up. It's not your problem, but I thought I should at least tell you since your niece and Rafe are . . . ' Gora's voice trailed off.

'She showed me the engagement ring,' Dominic said, understanding Gora's bias; he shared it in reverse. 'But if you're calling *me* about a serious fuck-up, it must be about Rafe. Is he alive?' Dominic wasn't naïve; Rafe wasn't in Bangkok on holiday.

'I think so. Zou has him. Rafe offered himself as ransom in place of Ganz.' Gora went on to tell Dominic what he knew. 'I'm flying to Bangkok in a few minutes. It's probably not wise to say anything to Nicole until we know more, but that's your call. I'm not mentioning it to Camelia.'

'Until you have to.'

'No, until Rafe comes home,' Gora said firmly. 'Alive.'

'Of course. Can I help?' Regardless of his reservations, the way Nicole had beamed with love when she looked at Rafe and said, *We're engaged*, was hard to forget.

'I'll take care of it myself.' Gora's voice was cold as ice.

Dominic was reminded of the Gora he'd first met years ago, how he'd thought he could buy him off, how he'd been wrong. How he'd met a man as ruthless as himself. 'If you change your mind, don't hesitate to call. Isabelle's on the mend. I can get away if necessary.'

'No, Rafe's my son. Zou is mine to kill. It's the way in my world.'

'I understand.' Dominic knew he'd fight to his last breath if Kate or his children were in danger. 'Look, Max is in Hong Kong. I'll have him fly in. He's knows Thailand better than either one of us.'

'I'm going after Rafe as soon as I land. Ransom or not, Zou can't be trusted.'

'Max will be waiting at the airport,' Dominic said. 'Tell him what you need, he'll get it for you.'

After his talk with Dominic, Gora sat at his desk for a moment, wondering what to say to Camelia, how to conceal his blinding fear. In his line of work, the jobs had always been impersonal. A matter of logistics: get in, do the hit, get out. This time it was so deeply personal he ran the risk of not functioning at his best.

He couldn't afford that weakness.

He couldn't afford one mistake.

In the end, the story he chose for Camelia was close to the truth at least in terms of destination. 'That was a supplier of teak from Bangkok,' he said when he walked back out to the pool. 'He'd promised me first pick of his newest shipment for the sailboat. But it's on a first come, first serve basis and he has other buyers so I'm going to have to leave immediately. If it wasn't for the political turmoil over there, I'd ask you to come along.'

'Luca can't handle it?'

'I'm too fussy.' Gora smiled. 'He might pick the wrong timbers.'

'You're sure?'

'I'm sure. I'll bring back some silks for the stateroom furniture. Tell me what colours. Better yet, I'll bring back a collection of colors. You can decide later.'

Camelia tipped her head, looked at him intently for a moment, then said, 'At least say goodbye to Titus before you go.'

His pulse rate subsided and he smiled. 'I'll see what he wants for a gift.'

'You spoil him,' she said softly.

'I know. I'm making up for all the years I missed Rafe growing up.'

She laughed. 'You still watch over Rafail even though he's grown.'

Not well enough. 'He's our son. I'm allowed.'

She nodded. 'You won't be gone long?'

'No.' Bending, he kissed her softly. 'I'll be back before you know it.'

Thirteen hours later, Gora came down the steps of his private jet onto the tarmac at Suvarnabhumi airport in Bangkok. Four of his old colleagues, leaders of their own organizations now, were with him. They, in turn, were accompanied by several large heavy-set men in para-military gear. Max was there with Carlos. They had SUVs waiting.

'Where is Rafe now?' Gora asked without preliminaries. He spoke in Italian, a language his colleagues understood.

'At the compound up north,' Carlos replied. 'Zou choppered in with Rafe and a dozen others. We have someone from the area in the kitchen, but Dao's other two spies are with Zou's troops driving up from Bangkok.'

'The prick knows Rafe is worth a lot of money alive.'

It was a question, no matter the declarative delivery. 'I'm sure Rafe has made that clear,' Carlos said.

'If I pay the motherfucker, will he keep his word? Will Rafe be safe?'

272

'Good question.'

Gora shot Carlos a hard look. 'That's a no.'

'He had Ganz shot after Rafe got into his car.'

'Okay, we're not going to screw around on this. The longer he has Rafe, the more likely he'll hurt him.'

'Agreed.' Lying to Gora was impractical.

'We go in now. Before the rest of his troops reach the compound. You chartered the helicopters?'

'Yes, ten as requested. Max got us military issue. New models.'

Gora nodded at Max. 'Thanks for the help. It's been a while.' They'd met once, in Rome after Titus had been born. Max had picked up the last divorce papers dissolving Dominic's marriage to Bianca.

'Glad I could help,' Max said, his Italian coloured with the soft intonations of an upper-class Brit. 'Dominic knew I was posted here years ago. The military doesn't change much.' Max had worked for MI6 before he became ADC to Dominic; he still looked the part. Tall, buff, blond buzz cut, shuttered gaze, his trademark desert boots. 'Speaking of military, Zou's rival, Colonel Chen, just arrived in town. He wants Zou dead more than you. I guarantee he'd be interested in a joint operation.'

Gora shook his head. 'I don't work with people I don't know.' Then he stepped back and made a quick round of introductions, his friends acknowledging Max and Carlos with nods and the requisite Italian courtesies. In contrast to Gora's tall, thin frame, his shorter colleagues had the mid-life beginnings of a paunch. Although no one would mistake that bit of flab as testament to any kind of softness. Even in their well-tailored suits, the subtle bulk of shoulder holsters was unmistakable. 'Everyone knows everyone now?' Gora waited a fraction of a second. 'Back to business then. I brought eight pilots with me, you said you fly, Carlos and . . . '

'Sasha, Basil's cousin.'

'Each chopper carries twenty?'

'Some more,' Max answered. 'Those require co-pilots, so I could round up some more fliers if you like or we could improvise. You don't necessarily need a co-pilot. I can take one of the seats.'

'Fine. I don't like outsiders. We leave from here?'

Carlos nodded. 'The choppers came in a few hours ago from the air base north of the city. We'll drive to where they're parked.'

Max rode shotgun in one SUV, Gora and Carlos in the back, the driver Dao's man.

'There's something else,' Carlos said as they drove away from Gora's jet. 'I wanted to tell you in private.'

Gora's head swivelled to Carlos, his gaze suddenly chill. 'They've hurt him. How badly?'

'We don't know. Rafe was in a metal box when they unloaded him from the chopper. The man Dao has in the kitchen saw the box unloaded but hasn't been able to get closer. He saw it carried into one of the outbuildings he doesn't have access to. He'll try, of course.'

'What kind of box?' Gora said, stiffly.

'One too small for comfort.'

CHAPTER 26

Rafe's initial spiking panic as the box lid came down instantly disappeared when he saw air holes above his head. He dragged in a quick breath as though testing his perception. Musty and damp but air. Good. That meant Zou wanted the money.

As for claustrophobia and stress, he had Maso to thank for his relative equanimity in the cramped confines of the box. The nannies his father had hired had disciplined him by locking him in closets, wardrobes, once a box much like this. Maso referred to it as building character.

Whether his character had improved was debatable, but he knew how to deal with trauma and dark, closed spaces. In his early years, after he'd decided that crying didn't help, he'd turned to images of storybook bunnies and talking dogs to keep him company. Later action heroes entered his escapist visions and by the time his mother

276

rescued him from his nanny hell, he could shut out the world with ease. Scientists called it resilience training he'd discovered later in life. In solitary you have two resources: free time and your mind. It was a skill set he'd honed to a fine edge.

Having been unloaded and carried to his new prison, images of Nicole sustained him now, her lush beauty, her teasing smile powerful antidote to the small niggling doubts. Would Gora arrive in time? Would he survive after the ransom money was delivered? If Zou's penchant for torture persisted, how much more could he take?

He'd been dropped on his side, his legs shoved in roughly, crammed against his chest; his shoulders had been too wide for the lid to close so someone had stepped on them and they'd been throbbing like a son-of-a-bitch ever since. His head and neck were bent so awkwardly the pressure sent racking spasms up his spine.

After hours in the stress position, the pain was excruciating, every muscle in agony and he'd rubbed the skin off his right arm trying to reach the knife blade on the inside of his boot. If he didn't snap his wrist with the degree of torque required to slide his hand between his ankles, he might succeed.

But success continued to elude him.

When the pain became unbearable, he'd take a break and run through his mental film clip of Nicole in all her sweet glory and damned if she wasn't the imaginary Oxy he needed to temper the agony. Breathe in, breathe out, begin again.

He couldn't afford to break his wrist, he cautioned himself. He was going to need two hands, two feet, a working body – everything in reasonably good order – to get the hell out of this compound.

Think positive, right.

Shoulder to the wheel, no pain, no gain.

Maybe it was that slight bit of humour that did it, or maybe he was sweating so much from his efforts that his arm finally slid down far enough to reach inside his ankle to the lining of his boot. He momentarily froze, fearful that the small metal knob between his thumb and fingers might slip away.

Concentrate, relax. Not exactly possible, he thought drily. Then he slowly drew Carlos' custom, miniature version of an all-purpose knife upward over his thigh to his chest and waited for his heart to stop pounding in his ears. Gripping the blade firmly in his fingers, he studied the two wide red nylon straps binding the cargo box, the fabric visible through some of the air holes. Drawing in a slow, calming breath, he forced his arm upward in the confined space and, with a hellish twist of his wrist, managed to place the knife blade on the edge of the strap.

He wasn't able to see his watch so he had no idea how long it took him to saw through the first strap. Pain consumed him, radiated through his body in continuous waves, his brain shutting down occasionally as though offering a moment of respite. He'd eventually regain consciousness and, teeth clenched, drenched in sweat, he'd command his senses to function and go back to cutting the nylon.

When he finally severed the second strap and gently eased back the lid, he lay completely inert, unable to move. The room was dark, although it had to be daylight by now. But the murky black was an advantage. He needed time to become mobile. And he really had to piss.

Not knowing whether a guard was posted outside the door, he half-climbed, half-rolled out of the metal cargo container as quietly as possible and lay in a sprawl on a dirt floor. He managed to move his arm just enough to see his inexpensive sports watch that no one had wanted. Unlike his wallet.

Eleven-fifteen.

Gora should be in Thailand by now; Zou should be waiting for his money. In the meantime, he had to bypass the gnawing agony gripping his body and get off the floor. Beginning with his fingers and toes, stifling an urge to groan, he systematically flexed and contracted his muscles until he was able to slowly sit up, then even more slowly, stand. Fuck, everything hurt. He'd pay a fortune for a couple Oxys right now.

A sliver of light was visible on the side of what appeared to be the door and once his eyes became more accustomed to the darkness, he examined his prison. It must have been a stable at one time; he was in one of two stalls. Moving quietly to the farthest corner, well away from the door, he relieved himself, zipped up again, walked to the other stall, sat down, leaned back against the half wall and considered his options.

Zou wanted the ransom, but whether he kept his bargain after that was debatable. A man without scruple, he'd abandoned his wife and family, his mistress and child, his country. Surely he'd view a captive's life as equally disposable once the ransom money had been paid. But, first things first – could he get out?

Staggering to his feet, not sure whether a guard was outside, Rafe carefully moved to the door and tugged on it, then waited to see whether the small pull had been noticed. Nothing – no sound, no movement. Zou had left only a skeleton crew behind at the compound when he and his troops had travelled to Bangkok. It was impossible to fly his entire force back. That would explain the lack of guards. It also meant the compound's security was compromised. Bruised and battered as he was, Rafe felt a sudden surge of elation at the thought.

Oh fuck.

The door suddenly opened and, blinking against the light, Rafe found himself facing Zou and two guards.

'Well, well, well,' Zou murmured. 'I thought you were just a pretty boy with more money than brains.'

'I thought you were an asshole and I was right.' Zou was relatively small and the two guards didn't exactly look like prize-fighters . . . he could take them.

'You have no manners,' Zou said, softly.

'I just climbed out of a box you put me in. So fuck manners. All we have to do is agree on a price and I'm out of here.'

'I've already talked to one of your people.' A thin smile curled into a malicious sneer and Zou's voice dropped. 'I'll wait to talk to him.' His eyes drilled into Rafe, then he turned to his guards. 'String him up.'

Rafe took out the first guard with a slashing elbow to his throat that crushed his windpipe. Spinning to his left, he kicked the second guard in the groin and as the man crumpled to the ground, screaming, Rafe turned to Zou and abruptly stopped, his heart beating hard. Another guard was leading Dao toward them. She looked exhausted, dazed, her hands tied behind her back, her face bruised.

'You're such good friends,' Zou said, smiling faintly. 'I thought she might be useful.'

'She's a very good friend,' Rafe said, keeping his voice level. 'You shouldn't have done that to her.'

'I disagree. It brought you to heel. ' He waved his hand. 'Take her away. Now, I suggest you cooperate with my guards or your friend will suffer more.'

Zou waited for two other guards to arrive and watched while they tied Rafe's arms behind his back and hung him from a pole in one of the stalls. His shoulders were already damaged, and if he hung from that position long, his shoulder joints would separate and tear from their sockets.

'You probably don't want to move too much.' Zou's smile was sly, like a well-fed fox. 'Such a shame you're not lighter. Your weight is a disadvantage.'

Sweat was streaming down Rafe's face, relentless waves of pain jackhammering his body; he set his jaw to speak. 'If you hurt Dao any more . . .' His voice was no more than a rasping whisper, each word took effort. 'I'll see that you die slowly.' He stared at Zou for a moment, a hard glitter in his amber eyes, his breathing, rough, panting. 'That's a . . . fucking . . . promise you piece of shit.' Then, as if he'd used up all his strength, his gaze went dull and he lost consciousness.

'We'll see who dies,' Zou murmured, then glanced at the two guards. 'Shoot him if anyone comes to his aid.'

CHAPTER 27

Gora's helicopter landed in the centre of the compound and he stepped down, Carlos and Max behind him. The other nine choppers hovered overhead in a close pattern as a show of force, although the troops had all been offloaded several miles away. They were surrounding the compound now, waiting for Carlos' signal to attack.

After being checked for weapons, Gora entered Zou's makeshift office in the main structure that long ago had been a clan chief's home. Gora could have been any tourist on holiday in Thailand: beige linen jacket, brown slacks, white open-neck shirt, brown leather lace-up shoes.

He sat down without being asked, set a leather-trimmed canvas bag on the floor by his feet, looked up at Zou standing in the centre of the windowless room. 'I'm Rafe Contini's father.'

'His father's dead.'

'That's not true. But Maso's dead. I watched him die,'

Gora said, his voice and manner relaxed. Did Zou really think he could be intimidated by the juvenile psychology of who was looking up at whom? 'How much do you want?'

Zou glanced at the bag on the floor. 'More than that.'

'How much?' Two expressionless words.

'Fifty million.'

Gora raised one brow. 'I'd have to see Rafe for fifty million.' His smile wasn't really a smile. 'Proof of life. You understand.'

Zou flicked his finger. 'Follow me.'

Gora didn't bother to pick up the canvas bag. He left the room, nodded to Carlos waiting outside in the corridor and said quietly, 'Come with me. We're going to see Rafe. You okay here?' He glanced at Max. Max and his crew were in charge of clearing out the main house once the signal was given.

Max smiled. 'No problem. I'll go sit with the pilot. Stay out of the way.'

Four of Zou's guards, stationed at the entrance to the house, fell in behind the small party as they left the house and walked across the compound yard.

'I hope you haven't harmed Rafe.' Gora's voice was so mild, he could have been remarking on the weather.

'He's alive.'

Gora's gaze flicked sideways briefly, the only indication he didn't like the answer he'd been given. 'That's good.'

He turned to Carlos who was on his right. 'Perhaps Alexei should be called.'

'Call anyone you want once I get my fifty million,' Zou said, acidly. 'You're in my compound. I make the rules here.' He held all the cards with Rafe Contini in his hands.

'Naturally.' No one did neutral like Gora. Although the sudden stillness in his shoulders was a time bomb ticking down. 'Once I see that Rafe is well, I just need your tracking number and we'll be on our way.'

'I didn't say he was well. Your son had to be subdued. He tried to escape.' Zou gave him a mocking smile. 'You understand.'

They'd reached a small outbuilding and, just before the door was opened, Gora glanced up, surveyed the tree line, then held Carlos' gaze for a second.

'See for yourself,' Zou said with a little wave of his hand as though showing off a prize tiger in a cage. 'Proof of life.'

The door was thrown open by one of the guards, the outside light poured into the shadowed interior and illuminated the single figure within.

Rafe was hanging from a pole strung under his bound arms, his T-shirt soaked with sweat, his jeans-clad legs limp, his booted feet hanging a deliberately cruel quarter inch above the ground. His head was sunk on his chest, his long hair falling in dark, damp tendrils over his face, his breathing barely visible, his pain so intense that even almost unconscious he was moaning softly.

There was absolute silence for a second, then Gora drew in a breath. 'Very well, he's alive. Now all we have to do is make the bank transfer. Carlos, cut him down.'

'Not until I have my money,' Zou snapped.

Gora gave Carlos a nod. 'Wait outside, then. I'll come for you.'

Zou left his four guards with Carlos when he and Gora returned to the house.

The moment Zou and Gora disappeared into the house, Carlos pressed a small electronic device in his pocket twice and the assault began. Waves of armed men rappelled over the walls, dropped to the ground and quickly and quietly killed Zou's minimal security force. The attackers used knives when they could get in close; if that wasn't possible, the silencers on their weapons suppressed the sound.

Meanwhile, it was Gora's job to keep Zou talking while the compound was overrun. Having jettisoned his psychological games now that the transfer was about to take place, Zou sat at a table he was using for a desk and Gora pulled up a chair across from him.

They agreed the ransom amount would be minus the cash Gora had carried in. Gora had opened the zipper, held up the bag, showed Zou the strapped packets of hundreds and asked whether he wanted to count them. Zou had shaken his head and Gora had moved on to the details of the delivery method for the remaining funds. Gora also requested that their doctor be allowed to land and see to Rafe before they left.

Zou shrugged. 'Why not?'

'I prefer using my bank account in Cyprus or Dubai,' Gora explained. 'Do you have a preference?'

'Dubai.'

Gora almost smiled. 'Dubai it is. Now, bear with me. I usually have people who take care of these things for me. But under the circumstances –' a slight grimace '– I'll do my best.' He handed his satellite phone to Zou. 'I have my Dubai bank online. If you'd put in your routing number, I'll key mine in next and we'll get this completed. I'd like to get Rafe home as soon as possible.'

Zou tapped in his routing number and handed the phone back.

Gora punched in his numbers, swore, then looked up and gave an eye roll. 'Where's your assistant when you need him, eh? Let me try this again.' He slowly entered one number at a time, then waited. 'Ah . . . finally. I think that did it. Check your account.'

As Zou was bringing up his account on his phone, Gora busied himself with the money in the canvas bag. 'Just a quick check that all the packets are there,' he said, looking up with a twenty grand strapped bundle in his hand, putting it back on top of the ceramic and plastic handgun, designed to beat metal detectors, hidden in the bag.

Zou suddenly smiled. 'There. It went through.'

Gora leaned over, picked up the canvas bag, held it out. 'Don't forget this.' Sliding the custom gun in his other hand under the table, he squeezed the trigger twice.

While Gora was dealing with Zou and the compound security force was being neutralized, Carlos, Gina and Webster slit the throats of the four guards at the stable. Quickly entering the small building, they moved to Rafe and, making a seat with their arms, Webster and Carlos lifted him to ease the pressure on his shoulders.

'Oxy,' Rafe whispered, his eyelids flickering. Everyone had a supply. His had been taken.

'Here.' Gina pushed two tablets into his mouth. 'Water.' She tipped her canteen to his lips. 'Come on,' she urged. 'Drink enough. You know the drill.'

Rafe swallowed a few more times, then shook away the canteen and half-opened his eyes. 'Dao's here.' His voice was hoarse. 'Find her. She's been hurt.'

Carlos spoke into the small hearing device in his left ear that gave him audio contact with everyone on their team. He listened for a few seconds. 'Dao's with Reggie. She's okay. They're waiting to be choppered out.'

'Good.' Rafe raised his head with visible effort, opened his eyes. 'Ganz?' he croaked and steeled himself for the answer.

'Stable. He's on the medivac plane.'

If it wouldn't have hurt to breathe a sigh of relief, Rafe

would have. But every muscle in his body was damaged, the pain crushing. He visibly rallied to speak. 'I'll likely pass out when you lift me down. Don't sweat it.'

'Alexei's on his way,' Carlos said as Gina scrambled up on the half wall. 'He'll give you a shot. Make the pain disappear.'

'Gora okay?'

'I'm sure. He's in with Zou.' Rafe's voice was getting weaker, his breathing more difficult. 'We're going to get you down. On three, Gina's going to pull out the pole, okay? You hear me?'

Rafe gritted his teeth and nodded.

Carlos kept his eyes on Gina. 'One. Two. *Three.*'

Rafe bit back his scream but he was gasping like a landed fish as he was gently lowered to the ground and his arms untied. Fighting back the darkness trying to smother him, his pain insupportable, he looked up at Gina kneeling beside him. 'One bump,' he whispered, his breath wheezing in and out, his fingers clenched against the relentless agony.

She hesitated. Rafe had given up blow a few years ago when he'd begun to chase it too much. No rehab, nothing; he just quit.

Rafe's gaze didn't waver. 'Come on.' Cocaine was Gina's last-resort painkiller; she always carried it on missions.

'Give it to him,' Carlos said.

Taking a vial from her pocket, Gina shook out most of

the contents into her palm, raised the white powder to Rafe's face, clamped her hand over his nose and mouth and rubbed it in hard.

The numbing sensation was instant; the person sitting on his chest got up and left. He could breathe. Nothing hurt. The world snapped back in full colour and a wild, sweeping energy uncoiled in his body, brain – and viewed through the Technicolor prism of a powerful rush – his formerly unrecognizable soul. Lifting Gina's hand away, he grinned, wiped his nose, mouth and chin stubble with his palm. 'Angel of mercy, babe. I'm back.' And he got to his feet in a stunning display of coked-up energy.

Alexei arrived with Henny, Basil and Sasha as they were leaving the stable. 'Looks like you don't need me,' Alexei said. 'Unless you want that arm looked at.' He indicated the raw wound where the skin had been rubbed off Rafe's right arm.

'It'll wait. Gina saved the day. You can give me a shot later when the coke wears off. Right now I could climb a fucking mountain. Everyone okay?' Rafe quickly scanned his friends for wounds.

'Way too easy,' Henny said, a smile creasing his blood-splattered face. 'We blew 'em away.'

'That's the way we want it. Nobody hurt. Or were they?' Rafe glanced at Alexei.

'Nothing major. Gora's waiting for you.' Alexei pointed to the main house.

'He's giving me the honour?'

'Something like that.'

Rafe had never looked for a fight in his life. He actually preferred avoiding them. But that hadn't always been possible; the years of boarding school, for instance, had been a constant battleground. And Maso had always chosen to incite. But by and large, he saw himself as a peaceful man. He wasn't sure he wanted the honour.

That was Gora's business, not his.

The compound was silent as they walked to the main house, while the corridor outside Zou's office was crowded. Gora's four colleagues were off to one side, quietly relaxed, looking no different than when they'd stepped off Gora's jet, their tailoring undisturbed, their expressions calm, every hair in place. Leo, Max and several other men were standing around, comparing notes, waiting for further instructions.

Rafe thanked everyone, shook their hands with only an occasional flinch. Coke aside, the pain in his shoulders was clawing its way back to the surface. The bloody laceration on his right arm where the skin had been torn away was visible; the damage to his shoulders was not.

When Rafe entered Zou's office, Gora pointed to the table and held out a conventional Glock someone had brought in. 'If you want him, he's yours.'

Rafe walked over. Zou was lying on his back, gut shot, blood frothing from his mouth, a red puddle widening on the floor, his eyes wide with fear. Gora could have targeted his head with a kill shot but he hadn't.

'Fuck it, leave him,' Rafe said. 'He'll bleed out.' He'd promised Zou a slow death. Maybe that was why he didn't take a shot, or maybe he'd have trouble sleeping at night if he shot a man in cold blood. 'Let's get out of here.' Turning, he moved toward the door.

Gora leaned over and picked up the canvas bag. As he passed the dying man, he looked down at him, raised the handgun hanging loose at his side and put a burst of rounds through Zou's head. 'I like to be certain,' he said.

CHAPTER 28

Max called Dominic as soon as they landed in Bangkok. 'We're done. No casualties on our side. We got there before Zou's troops returned and went in huge. Makes for an easy win.'

'Good to hear. Thanks for the help and thanks for calling. How's Rafe?' Max had told him about the cargo box before they left for the compound.

'Right now he's feeling no pain. Zou roughed him up a little so he's self-medicating,' Max explained. 'But I don't think it's anything that'll need surgery. He'll mend.'

'He's strong too. That helps.' The line went quiet for a moment, then Dominic said, 'I don't suppose you're in any position to suggest he call Nicole.'

Max snorted. 'No more than you. He's in a great mood though. You could ask.'

'Yeah, right,' Dominic muttered. 'Do you know his plans?'

'Nada. How's Isabelle doing?'

'She's doing well – out of ICU and on a regular nursing floor. There's talk of her leaving the hospital. She still has a lot of recuperating to do but the worst is over.'

'Nice. I'm going back to Hong Kong in about five minutes. I can't be gone long with the new baby. Liv likes me home. I'll see you in a month – just call me when you know where you'll be.'

'Probably in San Francisco. The children's school starts soon. How's your little girl doing?'

'Great. Precious, beautiful, looks like her mum. You know how that goes.'

Dominic chuckled. 'Yes I do. Makes life worth living, right?'

'Absolutely. As for Rafe, if it helps . . . and I'm no authority when it comes to anyone's love life – you and I both had to be hit over the head with a couple of hammers before we figured it out. Anyway, if I had to guess, I'd say Rafe isn't on the make. You said he and Gina had a thing going. Not here. He's friendly to her but no more. For what it's worth, that's my opinion.'

'Jesus, I hate this shit,' Dominic grumbled. 'Why do I have to worry about Nicole's love life?'

'She's family, that's why. You want the best for her.'

'If I wanted the best, I wouldn't put Rafe Contini on anyone's list for fiancé of the year.'

'But then you're not the one who's thinking about marrying him, are you?'

Dominic sighed. 'You're right. Maybe when things settle down I'll give Gora a call.'

'Talk about unintended consequences. When Gora was taking care of your factory in Bucharest, who would have thought you two might end up relatives?'

'Fuck. Don't remind me.'

'The level of corruption in the area aside, Gora always dealt with us honestly. And the guy's got balls. He walked into Zou's office alone to save the kid, no questions asked. In my book that excuses a lot. Neither of us had a relative like that on our side.'

'True. My old man was more apt to fuck me over. The asshole's still trying.'

'At least he noticed you. Mine never looked up from his bottle. I don't think he even knew how many children he had.'

'You had a mother who cared. Count your blessings.'

'Believe me, I do.' As ADC to Dominic for ten years, Max knew about his disastrous childhood. 'Rafe has a loving mother too and Gora will walk through hell for him. That's not a bad family to marry into. Just saying. Neither of us can afford to be too righteous or judgmental with the lives we've led.'

'So I should stop my bitching.'

'Your call, but Rafe really was tortured by that fucking prick Zou. He didn't fall apart. He didn't whine. He wasn't even vindictive. Gora left the kill shot for him and he walked away. The kid's solid. You could do worse for your niece.'

Dominic laughed. 'You'll be coming to the wedding then?'

'Damn right. Liv loves weddings. Honestly, it was the best day of my life when Liv agreed to marry me.'

'Amen to that. Katherine's given me everything I could ever want.' Dominic blew out a breath. 'What the hell, I'll call Rafe. Be polite. Ask him how he's doing.'

Max chuckled. 'Ask him when he's getting married.'

'I'm pleased this amuses you,' Dominic drawled.

'You have to admit, you in the role of protector of young ladies is damned entertaining. I can hardly wait until Rosie grows up.'

'She won't be dating until she's out of college,' Dominic growled.

Max hooted. 'That'll be the day. She's had you wrapped around her little finger from the day she was born.'

'You won't find it so amusing when it happens to you. You have a daughter now too.'

'But then I'm not a complete control freak like you. I'm thinking Cressy can go on a date when she's eighteen – as long as I chaperone her.'

'Jesus, how did this happen to us?' Dominic muttered. 'There we were, busy fucking our way through endless crowds of women and suddenly – pow!'

'Would you change it?'

There was a small pause, then Dominic spoke as softly as Max. 'Not a chance.'

'Maybe Rafe's smarter than us.' Max said, a new thoughtfulness in his tone. 'Maybe he realized long before we ever did that you can be surrounded by people and still be lonely.'

'Or he got lucky like us . . .' Dominic's voice gentled, the memory of Katherine sitting across his desk from him in Palo Alto unforgettable. 'And the right woman walked into his life.'

'The bar at the Connaught.'

'My office in Palo Alto.'

'Rafe's yacht in Monte Carlo,' Max said.

Dominic sighed. 'Yeah.'

After the call ended, both men sat briefly silent in their respective cities, considering the impressive role chance and fate had played in their lives. How hollow the notion of practical, responsible choice. How happy they were to have escaped the sterile philosophy. How genuinely happy they were.

CHAPTER 29

After their return to Bangkok, Gora left directly from the airport. Camelia would worry if he was gone too long and he missed her terribly when they were apart.

'You'll come see your mother soon now,' Gora urged, smiling at Rafe as they stood on the tarmac. He was the last to board his jet; the engines were powered up, belching a high-test vapour.

'I will.' Rafe shrugged, winced, always forgetting. 'As soon as Ganz is stable enough.'

'And have your shoulders looked at. A specialist.'

Rafe smiled. 'Yes, sir.'

'I can tell that means no,' Gora grumbled.

'If they don't get better I will. How's that?'

Gora sighed. 'Fine.'

'Thank you for coming to my aid so quickly. I mean it sincerely. You've always been there for Mum and me. I owe you.' Rafe put out his hand and when Gora took it, Rafe pulled him close in a hug, then quickly stepped back.

'You don't owe me,' Gora said smoothly, seeing that Rafe was embarrassed by his unprecedented embrace. 'I'm glad I could help.' But he was deeply touched; he'd never held his son before. He'd almost told Rafe that he was his father a dozen times since finding him at the compound. The sight of Rafe hanging in that outbuilding had been horrifying, the possibility of losing him all too real. And if Zou had been even slightly more zealous, the box smaller, less air available, had Rafe been left hanging in the stable too long, he might have died. It would have broken his heart. But Gora had stifled the impulse to disclose the truth then as now; there was no up-side to revealing his parentage. 'So Ganz is about to begin a new life or a different one at least,' Gora said with admirable control and an easy smile.

'That's the plan,' Rafe said, pleasantly, once again in command of his feelings. 'We're taking him back to the island. We'll be there to help him. He's never good around people he doesn't know. And Alexei's managing some of the detox symptoms in Ganz's IVs, monitoring both the bullet wound and withdrawal with drugs.'

Gora nodded. 'Sounds like he's going to pull through. Once you're back on the island though, think about flying up to Trieste for the day. Your mother would like that.'

'I will, I promise, but my schedule depends on Ganz. There's still bleeding in his liver and no one's told Ganz we're doing an intervention. All hell's gonna break loose when he finds out.'

Gora sighed. 'I don't envy you. I'll tell your mother you sent her a kiss. Call her when you can.'

Rafe grinned. 'You deliver the kisses for me. Thanks again for coming to the rescue. And I'll call Mum soon.'

By the time Gora's jet had moved up the long line of planes on the runway waiting to take off and was finally airborne, Rafe was half way to Dao's house. Simon was driving. Carlos and all Rafe's friends were already on his Airbus. Ganz, the few walking wounded and the medical team were on the medivac plane travelling back to the island. Webster and Gina were on a chartered flight that would drop Gina in Paris, then fly on to England. Leo had flown out with Max; he'd catch a flight back to San Francisco from Hong Kong.

When they drove through the gates into Dao's walled property, Rafe glanced at Simon. 'You coming in? Feel free.'

'Nah.' Simon held up his phone. 'If we're heading back to the island, I'll give Angelina a call. Her teaching job doesn't start for another week.'

'Tell her we'll be there by morning. And consider yourself off duty. Ganz will have enough babysitters.' Rafe had his car door open before Simon came to a complete stop. 'Be back soon.'

A man with a briefcase chained to his wrist had been

waiting at Rafe's plane when he'd stopped there to freshen up. Simon had dealt with the messenger while Rafe had quickly showered and changed. But the stifling air hit him like a blast the moment he stepped out of the SUV and his T-shirt was sticking to him before he reached the front door.

The interior of Dao's home was blessedly cool, the houseboy, long in Dao's employ, greeted Rafe like an old friend. And as he escorted Rafe up the stairs and down a long hallway, he took the liberties of friendship to chide Rafe for involving his mistress in such dangerous activities.

'I've said all that and more to myself already, Ayu,' Rafe noted. 'I'm sorry as hell and I've come to apologize.' He held up the package in his hand. 'My gift of atonement.'

Rafe received a brisk nod.

'Then you're forgiven or semi-forgiven.'

Rafe laughed. 'By you or Dao?'

'By me. Remember, you don't get in the door if I don't open it,' the slender man said without pretence or conceit.

'Then I'd better apologize to you as well,' Rafe said with a grin. Taking a large bill from the roll in his shorts pocket, he handed it over just as they reached the double doors to Dao's sitting room.

Slipping the bill in his pocket, Ayu gave Rafe a graceful bow. 'I'll say a prayer for you at the temple. If anyone needs prayers, you do,' he said with a wink. Then he flung the doors open and announced, 'Mr Rafe Contini.'

Dao was sitting on a sea-green silk chaise near the windows, a light throw over her legs, a cup of tea at her elbow. Looking bruised and battered.

'I'm so sorry,' Rafe said, walking across the pretty sunfilled room. 'I never thought you'd be involved in this mess. I should have known better.'

'*I* should have known better. I've lived in this city most of my life. Everything and everyone's for sale.'

'Still, I blame myself.' Leaning over, Rafe set his small package in her lap. 'An apology gift. It's not enough, of course, for all you went through.' He dipped his head. 'A gesture only.'

'Thank you.' She waved at a chair. 'Sit. Would you like tea or are you in a hurry?'

I'm in a hurry. 'Tea would be excellent,' he said, sitting gingerly on a small, puffy chair upholstered in white silk, while she poured him a cup and handed it over. 'You've seen a doctor?'

She set the teapot down and nodded. 'Nothing's broken. The bruises will heal. I'm glad Zou's dead or I'd have to send someone to kill him,' she said, beginning to unwrap Rafe's gift.

'Gora emptied a clip in Zou's head. He's definitely dead.' Rafe drained his small cup of tea and set the cup aside.

'Did you kill – *everyone*? I'm only asking because Zou had a private hit squad who worked for him on personal matters.'

'We took care of everyone at the compound but some of Zou's troops were still in transit from Bangkok.' He held her gaze for a moment. 'You think some of his private squad are still loyal even after he's *dead*?'

She shrugged. 'It's just a thought. I might do some checking. For myself if no one else.'

'Would you like me to leave some troops behind for extra security? It's easy enough to do.'

'No, I'm increasing my own team. I'll deal with it. If I hear anything though, I'll let you know. If one of Zou's bodyguards decides to hold a grudge, you might be a target as well. You financed this whole mission for Ganz.'

'Crap.' Rafe exhaled. 'Don't tell me it's not over.'

'I'm sure it is. I just want a little more certainty to put my nightmares to rest once and for all.'

'Jesus, Dao,' Rafe said, softly, 'I can't tell you how sorry I am.'

'Zou's to blame, not you. This isn't your fault,' she said with a glance at her bruised arms. 'Now enough about vile men and their vile deeds.' She gave him a playful wink. 'Let's see your apology.' Casting the flowered paper aside, she opened the lid on a mother-of-pearl inlaid box. 'Oh heavens!' She looked up, wide-eyed. 'So many!' She held up a handful of sparkling rubies, then dipped in her other hand and pulled out more.

'It's not nearly enough for all you endured.'

'Everything ended well, darling. That's all that matters.'

She smiled, letting the rubies pour through her fingers back into the box. 'I'll have an extravagant necklace made from these gorgeous gems. Thank you. You've always been a darling man. I hope your fiancée appreciates you.'

'You and me both.' Rafe held up crossed fingers. 'I'm going to call her from the plane once we're in the air.'

Dao's brows rose. 'You expect problems?'

He shook his head. He didn't say Nicole was temperamental, he was temperamental, they hadn't known each other more than a few days, neither of them had ever been in anything resembling a relationship before and other than being mad about her, he didn't know her very well. 'I have to tell her I can't come to San Francisco until Ganz is better,' he said instead. 'She might not like that.'

'I'm sure she'll understand. Now you're excused.' She smiled. 'You remind me of Charlie when he's at one of those dance classes where they teach you how to be polite to little girls. Well behaved but fidgety. Go.' She waved her hand. 'And if your fiancée approves—'

'Nicole.'

'If Nicole approves, Charlie and I will come to your wedding. If she doesn't, I understand.'

'You're a friend. Of course she'll understand.'

'Darling, really, if all your former *friends* were invited, the wedding list would be predominantly female. I'm not sure even a saint would understand. So I won't be offended if I don't get an invitation. You have all my good wishes and you know it.'

'Thanks,' Rafe said, coming to his feet. 'But plan on coming to the wedding. You aren't like my other women friends.' Crossing the small distance between the chair and the chaise, he bent and kissed her cheek. 'And bring Charlie's papa if you like and if he's available. I doubt anyone will know him. I don't think *I'll* know very many people. Nicole's talking about an outdoor wedding somewhere. Hopefully it won't be in the middle of nowhere.'

She laughed. 'And if it is?'

He grinned. 'I'll fucking be there.'

CHAPTER 30

Rafe had the newest Airbus A350XWB for long-range flights. Built of lightweight material that allowed for better mileage, it was a practical purchase considering his heavy travel schedule for Contini Pharma. The wide body allowed for a greater variety of room configurations and if he wanted to be purely selfish, he now had space for an armoured SUV, a necessity in the outlands of the world.

He checked that everyone in the lounge was comfortable, announced that the kitchen was manned and open for the entire flight, pointed out the well-stocked bar and wine cooler, gave directions to the bedrooms. Then he held Carlos' gaze for a moment in silent query but was waved off. Even Carlos was taking some down time, socializing with several of his friends he'd recruited for the mission. After a last scan of the men relaxing with drinks in their hands, Rafe said, 'If everyone's settled in, I have some work to do. See you all when we land.'

'Work my ass,' Henny shouted, raising his spliff. 'Say hi to Nicole from me before you start your phone sex. Otherwise you'll forget.'

'Shut the fuck up.'

Henny smiled. 'I'm done. That's all I had to say.'

'Sleep well,' Basil said, looking up from his phone call with a smile. Now that he was back with Claudine, he was always smiling.

Rafe stood in the doorway to the lounge for a moment after everyone went back to their conversations, watching the various groups dispersed around the large area, grateful no one other than Ganz had been badly hurt, profoundly grateful Zou was dead, happy as hell that he'd soon see Nicole.

Life was fucking good.

And once Ganz was on the mend and drug free, he was looking at clear sailing to the mythical island where dreams came true.

Jesus H. Christ, what the hell had happened?

It was a rhetorical question, he knew the answer: he'd barrelled head-on into happiness. And happiness had a name.

Walking to his bedroom, he shut and locked the door against his inebriated friends who were likely to come knocking in the middle of the night. Being sober and listening to someone high or drunk wasn't his idea of a good time.

Sitting down on the bed, he kicked off his sandals, pulled his T-shirt over his head with a small grunt of pain, dropped it on the carpet next to his shoes, lay back in a careful unrolling of bruised muscles and exhaled a soft sigh. He needed another hit of Oxy but it could wait until he was off the phone. Sliding his cell phone from his shorts pocket, he punched in a number.

Nicole answered sleepily, her soft greeting trailing off in a yawn.

'I apologize for waking you,' Rafe said.

'Rafe? Really!' Nicole squealed, coming awake in a flash. 'I missed you! I missed you! Where are you? When can I see you?'

'I'm on my plane. We just took off from Bangkok. I'll be back on the island in the morning. Where are you?'

'At home.' She pushed herself up higher on her pillows. 'God, you sound good – just hearing your voice and suddenly the world is all sunshine and roses. Funny about that, right?'

'Same here, Tiger. We're good together, sunshine and roses and nothing but blue skies from now on.' Then his voice took on a small gravity. 'You said you were home. Do I dare ask if Isabelle is okay?'

'Dare away. She was released from the hospital today; she's sleeping in the bedroom next door. She doesn't remember the accident but otherwise she's doing pretty well. We're all really grateful. I told you she'd make it though, remember?'

He could hear the smile in Nicole's voice. 'Yup. You're one smart lady.'

'Nah, I just stream ESP with my sister.' She laughed. 'It's our own special magic.'

Her soft laughter warmed him bone deep. She lived life without pretence, her feelings and enthusiasms out there for all to see. 'You're *my* magic, Pussycat,' he said, softly. 'I missed you like crazy.'

She inhaled, trying to keep it together when she missed him desperately. 'Will I see you tomorrow? You have to say yes.' She took a little breath and her voice dropped to a whisper. 'I *need* you to say yes.'

'I can't.'

'Oh God, don't.' She bit her lip, trying to suppress her surge of temper and the countless images of Rafe with women racing through her brain; so sue her, she'd been Googling him, missing him and needing to see him. And now – here he was, living up to his reputation. 'So tell me, what's your excuse? Has the energy sector run out of aviation fuel? An important business meeting came up? Or maybe,' she said, with a little sniff, 'you didn't mean anything you just said to me.'

'No, none of the above,' he said, understanding her testiness; he'd *lived* on excuses in the past. 'It's about Ganz. Hear me out,' he quickly added because the empty hum on the line was ominous. He swiftly explained the situation, how Ganz would die without the intervention, how he needed his friends around him, how he'd come to San Francisco just as soon as Ganz was even semi-stable. He was careful not to mention the bullet wound.

'Oh Jeez, oh God, I'm sorry,' she murmured when he finished. 'You're right to stay, you have to. I understand. But you're not leaving something out, are you?' His heart did a little stutter. 'I mean besides having to stay with Ganz, are *you* okay? I know you can't tell me what you did, but Dominic and Leo were on the phone a lot. I'm nervous that's all.'

Head to toe, his tension faded away. 'No, I'm not hurt.' *Badly.* 'I'm good.'

'Okay, then I'm good too,' she said with a pitiful little sigh.

She was so not good. 'Tell me what I can do to make you feel better. Would you like to come here?' He'd figure out some story about Ganz's wound.

'I can't. Isabelle needs me.'

'So you do understand?'

Another sigh. 'Of course. I just don't like it. You know how long it's been since I touched you?'

'Six days, nine hours, twenty-two minutes. I'm not sure about the seconds.'

She giggled. 'Okay, you pass the love-me-madly test. But word of warning – when you finally get here, I'm going to hang on you like a lemming. Well, maybe more like a fanatically obsessed maniac. I'll have you know I thought of you every second I wasn't busy making sure Isabelle didn't slide deeper into her coma. The first five hours after I got to the hospital, I didn't dare stop talking. Then she moved her finger just a teeny, tiny bit and I knew she'd heard me.'

'That's amazing, Pussycat. She's better thanks to you.'

'Yeah, maybe. Isabelle still has double vision once in a while, some dizziness here and there, but that's supposed to go away eventually. And therapists are supposed to deal with whatever survivor's guilt issues she might have. So tell me again when you're going to be here.'

'As soon as I can.'

'That's not the right answer,' she grumbled.

'I know. But I love you and that keeps me going, gives me hope. Have you decided on the wedding stuff?' he asked, wanting to change the subject.

'No offence, but with your reputation as a player I thought it might be wise to wait until you got here. In case you changed your mind.'

'And?' An ultra-soft query.

'What do you mean and?'

'Come on, we've been crazy about each other from minute one. Player my ass. What's going on? Tell me and I'll fix it.'

After a slight pause, Nicole said, 'Other than having you at my side, I don't know exactly what kind of wedding I want. Isabelle's a great ideas person and planner, but—'

'You'd rather do it yourself. Want me to help?'

'Could you?'

'Sure. How hard can it be? You decide on a venue and if I get a vote, I say Paris. But wherever – your decision. Then you buy a dress, we order flowers, music, a church if you like and run through the friends you actually want at your wedding. My list is small.'

'You make it sound easy.'

'It is. I have buildings full of employees who can discharge whatever duties they're given.'

Nicole softly exhaled. 'There's my mother too. I'm the first one in the family to get married. When I tell her, she might want input.'

'You haven't told your parents?'

'Honestly, you *are* a player whether you like it or not, so I wanted you with me looking like a real fiancé when I gave my parents the news. In addition, when I left the island everyone was getting ready for something massive, clearly you were involved, there was a level of uncertainty to your world that spilled over to mine; another reason I didn't tell them.'

'Gotcha. We'll both tell your parents about the wedding. Now about this *input* of your mother's.' Rafe recognized the unspoken implications in Nicole's comment. 'Want me to talk to your uncle? Tell him it's your wedding day and you want to orchestrate it yourself? He's tight with your mom, right? He can make her understand.' He'd make sure Dominic understood.

'Could you really?'

'Of course.' His confidence was based on past perfor-mance; he'd wielded unlimited authority from a young age.

'I love my mom,' Nicole said. 'She's really sweet, but sometimes she takes her parenting role too seriously.'

'Consider the problem solved. Okay?'

'You're amazing at everything. How do you do it?'

Who the hell else would have if he hadn't. Story of my life. 'Practice, I guess,' he said in lieu of the truth. 'Now, if you want to give me a little reward for my assistance tell me Paris is fine with you for the wedding and I'll have the house decorated for the reception. If the weather's good we can have the ceremony in the cloister. Other-wise in the chapel.'

'You have a chapel?'

'Religious orders generally do, Pussycat. So, done deal?'

'I love being steamrolled by you. Seriously, thanks.'

'Anytime. Speaking of steamrolling, what are you wearing?'

She laughed. 'My Supergirl T-shirt. What are you wearing?'

'Nothing,' he said, unzipping his shorts. 'Why don't you take off Supergirl?'

'Send me a selfie.'

'Fuck no,' Rafe growled. 'You know how many hackers there are in the world?'

'You're shy.'

'No, I'm not shy, I'm sensible. I don't care to see my dick in the tabloids. And don't send me a selfie for the same reason. Now, do you want your vibrator or should we play this game the old fashioned way?' While she was going, 'Hmmmm,' he said, 'It's just getting light there, isn't it? Tell me what you look like.'

'Where?' A playful note in the single word.

A quick breath, a smile in his voice. 'Pricktease. My dick just fucking maxed out. Got a mirror?'

'No.'

'Go get one,' he said with casual authority. 'You have five seconds.'

'Yes, sir, anything else, sir?'

He laughed. 'That must be why I love you. You're clear on who runs the show.' He was sliding his curled fingers lightly up and down his dick – slowly up, then down, unhurried.

'Only when there's something in it for me,' she said, sweet as honey.

'That's what I meant. Now go.'

A breathless little catch in her voice when she came back. 'There, mirror in hand.'

'Good girl.' He traced the solid length of his erection with a fingertip. 'Now find your little clit, I'll wait, take your time, ah – sounds like you found it. Tell me what it looks like. Pink and pretty, ready for some fun?' Reaching down, he cupped his balls, squeezed lightly, softly exhaled.

'I heard that. What are you doing?'

'Getting my dick ready for you.'

'You've done this before, haven't you? Not that you'd tell me.'

'Have you?'

'Is that your answer?'

'You first.'

'No,' she said.

It surprised him how much it mattered. 'Me either.'

'I don't believe you.'

He didn't want to say sex had always meant getting off with a woman you could touch. 'It's the truth.'

'Not even when you were young?'

He never actually was young; he'd missed that stage. 'Nope.'

'Am I asking too many questions?'

'I could say no but my dick's not as diplomatic, so yes. Lie back on your pillows, put the mirror between your legs and describe your sweet pussy to me.'

'You give the orders and I have to obey them?'

'That's how the game works,' he said, mildly. 'Do what you're told, I'll make you feel good. Now, give me a point-by-point, graphic description: all the soft folds and pouty pinkness, your impatient little clit beginning to pulse. We clear?'

'Then I want a visual too. Are you getting hard?'

'Been there since you said hello. And right now . . .' He glanced down at his raging hard-on, the dark-red crest stretched taut, glistening above the softer hues of his painted tattoo –'it looks like all the blood in my body is in my dick.' Flexing his fingers down the wildly pulsing veins, he pressed slightly, stopped breathing for a second.

'So you both miss me? How much?'

Sucking in a breath, Rafe answered, 'He's fucking huge and twitching to get inside your tight little pussy, that's how much.'

You could hear her grin. 'Define huge.'

His grasp had tightened on his erection, his hand moving up and down firmly now in smooth, deliberate strokes. 'More than you can take, Jesus,' he said under his breath. 'Fuck . . .'

'Hey!' She heard the throaty heat in his voice. 'Wait for me!'

He sucked in a breath, loosened his grip, waited a fraction of a second for the shock to clear from his brain, then tempered his voice to neutral. 'Sorry, it's been awhile. Okay, I'll wait. You've been rubbing your clit, right? This isn't all about talking. You have to do some work on your end. Now touch your clit, feather light, up and down, some side to side, slowly now, no rush, then run your finger around that sensitive little bundle of nerves a few times – want me to count?' He laughed softly. 'Sounds like no counting required. Tell me how it feels, Pussycat.'

'Golly gee whiz and a thousand flashing bells,' she breathed all in one word, her body buzzing.

He laughed. 'So we're not wasting our time. I need you to keep stroking your clit until it's throbbing so hard you can feel every pulse beat ripple up your pussy. Then we'll see if you can reach your G-spot. You working your clit now, yeah? Don't stop. I need you slippery wet to take my insanely stiff dick. We're going to have to go real slowly so I don't hurt you. I'm thinking you're going to have to take a deep breath and relax each time before I push in a little deeper. Think you can do that?'

'Love to,' she panted, tracing the length of her slick, swollen clit with her fingertip, feeling the heated flutters shimmer up her sex, her body quivering at fever pitch.

'Okay, let's work on getting you just a little wider, make sure I can fit. My dick is seriously out of control. Two fingers now, Pussycat. Add your thumb, squeeze your clit lightly, not too hard, pretend I'm sucking on it. Can you feel my mouth, my tongue? Hey, you still there?'

She said, 'Here,' in a jagged breath, tense and shaky, compressing her clit with her thumb and index finger, flattening it – a deep groan escaping her at the raw flagrant jolt ripping through her senses.

Sprawled on his bed thirty-thousand feet over the Indian Ocean, Rafe grinned. 'Having fun?'

'Just a little bit,' she purred, as the aftershock subsided.

'Little's not good enough. I need you hotter and wetter

than ever or I won't be able to get my crazy-ass dick in all the way. You're going to have to show me you can take four fingers.'

'Four? I can't!' But there was a sting of excitement beneath the alarm.

He heard it. 'Course you can,' he said, gently. 'Your hands are small.' The fucking hot image of four fingers buried in her cunt sent fresh blood to his dick at warp speed. 'Come on. Give it a try.'

His voice was low and steady like he knew something she didn't. 'So I'm supposed to try to jam four fingers inside me while you're just lying there taking it easy?'

'Nothing easy about my goddamn aching dick,' he said on a soft inhalation. 'My tattoo is laid out flat. If I was there, I'd be doing it for you. Come on, start with one finger.'

She hesitated. 'I'm getting my vibrator.'

'Trust me, you're not.'

'I can if I want.' But her heart beat faster and her body began to hum.

'Sorry, not gonna happen.' No equivocation; he gave orders for a living. 'Now slide one finger all the way up your pussy. Consider this a learning experience.'

'And you're the professor, I suppose.'

'Fuck no. Jesus, I think my dick went limp,' he muttered. 'That's gross.'

She laughed. 'You were awful pretty and sexy as hell

two years ago when I saw you at that Stanford conference.'

'I wasn't your professor,' he said, crisply, 'or anyone's professor. Jesus, talk about putting someone off their game. Fuck, where were we? One finger or two?'

'No fingers.'

'Then you better get your ass in gear,' he growled.

'Yeah, or?'

'Or I'll come without you.'

'No, no, no, no, no!' she shrieked. 'Don't you dare!'

If only she knew what he dared. On the other hand, this was for her, not him. He'd learned long ago to control his dick. 'Hey, relax. I didn't mean that. Becoming a husband is going to be a steep fucking learning curve, so be patient, okay?'

'You too. I'm pretty headstrong.'

He bit back about a dozen unsuitable replies. 'We'll work on it together,' he said, politely. 'Now, do you want me to walk you through this or would you rather fly solo with your vibrator? Seriously, your call. I'm just happy to be talking to you. I can jack off anytime.'

'Do you?'

'What?' he said, instead of answering.

'Jack off often?'

'Sometimes.' He had all the ass he ever wanted. So no was the real answer. 'Want to get your vibrator?'

'Are you changing the subject?'

'Yeah.'

Anything personal and he immediately shut the door. 'Some day you'll have to answer my questions.'

'Okay.'

She laughed. 'But not today.'

'If it's not going to blow up the world as we know it, I'd rather not today.'

'Gotcha. Would you mind talking me to orgasm?'

'My pleasure,' he said, smoothly. 'And, Pussycat, your hands *are* small. It's gonna work out just fine. All you have to do is shut your eyes, and use your imagination, 'cause I'm going to be touching you. Now, we'll take this real slow.'

By the time she was trying to force her fourth finger into her drenched sex, everything in her body was wildly throbbing from her hair roots to her ruby-red toenails. Her hand was wet past her knuckles and all she could hear was Rafe's low quiet voice saying, 'I'm going to put my last finger in so give me a little more room, okay? Can you do that for me? Breathe in, relax, there, that's my girl, I'm almost where I want to be.'

She gasped as her fourth finger slid in.

'Perfect,' he whispered. 'Does it ache a little?'

'Ummm.' A little catch of breath. 'Sorta.'

'It won't for long. You just have a really tight pussy. Spectacular, hot, smooth as silk. I'm going to put my mouth on you right now. See if you're wet enough . . . Oh yeah – definitely wet. Now I'm going to watch you bring your

G-spot to life. Curl your finger a bit, brush that tiny feel-good spot lightly, take it easy, that little baby doesn't like rough stuff. Feels good, right, amazing, beautiful. Slowly now, you're still tight, don't worry, once your pussy gets sexed up, no problem; roll your fingers back and forth, your clit, your G-spot, got it? – back and forth, nice and smooth, velvety, slick, nothing so good in the world as your sweet little pussy wanting some love. Now push into my hand, it's my hand in your aching hotness. Want me to finish you off? Come on, push.'

She whimpered, groaned, pushed.

'There you go, almost there. I can feel your clit's frantic pulse, can you feel my fingers on you?' An inaudible gasping sound. 'Perfect,' he whispered. 'Now we're just waiting for you to come, then afterward, I'm going to spread your legs wide, hold you down and shove my big, stiff cock into your greedy pussy and fuck you hard and fast, caveman, wild, out of control, filling you to the brim with cum over and over again, not stopping. Even when you beg me to,' he said in a low, quiet rasp. 'Got it? I. Will. Not. Stop.'

The hot, brilliant delirium surged, peaked, burst and Nicole's climax broke in a wild, mindless scream that echoed in Rafe's ear, drummed through his senses, struck his long-abstinent libido like a hammer blow. Grabbing his rock hard dick, Rafe jerked himself off in a heart-stopping ten seconds flat. *Fuuuuck.* Like a teenager with his first taste of pussy.

But a moment later, he dragged in a breath, got himself under control; force of habit. 'How do you feel?' he murmured. 'Everything good?'

'I love you to pieces good, all melty and soft.' Nicole's voice was a wisp of sound. 'Hurry, come see me for real.'

'Love you too, every which way. I'll be there as soon as I can. I'm working on it.'

'Good.' Her voice drifted off. 'I'm going back to sleep. You wore me out.'

He smiled. 'Sleep well, Pussycat.'

CHAPTER 31

By the time Rafe said goodbye to Nicole, it was almost eight a.m. in San Francisco. With the Oxy in his system, he was lazy but not in the mood to sleep so he Googled high-end realtors in San Francisco, scrolled through websites and selected a realtor from the area where Nicole lived. Then he called the cell phone listed on the realtor's website.

'Chris Fellows here.' The man's voice was bright and cheery. 'You're an early riser. How are you this morning?'

There was no point in explaining that it wasn't morning in his current time zone. 'I'm fine, thank you,' Rafe said, not as brightly, but politely. 'I'm looking for a house in Cliffside. I'd like a property within walking distance of an address I'll give you. Price isn't an issue. I'll pay cash. Any architectural style will do except for a severely minimalist design. The house has to be available for immediate occupancy. That's about it.'

'Ocean front?' the realtor asked smoothly, cha-ching ringing in his ears; he'd move the owners out himself for a client who wasn't going to quibble over price.

'If possible. No, actually yes, I'd like ocean front. Although I'm in a hurry so if ocean front's a problem, I'll settle for something inland,' Rafe said, changing his mind again. It wasn't as though he didn't own ocean front properties.

'How soon are you looking to move in?'

'Four, five days if all goes well. My schedule is uncertain.'

'Give me your email address and I'll send you videos of available properties. Your phone number too if you don't mind.' Chris was looking at an *unknown caller* ID.

'I'm available at this phone number. Rafe Contini.' Rafe gave the realtor his business cell phone number and Nicole's parents' address.

'I'll get on it right away. Expect a response within the hour.'

'Thanks. I appreciate you taking my call. I know it's early there. But I'm hoping to be in San Francisco soon and I prefer sleeping in my own bed.'

'Cliffside's a nice area,' the realtor said, mildly, as if clients bought houses on the spur of the minute everyday so they could sleep in their own beds. 'You'll enjoy living there.'

'That's what I hear. Ciao.'

Chris was left with a dead line. Not that he cared. Cash.

In that area? He was going to wake up his wife and give her the good news. With this commission she could do the kitchen remodel *and* add a chunk to the kids' college fund. 'Hey, Di, wake up! You won't believe this!' he shouted, walking back into the bedroom from the hallway where he'd gone to take the call so he wouldn't wake her. 'Christmas came early this year and Santa's name is Rafe Contini!'

Rafe stayed awake until the videos arrived, then scrolled through a dozen properties inside and out, selected an ocean front house two blocks west of Nicole's parent's home and called Chris Fellows. 'My banker will handle the paperwork,' Rafe said and gave the realtor a name and number in Geneva. 'He'll wire the money to you as soon as everything's signed. I also have a few small commissions. Hire someone to take care of them and send the invoice to Geneva. Here's what I need.' Rafe gave instructions for a bed to be purchased and set up in one of the bedrooms. To the list of necessary linens, towels, soap, shampoo, he added a number of grocery items for the refrigerator, among them several bottles of champagne – California sparkling wine was fine, he agreed. Also a bottle of Macallan 32. 'I appreciate your patience,' Rafe said when his list was complete. 'Thank you.'

'More than happy to be of assistance,' the realtor said with genuine delight. Contini had given him the name of a personal shopper in the city, mentioned he wanted something substantial – whatever that meant. Expensive, he figured.

'Sundlin will be waiting for your paperwork,' Rafe said. 'He's promised me to return it to you promptly. Thank you again. I'm delighted with the house.' Then he listened politely to Chris Fellows' gratitude, assured him the pleasure was all his and ended the call.

With a major item crossed off his list, Rafe set his phone aside with a sigh of relief. He had a house in San Francisco, or rather he and Nicole had a house; he'd had both names put on the title. Nicole could deal with the rest of the furniture if she chose, if not, someone else would.

Now that the purchase of the house itself, along with some basic household items was in capable hands, Rafe took enough Oxy to push him over into some serious sleep. He hadn't had a decent night's rest since he couldn't remember when.

In the morning, after landing at Split, Davey choppered Ganz and his medical team to the island first, then made additional trips from the airport, ferrying the rest of the passengers who were remaining. Most of the security forces were returning home, only a small contingent stayed behind. In fact, the majority of the tech people had already left when Rafe and Carlos returned to the operations room.

Rafe explained to the skeleton staff that there was a possibility some of Zou's personal bodyguards might still be
active. He'd double-checked the photos of the bodyguards
who'd accompanied Zou to Thailand in the event he'd
missed one when he scanned them on the plane. No, it
was still two dead at the compound. He set the other two
photos aside. 'Make sure all our contacts have these pictures. Tell them we need airports and other transportation
monitored as well as phone calls if they're still using their
phones, credit cards – they might need a car rental. We'll
do the same, but the more people looking the better.' Rafe
scowled. 'They could be anywhere. This is needle in a hay-
stack shit.'

'Only for us,' Jorge said. 'They have targets.'

'Unfortunately,' Rafe said grimly. 'So make sure you stay
in contact with Dao. She's looking for them too and she's
connected.' Rafe surveyed the array of cyber surveillance
professionals and softly exhaled. 'If you need more help,
ask. If there's some niche specialist you know who could
assist, get them here. I want this over yesterday, okay?'

Everyone nodded, but Rafe wished he still had Zander
and Webster. They could both do the work of ten men. He
said as much to Carlos as they walked back to the palazzo.

'Call them, ask them to return,' Carlos said.

'I fucked up their summer holiday enough already. Let's
see if we can manage. Jin worries me more than the other
guy who's older and less likely to be a firebrand. Also, he

wasn't saved from the streets by Zou like Jin. That kind of bond . . .' Rafe blew out a breath.

'Like you and your friends.'

'We were saved in a different way, but yeah. It makes you close, tighter than hell. And Jin could be driving, flying, grabbing sea transport. It's going to be really hard to see him coming if he's on some goddamn mission from God.'

'We're safe here. No one's getting on the island.'

'True.'

'But you aren't staying.'

'No. I wouldn't have even returned if it wasn't for Ganz.' Rafe gave Carlos a flash of a smile. 'I have a hot chick waiting for me in San Francisco and we have wedding plans to make. I just bought a house for her a few hours ago.'

'You really are fucking serious.'

Rafe looked surprised. 'You doubt my sincerity?'

'Not any more,' Carlos said with a roll of his eyes. 'A wedding, a house, you'll be a daddy soon.'

'No I won't.'

'Don't be so sure. Nicole has managed to turn your life upside down. She might not be in complete agreement with you when it comes to babies.'

'Jesus, Carlos. Stop. No one's talking about babies.'

'Fine.'

Rafe scowled at him. 'Goddamned right it's fine.'

Rafe might be surprised to find Nicole had a different

viewpoint on babies, Carlos reflected. Particularly when she was a woman with firm opinions of her own, came from a large family and happened to be at loose ends right now, according to the dossier he'd been sent. 'By the way,' Carlos said, moving to a more agreeable subject, 'Gora just texted. Saxe reversed Zou's wire transfer to the Dubai bank. The fifty mil's back in your Geneva account.'

'Great. Thank Saxe and give him a bonus.'

'How much?'

'Ten per cent. Hell, I probably should give him more. He saved us a ton of money. Make it twenty per cent. He deserves it.'

Carlos laughed. 'You bought yourself a friend for life.'

Rafe gave Carlos a sideways glance. 'Please. The man's for sale to the highest bidder.'

'Such a cynic.'

'Yeah, I know. What a fucking shame the world isn't all sweetness and light.'

For the next five days everyone rallied around Ganz, keeping him company when he was awake; even when he slept one of them stayed with him in case he woke up and needed company. Alexei had a large-bore IV in Ganz so the fluids he needed would run faster and also an arterial catheter in his other wrist to monitor his heart rate and blood pressure. Ganz needed drugs to lower his heart rate as he came off cocaine, but the pressure couldn't go too low or it would adversely affect the bleeding in his liver. So Alexei's treatment was a fine balance between controlling the bleeding and managing Ganz's withdrawal symptoms.

Rafe and Nicole talked on the phone whenever they could, although Nicole was as busy with Isabelle as Rafe was with Ganz. Isabelle had to be driven to physical and occupational therapy every day, the therapist every other day and she preferred Nicole's company at home as well. No one thought it strange. The two girls had always been close. They watched TV, movies, read, talked about Isabelle's slowly returning memories of the accident, had friends over occasionally as Isabelle's health improved. They also discussed the wedding, although Isabelle was pledged to secrecy until their parents were informed.

Isabelle initially had asked if the engagement was for real and Nicole had given her an affirmative answer. But as Rafe delayed his departure and their separation persisted, Nicole's doubts surfaced.

'Rafe's unpredictable schedule is another reason I'm not telling Mom and Dad about the wedding until he arrives. Just in case,' Nicole said, lounging in a chair in Isabelle's room late one afternoon.

Sitting cross-legged on her bed, Isabelle grinned. 'In case he finds someone else in the meantime.'

'Thanks, that's really helpful,' Nicole muttered. But a moment later, she sighed. 'It's not just Rafe. Sometimes

I wonder if I'm being stupid about this. I've only known him a few weeks. How serious can it be?'

'You mean you've never given a damn about a guy before and you're not so sure you know what you're doing.'

Nicole grimaced. 'I wouldn't say that exactly, but—'

'You've never had a clue about love.' Isabelle put up her hand. 'I can attest.'

'Maybe no one does until it happens. Still . . .' She took a small breath. 'When I'm in this limbo, I have doubts. What if I change my mind later? What if Rafe changes his mind? It's all happened so fast. How do I know for sure that our for ever is the real forever?'

'You could ask Mom. She and Dad are still in love.'

'But I'm not a bit like Mom,' Nicole murmured. 'Not even close.'

'You could ask Dominic. He likes to be boss all the time, same as you. And look what happened to him. He loves Kate like she's his whole world. He might have some good advice.'

'He already gave me his advice. He told me to dump Rafe.'

Isabelle laughed. 'Ordered you, you mean, and we know how that turned out. So, okay, we'll just figure it out ourselves, weigh the pros and cons – come to a logical conclusion. To begin with, you think about Rafe twenty-four/seven, right? Second, you practically glow when he calls. And third, you're all starry-eyed when you get off the phone. Not to mention, he's rich, gorgeous, smart. Are there any cons?' Isabelle paused for a moment. 'Voila! – done deal.'

Nicole sniffed. 'Don't forget all the women.'

'Hel-lo,' Isabelle countered. 'You should talk. You've had a few boyfriends.'

'Not like Rafe. You'd need a database to keep track of his playmates.'

'Hey, people change. You did. You're like a lost puppy when he doesn't call and a space cadet when you're thinking about him – which is all the fucking time. You almost drove us into a cop car the other day. And it was parked. So I'm asking you – has anyone else ever made you feel like you do about Rafe? Giddy, wildly delirious, dizzy with love?' Isabelle stared at her sister for a moment, then spread her arms wide. 'I rest my case.'

Nicole smiled. 'It is a pretty nice feeling.'

'Exactly,' Isabelle said, as though concluding the argument. 'So who cares what you call it when he makes you feel that good. Call it love, chocolate cake, Hindu Kush. He's your one and only gift from the gods. Don't question it, embrace it.'

Nicole grinned. 'Embrace it? Are you going out with that massage therapist again?'

'I will once I can see straight again. He's sooo hot.' Isabelle grinned from ear to ear. 'Did I say he was a massage therapist?'

'Only about a thousand times. He is cute.'

'Cute? I'm sorry, cute? He's six foot five of super-toned flawless male. Bunnies are cute. Bax is magnificent.'

Nicole lifted her brows. 'Everywhere?'

'Goddamned right, everywhere. He has tattoo sleeves though . . . ' Isabelle gazed at Nicole from under her lashes. 'Unlike your fiancé. Don't look so surprised, the rumours are all over the net. No pictures, but . . .' Isabelle gave her blonde curls a little shake. 'Everyone knows Rafe's got an inked dick.'

Nicole laughed. 'Okay, I'll embrace love, fulfilment, the beauty of the universe, the meaning of life, the perfection of tantric sex – what else does Bax talk about?'

Isabelle winked. 'Sometimes he doesn't talk at all. He just moves real, real slowly so every nerve in your body is just waiting for him to slide in that final—'

'Okay, that's enough. We have to change the subject or I'm going to need some me time with my vibrator.'

Isabelle held up her hand. 'Stow that thought. We're going to watch that Netflix series, the one with the gladiators in the skimpy outfits.' She grabbed the remote. 'That'll be almost as much fun.'

On day six after their return to the island, Alexei finally gave Rafe the news he'd been waiting for.

'Ganz's liver is on the mend. He hasn't had any bleeding for two days and his vital signs are approaching normal.

Lucky for him the peripheral areas of the liver aren't as difficult to heal. And the transfusions helped. I'm going to take out his IV later today.'

'Will he swallow his detox drugs?' Ganz had been getting Ativan through his IV.

'This is where those therapists Basil knows come in. They've been sitting around doing nothing; now they can start their sessions. And I'm here to remind Ganz that his body can't take any more coke. So you can say your goodbyes anytime. Ganz will be fine.'

Rafe waited until Alexei had removed the IV lines and monitors before he carried in a new top-end laptop. Ganz was sitting up in bed, thinner, paler, but on the road to recovery. 'This is one of the first ones off the line,' Rafe said, setting the sleek aluminum piece of hardware on Ganz's lap. 'Have fun.'

Ganz ran his fingers over the smooth metal, lifted it to gauge its feather-light weight, looked up and smiled. 'A new kind of fun?'

'That's what everyone's hoping. Your old kind of fun was killing you – and not slowly. We all want you to be happy, but maybe pick another way, okay?'

Ganz arched a brow. 'You're not gonna say I did it, you can too?'

Rafe shook his head. 'Doesn't work that way. You have to find your own way out of hell.' Rafe grinned. 'Speaking of ways out, Alexei says you're fit enough for company.

Not us, we don't count. Good company. Madeline's on her way here. Davey picked her up a couple hours ago. Ha! Now there's a fucking smile.'

'Thanks, Rafe.' Ganz's smile faded and his voice hushed. 'Thanks for everything. For Madeline now, for always being there when I got out of hand, for stepping in and saving me from Zou.'

'I didn't exactly save you,' Rafe murmured. 'Rat bastard shot you anyway.'

'Still, I owe my life to you.' Tears welled in Ganz's eyes.

'Hey, I owe my *company* to you,' Rafe replied. 'I wouldn't have a single drug formula left, present or future, without you stopping those assholes' attacks. Twelve times, don't forget. I should probably give you a partnership,' Rafe said, smiling. 'Seriously, you can have a piece of the action if you want. I mean it.'

Ganz smiled back. 'If Zou hadn't made me rich as hell, I might take you up on your offer. But you know he gave me that bundle of money when I left the unit.'

Rafe was pleased to see Ganz smile. 'I remember. So he wasn't all bad after all,' Rafe quipped. 'Although with the fortune he's left around the world, feel free to add to your exchequer. I was thinking his wife should have some, although that might not be very easy to accomplish. Certainly his son who's out of the country, at Oxford, could be a recipient. And maybe the nice young lady who had to pretend to be Zou's mistress all those years. That should be

335

worth some combat pay. What do you think?' Rafe wanted to distract Ganz. His emotions were clearly shaky as hell, his body struggling to regain its equilibrium. He needed a task to occupy his mind. 'I'd like you to think about disposing of those funds. Some charities of your choice as well. There's a fuck load of frozen assets in all of Zou's secret accounts. More than enough to benefit a whole lot of people.'

Ganz laughed. 'Smooth, Contini. You keeping me busy?'

'Preferably twenty-four/seven, dude. That's what it's gonna take to break the cycle. Let Madeline help. You said she's as good a hacker as you. Fuck, with Zou's money, you two could make some major changes in the world. So think about it, that's all I'm saying.' He deliberately made no mention of Jin. Ganz didn't need any further anxiety when he was going through withdrawal. And Carlos would take care of the island. Ganz was safe.

Ganz leaned back against this pillows. 'I'll give it a go. I like the idea of payback. Madeline can help too. It'll be super-nice to have her here. Henny says you've been missing your babe too, chafing at the bit.'

'Henny's right about missing my babe. But I'm in no rush. Nicole's busy helping nurse her sister back to health.'

'You really in love?' Ganz looked at Rafe, puzzled.

'Pretty much. No one's given me a definitive run down on love so I'm not sure about the details but, so far, it feels really fine. Like I got it right. I bought a house in San Francisco,' Rafe added. 'Didn't even question the impulse.'

'I don't suppose I'm allowed to suggest there's a sexual subtext to that impulse.'

Rafe gave him a steady look. 'No, you are not.'

Ganz raised both his hands, and smiled faintly. 'Then I am witness to an end of an era.'

Rafe knew what he meant, but his voice when he spoke was without humour. 'It lasted long enough . . . ' His voice trailed off, ruinous memory pulsing through his senses, cruel and pitiless. 'Too long.' He stopped to breathe, back in the past.

Rafe's naked regret was extraordinary. Clearly he was a man in love. 'You have my permission to go,' Ganz said.

Rafe's head came up sharply, his gaze ablaze. 'I don't need your permission. Oh fuck.' He blew out a breath. 'Sorry.' Another half second to gather himself, then a last flash of anger in his eyes. 'My fucking old man has a lot to answer for. But it's no excuse. I shouldn't have—'

'Forget it.' Ganz smiled. 'We've known each other a long time. I'm on a first name basis with your fucked-up psyche. And you with mine. But seriously, why don't you go to San Francisco? See your new house, your new fiancée. Madeline will be here soon and then I won't have time to talk to you anyway.'

'You sure? I have no problem staying as long as you like.'

'I'm sure. Go. You don't have to take care of everyone all the time. It's been a lot of years. Go take care of Nicole.' Ganz grinned. 'Or try. You have to admit – part of her charm is the fact that she says no to you more than she says yes. You love it. It's like having a sparring partner twenty-four/seven. A beautiful one you can f—' Rafe's sharp look stopped him.

'I'll give your regards to Nicole,' Rafe said, pleasantly. 'And if you fall off the wagon, I'm coming back and personally beating the shit out of you. Consider me your worst nightmare, okay?' He gave Ganz a hard, steady look. 'Now be good.'

Ganz shot Rafe a teasing glance. 'I'm getting stronger. Pretty soon I'll be able to take you on.'

'Lots of luck with that,' Rafe drawled. 'Now eat, take your meds, sleep well and say your prayers. God will save you.'

Rafe was halfway out the door when the book Ganz hurled at him whizzed by his head.

'Practise,' Rafe shouted as he raced down the hall. 'I'll be back.'

CHAPTER 32

Nicole had said she and Isabelle were going to their friend Maddy's birthday party at a bar in the city. Isabelle had been given permission by her doctor to attend so long as she promised to simply sit and observe the celebration. It was a family party: Maddy's parents, Nicole's parents, her aunt and uncle and other close friends of Maddy's mom and dad. Cocktails, dinner and opening presents were planned for the family festivities in the dining room. Later, the young crowd would arrive to party at the bar. A band was scheduled to begin playing at nine.

Rafe had heard all the details from Nicole over the past few days and he'd flown in to surprise her. But he was the one surprised when he walked into the downtown bar. Instead of the semi-sedate family affair he'd envisioned, the scene was a wild, raucous blow-out. Rafe recognized the band, famous for their music and their groupies; they'd just come off a world tour. His scowl had been in place since he'd walked through the door and was stopped by the wall of ear-splitting, lyric-screaming music. Jesus, they were dragging some woman down off the bar, the watching bartenders grinning up a storm; the dance floor was a writhing mass of bodies engaged in various forms of dry fucking and if there was anyone over thirty in the room, he'd personally hand them a million.

Family party, my ass.

His scowl deepening, he scanned the dimly lit room looking for Nicole. The half-dressed, sweating musicians on the stage were rockin'; the bar was elbow to elbow with beautiful people knocking back booze, the tables, ditto. He checked out the banquettes but couldn't see anyone resembling Nicole, although he knew Isabelle had blonde hair. Christ, he'd never seen so many blondes.

He began a second, slower scan of the room and almost hidden from view so he'd missed it the first time, at the very end of the bar Rafe glimpsed a familiar fishtail braid. The woman's back was to him, so he couldn't see her face, but the second she leaned over and kissed the man beside her, he launched himself forward, ploughing headlong into the crowd, pushing people aside, spilling drinks, leaving a trail of ticked-off people behind. Then Nicole stepped back from the bar, half-turned and a moment later disappeared down a corridor with a neon flashing sign above the entrance indicating the bathrooms.

What the *fuck* was she doing kissing some guy?

With half a room of solid people still in his way, Rafe continued to shoulder a path through the crowd. A couple of women squealed when he picked them up bodily and lifted them aside, but he swept past them a second later, immune to their caustic comments. Just as he escaped the last press of partygoers and reached the corridor, he caught a glimpse of the tag end of a fishtail braid swing out in a little arc and disappear through a doorway.

He was breathing hard when he reached the bathroom. And seriously pissed.

The corridor was quiet after the noisy crowd in the bar. Taking out his cell, Rafe called Simon who was waiting in the car, explained where he was and what he needed. 'Then come down here,' he said. 'I want you to run interference.'

While waiting for Simon, Rafe turned away a number of women wanting to use the bathroom. 'Sorry, it's under repairs,' he said, super-politely. 'Water on the floor. There's another bathroom near the dining room.' Then he'd smile and point; Simon had texted directions after talking to the bar owner.

Rafe counted the women exiting the bathroom, playing the percentages most would leave before Nicole. She'd gone in last.

When Simon arrived a few minutes later, Rafe relaxed. 'The owner good?' he asked. 'No problem shutting down one of his bathrooms?'

'No problem. You told me not to quibble on price. I

didn't. The guy said you can set up Housekeeping in there for that amount of money.'

'Thanks, well done.' Rafe nodded at the bathroom door. 'I'll get rid of whoever's left inside. Don't let anyone else in.'

'Got it.' Simon's brows rose faintly. 'Some family party.' Rafe had given him the party specifics per Nicole's description on the drive into the city.

'No shit. Makes you wonder what it's like when it's not a family party. Davey outside with Carlos' crew?' Jin had been sighted at the Tokyo airport a few days ago. Carlos had sent reinforcements.

'They're on watch. Along with Leo, so Dominic's around somewhere.'

Rafe grinned. 'Then I'd better see if there's a lock on the door.'

'Not a bad idea. But don't worry,' Simon said, firmly. 'No one's getting in.'

'If I have to hustle some women out, they might be spitting nails. Calm them down.'

'Doubt I'll have to. If anyone can sweet-talk a woman, you're the man.'

Rafe took a deep breath, slowly exhaled. 'Fuck. Life's getting way the hell too complicated.' A wave of disbelief rolled over him. 'I remember when I didn't give a shit.'

'Yeah, major changes. Higher highs, lower lows, but the rush is worth it.'

342

Rafe gave him a quizzical look. 'You too? Angelina?'

'Getting there.' Simon shrugged. 'Maybe. I'll let you—'

A woman suddenly walked out of the bathroom and both men stepped aside.

'Pardon me,' Rafe said, quickly. 'I'm waiting for my girlfriend. She's been in there a while. I'm wondering if she's okay. Long dark hair in a plait, bright-blue eyes, semi-tall.'

'I didn't see anyone. But there's a small lounge in back. She could be there.'

'Thanks.' A charming smile. 'Friend of Maddy's hey? Nice party.'

'I haven't seen you before.' The shapely blonde examined Rafe in a slow head-to-toe survey, as though he was for sale and she was buying.

'Just got into town. Distant cousin,' Rafe said, giving Simon a veiled look that said, get her the hell out of my way.

Pulling a flask out of his jacket pocket, Simon lifted it. 'Would you care for a drink?' he asked with a boyish grin. 'It's from my family's distillery in Scotland.'

'Ooohh,' the pretty blonde purred, clearly impressed with the scent of money. 'I'd *love* a drink.'

Rafe slipped into the bathroom before the woman finished purring. The elegant white marble, chandelier-lit room with mirrored walls and a line of sinks in startling flamingo pink, was empty. But Rafe peered under the stall doors too, just in case. Also empty. Shooting a look at the archway that presumably led to the lounge, he gambled on Nicole being alone, moved to the outside door and quietly turned the lock.

Game on.

Leaning back against the secured door, he slowly counted to ten, told himself to calm down, don't do anything rash; there could be a perfectly good reason for that kiss. But a little voice inside his head snarled, *Bull . . . shit*, so it took another ten count before he had himself under control. Although a muscle was still twitching in his jaw as he pushed away from the door and walked across the bathroom.

He came to a stop in the archway.

And there she was.

Even in the ever-changing tangle of his thoughts, he was grateful.

She was alone. Slumped in an upholstered flamingo-print chair, head thrown back, eyes shut, her arms resting lax on the chair arms, her long legs stretched out in front of her. She wore a blue and white striped silk T-shirt tucked into a belted blue and white silk jacquard-print skirt he didn't recognize. He'd seen the blue platform heels before. Alessandra had sent them from Rome.

'Bonsoir,' he said, quietly.

At the sound of his voice, Nicole's eyes snapped open. 'Rafe!' she cried and began to rise.

He held his hand up. 'Not yet, sit. I have a question. Who were you kissing?'

She sank back down. A blush rose up her neck to her cheeks like a flaming mark of infidelity, he thought, and an unprecedented sense of betrayal washed over him.

'I don't know who he was.' Unsettled by Rafe's chill, watchful gaze, she shoved her hair behind her ear in a small, restless gesture. 'Some friend of Maddy's from UC Santa Barbara.'

She was nervous but at least she hadn't lied. Maybe he should be grateful. 'I suppose the next question then is, why?' he asked, soft as silk.

She didn't answer for a second, not wanting to make excuses with Rafe's hard gaze on her. 'I felt sorry for him. His friend was needling him about how he couldn't get a woman. So I said, "I think you're cute," and kissed him. That's it. Don't be mad.'

'A pity kiss for someone you didn't even know.' His voice was no more than a whisper. 'But then you're into strangers, aren't you? That's how we met.'

'No. You're wrong.'

He smiled a smile without humour. 'Are you going to kiss guys you feel sorry for after we're married?'

'No!'

'Why should I believe you?' He paused fractionally. 'I flew in for this party and thought I'd surprise you and instead . . . ?' Rafe spread his hands. 'Here you are, surprising me.'

'I'm sorry I kissed him. I'm sorry you saw it. I'm sorry

you're pissed.' Nicole took a breath, not sure how to go on when he stood there unmoving, filling the entrance to the lounge: tall, powerful, his dark hair loose on his shoulders, his booted feet firmly planted, the silver grommets running down the front of the black leather boots strangely mesmerizing. As if they symbolized the magnetic strength and spirit of the man.

She wanted to say, *You look beautiful, you always do.* Even casually dressed in black slacks, a white T-shirt with a faded red drug logo and a lightweight black topcoat, he was breath-taking. But instead, she said, 'Don't just stand there. Say something, please. Talk to me.'

'Do you like the band?'

The question startled her, the forbidding look in his eyes made her cautious. 'They're okay.'

'They fuck a lot of women. They actually compete amongst themselves. Weekly prize for the most ass.'

Her gaze sharpened. She'd done nothing wrong; you either stood up or you didn't. 'Is there a point to this conversation?' she asked icily.

He stared at her. 'The point is, I'm viciously jealous,' he said, irritably. 'I wish I wasn't. It disgusts me. But I am, so even though I know how hypocritical it sounds, I don't want you looking at a band that fucks their way through every town on their tour. I don't want you touching another man. I don't want you kissing anyone – pity kiss, air kiss, nothing. You touch only me, you kiss only me.'

Admittedly, the raw emotion in Rafe's words was satisfying; she too was unlikely to share the man she loved. But there was a price to be paid for such unlimited authority. 'I don't know if I should be flattered or angry. It sounds as though you want to own me.'

'Let me make it clear,' he said, flatly. 'I do.'

'You understand it's no longer the Middle Ages,' she noted, sardonically.

'Certainly. Just so long as you understand you're mine,' he returned, ignoring the self-contradictory statement. 'Not just a little. Not just sometimes. Not just when you're in a good mood. Always.'

She bristled, her temper like a force of nature. 'I'd expect the same total commitment from you.'

'I haven't kissed anyone but you since Monte Carlo. If only you could say the same,' he drawled. 'So I'll require a renewed commitment from you – verbally.' She was sitting up straight now, her snapping gaze trained on him, the flush on her cheeks not from guilt, but the familiar one he liked. She was fighting back. He put his hand to his ear and smiled faintly.

'I shouldn't,' she muttered.

'Why the fuck not?' His smile disappeared. 'I'm in this for ever. I need the same from you.'

She stared, her eyes throwing off sparks. 'Are we negotiating?'

'If that's what you want to call it. I prefer capitulation.'

She was up on her feet in a flash and coming at him like a fierce little wildcat. He caught her hands easily as she lunged at him, shoved them behind her back and dragged her close. 'Now then, Pussycat,' he said, smiling again, the feel of her – soft and scented, the mythical girl of his dreams – crushed against his body like coming home, 'tell me what I want to hear. Tell me you're mine.'

Her lips twitched, a tiny smile appeared, then a big, proper smile broke. 'Okay, I'm yours. But it's not capitulation. I hate that word. It's a mutual agreement. By the way, you feel really good, divine, heavenly hot,' she added at the last in a low, sexy murmur, moving her hips gently against his rising erection. 'Could we get out of here?'

'No problem.' His dick seconded the motion, swelling larger. 'I bought you a house in Cliffside. We could go there.'

'Okay, wait, what?'

Her wide-eyed, open-mouthed surprise was worth the price of the house. 'It's down the block from your parents. So you can walk over and visit your family when you want. I had a bed set up, but otherwise it's damned empty. Your voice echoes.' He'd showered and changed there before coming to the party.

'Really? You're not kidding?' Tiny breathless queries.

'Nope. This is really for ever for me, Pussycat. No changes, no going back, no reorgs or modifications. I'm in this for the long haul.' He lifted a brow. 'Your turn.'

She smiled. 'I hope you know what you're doing because you're never getting rid of me. I want you for myself; no one else gets to touch the merchandise.'

'We understand each other then,' he said simply. Dipping his head, he kissed her gently, sealing the deal. 'Now, introduce me to your parents.' He released her, stepped back and took her hand. 'We'll make this official. I want you to stay with me tonight ... ' He tilted his head. 'If that's okay with Isabelle.'

Nicole squeezed his hand. 'It'll have to be all right. I'm not letting you out of my sight. But seriously, she's feeling fine. The doctor just doesn't want her drinking yet.'

'Makes sense.' He picked up Nicole's small purse from the chair and slipped it in his coat pocket. 'I'll follow you. Lead the way.'

Her parents were in the dining room, seated at a table with Dominic, Kate and the birthday girl's parents. A few other guests were at a small bar that overlooked a decoratively lit courtyard, but most of the parent contingent had left.

The dining room was largely empty, so the instant Nicole and Rafe entered the room, they were immediately the focus of all eyes.

'Christ, now I know what it feels like to walk to the guillotine,' Rafe teased.

Nicole gave him a little smile. 'I wonder if Dominic said something?'

'I'd say likely from the stares.'

When they reached the table, Nicole smiled at her parents. 'Mom and Dad, may I introduce Rafe Contini, Rafe, my mom and dad, Melanie and Matt. I met Rafe in Monte Carlo a few weeks ago and he was with the holiday group in Croatia too. He just flew into town.' She leaned into his arm. 'It was a nice surprise.'

'It's a pleasure to meet you, Mr and Mrs Parrish,' Rafe said, with well-mannered smile.

'You know Dominic,' Nicole said, with a little wave at her uncle.

'Yes.' Rafe nodded and received a cool nod in return.

'And this is Kate, Dominic's wife,' Nicole went on, quickly, recognizing Dominic's moody frown.

'I've heard such good things about you.' Kate smiled warmly. She and Nicole were confidantes; she knew about the engagement. 'Dominic told me about your lovely Adriatic home,' she added, not wishing to embarrass Melanie, who was clearly surprised at her daughter's new boyfriend.

Nicole introduced Maddy's parents next, then an awkward silence fell.

Never at a loss in social situations, Rafe was about to make an innocuous remark about San Francisco, when Nicole squeezed his fingers hard and took a quick breath. 'I have some other good news.' She held up her left hand. 'I'm engaged, or rather, Rafe and I are engaged.' She gazed up at him and smiled. 'We're very happy.'

'Ecstatic,' Rafe said softly, smiling down at her, not caring about the silence, the astonished looks, Dominic's frown. 'I bought Nicole a house in Cliffside,' he added, looking up. Taking note of Nicole's father staring at him as if he might raise some objection, he said, simply, 'We hope to marry soon.' He glanced at Nicole. 'We do, don't we?' Putting his arm around her shoulder, he pulled her close.

She looked up, startled and pleased. 'If you want to.'

He nodded, and for a moment they were alone in the room. 'I do, very much.'

'Well,' Melanie said, softly. 'What a surprise.'

'Where in Cliffside,' Matt asked, gruffly.

Rafe turned to Nicole's father. 'I forget the exact address. The realtor referred to it as the Merchants' house.'

'Nice place.' Matt turned to his wife. 'It's close by, Mel,' he said, taking his wife's hand and smiling at her.

Nicole softly exhaled, understanding her father had given his approval.

Recognizing he'd passed at least Nicole's father's inspection, Rafe said, 'I was hoping Nicole could find time to furnish it. It's standing empty.'

'My goodness,' Melanie said. 'I saw the Merchants pull into their driveway just a few days ago.'

'Chris Fellows, the realtor who handled the sale, didn't mention any of the moving arrangements,' Rafe said, smoothly.

Don Merchant, however, had mentioned them at the yacht club, Dominic reflected. So Rafe was the buyer who'd insisted the house be vacated immediately. Not that Don had minded. He'd been given an extra ten per cent mark-up for moving out quickly. 'Are you in the city long?' Dominic asked, his gaze unreadable. Leo had heard the rumours about Jin.

'I'm hoping to stay for a week or so. Nicole and I have to coordinate our schedules.' Rafe looked at her. 'School starts soon, right?'

'I could go to school in Geneva.'

A smile lit up his face. He hadn't wanted to ask. 'I'd like that.'

Nicole turned back to her parents who, each at their own pace, were digesting their daughter's unexpected news. 'We're going to go now. I'm staying at *our* house tonight,' she said with a quick grin for Rafe, taking the world in stride with her usual unequivocal confidence. 'I'll stop and see Isabelle on our way out.'

'I think we'll leave now too,' Dominic said, wanting to talk to Rafe about Jin before he left. 'If that's okay with you, Katherine,' he added smiling at his wife.

'I'm ready.' Getting to her feet alongside her husband, she gave a little wave to their hosts and Nicole's parents. 'Thank you, it was a lovely party. But the children get up early.'

Dominic and Kate were a dozen yards behind Rafe and Nicole when they exited the dining room.

'I have a few questions for Rafe,' Dominic said.

'I must be a mind-reader.' Kate's tone was light. 'I could tell. Also, Leo's here tonight. Something's in the air.'

'Nothing for you to worry about.'

Kate smiled. 'What makes you think I'm worried?'

Dominic shot her a narrowed-eyed look. 'Cute. There's Contini.' Rafe and Nicole were within a few feet of the banquette where Isabelle sat. 'Come on, this'll just take a minute. You can visit with Isabelle.'

'Thank you, sweetie, but I'm not one of your employees. I don't need instructions.'

'Sorry.' Dominic grinned. 'I always forget you're the boss.'

Kate laughed. 'Don't worry, I'll remind you.'

Dominic and Kate were making their way through the crowd when a waiter carrying a tray suddenly dropped it; drinks spilled, glasses fell to the floor, partygoers jumped out of the way. As a space opened up around the man, he flung away the towel on his arm, swung up the Chinese-type 54 semi-automatic pistol in his hand and aimed it at Rafe.

Rafe heard the low mumbled curse in Mandarin as if a moment of silence had materialized in the vibrating waves of music and, in a single uninterrupted flow of motion, he shoved Nicole aside, spun around, slid his hand under his coat, grabbed his Glock from his waistband in back, ripped off the safety and fired.

Three shots exploded, the sharp retorts blasting through the music.

The waiter slowly crumbled to the floor, a star-shaped hole in the back of his head, his right eye blown out, brains and bone fragments misting the shrieking guests in bloody carnage.

The third round had smashed into the wall, the thirty-eight super-cartridge punching a hole in the concrete.

Leaping into the expanding gap around the fallen man, Rafe stood astride the bloodied form, weapon drawn, until the body stopped twitching.

The band had fallen silent, people were pouring out into the night, the party literally exploding with gunfire.

A few feet distant from the corpse, Dominic was staring at Kate as she slid her handgun back in her purse. 'What the fuck?' he growled.

'Gramps said only if you have to,' Kate said, calmly, snapping the closure shut. 'This was one of those times.'

'I meant where the *hell* did you get that Beretta?'

'Max.'

His scowl deepened. 'You're kidding.'

'I'm not. Could we talk about this later? Someone should call the police.'

Leo, Simon, Davey and Carlos' security team were already moving people aside, cordoning off the area around the dead man. Pocketing his Glock, Rafe returned to Nicole and, pulling her into his arms, bent his head so their eyes were level. 'I'm sorry you had to see that,' he murmured. 'You okay?'

She nodded.

'Want me to call a doctor? I didn't bring Alexei with me. Give me a name and I'll get someone here.'

'No doctor,' Nicole whispered.

Concerned with her dazed look, he asked, 'Want your Mom?'

She shook her head.

'Can I carry you out of here? I'd really like to,' he added, not sure she heard him.

Instead, she said, slowly, as if unlocking some mystery, 'Is this part of what you were doing on the island?'

'The very last part. It's over now. Word of God,' he said because she was trying not to shake. 'Come on, let's go.' He waited until she nodded, then picked her up in his arms, met Simon's gaze and beckoned him over with a lift of his chin. 'Have Davey escort Isabelle to her parents. She's the blonde in the red dress over there. The Parrishes *were* in the dining room. If they need to be driven home, have Davey do it. We have enough cars, right?'

'Plenty. I'll let him know. You stay in here until I bring the car up.' Simon held Rafe's gaze, his meaning clear: *Don't come out, I'll come in to get you.*

'Will do,' Rafe said, then glanced at Nicole. 'You gonna make it?'

She made a pathetic attempt at a smile. 'As soon as we get out of here I'll be fine.'

'Simon will have the car waiting in just a few minutes,' he promised. 'Can you hang on a little longer? I'd like to thank Kate before we go.'

Nicole dragged in a breath, rallied enough to quip feebly, 'Just don't ask me to be witty.'

He brushed her nose with a kiss. 'Thanks, you're a trooper. I'll make this quick.' Rafe carried Nicole to where Kate and Dominic were standing just beyond the cordoned-off area. Dominic was on his phone. Rafe spoke quietly to Kate. 'I just wanted to say thanks. Appreciate it.' He would have said more if Nicole wasn't there. But he didn't want to upset her.

Kate could read between the lines. 'Glad I could help,' she replied in the same mild tone. Everyone hadn't had a grandfather who'd been a legendary sniper like she had. Firearms could be traumatic to those unfamiliar with them.

Dominic finished his call. 'Leo will take care of things here with law enforcement,' he said, sliding his phone into his jacket pocket. Targeting Rafe with a glance, he said, 'Nicole looks a little pale. Why don't I tell her mother you took her home?'

'Thanks, that'd be great. Nicole will give her mother a call later.' Rafe dipped his head, held her gaze. 'Right? In the morning?'

'Right, the fuck after you *explain* all this to me,' she said, tartly.

Rafe grinned. 'There's my girl. Back in the game.' Although when it came to an explanation, she'd be getting the sanitized version.

Nicole turned to Kate. 'You're going to have to take me to your target range. Apparently, I have to learn some new skills.'

'No!' Rafe and Dominic said in unison.

Nicole sniffed. 'They like to give orders, don't they?'

Kate winked. 'Best to ignore them.'

But later, once Kate was sleeping, Dominic called Max.

'I should fire you,' he growled.

'You saw Kate's Beretta.'

'I also saw her blow off the back of a guy's head.'

'She's good, isn't she,' Max said, unfazed. 'She's better than any of us.'

'I still should fire you for not telling me,' Dominic muttered.

'You might have to run that by your wife first,' Max drawled.

'Shut the fuck up.'

'Hey, relax. Kate knows what she's doing. She's not going to shoot her foot off.'

Dominic dragged in air through his teeth. 'When would you have told me?'

'Come on, Nick, don't put me in the middle. She wanted a weapon. She knew that you were always caught up in some shit. You can't blame her. And look,' Max said with a chuckle, 'if you ever need a freelancer in a pinch you're sleeping with one.'

'Fuck you. I'm taking that Beretta away from Katherine in the morning.'

Max was still laughing when Dominic hung up the phone.

CHAPTER 33

Simon parked the car in front of the sprawling Mediterranean-influenced, California-style house, then came around and opened Rafe's door. 'Everyone's back but Davey. We'll keep an eye on things tonight.'

'Sorry about the sleeping conditions,' Rafe said, stepping out with Nicole in his arms. 'We'll get everything in shape tomorrow.' The security crew was sleeping in the pool house.

'Hey, we've all seen worse. Not a problem. Unlike the bush, we have take-out here.'

'I left a couple of things in the car,' Rafe said, cryptically, moving toward the front entrance. He'd set his Glock and extra mag on the floor.

Simon nodded. 'Got it.'

'I'll talk to you in the morning. Late, probably.'

'Anytime. We're not going anywhere.' Simon reached

359

the entrance first, punched in the code and pushed the door open. 'Sleep well, guys.'

'Thanks, you too.' Then Rafe stepped into the large foyer and kicked the door shut. 'I'll carry you over the threshold officially later when we don't have an audience,' Rafe murmured. 'Or if you want I'll go back out and, no?' Nicole was shaking her head. 'So what can I offer you? Want something to eat, want the grand tour, a glass of champagne, or—'

'I'll take the or,' she interrupted with a tiny smile.

'There you go,' he murmured, walking toward the broad carpeted staircase. 'We've always agreed on that.'

'Nice, hey?'

'Nothing nicer.' He suddenly stopped and gazed down at her, his brow furrowed, as if he'd forgotten something. Then his smile suddenly blazed, beautiful and clean. 'I've never been so happy, never even knew I could be this happy. You and me in our own house. I get to come home to you every night, walk in the door and, hey, don't cry, come on, life's good, everything's gonna be perfect.'

'I know,' Nicole whispered, her eyes suddenly bright with unshed tears. 'But do you ever worry that it's all going to slip away? That something might happen to steal our happiness.' *Like tonight*, she thought but didn't dare say it. The man posing as a waiter had come to *kill* Rafe.

'No, never,' he answered, rapid fire and sure. 'We, us, the soon-to-be-married, deep-in-love us is *forever*. And,' he added with a flashing grin, intent on diverting her fear, 'you might want to think about taking cooking lessons because my coming-home-every-night scenario has my wife serving dinner to me.'

Nicole giggled. 'With my hair done and makeup on.'

'Apparently we saw the same old TV shows,' he murmured, pleased to see her playful again. 'Although in a modern version, I could bring home take-out and we could eat in bed.' His leer was pure farce. 'Afterward.'

'Goddamn, I'll marry you right now.'

'Sex and food, I'll say, when they ask how I got you to the altar.'

'In that order please,' she said, sweetly.

'Yes, ma'am,' he drawled. 'Let me show you my bedroom.' He took the stairs two at a time, then walked down a long corridor and entered an enormous room with a window wall facing the bay. 'Voila, Pussycat! That's what we see from our bed.'

Lights sparkled on the opposite shore, ships with their running lights on were moving out to sea, the Golden Gate Bridge blazed and sparkled far to the right.

'Feel like home?' There was a tenderness in his voice. 'I thought you'd like something in your neighbourhood.'

'It couldn't be more perfect. You're going to make me cry again. You're so good to me.'

'Uh-uh, other way around. I never knew what goodness was until you came into my life.' He took a small breath because he never cried and damned if he was going to now. 'We just lucked out, you and I,' he said in a different tone of voice, light, teasing. 'I think it was your killer body in that blue flowered bikini that day on the yacht. Blew my mind.'

'You have to hold me.' Her voice was thick, a flicker of distress in her gaze.

'I am,' he said, his voice soothing.

She shook her head. 'That's not what I mean.' She was restless, agitated, needing reassurance that the events of the evening were outliers. 'I need you in my arms, me in yours, the warmth of your body close to mine.'

'Ah . . . let me see what you think about the bed, then,' he said, knowing she was asking him for oblivion from the horror she'd witnessed. Moving quickly from the doorway, he strode across the room. 'If you don't like it, we'll move the bed to another room.' He spoke mildly, as if they were actually having a conversation. 'The realtor and some personal shopper picked it out.'

'I don't care what the bed looks like. I just want you to distract me in all my favourite ways or your favourite ways – I'm not fussy just so long as it's five minutes ago.'

He smiled. 'You're feeling a little better?'

'Not quite good enough *yet*.' She was tempted to talk about why she was shaky, but it was pointless; he'd be evasive about the killing. 'I'm guessing you can remedy that,' she added, going with Plan B in lieu of full disclosure.

He laughed. 'Sounds like I'm on the clock. Give me a second.' Placing her on the bed, he turned on the bed-side lamp, shrugged out of his topcoat, looked around for someplace to toss it and hung it on the spiral bedpost. 'Seriously, we need some furniture. Put it on your list.'

'*Our* list. I have no idea what you like – in furniture,' she added at the delicate lift of his brows. 'This is nice though.' Lying back against the pillows, Nicole stroked the blue flowered quilt.

'I may have mentioned to the personal shopper that you have blue eyes and you had a blue flowered bikini that I liked.' Unbuckling his belt, he stripped it free and dropped it to the floor. 'You standing in the doorway of my stateroom that first day is one of my all-time favourite memories.'

'I remember you were wearing khaki shorts, nothing else and looking good enough to eat even with Sylvie glaring in the background.'

'Who?' He turned from shoving his wallet in his coat pocket.

'God I love you.'

'Same.' He smiled. 'Maybe a little more, but I'm bigger, so it's allowed.'

'Speaking of big.' She raised her hand slightly and pointed.

'He really likes you, what can I say?' Moving to the edge of the bed, he held out his hands. 'Sit up, Pussycat. I'm going to undress you very, very slowly because it's been almost two weeks and I've been dreaming about this.' He didn't say that thinking about her had been his salvation crammed in that small metal box in Thailand. Nor would he ever.

But he kissed her gently after he pulled her up into a seated position. 'I've missed you,' he whispered, 'more than you could ever know.'

'You were gone too long,' she murmured, her heart in her eyes.

Standing upright, he nodded. 'Won't happen again. I promise.'

'Good.' She was mollified by his blunt absolutism, cheered as well. He saw the world as his to command; there was safety in that. 'I'm really glad I'm going to school in Geneva.'

'Not as much as me,' Rafe said, tugging her T-shirt free of her skirt. 'There are no words.' Then his eyes flared wide as he pulled her silk T-shirt over her head. 'A bra. That's new.'

She wrinkled her nose. 'My mom. She doesn't like to see my nipples showing or my boobs bouncing. She says it's unladylike.'

Rafe grinned. 'Unladylike?'

'I don't suppose that word's familiar to you.'

He looked amused. 'Is there a correct answer? Give me a hint.'

'Fuck you.' But his lazy smile was firing up all her hot and heavy party zones.

'No problem there,' he drawled, as though he hadn't noticed her catch her breath. 'Come on, stand up first. I've never had the pleasure. I'll bet your panties match.'

'Christ, are you a voyeur?'

'I am with you.' He lifted her bodily from the bed, unbuckled her belt and stripped off her skirt in two seconds flat, then stood back and whistled softly. 'Very nice. Is that lace blue or black or what?'

'Blueberry.'

His brows rose. 'Sweet. We should get you strawberry, cherry, blackberry, chokecherry, whatever.' His voice drifted lower. 'You have the nicest tits, Pussycat, seriously, best ever.' He sucked in a breath, shifted his stance as his erection surged. 'Sorry, it's been a while,' he murmured, sliding his fingers down the prominent bulge straining the fabric of his slacks, pushing his dick over a little to give it more room to expand. A quick smile. 'Obviously, he's missed you.' Then he lifted his chin. 'Do me a favour. Walk to the windows and back.'

Lacing her hands on the top of her head, she offered him a centre-fold pose, a flicker of a smile on her lips. 'Then you'll do me a favour?' She nodded at his crotch. 'I need to feel your humungous dick deep inside me.'

'Lucky him,' he murmured, smiling faintly as his cock punched up higher. 'He'll give you all the favours you want, anywhere you want, as long as you want.' He lifted his finger and twirled it. 'But first – give us a little show.'

Nicole wiggled her hips in a delectable little grind, then blew him a kiss, turned and walked to the windows.

'You tease, no guarantees,' he gently said. 'After almost two weeks I'm on a tight leash.'

'No need for that,' she tossed back over her shoulder. 'It's been two weeks for me too.'

'Good news,' Rafe murmured, dropping down on the bed, quickly unlacing his boots, kicking them off, pulling off his socks and jerking his T-shirt over his head. 'I was thinking I might have to take it down a notch.'

Turning to face him, Nicole smiled. 'That won't be necessary.' He was all lean, hard muscle, sleekly modelled down the length of his torso, his arms resting on the bed, powerful and strong. Feeling her body open in welcome, a lush heat lick at her senses, she stirred, antsy and aglow, wondering how many women had seen him like that – naked, at ease, impossible to resist. 'Take off your slacks,' she said, a new testiness in her tone.

Living the life he had, he was pretty much immune to female pique. 'Sure.' He leaped to his feet, comfortable in his own skin, not a prudish bone in his body, his openness bought at a price so long ago it seemed natural. He unbuttoned, unzipped, slid his slacks and boxers off, and kicked them aside. 'You need anything else?' he drawled.

A small flash of resentment narrowed Nicole's eyes. 'You've said that a lot?'

He could have asked her something equally snarky. She was every male fantasy come to life in her *blueberry* scraps of lace. 'I'll say it as often as you like,' he replied, not answering her question.

She raised her chin slightly 'One more thing. How you'd get that nasty scab on your arm?' His entire right forearm and a portion of his upper arm had been scraped raw. The reason, no doubt, for his long-sleeved T-shirt.

Knowing an explanation would be required, he'd already decided on a story. 'Stumbled coming off the helicopter. Tired, I guess. It's healing.'

'You don't feel like telling me.'

He sighed. 'I would if I could. It's over.' He held out his hand. 'Come on, we're on our pre-honeymoon. I'm going to make you feel good, you're going to make me feel good and when we finally collapse . . .' He smiled. 'I'll recite some Hafiz in your ear. Deal?'

A smile slid across the corner of her mouth. 'No one negotiates like you, Contini,' she murmured, the prickle gone from her voice at the incredible sweetness of his offer.

'And no one but you, Miss Parrish, is worth memorizing eight pages of Hafiz.'

She giggled. 'Wow, eight pages?'

'Parts of the ninth too. That's how much I love you, Pussycat.' He started to raise his hand to beckon her forward, but his heart beat suddenly quickened at the irresistible little wobble of her barely covered tits; a spiking surge of lust ripped through his senses, and a gut-deep, chafing resentment too headstrong to deny, reminded him that any man who saw her, naked or not, would feel the same. Like the man she'd kissed at the party, or maybe it had been *men* plural she'd kissed before his arrival, an unhelpful little voice pointed out.

Let it go, he told himself, dropping his hand back on the bed. So she was stupefyingly desirable, all soft curves, sumptuous tits, long legs, hot cunt; she was his. *Except maybe when he wasn't around.* Seriously, how well did he know her?

He was frowning when he summoned her back with a flick of his finger. 'This way now, nice and slow.' But a flash of temper lay beneath his quiet utterance, a tiny whiplash of sound.

She didn't move, offended by the casual flick of his finger, by the naked reprimand in his voice. 'I should say no.'

He didn't answer for so long, she wondered if there were limits to his love, whether she'd drive him away. If even this extravagant house could be jettisoned for the sake of his resentments.

His gaze, focused somewhere beyond her head, finally slid back to her face, his voice when he spoke, was restrained. 'You probably shouldn't.'

Her brows lifted faintly. 'Equivocation? From you?'

'Courtesy.' His smile was fleeting. 'Now are we going to continue this conversation or . . .' He beckoned again. 'Can we move on?'

She remained utterly still. 'If you have some problem, why don't we talk about it?'

'No thanks,' he said, gruffly.

'Or I could go downstairs until you get over your sulkiness.' She smiled tightly. 'Rudeness, whatever.'

'No you couldn't.'

'No? Should I call for help?' She indicated a phone on the floor where a desk might have once stood.

'The phones aren't hooked up yet.'

'I have my phone.' She gestured at his coat on the bedpost.

'Think you can reach it?' he said very softly.

She sighed. 'Look, we might as well talk about what's on your mind or you're never going to stop being an asshole. You're still pissed about me kissing Maddy's friend, aren't you?'

'Partly.' He exhaled softly. 'And all the men you might kiss in the future.'

'Do you know what Isabelle and I talked about most?'

That tone of voice in a woman made him automatically wary. 'I have a feeling you're going to tell me.'

'We talked about how you might find someone else and not even come to San Francisco,' Nicole said, as if he'd not spoken. 'How you viewed women as entertainment, how a man like you isn't likely to change, how everything's happened so fast maybe we'll both realize we've made a mistake. What do you think? You're the poster boy for unreliable; should I be pissed too?'

His hesitation was minute, then he asked, 'Have you? Made a mistake?' She didn't answer for so long, he was thinking about getting up and locking the bedroom door.

Finally, she said very softly, 'No.'

His eyes drilled into hers. 'Louder.'

'No,' she repeated sharply, as sullen and moody as the man watching her intently. 'Satisfied now?'

He drew in a very slow, deep breath, then exhaled. 'You can't ever leave me,' he said, bluntly. 'I won't let you.' He shut his eyes for a moment and when he opened them a flicker of anger still shimmered in the amber depths. 'Look, I wish I was better at this, more reasonable, conciliatory. I *am* sorry for being such a dickhead but . . .' He shrugged. 'I love you so much – too much, I think sometimes. My jealousy borders on manic. So I can apologize but I can't change how I feel. I'm obsessive about you in a seriously fucked-up way.' He blew out a breath, opened his mouth to speak, shut it again, then said, 'What the hell, I might as well say it. If someone had told me I'd feel this way about a woman, about you in particular, that I'd be married soon, not a decade or two from now, but soon, I would have asked them what they were on. So give me a little slack when I'm struggling with the . . .' He stopped and spread his hands.

'Scary-as-hell future with me?' she contributed with a grin.

'You're such a bitch,' he said with an answering grin. 'But yeah, you nailed it. Jealous, crazy in love and not a clue.'

'Same.' She gave him a considering look from under her lashes, then smiled. 'We're lucky though. Lots of people never have the crazy in love.'

'The luck I understand. As for the rest,' he said, thinking her smile alone was reason for living, 'we'll just have to work at it till we get it right. Now, please,' he added with great gentleness, 'come closer and tell me what I can do for you.'

Even had she not been deep in love, his charming offer and breathtaking beauty would have been enough to overwhelm her with longing. He was smiling faintly, leaning back with a careless grace, his weight resting on his hands, his legs slightly spread, his colourful, inked dick arched high against his stomach. 'That's mine,' she said on a small caught breath, moving toward him, pointing at her all-time favourite Hokusai reproduction tattooed on Rafe's rampant erection. 'Nothing on this planet is hotter and I want it.'

He smiled at her breathy fervour. 'Any special place?'

'I'll show you,' she whispered, starting to slide her fingers under the blue lace of her panties.

'Come here,' he said, quietly, sitting up and pointing at the floor between his legs.

She crossed the small distance that separated them, restive, hot-blooded, mesmerized by the tossing boats and foam-flecked blue waves undulating on Rafe's massive, surging dick. 'And I don't want to wait.' A heated flutter slid up her spine. 'You hear?'

'Just a little longer, Pussycat,' he replied, calmly, slipping her tiny lace panties down her thighs and letting them drop to the floor. Leaning over, he lifted one of her feet, then the other, tossed the bit of blue lace aside, then sat up and smiled. 'Comfortable?'

'I'm not looking for comfort,' she said on a suffocated breath.

'Come on,' he murmured, running his hands up the outside of her thighs. 'It's always better if you don't rush.'

'I'm not interested in patience either.'

He laughed. 'You're so fucking adorable. Seriously, you have no sense of recall.'

She glared at him. 'I haven't had as much practice.'

True that. He smiled faintly. 'How about we practise together?' Taking her hips in his hands, he pulled her close, dipped his head, slid his tongue into her slick heat, gave the little nub of her clit his full attention until it was rock hard, then sat back and watched her shiver under his hands. 'Actually, we have all the time in the world now,' he said, issuing his fiat in a silken murmur, his demons never completely locked away, 'because I'm never letting you go.'

'Do that again,' she whispered, immune to fiats with flame-hot bliss strumming through her body, and the focus of her world centred on the jolting rapture pulsing through her clit.

His long lashes drifted upward and Rafe gazed at her from under their dark fringe. 'Let's give this a try first.' Sliding his hand between her legs, he parted her pouty folds, slipped one finger inside her velvety, soaking-wet pussy, then a second, reaching deep into her sleek heat, gently stroking the slippery flesh, the rough little patch of her G-spot, the hard, swollen length of her clit until she was squirming, panting, desperate, until his fingers were drenched.

'Please, please, I can't wait,' she panted, her body on fire, her skin flushed, ravenous desire scorching her brain.

'Ready to move on?' he murmured, not really expecting an answer. Cupping one of her ass cheeks with his free hand, he hauled her close, bent low, gave the tender skin of her inner thigh a quick nip, marking his territory. Then, fractionally easing aside his two fingers sunk palm deep in her melting hot pussy, he shoved his tongue way the hell up her silky wetness and hit her G-spot. Pow.

She whimpered, her knees went weak. Rafe caught her weight with his hand spread wide on her ass and glancing up, checked to see whether she'd reached the point of no return. Not yet, he decided, adept at reading female arousal. With her firmly in his grasp, he returned to the molten heat beneath his tongue, measuring her throbbing clit with slow, leisurely licks, up and down, around and around while she moaned and quivered. And when his lips finally closed over her hard clit and he gently sucked, she grabbed his head and frantically whispered, 'Please, please, please.'

Leaving his fingers in place, he shook his head free and looked up. 'I have a request.' he said, continuing to massage her slick tissue with casual expertise. He waited for what he considered a polite interval as she trembled under his touch, eyes shut and whimpering, then withdrew his fingers.

Her eyes snapped open. 'What are you doing?' Feverish, shuddering, so damned close she could see nirvana, she grabbed his wrist and tried to jerk his hand back.

'I have a request,' he repeated, peeling her fingers off his wrist.

'Could it wait?' she snapped, planning vengeance for this torture right *after* she came.

'No.'

'God, Rafe!' she wailed, squirming, impatient, overwhelming lust spiking through her senses. 'Don't *do* this. I don't *want* to wait.'

'You never do,' he said. 'Show me your breasts.'

She froze, struggling to understand, her frenzied desires

at odds with his cool demand. 'Jesus,' she exploded, frustration blazing in her eyes. 'Here, dammit!' She swung her arms open wide. 'Take a good look!'

He sucked in a breath, the word 'opulent' always completely inadequate when it came to Nicole's tits. The blueberry lace bra – two scant half-cups held up by ribbons – was filled to overflowing with her pale mounded breasts, the ribbon straps barely supporting the sumptuous weight.

With considerable effort, Rafe tamped down the jealous fiend inside him that regarded both her and her tits as his personal property and spoke, softly. 'Now I want to see your nipples.'

She shivered, blew out a shaky breath. 'If I do this, do I get your dick?'

'Here's what I need you to do,' he said, ignoring her question. Sliding one finger under the scalloped border of one lacy half-cup, he pushed up her nipple so it was visible above the lace. 'This little baby is stiff,' he murmured, stroking the distended crest, taking the tip between his thumb and forefinger, squeezing gently. 'But then you're always ready to fuck, aren't you?'

A piercing sensation raced downward from the pressure of his fingers on her nipple, further ignited the fierce throbbing between her legs, and she whimpered in soft, breathless appeal.

'Uh-uh,' he said, running his palm over the swell of her

breast. 'Show me your other nipple first.' He pinched her exposed jewel-hard crest hard, watched it swell, watched her quiver under the rough treatment. 'Do it now,' he said, a sudden harshness in the voice, 'or you won't get my dick.'

The distinct threat of withdrawal, the bitterness in his tone jerked her out of her carnal haze as effectively as an ice-cold shower. 'How much longer am I going to have to pay for that stupid kiss?' she hissed.

He dropped his hand, sat motionless. 'I don't know.' He took a deep breath because he'd never experienced such uncompromising feelings. 'I wish I did. It would make the next fifty years a helluva lot easier.'

Suddenly aware of the huge changes he'd made in his life for her, ashamed of what she'd so thoughtlessly done, even more frightened he might decide to stop loving her, she whispered, 'Oh God, I'm so sorry. I'll make it up to you. I promise.' She readjusted her bra, covering herself, as though niceties of decorum mattered. Then she searched his face, wanting to know his thoughts, so she could make him understand how much she regretted her actions. What she'd naïvely viewed as casual, was of marked significance to him.

He didn't speak for a long time and when he finally did, he said, simply, 'You can't kiss anyone but me. If you do, I can't promise I'll be sensible.'

'I won't, not ever. And I'm not just saying it because you not being sensible is supposed to frighten me.'

'It should,' he said, darkly.

'I understand. But I love you and you love me and that can't just stop – can it – because I did something thoughtless?' Her voice was grave, intent, as though this was a test she dare not fail; she wasn't sure he might not get up and walk away. 'I didn't know how much my kissing that guy bothered you but now—'

A blazing amber stare hit her so hard she flinched.

'Now that you know,' Rafe said, finishing her sentence, each word raw-edged and gritty, 'we'll have to find some salvageable area of agreement because, gun to my head, I'll never love you sweetly. I love you gut deep and burning hot with a mammoth side of crazy and that's never going to change.' He pinned her with his gaze. 'So take it or leave it.'

'I'll take it,' Nicole said, her smile breaking like sunshine after a storm now that she knew he was going to stay. 'But on that same street of crazy love, I have a ground rule or two myself. If I ever find you with a woman, I won't wait for some bullshit explanation about we're just friends, or I bumped into her at the grocery store. I'll do violence to the bitch first, then to you. Kate's going to teach me to shoot. So you better be scared.'

Rafe laughed. 'Goddamn you're high maintenance, Pussycat, but worth every second of angst. I don't go to grocery stores though.'

'Then I'll have to take you, show you how the rest of

the world lives.' She smiled. 'At least we'll never be bored, right?' Taking his face in her hands, she leaned over and taking charge, crowded in close and kissed him, teeth and tongue, hard and deep.

Her fine, lace-wrapped tits pressed into his shoulders were a fucking bonus and he was smiling when she relinquished his mouth. 'I'm guessing it'll be pretty tough being bored with the mind-blowing, breath-stealing, world-shattering sex.' Pulling her down on his lap, he unhooked her bra. 'Now, one last question before my focus goes all to hell – when do you want to get married? I have to tell some people in Geneva I might be taking off a few days.'

'Depends on how nice you are to me now.'

'Tomorrow then. I intend to be excessively nice to you tonight.' Dropping the bra on the floor, he lifted her up, repositioned her on his lap so she was straddling his thighs, facing him, and gave her butt a little slap. 'Up a little.' But he helped her to her knees, smoothly eased his dick into place, circled her waist with his hands and kept her from taking a kamikaze dive.

'Hey,' she pouted, fighting against his restrictive hold. 'Are we ever doing it my way?'

'Sure,' he murmured, forcing her to descend slowly.

'Liar.'

'I just have a better memory than you. There now,' he said as she finally settled on his thighs, completely impaled on his dick and uttered a blissful sigh. 'Admit it, every sensation is purer, sharper when you slow things down.'

She raised her lashes enough to take in his smile. 'At the risk of augmenting your considerable ego, you might be right this once. Although it could just be your really huge cock that makes it so goddamn good.' She moved her hips in a slow undulation, shut her eyes and softly groaned.

Closing his fist around her braid, Rafe tugged, forcing her head back so his gaze was full on her face. 'Tell me it's not just sex,' he whispered, when a good deal of his life had been about sex, when he had more reason than anyone to be sceptical, because he'd never been in love before and it mattered. 'Hey, look at me.' Whether he was testing her single-minded focus or his control, he flexed his hips, thrust solidly, powerfully upward.

She gasped at the fierce, stabbing pleasure, the dizzying sensation brought the world to a stop and, a moment later, when Rafe said, 'Answer me,' she panted, 'What?'

Clearly she wasn't capable of an extended conversation right now. 'Simple question. Are you mine?' Maintaining the tension on her plait, he rocked gently from side to side, slowly, slowly, magnifying the taut, blissful pressure, casually eliciting the answer he wanted. 'Say it.'

The riveting sensation of his erection cramming her full, her distended flesh pulsing and throbbing under Rafe's delicate shifting movement, obliterated all but a sliver of rational thought. 'Yes – is that right?' she breathed.

'Pay attention, Pussycat.' He forced his cock higher, deeper, gaining her attention in one area at least. 'I want you to say, I'm yours.' And arching his back, he pushed into her that last shocking distance more where the world disappeared and the drama of life was purified into a single moment of all-consuming ecstasy.

'Yes, oh God, oh God, oh God, I'm yours!' Her rush of words rose into a wild cry as her orgasm slammed through her body, clawed through her senses, jolted her brain with such intense, unbridled pleasure that her cry at the end turned into a shrill, ear-piercing shriek.

A few moments later, his ears ringing, a smile on his face, Rafe released her braid, bent his head, lowered his mouth to her, whispered, 'Thank you,' and kissed her slowly as though committing the satisfying moment to memory. Then, no longer prey to inchoate resentments, he lifted his head, brushed Nicole's flushed cheek with the back of his fingers and smiled a warm, unhurried smile. 'Now, how many more times would you like to come?'

'God, you're a Neanderthal. Although,' she murmured, with a flicker of a grin, still drifting in a soft, sensual daze, 'that's not all bad. And I'll let you know when I've had enough, okay?'

He laughed. 'My darling no-limit girl.'

Moving her hips gently, she winked. 'So, I'm getting my way?'

'Absolutely,' he said, his smile brilliant. *And I'm getting mine.*

Rafe brought her up to climax so fast, she gasped and was still basking in the tremulous afterglow when he fell back on the bed, rolled her under him without dislodging himself and took them both over the edge that time with the practised virtuosity of a man who'd done this once or twice before. Her fourth and fifth orgasm followed in quick succession, the fifth for both of them again and still on a roll, it took a few moments before he registered that the pounding on his chest was Nicole's fist. He looked down. 'What?'

'Do you mind?'

His heart was hammering like a son-of-a-bitch, his dick was rock hard, his libido was telling him two weeks had been way the hell too long; he needed a second to replay her question in his mind. Didn't help. 'What the hell does that mean?' he muttered, balancing lightly above her, trying his damnedest to be polite.

'It means I'd like to introduce myself. Nicole Parrish and you are?'

He locked it down in a nanosecond, rolled off her and lay in a sprawl, breathing hard. 'I know who you are,' he said to the ceiling.

Sitting up, she stared at him. 'Then I suppose the next question is: do you care who I am?'

He turned his head and tried not to look at her awesome boobs. 'Jesus, Tiger, give me a break. I missed you like hell, okay? It's been at least two shitty weeks and you said no limits. So you changed your mind, I get it. We could reschedule and watch TV if we had one.'

'You're pissed.'

'You stopped me at a fucking inconvenient time.'

'Sorry.' It was going to take her a while to forget the scores of women with Rafe in all the tabloid photos, like he was going to have to forget about the guy she'd kissed. But at least his explanation for his non-stop screwing agenda made sense. 'Let me make it up to you.'

'It's okay,' he grunted. 'I'll live.' But a moment later, he felt her fingers trace a slow path up his dick and living became a whole lot better. Then he felt her lips slid over the head of his erection, brush over the swollen, sensitive rim and the world turned golden. His fingers threaded lightly through her hair as she drew his rigid dick into her mouth and every muscle in his body relaxed.

When she heard his soft sigh, she almost stopped to ask, 'Feeling good?' But obviously he *was* feeling good, so she concentrated instead on seeing how much of his fine tattoo she could swallow. Considering the huge un-inked crest of his erection was an added extra to the colourful artwork sliding toward her throat, she remembered it was half at best. In his more-bossy-than-usual mood tonight, she thought about asking him if half was okay but decided against it. He was kinda softly purring now, the throaty resonance coming from deep in his chest, so everything was probably going well for him. Such a nice sound; she hadn't heard it before; part growl, part mellow. Like a big jungle cat having his dick sucked. She'd have to ask him about that feeling later too. Really, she had a ton of questions. But, right now, she'd better concentrate. He'd just made her come five times. The least she could do was pay him back once.

Wait, what? He was slowly unbraiding her hair. Talk about multi-tasking, because he was beginning to breathe hard now too, and his stomach muscles were doing that little flutter that meant he was getting where he wanted to go. Okay, now, take a big breath, relax, see how deep you can take him.

She choked.

He laughed. 'Thanks for trying, Pussycat.'

She looked up at him, mouth full, her brows raised halfway between a query and a frown. But then he slid his hands over her cheeks gently and set the pace. In her current accommodating mood, she jettisoned all irrelevant thoughts, and paid close attention to the rhythm. There was another question she'd have to ask later. Did he have a preference?

It was fortunate she didn't ask because Rafe couldn't have said – twenty or so out of fifty or more options. He also couldn't have said he really didn't care one way or the other. He absolutely could not have said there had been a woman once in Japan he'd never forget. But the Japanese experience had been about technique not love. Nicole did this for love and that made it the best ever.

He said as much afterward. Then he lifted her up on his chest and added, 'You didn't have to swallow. I wouldn't have minded.'

'I wanted to,' she replied, smiling with a trickle of cum on her chin.

He found some towels stacked under the bedside table, wiped her mouth, wiped himself, pulled her back into his arms and said, 'Seriously, that was stellar, Pussycat. Thanks so much.'

'You're welcome.' Her smile was sunny and warm. 'It was my fault you were left, well . . .'

'Not a problem. We have a lifetime to figure out who likes what, when. Yeah?'

She nodded, the solid feel of his hard, muscled body beneath her, his strong arms holding her close, was unalloyed happiness. Life was sweet. 'Tell me we can just stay here for ever,' she whispered. 'Like for a thousand million years.'

He smiled. 'Whatever you want, Pussycat, it's yours.' He could do that too; he could give her anything. 'For instance,' he added, softly, brushing her lower lip with his finger, 'whenever you're rested up, just let me know. It's your turn again if you're interested.'

Was he a mind-reader or what? 'You don't have to.'

He laughed. 'Jesus, so polite. What happened with, "Hey, it's my turn first"?'

'It's just that you're making a lot more changes for me than I am for you. I feel I should be more appreciative and understanding.'

'If making changes is code for all the women, forget it. You found me or I found you and I couldn't be happier. You know how close we were to never meeting?' He held up his hand, his thumb and forefinger only a sliver apart. 'Like that. I was getting bored that day at the party. There was a good chance I would have gone ashore within the hour. You saved me and I'll be forever grateful.'

She smiled. 'So I'm your angel of mercy?'

'No, you're my pain-in-the-ass angel, but I love you for it. You make my life interesting in a whole lot of good ways,' he added, reminded of the various ways his life was *interesting* in negative terms – his recent trip to Thailand a case in point. 'So what do you say? Feel like screaming the house down?'

'How did you know?'

He grinned. 'It's a gift.'

Much later, after numerous orgasms, after an impressive recitation of Hafiz poetry, they were lying in bed, the debris of the picnic food Rafe had ordered, as well as an empty bottle of sparkling wine and a half-drunk bottle of Macallan pushed to the foot of the bed.

'Happy, happy?' Rafe murmured, holding her in the crook of his arm.

'Times a gazillion,' Nicole whispered, reaching up to brush his cheek.

'More.' Contentment echoed in Rafe's voice.

A small silence fell.

'What about children?'

No matter Nicole's voice was pitched low, it burned into Rafe's brain like white fire. He tensed. 'What do you mean, what about children?'

She moved a little, propped her chin on his chest. 'That's not an answer. That's another question.'

'I don't know how to answer.' He remembered Carlos asking about children. Maybe he should have read the dossiers on Nicole that Gora and Carlos had assembled. On the other hand, he was the last person in the world who wanted to dwell on the past. Count his goddamn blessings, that was his mantra.

'Come on, relax,' Nicole said. A tiny smile. 'You must have some opinion.'

Relax, my ass. 'How about I don't want to think about it?'

'Then the decision is mine?'

'No, I didn't say that.' He felt like he was walking a tightrope without a net. 'Look, we have a wedding to plan. First things first, okay?'

EPILOGUE

Paris, the night before the wedding

Rafe sat up in bed and stared at Nicole. 'You could have told me what you were going to do,' he said, trying to keep the fury from his voice.

Nicole came up on one elbow and stared right back. 'You might have said no.'

'Damn right I would have.' He jerked the sheet up over her nakedness; his life was being blown to shit. He didn't need the distraction.

'Then see. I was right.'

His nostrils flared. 'As in?'

'*As in* I wouldn't be pregnant if I'd told you I was going off my birth control.'

He was trying hard to hold it together, but he felt the world shifting under his feet. 'Jesus, are we ready for this?'

'I am.' Nicole's voice was smooth and easy, like her

smile. 'And you don't have to do anything. Your job is done.'

He lifted one brow. 'You gonna eat me now like some of those insects do?'

'I could eat you if you like,' she said with a flirtatious little grin.

His hooded gaze darkened. 'Don't fuck with me. I'm not in the mood.'

'I'm sorry,' she said, unintimidated. 'But you never would have said yes. You've lived a different life. Children weren't something you'd miss. They'd never been part of your world. You know I'm right.'

He was watching her, cool and unblinking. 'Out of curiosity. Why didn't you wait until after the wedding?'

'You mean once I'd snared you?'

'Yeah, that's what I meant.'

Her eyebrows pulled together just a touch. 'Let me ask you this? Do you love me less now that you know?'

He took his time before he answered; you could practically see the struggle going on. 'No.'

'Then there's something else I have to tell you.'

His head came up as if he scented danger. 'Are you okay? I mean other than . . .' He jabbed a finger toward her stomach.

'I'm fine, but . . .' She took a small breath, then sat up.

He didn't even notice the sheet falling away; his pulse was spiking, his heart suddenly drumming in his chest.

Something *was* wrong. What if he lost her? He couldn't bear it. His life would be over. Scooping her up in his arms, he dropped her on his lap and held her close. 'Whatever it is, we'll deal with it,' he said, soft and low. 'I won't let anything happen to you. Just tell—'

She put a finger over his mouth to silence him. 'It's not me; this is about you and my fears. Ever since the night of Maddy's birthday, I've lived in terror that you could be taken from me. You think you're indestructible, that you can handle any crisis that comes your way, but I wasn't so sure.' The words were tumbling out in a rush, as if she'd been holding them back a long time. 'I was selfish. I wanted your child so even if, God forbid, something happened to you, I'd still have part of you. Don't tell me I shouldn't feel this way because I do. It's not something you can talk yourself out of. So there.' She sucked in a breath. 'That's my reason for not telling you before.' She stared at him, her blue gaze straight on. 'And if you don't want to marry me, I understand.'

'There's not a chance in hell you're getting out of this marriage,' Rafe said, brusquely. 'You can forget about that.' He shut his eyes for a second, took a hard in-breath through his nose, sorted through the tumult in his brain, finally got a grip on the I-can't-believe-this-is-happening. She was and always would be the only person he loved with every fibre of his being. He moved his hand down to her stomach and gently spread his fingers over the beginnings of a new life. 'So we made a baby,' he said, a touch of wonder slowly rising in his voice. 'How about that?'

She watched him, her eyes wary. 'You sure you don't mind?'

He shook his head. 'I've loved you from the first time I saw you. I'll always love you.'

'Me *and* the baby – both of us, right?' She was less uncertain now, a dawning happiness in her eyes; he'd said he'd always love her.

'Yes, both of you,' he said, his voice deep and sure, his large hand warm on her stomach. 'How much time before—'

'You're a daddy?' Her smile was sunshine bright. 'Eight months. So you have plenty of time to get used to the idea.'

'You'll have to help me out,' he said, with a wry twitch of his mouth. 'I've had zero role models.'

'You're so good with Titus. It's the same thing, only you have to be a little more careful when the baby's tiny.' She threw her arms around his neck and kissed him hard. 'I'm so excited! Tell me you're excited too! You are, aren't you?'

He adored her full steam ahead persona, the one that assumed the world shared her enthusiasm. 'I'm getting more excited by the minute,' he said, only half teasing. The thought of Nicole having his baby was like staring out the window and suddenly seeing a new world: the sun warmer, the grass greener, the sky bluer. His child would be loved unconditionally; he'd make sure of it. 'I'll try to be a good father,' he said, quietly.

Immune to his reservations, she spoke with jubilation. 'You're going to be just perfect!' Then she laughed, a little breathless sound. 'May I announce the baby at the wedding reception? Say you don't mind,' she added without waiting for his answer. 'I'm just over the moon happy and I want everyone to share in our joy.'

He smiled. 'I don't mind. Say the word and we'll have fireworks to celebrate.'

'Really?' she said, her eyes huge. 'Can you do that in the city?'

She took such pleasure in life; she'd even taken charge of her fear and had his baby. She loved him and for that he'd give her the world. Fireworks were nothing. Short notice if he needed permits for tomorrow, but make a few calls – the mayor of Paris, the president of France if necessary. 'If you want fireworks, Pussycat,' he said, calmly, 'piece of cake. I'll arrange it.'